S0-AFS-956

The New Messiah is Closer Than You Think

Not since Dante has anyone so masterfully captured the truths of Heaven and Hell in a single work. Take a soul-gripping ride with this action-packed adventure and discover never-before-published mystical techniques and principles that will change your life.

Journey into the dark world of demons to find King Solomon's magical ring ... solve an ancient riddle to unearth Samuel's Oil ... discover a powerful gold medallion in The Well of the Souls ... and stand before the Ark of the Covenant to hear God's surprising message about the new messiah.

Richard Behrens' stunning triumph is the spiritual action adventure of a lifetime. Hold on—his revolutionary visions will take you to new levels of spiritual enlightenment.

"Master Behrens is a true spiritual master in every sense of the word. He knows more about the human mind and spiritual truths of existence than anyone I have ever met before."
— *Kevin Celestin, recording artist*

"What Master Behrens teaches is one hundred percent real, it all works!"
—*Larry Webster, defensive tackle, Cleveland Browns*

"I'm hooked on Master Behrens!"
— *John "Spider" Salley, Miami Heat*

About the Author

Richard Behrens is an authority on Jewish Mysticism, the Occult, and the Nature of the Mind. For thirty years, he has been teaching and lecturing, bringing his knowledge and wisdom to the public. He has lectured at colleges, universities, and hospitals, and has appeared on radio and television. He is also the Grand Master Tenth Degree Black Belt of the esoteric martial art of Torishimaru Aiki Jutsu and Head of the World Torishimaru Aiki Jutsu Federation. Behrens has met with and counseled numerous men and women around the world ranging from Islamic generals to hand-to-hand combat instructors of the Israeli Army, from Wall Street moguls to recording artists and movie stars.

To Write to the Author

If you wish to contact the author or would like more information about this book, please write to the author in care of Llewellyn Worldwide and we will forward your request. Both the author and the publisher appreciate hearing from you and learning of your enjoyment of this book and how it has helped you. Llewellyn Worldwide cannot guarantee that every letter written to the author can be answered, but all will be forwarded. Please write to:

Richard Behrens
c/o Llewellyn Worldwide
P.O. Box 64383, Dept. K059-0
St. Paul, MN 55164-0383, U.S.A.

Please enclose a self-addressed, stamped envelope for reply, or $1.00 to cover costs. If outside U.S.A., enclose international postal reply coupon.

The Lost Scrolls of King Solomon

Richard Behrens

1998
Llewellyn Publications
St. Paul, Minnesota 55164-0383

The Lost Scrolls of King Solomon © 1998 by Richard Behrens. All rights reserved. No part of this book may be used or reproduced in any manner whatsoever without permission from Llewellyn Publications except in the case of brief quotations embodied in critical articles and reviews.

FIRST EDITION
First Printing, 1998

Cover illustration by Rijalynne
Book editing and design by Astrid Sandell

Library of Congress Cataloging-in-Publication Data
Behrens, Richard, 1946-
    The lost scrolls of King Solomon : discovering the treasure /
Richard Behrens. — 1st ed.
        p.   cm.
    ISBN 1-56718-059-0
    1. Bible. O.T.—Antiquities—Fiction. I. Title.
PS3552.E417L6   1998   98-5386
813'. 54—dc21   CIP

Publisher's Note: Llewellyn Worldwide does not participate in, endorse, or have any authority or responsibility concerning private business transactions between our authors and the public.
    All mail addressed to the author is forwarded but the publisher cannot, unless specifically instructed by the author, give out an address or phone number.

Llewellyn Publications
A Division of Llewellyn Worldwide, Ltd.
P.O. Box 64383, Dept. K059-0
St. Paul, MN 55164-0383

Printed in the United States of America

Forthcoming Books by Richard Behrens

The Esoteric Teachings of a Grand Master
Golf: A New Dimension

Dedication

To God, as promised . . . the Great Healing River has begun!
To my wife, Sandra, thank you for your love, trust, and faith
in me, and the Great Work that lies before us!

Contents

Author's Note

As a Jewish mystic, I have long been aware of the latest trends in spiritual thought. As modern Western society degenerates before our eyes, I have watched more and more people begin their search for true spirituality. In their quest, numerous adherents have come across many of those truths ready and waiting for them as they pursued their various spiritual disciplines. Still, there sometimes comes a point on a spiritual path where the spiritual information handed to them orally from their teachers slows or even stops and they must, themselves, continue the journey deeper and deeper into the mysteries of existence, not only with the tools that their spiritual preceptors have provided them, but with the tools and information that they, themselves, have uncovered along the way.

Fortunately, a modern seeker of spiritual truth has the enormous benefit of being able to acquire volumes upon volumes of well written books containing not only doctrinal information, but accounts of spiritual "breakthroughs" uncovered by leaders in the various disciplines. In the ancient world, this was not possible. Happily, we live in modern times when, in order to delve further and further into the truths of existence, you need only travel to your local bookstore. This is a blessing. Why? Because, as they say, it allows you to "stand on the shoulders of giants" in order for you, personally, to spiritually advance and put more and more of the pieces into the puzzle in place. It allows you the ability to explore esoteric mysteries uncovered by those pursuing other disciplines. To do so may very well enhance the discipline that you are following and thereby propel you further along your personal spiritual path-further than you had ever hoped or anticipated.

Of course, nomenclatures vary, doctrinal differences proliferate, procedural disputes arise, and variations occur, not only between the many different disciplines, but often even within a single discipline. For example, in Hindu disciplines, a very important Chakra or spiritual center, located between the eyebrows is called the Ajna Chakra. In my discipline, we call this center the "Daath Gate." In other Jewish disciplines, such as Safed Kabbalism, the "Daath Gate" is located in the area of the throat. In fact, even the names of the different divisions of Heaven and Hell may be at variance. Is this wrong? Is this bad? No, not at all! This is the way of things. This is testament to man's acute ability to probe the infinite mysteries of existence and uncover various esoteric truths.

The point is, no matter what your particular spiritual path, no matter what your individual degree of spiritual attainment, you should endeavor to maintain an open mind and a special tolerance for the spiritual truths uncovered by others. Even if you disagree on certain doctrinal points or stated truths, you owe it to yourself to at least inquire into them. Remember, personal spiritual growth and intellectual advancement is just a book away. A barrel fills drop by drop, you advance book by book. Read and learn.

In writing *The Lost Scrolls of King Solomon*, I have woven throughout the fabric of the adventure a factual account of my own experiences in the various Heavens and Hells, as well as what I learned through my various encounters with certain demonic beings. The angels, their descriptions, and their teachings that I submit in the adventure are accurately and faithfully presented. Until this writing, I have never revealed this information to the general public. For your convenience, I have placed a full description of the techniques and principles in an appendix with step-by-step instructions that, if followed correctly, will allow you to experience for yourself the Presence of God and some of the deeper esoteric truths mentioned in the novel.

Regardless of which spiritual discipline you follow, I am one hundred percent sure that the techniques and principles presented here will significantly further your endeavors and, perhaps, grant you a new understanding of the nature of the world that you live in.

This is the beginning of a new spiritual renaissance, one that will transcend in both wisdom and enlightenment anything that has come before. What I present in *The Lost Scrolls of King Solomon* is the humble beginnings of the "Great Healing River" that will, if understood properly, change lives and offer new understandings concerning God. This is my hope! This is my work! This is part of God's initial response to the innumerable prayers of so many good and faithful people requesting redemption, understanding, and closer contact with Him.

Richard Behrens
Winter 1997

1

The Dokusan

"SENSEI, MASTER WANTS YOU IN HIS QUARTERS FOR *DOKUSAN*," Jerry said, bowing sharply. "He told me to take over your class."

"Do you know what he wants to speak to me about?" I asked, returning Jerry's bow.

"No, Sensei. He didn't say."

"All right, thanks."

"What do you have the class doing?"

"I have the novices going over nerve center techniques. The blackbelts are working on *osae dore* from wrists grabs and *koshi nage* from straight knife lunges. They're all yours."

"Sensei," Jerry said as I turned to go into the master's quarters.

"What?" I asked, pausing to turn around.

"I think Master's a little annoyed."

"How do you know? You can't always tell with him."

"I know," said Jerry, glancing at the class, "but it was the way he asked me to send you in. There was something in his voice besides his annoyance."

"What did you pick up?"

1

"I'm not sure, I couldn't put my finger on it. You know how hard it is to figure him out sometimes. I wouldn't keep him waiting."

"Okay, thanks." I went to the Master's quarters, took a deep breath, and knocked on his door.

"Come in, Benjamin," he said, sternly.

I entered quietly, centered myself in front of him, and bowed deeply. "Master, Jerry said that you wanted to see me."

"Yes, Benjamin, please sit down."

The Grand Master was a slight man, maybe five feet five inches tall, one hundred fifty pounds or so. His forty years in the mystical Art of Torishimaru Aiki Jutsu had not only made him a redoubtable fighter, but had given him deep, mystical insights into the nature of things beyond that of anyone that I had ever known. I knelt in front of him in the traditional *seiza* position, straightened my *hakama*, squared myself up, and waited for him to speak as his eyes bore into mine, penetrating my inner being as if he were searching for something that even I didn't know existed there. After what seemed an eternity, he broke the silence.

"Benjamin, tell me, how long have you been studying here?"

"Eleven years, Master."

"In those eleven years, I've watched you grow from an awkward novice to an accomplished and deadly practitioner. You are a *San Dan*, a third degree blackbelt, and one of my best students."

"Thank you, Master. I've always tried to—"

"And in those eleven years," he interrupted, "how many times have we had dokusan, a private talk like this?"

"I don't know, Master, maybe hundreds."

"Yes, hundreds. So tell me, what is the purpose of dokusan?"

"Well, dokusan is a private talk between Master and student where the Master not only leads the student spiritually, but helps the student cope with his day-to-day problems."

"And what is expected of the student during dokusan?"

"Respect and undivided attention."

"True, but what else does the Master expect?"

"What else?"

"Yes. What else?"

"Er . . . honesty."

"That's right, honesty. You've been honest with me in most things, Benjamin," said the Master, his eyes suddenly narrowing, "but not honest in all things."

"Master, I don't understand. I've always been honest with you."

"Have you? For eleven years I have tried to get you to tell me what's been bothering you, really bothering you. We have spoken about many things, minor things in my estimation, but never that. Lately, I've noticed a change in you that concerns me. For the past two months, I have watched you become more and more agitated and short-tempered. Last night in class, I noticed bruises on your knuckles. Tell me what's happening in your life, Benjamin."

"The knuckles? Oh, the knuckles." I said, glancing at my hands. "I got into a fight two nights ago and . . . ."

"You know that we have to avoid fights."

"I know, Master, but I couldn't avoid this one."

"Tell me about it."

"It was nothing, really."

"Is that your opinion, Benjamin?" asked the Master, his eyes narrowing again.

"Yes, but—"

"But?" the master interrupted. "Am I hearing correctly? Did you say 'but'? Benjamin, I know that you are trying to be humble about this business, but there is such a thing as being too humble, correct?"

"Yes, Master."

"Now, do as I asked and tell me about the fight."

"Yes, Master, I'm sorry," I said, bowing apologetically.

"Good, now tell me what happened."

"Well, I had trouble sleeping the other night and decided to take a walk around the neighborhood to unwind, I've actually been doing that a lot lately. When I passed the parking lot of a convenience store near my apartment building, I noticed three large men roughing up a young kid and his girlfriend. The kid was in trouble, I could tell right away that he couldn't defend himself against them. The girl was obviously terrified."

"Were they striking the boy?"

"No. They were pushing him around. The girl was crying and begging them to stop. I went over to see if I could talk some sense into the three men and get the kids off the hook. As soon as they saw me, all three men turned their focus on me. When they did, the two kids took off, suddenly leaving me the center of attention."

"Not the best place to be."

"No."

"Did you offer them the Three Pearls to try to avert the fight?"

"Yes, Master. I asked them if I could talk my way out of this, and they laughed. When I asked them if they would let me walk away, they laughed again. I asked them if I run, would they chase me, they laughed, looked at each other, and then started to move towards me."

"What did you do?"

"I didn't have any choice. The largest of the three reached out to push me, so I executed a koshe nage that sent him flying. The second man drew a knife and charged at me. I parried the knife and executed a breath throw. In the process of the projection, I brought the knife across the face of the third man. The breath throw sent him across the hood of a parked car and onto the pavement on the other side. The guy with the slashed face fled, but the first man came back at me. He walked right into my back-kick and combination back-fists, he went down hard. I turned and dropped down, and continued working him over with vertical fist strikes. Just as I was finishing, the other man came around the car, picked up the knife again and we squared off. He was stalking me, and kept switching the knife from hand to hand. I think that he'd seen too many hoodlum movies. When I dropped my hands and offered him my chest, he found the target so tempting that he made his play and lunged at me. I parried his lunge and went into combination hand strikes, elbow strikes, and knee strikes. He went down and was out cold. They weren't so tough, just punks. Like I said, it really wasn't all that much, Master, you've had me training for much more difficult situations here in class."

"Did you go right home?"

"No, Master, I finished my walk."

"The way you tell it, I suppose that the fight couldn't have been avoided honorably. Still, always remember that here in the art of Torishimaru Aiki Jutsu, we must try to avoid confrontations."

"Yes, Master."

"Now tell me, Benjamin, why you couldn't sleep."

"It's nothing. Dreams, that's all."

"About what? Have you had them before?"

"Master, it's nothing, really, I . . . ."

"Benjamin, this is just what I mean. I'm trying to help you and you're not helping me do that. You have to be honest with me or I can't help you," the Master said, his voice growing stern.

"You're right. I'm sorry. It's just that . . . ."

"Tell me about the dreams."

"I've been having them since I was a boy. Lately, they've become a real problem. Some of them I can deal with, but the others are real nightmares."

"Tell me about them."

"The light ones are just fleeting images of people, places, and things."

"Who are the people?"

"My father, mother, my uncle Mort, you know, light things."

"Your uncle Mort?"

"Yes, he's my father's brother. He's a rabbi in Brooklyn."

"Go on. What about the places and things?"

"Well, I dream of places like the beach, school, the synagogue, my father's old beat-up bible, and . . ."

"What about the nightmares?"

"Those are something else entirely. For the last two months I've been having strange dreams about people, places, and things that I don't even know. The places are often dark, claustrophobic, and filled with horrors. Sometimes, I dream that I'm locked in the basement of a synagogue and can't get out. As I pound on the door, the walls start to close in on me until I have no choice but to jump in a hole in the floor just to keep from getting killed. When I jump in the hole, I fall forever, never hitting bottom. I've had that dream over and over, and I always wake up in a cold sweat. In another dream, I was picked up by some invisible hand and put into a black case, like a big cylinder or something."

"Cylinder?" asked the Master.

"Yes, a black cylinder."

"Interesting."

"Master, I couldn't even begin to tell you how many times I had that one. I don't know, I dream of exploding Stars of David, strange mountains, and grotesque, inhuman creatures. What's happening to me, Master? Are these dreams just *makyo* or am I going crazy?"

"As you know, makyo are illusions often experienced in deeper levels of meditation, Benjamin. Of course, most dreams could be considered nothing but makyo, but sometimes dreams are visions, messages from a divine source."

"Prophecies?"

"Sometimes prophecies, sometimes warnings. And sometimes they're divine guides telling us to take a certain path."

"Why me? Why now?"

"I don't know, Benjamin. I need to know more about your circumstances. Tell me, how do you get along with your parents?"

"I love my parents. My mother is a second generation Austrian-American and my father is a second generation German-American. They're two orthodox Jews living in a world of their own. My mother lives for my father, and my father lives for God. Growing up, I just tried to live."

"That's fine, but it's not what I asked. How do you get along with them?"

"I have no real problems with my mother, but I haven't spoken to my father since I was eighteen."

"Eighteen? How old are you now?"

"Thirty-four."

"Sixteen years is a long time. What happened?"

"When I was eighteen I was supposed to enter Yeshiva and become a rabbi. He's always wanted that. I couldn't stand the thought of it and backed out. It wasn't what I wanted. I didn't want to become a rabbi."

"What did you want?"

"I wanted to study history."

"Did you ever talk to your father about it?"

"Yes, but every time I mentioned going to NYU to study history, we'd have these big fights. They used to break my mother's heart. Since I had a full scholarship to NYU that covered room, board, tuition, and books, I didn't need their money. I left home and studied history, working part-time for spending money."

"How did your parents react to that?"

"Let me put it this way, Master, the last thing that my father said to me was 'You are not a Jew, you're a pagan. I have no son, my son is dead.' Then he ripped his shirt over his heart."

"Ripped his shirt?"

"Yes. In Orthodox Judaism, when someone close to you dies, it's customary to tear a piece of your clothing. It's a sign of mourning. To my father, I was dead. Imagine, my own father doing that. Growing up Orthodox, I thought I was dead already."

"What do you mean?" asked the Master.

"I mean, there I was, eighteen years old, living in an old world community so long that I couldn't even identify with the modern world."

"What about girls?"

"Girls? Most of the girls that I knew were Orthodox and lived quiet, austere, proper lives. You know, everything in its place. I didn't know how to relate to girls on the outside. To this day, I still can't deal with them. I don't understand them. I date them, make love to them, and work with them, but they're a mystery to me."

"Do you see your mother?"

"I see her a couple, maybe three times a month when my father isn't there."

"Does your father know that you see her?"

"Yes, he knows. He makes sure that he isn't home when I go over."

"I see."

"Master, what's wrong with me? I feel like I'm falling apart. I don't want to . . . ."

"Guilt."

"What?"

"Guilt, Benjamin, guilt."

"Guilt?"

"Yes, guilt. You can call it a sort of spiritual guilt. There's a pattern here, Benjamin. What your dreams tell me is that you are going through some kind of spiritual dilemma—synagogues, exploding Stars of David, your father's old bible, your Uncle Mort. It's the kind of spiritual crisis that has to be resolved or you'll never find peace, believe me."

"What should I do? Should I meditate more? Will that do it?"

"No. For a great many situations, meditation would be the answer. For this, my intuition tells me that you have to do more than that." The Master suddenly went silent and closed his eyes, seemingly lost in thought. A moment later he looked at me and continued. "You have to reexamine your roots, Benjamin, that's where the problem lies. You have to find out who and what you are spiritually."

"I don't understand."

"Benjamin, everyone has a path in life, a path that is solely their own. Yours may be a special one, maybe a very special one. To find out for certain, you must learn more about your roots. I believe that the problems you have could be settled once and for all."

"Do you mean talk to a rabbi?"

"Well, you could do that, but what I mean is that you have to do more, much more. You have to go to the source of your religion and learn about it at the most basic level. I don't think that your dreams are makyo, I think that they might be visions. If they are visions, then you have to resolve this."

"Do you mean that I should go to Israel?"

"Why not? Don't you have a vacation coming up soon?"

"Yes, school's out next week, but I was planning to teach summer school at the college. I've done it every year and . . . ."

"What's more important, putting this matter to rest, or earning a few extra dollars? Besides, at the very least you'll have an interesting vacation. Jerry can take over your classes here while you're away. You know, of course," he continued, "the government of Israel sends me some of their special Mossad agents to train every year."

"I know, Master, but they're here for only two weeks and train during the day. I teach history during the day and never had the opportunity to meet any of them."

"They're very interesting fellows, excellent at what they do. They love their country and from what they tell me about it, I think that you could have a very nice stay there. You can call it intuition or just plain insight, but I advise you to go there and resolve all of this, Benjamin. In my opinion, until you do, I don't think that you'll be released from these dreams of yours. Benjamin, a journey of a thousand miles begins where?"

"Well, according to Confucius, it begins with the first step, Master."

"No. Confucius was a clever fellow, Benjamin, but he was mistaken in this instance. A journey of a thousand miles does not begin with the first step, it begins with the thought of the first step."

"I understand."

"Good. Dokusan is ended. I wish you well, Benjamin," said the Master with a knowing look.

I nodded and bowed deeply.

Go to Israel and investigate my roots? I'd never known the Master to be wrong about anything before, so perhaps he was right now, that I should discover more about these dreams and nightmares. Whether they're divine visions or just constantly recurring nightmares brought on by guilt, they'd been torment-ing me long enough. If going to Israel could possibly end them forever, then it would be more than worth the trip.

2

Strange Beginnings

I'D HAD EVERY INTENTION OF SPENDING THE SUMMER TEACHING, I thought to myself. Everyone who knows me knows that when I make my mind up about something, it's a done deal. I had been set on teaching, I'd developed lesson plans, even started preparing my class notes. Instead, there I was, sitting in the gate lobby at JFK, ready to board an El Al jumbo jet bound for Israel. My friends were taken aback by my sudden about-face, and even to me it seemed incredible that I would be spending my vacation in the Holy Land, searching for my spiritual roots. It was something I'd never even imagined doing. But, ever since that dokusan when the Master suggested that my dreams and nightmares may be the result of divine visions or caused by some kind of spiritual guilt, I couldn't get the idea out of my mind. For a lack of anything better to call it, this seemed a sort of visionary's spiritual "guilt" trip. Whatever the cause, the fact remained—I was going to the Holy Land.

I lingered at the gate, dreading the long, overseas flight. I'd never liked flying. The cabins were tight, claustrophobic places, much like the dark, inescapable places that had always been part of my recurring nightmares. But flying to Israel was

11

my only viable choice, a necessary evil that I had no way of avoiding.

I was the last passenger to board the plane. The coach compartment, where I'd been assigned an aisle seat, was crowded. A window seat would have at least given me a view of the wide open spaces, perhaps helped to ease the unsettled feeling I knew would overtake me as the flight wore on. I located my seat and was putting my carry-on bag in the overhead compartment as the heaving clanging of the plane door slamming shut echoed in my head. I'd heard the sound many times before, always in my nightmares. For a moment, my uneasiness was intensified. I sat down, buckled my seatbelt, and waited for the captain to announce our departure. Soon the engines began to roar and my heart started to pound. I gripped the arm rests and noticed a young couple next to me. They had the luxury of holding hands to ease their nervousness, and I envied them.

After we'd been airborne for a while, the flight crew began handing out pillows and blankets. I had to use the washroom and began to make my way toward the washrooms at the rear of the plane. All were occupied, but I heard someone in the lavatory behind me begin to fidget with the door latch. Someone else was coming down the aisle toward me, so I quickly turned and stepped right in front of the door to keep the other passenger from getting at it first. I was so close to the door that when it opened, I found myself standing practically nose to nose with an elderly gentleman. The space was so tight, we seemed to be frozen in place.

"Well?" said the old man, raising an eyebrow. "Are you going to let me pass or are you here to rob me?"

"Sorry," I said, breaking into a smile and stepping back.

I watched him walk down the aisle, and then I spotted it—hanging at his side was a black leather cylinder. I stepped into the lavatory and my mind was flooded with images. It was a shock, the old man's cylinder was identical to the one in my recurring dreams. As I returned to my seat, I checked both sides of the aisle, searching for the old man along the way. I found him sitting in an aisle seat just three rows behind me. I hesitated, then returned to my seat.

I couldn't keep my mind off of it. I knew that I had to take another look at the cylinder. I waited an hour and decided to go to the lavatory again just so I could get another peek at it. Just as I reached the old man, the plane hit an air pocket and jerked, causing me to lose my balance and fall toward him. To steady myself I instinctively reached for the armrest, but wound up grabbing the old man's arm instead, bringing us nose to nose again.

"Look, young man," he said, our noses practically touching and our eyes locked, "if you're not with anyone, why don't you come sit next to me. The seat is vacant and I would feel much safer with you next to me than to have you wandering around the plane like a nomad, always surprising me like this. Besides, I would really like the company."

"I accept," I found myself saying, still nose to nose with him.

"Good, my boy," he said, standing up. I eased my way past him and into the narrow row of seats.

"Shalom," he said, extending his hand, "I am Rabbi Ani. With all our chance meetings, I really feel like we know each other already."

"Shalom, Rabbi, I'm Benjamin Stein," I said, reaching out and shaking his hand. I knew that he was kidding about us knowing each other, but still there was something familiar about him, something that I couldn't quite put my finger on. It was something that told me that somewhere, somehow, some way, I had seen him before.

The rabbi, like my martial arts master, was a slight man, maybe five feet six inches tall and I guessed he was in his mid-seventies. He wore round wire-frame glasses and a dark gray suit that matched the color of his deeply set eyes. His face was thin and he had a neatly trimmed gray mustache and goatee. He cradled the black leather cylinder in his lap.

"Is this your first trip to Israel, Benjamin?"

"Yes, Rabbi. You?"

"Oh, I've made this trip many, many times," he said, a broad friendly smile stretching across his face. "Israel is my love, my second home, one could say. So tell me, are you going there on business or pleasure?"

"Pleasure."

"You are going to love it there!" he said, scratching his chin. "I wouldn't exactly call it the pleasure capital of the world, but still, there are many things to keep a young man like you entertained."

I simply nodded and when he noticed me glancing at the black leather cylinder nestled in his lap, his grip tightened on it. During our conversation, my eyes kept wandering back to it.

"Are you married, Benjamin?"

"No, Rabbi. I suppose I just never found the time."

"You sound like a very busy young man. Perhaps it's that you haven't found the right young lady yet? What do you do for a living that keeps you so busy?"

"I'm a professor of history at Welk University in New York."

"My, my, so young to be a professor and of history no less . . ."

"I'm thirty-four!" I replied, almost defensively.

"Yes, thirty-four, a very responsible age, indeed."

I had to know what he was carrying in that cylinder, it was just too much of a coincidence. The mysterious black cylinder kept beckoning me to take action. I took a deep breath and was just about to ask him about the cylinder when our conversation was untimely interrupted by another offer for pillows and blankets. Politely accepting the offer, we quickly returned to our conversation. I tried to ask my question again.

"Rabbi, about the—"

"Benjamin Stein, a Jew returning to his roots," he said, interrupting me. "Certainly, you're going to like Israel."

"I hope so, Rabbi," I said, wondering how he knew my reason for traveling.

"I am seventy-six years young and have been traveling back and forth since I was twenty. More than fifty years," he mused, giving a little chuckle. "I feel like a Sabra already. Really, a Sabra."

"A Sabra?"

"A native, someone born in Israel."

Our conversation was light and went on for hours. We spoke of history, music, sports, travel, and the arts. Not even dinner stopped us. But all the time we were talking, I couldn't help feeling that there was more to this convivial old rabbi than met the eye. Why did he tighten his grip around the black cylinder every time my eyes wandered to it? Why did he cut me off mid-sentence every time I was about to mention it, steering the conversation in an entirely different direction? Clearly he didn't want to discuss whatever secrets that cylinder held. After a while, I began to believe, uncomfortably, that he was some sort of psychic and could actually read my thoughts. Still, I was sure of two things—first, the cylinder he was carrying had something to do with my recurring dreams; and second, I was going to do everything within propriety to find out what was inside.

Around two o'clock in the morning I found myself staring out the window into the blackness. The plane's cabin was steeped in a twilight glow broken only by random reading lights kept on by other sleepless passengers. I had no idea how high we were or where we were. The rabbi had been sleeping peacefully for a couple of hours, all the time clutching the mysterious cylinder in his hands. I imagined it falling from his lap and popping open on the floor of the plane spilling a large fortune in diamonds. He could have diamonds in the cylinder, I mused. After all, Israel is a major world center for diamond cutting. But what about my dreams? The thought even crossed my mind to slowly ease the cylinder from his hands while he slept to peek inside—but I didn't have the answers to the questions that I would have to face if he caught me. I closed my eyes, adjusted my seat, and fell into an uneasy sleep as I tried to force the cylinder from my thoughts.

My sleep was plagued with nightmares—great barrages of fleeting images of people, places, and things—but this time there was a new element added to my nightmares. Dark, ominous images of the rabbi and the cylinder became part of the recurring dream of the invisible hand picking me up and dropping me down into the depths of a huge black cylinder.

I awoke at about six-thirty only to find the Rabbi bright, chipper, and full of energy. As I stretched and tried to muster some semblance of strength, I looked at the Rabbi and smiled my good morning, which he returned with the limitless energy of a teenager.

"Good morning, Benjamin, *boker tov*," he said, adjusting his tie. "Did you sleep well?"

"Good morning, Rabbi," I stammered, rubbing my eyes. "I slept all right."

The rabbi was too cheerful so early in the morning. At six-thirty in the morning, after hours of dreams and nightmares, I was a wreck.

"We'll be in Israel soon. I'm sure that you're going to enjoy your stay there."

"I sure hope so, Rabbi," I said, stretching clumsily in my seat. "Now, if you'll excuse me, I think I'll go freshen up a little before we land." We exchanged smiles as I stood and eased my way into the aisle.

"Of course, Benjamin, I did the same thing about an hour ago. It made a world of difference."

I made my way to the lavatory. Leaning over the sink, I stared at myself in the mirror and shook my head. I looked terrible. "Damn, I look like a zombie," I said aloud, pulling at my lower eyelids and staring at the little red lines. "I'm the first Jewish zombie in history!"

The little sleep that I had managed to get, plagued with those odd dreams, had only sapped my energy and every uneasy moment of it showed in my face. I washed with cold water in an attempt to shake off the vestiges of a restless sleep. I felt better, but only made marginal progress with my looks. I combed my hair and returned to my seat.

"There, you look much more refreshed," the rabbi said, repositioning the cylinder after noticing me glance at it.

"Thank you. I feel a lot better."

"Didn't you sleep well last night, Benjamin?" he asked, raising both of his eyebrows.

"Well . . . er . . . ."

"You had dreams, didn't you?"

"How did you—"

"So, tell me, Benjamin," he interrupted, his demeanor suddenly becoming more serious as he changed the subject, "are you an observant Jew? Do you believe in God?"

I had known that the subject of religion would come up sooner or later. It was inevitable, I supposed. I had tried to avoid talking about my faith since I'd left home to go to college. Of course I'd always believed in God. After all, I grew up in a house where belief in God was not only expected, but demanded. But somehow, the way the rabbi asked the question, I knew that it was more than just a cleric's way of passing the time.

"Yes, Rabbi, I believe in God," I said, "but I'm not what many people would consider to be observant."

"Just so!" he said, leaning over towards me and dropping his voice to a whisper, as if to make our conversation a little more private. "We are living in exciting times, my son! Very exciting times!"

I found myself leaning toward him and whispering back. It made me feel like some kind of secret agent. "Do you mean exciting because of all the technological advances in . . . ."

"No! No!" he said, cutting me off. "I mean because of what is going to take place within our present lifetimes."

I noticed that the more secretive he grew, the more protective he became of the black leather cylinder, and the more he looked around to make sure that we weren't being overheard. I had to admit that I was becoming increasingly intrigued by his theatrics. "Please, go on, Rabbi," I whispered to him.

"Not now!" he said, his voice suddenly assuming normal volume again. "This isn't the place to talk about such things. It's best to speak of these things elsewhere. Perhaps we could meet under more favorable circumstances, somewhere more private. Where will you be staying in Israel, Benjamin?"

I was disappointed. I knew that whatever he was going to tell me had something to do with the contents of the cylinder. I wondered what could have been so secretive that it had to be whispered. Could the elderly gentleman be some sort of spy carrying secret papers in his black cylinder? No, that was ridiculous. If this was the cylinder of my nightmares then I knew that I had no choice but to go along with whatever he was going to propose.

"I'll be staying at the King David Hotel in Jerusalem, Rabbi."

"It is a very nice hotel," he said, scratching his beard and looking as if he were calculating his next thought. "It is very expensive there, though?"

"Yes, it is expensive. I made my plans at the last minute and all of the less expensive hotels were full so . . . ."

"So, the King David."

"Right."

"Benjamin, how would you like to get together during your stay? I really think that we should talk some more. I promise you that you won't be sorry."

He adjusted the cylinder in his lap and tapped it with his fingers. It was apparent that he had recognized my preoccupation with the cylinder and was using it to get me to agree to the meeting.

"Yes, Rabbi, I would like that."

"Fine, my son. Perhaps tomorrow?"

"Yes, Rabbi, tomorrow."

"Good. Suppose we meet in the lobby of the King David at, say, six o'clock tomorrow evening. Is that okay?"

"Yes, Rabbi, that would be fine."

"Good, it's done then!" said the Rabbi, peering at me over his glasses. "Oh, by the way, please dress casually. Wear clothes that you don't mind getting soiled."

He leaned back in his seat with an expression of contentment on his face. Or was it an expression of relief? And why the casual clothes? No matter, I supposed I'd find out about that tomorrow night—and hopefully about the cylinder, as well.

The captain's voice startled me from my musings as he announced our approach for landing and welcomed us to Israel.

In the terminal the rabbi and I shook hands and said our goodbyes. "Shalom, Rabbi," I said, "I'll be looking forward to seeing you again."

"Until tomorrow evening," said the rabbi, with a mischievous smile spreading across his face. "Shalom Aleichem."

We parted company and I took the next shuttle bus leaving the airport and headed straight for the King David Hotel in Jerusalem.

3

The Offer

THE ABRUPT RING OF THE TELEPHONE WOKE ME FROM MY AFTER-
noon nap. I picked it up and heard Rabbi Ani on the other end.

"Have you changed your mind about tonight, Benjamin? I
hope that we will still have a chance to talk."

"No, Yusef, I haven't. I'm looking forward to it," I answered.

"Good, good." he seemed quite pleased. "Certain circumstances, however, prevent me from picking you up personally.
Instead, I will send Ali. He is the son of my good friend Muhammad. He will meet you in the hotel lobby at six o'clock."

"Okay. How will I recognize him? What does he look like?"

"Don't worry, the boy has your description. He should have
no trouble finding you. Remember to dress very casually, Benjamin, and trust Ali."

I shaved, showered, dressed, and sat down to the dinner I'd
ordered from room service. Suddenly, my mind was racing. Was I
having second thoughts about going along tonight? Was this why
I came to Israel? Could the kindly old Rabbi actually be some
kind of spy? What extenuating circumstances were preventing the
Rabbi from coming here himself? Was it something dangerous? I
shook my head sharply as if to clear it. *You're just being paranoid,*

I thought to myself. Anxiety nagged me. I knew that my fears were nothing but the product of a wild imagination, but still . . . .

A bit before six o'clock, I was seated in a large brown leather chair in the lobby waiting for my escort to arrive. As I waited, I imagined all the possibilities concerning the contents of the black leather cylinder—diamonds, rubies, secret government documents, a bottle of expensive wine, a stolen Matisse, anything seemed possible. A hand on my shoulder jostled me back into reality.

A young Arab boy, not more than sixteen years old, stood in front of me. He had a dark wiry frame, stood about five-feet eight inches tall, had big brown eyes, and was crowned with long curly dark brown hair. He was wearing a washed-out pair of blue jeans and a short-sleeved khaki shirt a little frayed around the collar. All in all, he was rather handsome in a boyish sort of way.

"Mr. Stein?" the boy said rather seriously.

"Yes, I'm Stein. Are you Ali?"

"Yes, I'm Ali," he said, making a small anxious bow. "Didn't Rabbi Ani tell you to dress casually?"

I was wearing a pair of slacks and a golf shirt, the epitome of casual back in the States, but Ali was looking at me like I was dressed for dinner with the prime minister.

"Yes, the rabbi told me to dress casually," I said, self-consciously unbuttoning the top two buttons on my shirt, attempting to look a little more casual.

"Well, never mind. We have to go."

"Where are we going?" I asked, smiling and trying to seem confident. He didn't smile back.

"Please, Mr. Stein, we must be going, " he said, nervously looking around the lobby.

"But, Rabbi Ani said that—"

"The Rabbi wants you to trust me! Come! Please, we must be going."

The way he kept looking around the lobby should have set alarms off in my head, but the boy's nervousness only heightened my intrigue. I had never thought of myself as a particularly fool-hardy person, but the images of the Rabbi's black leather cylinder kept flashing across my mind, taunting me, and motivating me to go with the boy.

"Is the rabbi going to—"

"Sssh!" Ali hissed, holding his index finger up to his lips and taking another quick look around the lobby. "Come, we have to go."

We left the hotel and climbed into a late-model four-wheel-drive vehicle. Ali climbed into the back seat and directed me to sit up front. I slammed the door shut and turned to find the most beautiful woman I'd ever seen sitting behind the steering wheel. She was slender and had long straight dark brown hair with bangs that highlighted her penetrating brown eyes. She was wearing a white tank-top shirt and khaki shorts that revealed the longest, sexiest pair of legs imaginable. I guessed she was about twenty-seven years old. It was hard not to stare at her, which is what I was doing when Ali interrupted my thoughts.

"Mr. Stein, this is my older sister, Mara," said Ali, leaning forward in his seat and tapping his sister on the shoulders with both hands.

Mara didn't say anything, she just slipped on a pair of sun-glasses, casually looked over to me, and nodded a cool hello. I nodded back.

"Where are we going?" I asked, hoping to get an answer before we pulled onto the highway.

"Please, Mr. Stein, you must trust us," said Ali, leaning back in his seat and running his fingers through his thick curly hair.

"Okay, but as long as I'm putting all my trust in you guys, you might as well call me Benjamin."

"Yes, Benjamin, now we have to take a little ride, okay?"

We slowly made our way through the crowded streets of Jerusalem, and before long we were headed north, away from the city, on a well-constructed road, which seemed to help us make better time. I was enjoying the ride until we hit the city of Ramallah, just north of El Bira. Now the luxury of cruising a wide, modern, well-paved road ended. North of Ramallah we took Israeli Road 60, a smaller, less accommodating road that zig-zagged through some pretty rough terrain. All through the trip the car was silent. No one spoke, no one even turned on the radio. Looking over at the straight-faced Mara, as beautiful as she was, I wouldn't have been surprised if she would have reached over, ripped the radio out of the console and thrown it out of the window had I turned it on. I wasn't prepared to deal with that, so instead I occupied myself by studying the passing terrain.

We eventually reached a fork in the road, and Mara turned onto a stretch of wheel-rutted, dried mud that was littered with rocks—some the size of softballs. I imagined that something this crude could hardly be called a road, except, perhaps, by ancient caravans, or nomads having little experience with the pleasures and conveniences of driving on modern highways.

When we finally came to stop, we were in the middle of the wilderness. This remote locale was not quite something I was accustomed to, *but,* I told myself, *I am on an adventure of discovery, after all.* I trusted the rabbi, and Ali and Mara seemed to be safe enough—if they were going to rob me, or kill me, or both, they would have had plenty of opportunities to do it before now.

We got out of the car and I stretched out my stiff limbs. The ride hadn't been very long, but it hadn't been very comfortable, either. Mara came around to my side of the vehicle and Ali walked off into the distance. I smiled at Mara, who raised an eyebrow, nodded, and managed to return a cool half-smile back. A serious woman, I thought. I surveyed my surroundings, which seemed dry, foreign, and unfriendly. *Who but nomads and lizards could possibly live out here,* I wondered. It was a semi-mountainous area filled not with majestic mountains like the Alps or Himalayas, but rather with ranges of lifeless, sunbaked desert mountains, variously cut by numerous narrow waterless wadis, gouged seemingly haphazardly by the passage of time.

There were none of the luscious greens and blues of the mountains that I was accustomed to, just dull browns and tans.

Within a few minutes, Ali returned to the truck with the rabbi and another gentleman. The other gentleman was an Arab, in his mid-fifties, stocky, sporting a full but rather unkempt salt-and-pepper beard, and dressed like Ali, in worn blue jeans and short-sleeved shirt. The big surprise was the rabbi! He looked like someone on safari in Africa, khaki colored short sleeve shirt, khaki colored short Bermuda shorts—khaki everything, right down to his knee-length socks. For a man of his age, he cut quite a dashing figure.

"Benjamin, Benjamin, my boy," said the Rabbi, clasping his hands together and walking towards me. "I'm so very happy you could make it. Happy, indeed. I hope your journey out here wasn't too uncomfortable."

"It was fine, Rabbi. I hope that—"

"Benjamin," the Rabbi interrupted, "this is my very dear friend Muhammad, the father of Mara and Ali."

We shook hands.

"Benjamin, your clothes," said the Rabbi, shaking his head. "Well . . . ." He broke off and then turned and nodded to Muhammad. Muhammad, raised an eyebrow, turned, and quickly walked away from us.

"My clothes?" I asked. "Didn't I dress right? You told me to dress casually. I didn't know that . . . ."

"Casual yes, Benjamin, but your clothes just won't do for this sort of country. I took the liberty of bringing you clothes more suitable for the terrain. I'm sorry, I should have been more specific. You don't mind that I took it upon myself to bring you a change of clothing, do you?"

"No, not at all."

"Good! Very good!"

A moment later, Muhammad returned carrying a small bundle wrapped in plain brown paper, which I assumed were the clothes that the rabbi had picked up for me. Muhammad handed it to me and I opened it, and, as I'd guessed, it was a bundle of khaki clothing. The shirt was short-sleeved, but thank heavens, the pants were long. Short pants would have made me feel too self-conscious. They even supplied me with a khaki-colored adjustable canvas military belt with a shiny brass buckle. I stood at the back of the Land Rover and changed into them. *This was going to be interesting,* I thought. *I wonder if the Rabbi will mention the contents of that damned cylinder.* I finished dressing, tightened my belt, and walked over to rejoin my new friends. This was a new look for me. I felt like a cross between Bugs Bunny and Indiana Jones.

"Benjamin," said the rabbi, linking his arm through mine and patting me on the shoulder with his free hand, "we have much to talk about. Come, my son, take a little walk with me."

I didn't even have a chance to respond to him, not even an "okay." He just turned and began walking, expecting me to be alongside him.

The sun was setting, lending a purple hue to the tawny landscape, and the peaks of the mountains cast their dark shadows across the dry wadis below. As the Rabbi and I walked away, the others began to pull camping equipment and folding chairs out of the rear of the van. We walked for a few minutes without saying a word, passing dry bramble bushes and sparsely scattered cacti. When we came to a small, odd arrangement of boulders, Rabbi Ani asked me to sit down. I chose the most agreeable-looking rock and made myself as comfortable as I could.

"Benjamin," said the Rabbi, peering at me over his glasses, "yesterday, on the plane, I asked you if you believed in God. You said that you did. My question to you now is how much do you trust in God?"

I started to squirm a bit. It seemed like a perfectly legitimate question, but I wasn't prepared for it and my mind raced. *Yes, I believe in God,* I told myself, *but trusting in God requires more than belief.* Even though my father never thought so, I knew that in my own way, I did trust God.

"Yes, Rabbi," I finally answered, "I do trust God."

"Good, Benjamin," he said. "Do you trust God enough to work for Him?" He raised an eyebrow as if he was concerned about how I was going to receive his question.

"Do you mean missionary work?" Suddenly, I imagined myself, Torah in hand, marching into obscure regions of the South American rain forest, converting the local Indian populations to Judaism while dodging steel-tipped spears, Brazilian machetes, and poisoned darts.

"No! No!" he said, breaking into a smile that faded quickly into a more serious expression as he continued to speak. "I mean, would you put your trust in God to the test, perhaps by retrieving a few holy objects for Him?"

Was this why I came to Israel? Did this have something to do with the recurring dreams? Was I here to actually work for God by retrieving a few holy relics? Suddenly, it dawned on me that it was a possibility, but why me? I'm not an archeologist, and my Hebrew is so rusty that it wouldn't be of much use if needed.

"I don't know, Rabbi. This whole thing sounds very—"

"Wait, Benjamin" the rabbi cut me off. "Before you answer, I have a couple of stories to tell you. You may find them interesting, maybe even enlightening," he said as he brushed off the surface of the rock next to me with his hand and sat down.

I wanted to hear his stories, but I wasn't crazy about getting involved in this. I had a feeling that this whole thing wasn't going to be as simple as he was trying to make it out to be. I pulled out my handkerchief and wiped the sweat from my forehead as I waited for him to collect his thoughts and begin his stories.

"Back in the days of Israel's glory," he began, "King Solomon had in his possession a number of religious artifacts sacred to the Jewish people. Among these holy items were Aaron's Rod, the remainder of the oil with which the prophet Samuel anointed his father David, and so on. He kept them safe all of his life. It really wasn't a problem. As he grew older, however, he began to be concerned about the safety of these holy relics. He knew that the enemies of Israel that feared to attack Israel during his lifetime wouldn't hesitate a minute to go to war against Israel after his death. Fearing that the holy objects that he had promised God to protect might fall into pagan hands, he went to great lengths to hide those objects in various places around Israel. Do you understand, Benjamin?"

"Yes, it's very interesting," I said, readjusting myself on the rock. "I didn't know that King Solomon had those things in his possession."

"Not many people did. Even those who were closest to him had no idea. But, that brings me to my second story. In 1963, I was driving a jeep on my way across the Negev to visit a couple of archeologist friends of mine. I was young then, and quite adventurous. My friends were out in the Negev looking for some lost city, which they never found. On the way to their dig, my jeep became bogged down in a small tract of sand. I couldn't move the stupid machine. I pounded on the steering wheel once or twice, wishing that I had taken a half-track instead of the four-wheel drive. When I got out of the jeep I was still angry and kicked the jeep a couple of times. That's when it happened. The sand gave way and half of my vehicle disappeared. There I was, in the middle of nowhere, staring at my half-buried jeep, when the sand suddenly shifted again, this time uncovering what appeared to be a small cave entrance just large enough to pass a man's body through. I grabbed a flashlight from the jeep. Peering down into the hole, I saw that it was a cave consisting of just one very small chamber. The ceiling seemed just high enough to allow a man to stand upright. In the center, I noticed a large rock hewn into some sort of altar holding a golden urn. This was something special, I thought, a real find! I slipped through the opening and dropped into the chamber. On my way to the urn, I looked around to see what else was down there. I could see nothing, just the altar and the urn. The urn, itself, was quite a find, of course. It was obviously very old, made of gold, and studded with precious gems. But, Benjamin, what the urn contained turned out to be much more valuable. Inside were a set of scrolls.

"The scrolls appeared to be quite old, but they were remarkably well preserved. They had been carefully rolled and tied together with an indigo-colored binding. I can't begin to tell you how really excited I was. I wiped my hands on my shirt so I wouldn't damage the scrolls with the dirt and sand and sweat, then I untied the binding and unrolled the scrolls. To my utter amazement, they seemed to have been written by none other than King Solomon, himself. I couldn't wait to read them, but there was a problem. A big problem. The difficulty was that I was only able to read part of them, only the introduction. The rest of the scrolls were written in some sort of sophisticated code that I was unable to decipher. In fact, Benjamin, to this day I am still unable to decipher it, Believe me, I've tried. It's been very frustrating. Anyway, I realized that I wasn't doing much good there, so I carefully rolled the scrolls up and placed them back into the urn.

"Apparently, I left the chamber at the right time. Just as I climbed out there was a slight rumbling of the ground, and not only did the hole disappear, but the desert swallowed up my jeep, too. It was almost as if the desert had waited for me to come out before destroying the hole. I just wished that the Negev hadn't destroyed my jeep too.

"So, there I was, alone in the desert with a priceless urn containing priceless scrolls, and not a drop of water or ounce of food. Let me tell you, Benjamin, it took me two full days of walking before I was found. Thank God that it was Muhammad who found me, he was quite a young man in those days. Maybe seventeen or eighteen years old. Anyone else would probably have killed me and taken the urn. Apparently, I had wandered north. He found me just a kilometer or so from his village. I was dehydrated, hungry, and sun-beaten. He brought me to his home and he and his mother nursed me back to health. Thank God for them both.

"Benjamin, I have never shown anyone else the urn or the scrolls that I found that day. I didn't even report my find to the authorities, knowing that they would have taken them from me. Instead, through the offices of some of my influential Sabra friends, I was able to leave the country with them by gaining passage on a dilapidated old American cargo ship whose captain often involved himself in questionable cargo. He was well paid for his efforts, and figured I was some sort of political refugee fleeing the authorities. I did nothing to break that illusion. I think that if he knew about the urn and the scrolls I was carrying, I would have been a Kosher dinner for the fishes."

"Is that what you keep in the black leather cylinder, Rabbi?" I asked, hoping finally to find out the truth about the cylinder.

"Yes, Benjamin, the scrolls are so important that I'm too terrified to put them down anywhere, so I keep them with me always. You noticed that on the plane, no?" he said, lightly tapping the cylinder strapped to his side. "Of course, the urn itself is safe back home. I didn't see any reason to carry it around Israel. It would have been more of a liability than an asset."

"That's quite a story, Rabbi. What were you able to read on the scrolls?" I asked, my pulse suddenly quickening.

He stood up, turned his back to me, and then took a few steps. He stared at the last vestiges of sunlight peeking over a small western ridge. I knew that he was mulling over what he was going to say and how he was going to say it.

Finally, turning to me, he said, "My boy, the first section of the first scroll related the story that I told you about Solomon's dilemma, but the second section of the first scroll spoke of something quite different. It is something that I have never told another living soul, except Muhammad."

I couldn't help noticing the change in his demeanor. Suddenly, he'd taken on the look of someone who had a mission to accomplish—a very important mission, something oddly wonderful.

"The second section," he continued, "told of a prophecy. It read: 'Know thee, that God's own hand shall direct the finder to these scrolls, and for God's own sake, as well as that of all of mankind, must that finder collect the Holy Objects that I have hidden to keep them safe, lest the Messiah, in future days go untutored. Know thee more, that he, in whose hands God Almighty shall place these scrolls, shall be he whom God Almighty has chosen to train the Messiah. Signed: Solomon, son of David, King over Israel. Blessed be the name of the Lord for ever and ever.'

"Benjamin, the Messiah is about to make himself known to the world, and I must hurry to fulfill Solomon's prophecy and gather the sacred relics. This is where I need your help. Unfortunately, I'm too old to retrieve the holy relics alone. I need someone younger, stronger. Someone like yourself to help me."

"But, what about Muhammad, or one of his kids? Why can't you use one of them? Why me?"

"Because they aren't one of us. No one other than a Jew is allowed to take these objects from their resting places. Solomon warns that it would be a sacrilege for anyone outside of the Covenant to remove them, that if a non-Jew attempts to remove the objects, he will be punished by God, and that punishment will be severe. I believe him and don't want to place Muhammad and his children in jeopardy. Benjamin, I believe that the Lord has sent you to me for this purpose. Do you understand?"

"Yes, but . . ."

"But, are you saying that you won't help me? You won't help God?" he said, turning his back on me again, staring out toward a now night-black horizon.

This wasn't just his way of giving me a private moment to think. Suddenly, he'd turned into a wounded lamb suffering in the wilderness, using the moment to make me feel guilty. My martial arts master spoke of my dreams as possibly being visions. Was this what I was here to do? If this was my path, then I had no choice. After all, the black cylinder was a large part of my recurring dreams and that turned out to be real. Maybe this was something that I had to do to resolve everything once and for all?

"Okay, Rabbi," I said, tossing my hands in the air like a felon giving himself up to the police, "what do you want me to do?"

He turned back and faced me with a serious expression. He took out his handkerchief and wiped the perspiration from his forehead. Relief and joy overtook his face. "Good! Good, my boy! I knew you would volunteer to help me. This is very serious work, you know. We have much to do!" Tears welled up in his eyes. He put both of his hands on my shoulders and gave me a squeeze. "You must be brave, and trust God!"

Why would I have to be brave? I'd never thought of myself as a particularly reckless person. I had always thought things through before acting, but here I was, a reluctant hero, a volunteer, suddenly with more faith than common sense.

"When do we start?" I asked, hoping for a few days to prepare.

"We start tonight, my boy, tonight!"

"Umm . . . great! I . . . er . . . I can't wait to get started," I stammered, suddenly feeling like the guest of honor at my own lynching.

"Good, Benjamin, good. You're making an old man really happy."

"What do I—"

"Not to worry, Benjamin, not to worry. Muhammad, Mara, and Ali are already preparing for your descent into the well."

"Well? What well?"

"The Well of Souls, of course, didn't I tell you? Oh how stupid of me . . . ." The rabbi turned his head heavenward and lightly tapped his forehead with his fist, then peered down at me to see how I was reacting to his news.

The old man was as sly as a fox, all right. He knew before I did what my decision would be before we even started our conversation. I mean, with Muhammad and the others already preparing to lower me down into some hole in the ground—called The Well of Souls, no less. But I was hooked, and we both knew it. All the same, my throat was as dry as dust, my palms were sweating, and my pulse was pounding.

"Rabbi . . . ."

"Please, call me Yusef."

"All right, Yusef, what about the well? You mentioned some-thing about a . . . er . . . a well . . . ."

"Benjamin, we have so much to do," said Yusef, turning to leave. "I promise that I'll tell you what I know about the well as soon as I return from the city."

"Wait! Rabbi . . . ." I said, jumping to my feet.

"Yusef, my son. Please, call me Yusef."

"All right, Yusef. Where are you going? What city?"

"I'm going to Jerusalem to move you out of the King David. Why pay for such an expensive room if you won't be staying there anymore? I'm going to move your things into my house. They'll be safe there, trust me."

"Let me give you money."

"Nonsense, I'll take care of the bill."

What could I say? Yusef had a certain way of maneuvering things. Sure, I trusted him, but I also felt like I'd just been finessed. God, the Messiah, King Solomon, and guilt trips . . . he had my number. He took away all of my arguments before I could come up with them. So I did the only thing I could do—I nodded my agreement.

"Excellent! Excellent, my boy," said Yusef, putting his hand on my shoulder and walking me back to rejoin the others. "God will bless you for this. Yes, He'll bless you, indeed."

When we walked into camp everybody immediately stopped what they were doing and looked at Yusef, probably to find out whether or not they were wasting their time setting up the appa-ratus. They didn't have to wait long for Yusef's report.

"Muhammad, my friend, guess what!" said Yusef, clasping his hands together. "I have some very good news for you, very good news, indeed! Our good friend, Benjamin, has volunteered to help us."

Muhammad took a handkerchief out of his back pocket, wiped his forehead and smiled at Yusef.

"Muhammad, I'm going to Jerusalem to move Benjamin out of the King David. I'm going to take Ali and we'll be back as soon as possible. You and Mara please continue to make the necessary preparations."

I handed the key to my hotel room to Yusef and gave him a quick, nervous smile.

"My boy, get some rest, it's going to be a very exciting night," said Yusef, turning to me with a more serious look on his face. "I'll see you when I return. And . . . oh yes, then I'll tell you what I know about the well. Until then, shalom, and put your trust in God."

Yusef and Ali headed for the Land Rover, climbed in, and in a matter of seconds were off for Jerusalem. I watched them drive out of sight and turned just in time to catch a sleeping bag tossed to me by Mara.

"Better get some rest," she said over her shoulder as she turned to walk away.

4

The Well of Souls

I LAY ON TOP OF THE SLEEPING BAG STARING UP AT THE STARRY Israeli sky trying to figure out just how I had wound up in this situation. I thought about everything—my dreams and night-mares, my master, the plane trip, the scrolls, Yusef, the Messiah, God, Muhammad, Mara, everything. I even briefly thought of sneaking off before Yusef got back.

Then I remembered the time my Uncle Nathan took me to the circus at Madison Square Garden when I was ten years old. I remembered telling my uncle how brave I thought the lion tamer was as he put his head into the lion's mouth. My uncle's response echoed in my head. "Benny, he's only brave until the lion closes his mouth. Then, he becomes something else entirely."

"What does he become then?" I asked.

"He becomes lunch, no?"

That seemed to be the essence of the dilemma I was fighting with now. Am I a brave man on the verge of a terrific adven-ture? Or am I just lunch?

I propped myself up on my elbows and took a good look around the camp. There was no one around to talk to, I was completely alone. Muhammad and Mara had long since finished putting together their mechanical contraption and had carried it out of the camp site. I thought of wandering out to see what they were doing, but decided I didn't want to get lost and have everybody searching for me all night.

It was nearly one in the morning when Yusef and Ali returned to camp. I got up as quickly as I could and greeted them as they stepped out of the Land Rover.

"Shalom, Yusef," I said, tucking my shirt tails back into my pants.

"Shalom, my boy," said Yusef, nodding to Ali that he should go and join Muhammad and Mara.

"Yusef, you told me that you would tell me all about the well when you got back. I'm looking forward to—"

"Come, Benjamin, let's sit over there," he said, pointing to two director's chairs that Muhammad had set up when he unloaded the van.

We arranged the chairs so that they were facing each other and sat down. Yusef closed his eyes for a moment, seemingly trying to figure out just how to tell me about the well. Seeing him so lost in thought didn't exactly fill me with confidence. Finally, he opened his eyes and leaned slightly forward in his seat.

"Benjamin," he began slowly, "you remember, of course, what I told you about Solomon's scrolls and how the great king indicated that the finder of his scrolls would be the one that God has chosen to train the Messiah. Well, Solomon went on to explain that the key to unlocking the code that he used to write the remainder of the scrolls is to be found in a place called HaYa'fey HaNesha'mot, the Well of Souls. I had always heard legends and hearsay about the possible existence of the Well of Souls. Up until the time that I came into possession of Solomon's scrolls, the Well of Souls was just a fairy tale to me. The part of the scrolls that wasn't written in code gave me its exact location. Do you understand, Benjamin?"

"Yes, Yusef, of course, but what exactly is the 'Well of Souls'?"

I watched him lean back in his seat and pull on his beard, again lost in thought.

"My son," he said, at last, "let's take a walk. I think that the best way for me to explain it is to simply show it to you and let you experience a few things."

I nodded. We left the camp area and headed for the well, which turned out to be only some twenty yards from us but past a thick mass of bramble bushes that had obscured it from view. Our vehicles had been arranged so that the headlights lit up the whole area, and Muhammad and Mara were making adjustments to a compound pulley device that was centered about eight feet over the opening to the well and supported by two steel tripods anchored to the ground. It looked like a cross between a miniature oil well and the pulley devices used in car manufacturing plants to move heavy car engines. Ali was off to the side preparing an astoundingly large coil of rope. A second coil of rope, just as large, was already lying on the ground by the well.

When Ali finished, he brought one end of the rope over to his father, who deftly threaded it through the pulley. Now I knew how I was going to descend into the well.

Being born and raised in New York City, I'd never seen a real well. To me, a well was a hole in the ground surrounded by neatly mortared stone. It should have a crank and a wooden bucket, and be covered by a shingled A-frame roof. It was something that you threw loose pocket change into in order to have a wish granted. This well was something else entirely. It consisted of an irregularly shaped hole in the ground with just a few flattened reddish rocks around it. I couldn't imagine anyone throwing money into this thing.

We'd been watching the preparations in silence for a few minutes when Yusef asked me to step over to the well with him. "So, what do you think of it?" he asked, with a big smile on his face. "She's something else, no?"

Staring at the hole in the ground that Yusef called a well, knowing that soon—too soon—my six-foot, hundred eighty pound frame would be going down into that thing. I blurted out the first thought that came to mind. "Yeah, she's a real beauty, all right . . . a hell of a well!"

"Come closer, Benjamin, and tell me what you hear," said Yusef, bending down and picking up a large gray stone. He dropped it into the well.

I leaned over the hole and listened, expecting to hear the splashing sound of the stone striking. There was nothing. Not a sound. I continued to listen and wait, hoping that it would strike something, anything-if not water, then at least solid ground. Still, there was no sound. I looked up at Yusef.

"Isn't it wonderful?" he said proudly, as if he were the one responsible for designing the well.

"Er . . . yeah, it's wonderful all right. Where's the bottom?" I said, trying to force a smile.

Yusef's expression changed from a reasonably broad grin to an absolute beam. "Don't you see? That's what makes it so wonderful, so remarkable, my boy. It doesn't have a bottom, it's bottomless. Isn't it great?"

"Great! Yeah, really great! It's a great well, all right!" I said, giving him the most enthusiasm I could muster.

Yeah, great. That's what I said, but that wasn't what I was thinking. It was bad enough that I was going to be lowered into some ancient hole in the ground that they call a well, but a bottomless pit? An abyss? I swallowed hard. I had just accepted this whole thing, thinking that if something went wrong—a rope broke, or the pulley malfunctioned, or the tripod collapsed—that the worst that would happen would be that I would get soaked and have to splash around in a lot of water while they arranged for my rescue. Now, if something unforeseen did happen, I'd be lost forever! I tried to clear my thoughts, but images of me falling through eternal blackness kept flashing through my mind. I saw people that I knew and loved growing old and dying; continents that have been drifting on the oceans of the world for millions of years finally coming together; great civilizations being born, flourishing, and decaying; enormous evolutionary strides being taken by Mother Nature; and the sun growing old and super-novering; and through it all, there I would be, still falling down this damn well.

I also imagined the great tales that Yusef, Muhammad, Mara, and Ali would have to tell their friends and grandchildren about the fool they conned into going down that well. "He's still falling to this day," they would say, sipping their tea and tossing another log on the fire.

"Look, Yusef, I don't know whether this is a good idea. I mean . . . ."

"Benjamin, you must trust God!" said Yusef.

"I do, but going down wells isn't my thing. Maybe I could do something else to help? I could . . . ."

"We need you to go down into the well. We can't—"

"All right, suppose I do this," I interrupted. "When I'm lowered into the well, what would I be looking for?"

Yusef peered at me over his glasses. "The scrolls didn't say exactly, but I'm sure you'll know it when you see it. Not to worry, my son. Just trust God."

Fine. I was about to be lowered into a bottomless abyss, and no one had any idea what I was supposed to be looking for. I was just about to express more second thoughts on the matter when Muhammad showed up and handed me a flashlight and Yusef shoved a small notepad and pencil into my hand.

"Here, son. Take these as well, you may need to take notes."

"Yusef," I said, looking at him squarely, "isn't there another way to do this?"

"What do you mean?" he said, exchanging glances with Muhammad.

"I mean . . . well . . . I . . . ."

I was just about to tell them that I didn't want to go down that hole any more than I wanted to douse myself with gasoline and set myself on fire when I caught Mara's smirk, which told me she knew how terrified I was. She knew it! It was there in her face, her expression challenging me to do it or be thought of as a coward for the rest of my life. *There's no way out now,* I thought, *at least no honorable way out.* Mara knew it, too.

"All right, I'm ready," I said, meeting Mara's challenging glare and stuffing the pad and pencil into my pocket.

"Good!" said Muhammad, watching us as Yusef put his arm around my shoulder and ushered me toward Yusef.

"Remember," Yusef whispered to me, "we are doing this for God and the Messiah."

"Yes, Yusef, God and the Messiah," I said, looking around for the little seat I supposed I'd ride down the well on. I couldn't see one. I turned to Yusef. "What am I going to sit in?"

"Slip this around one of your feet." Mara said to me as she twirled the end of the rope that had been threaded through the pulley. There was a small loop at the end. "A brave man like you doesn't need a seat. Besides, we don't have one. It would be useless, anyway. You could never fit through the opening in a seated position."

It seemed awkward, but it was the only way to go down. I slipped my right foot into the loop of rope. It would be a lot faster to just slip this loop around my neck, I thought as Mara tightened the foothold. I bet she'd love that!

Yusef interrupted my dark thoughts, "Do you have the pad, pencil and flashlight?"

I nodded, tapped my shirt pocket and held up the flashlight. As I flicked the switch of the flashlight on and off to make certain it was in working order, someone's hands touched my back and a second line was slipped around my waist. It was Ali, tying a safety rope to me. The other end of the of this rope was secured to a large boulder about twenty feet from the hole.

"This is for your safe return," said Ali, "also, use it to signal with. Two tugs to stop, one tug to go, and three tugs to bring you up. Got it?"

"Got it. One tug to go, two to stop, and three to bring me up. Listen, if I tug more than three times on the rope, that means bring me up fast. Very fast! Got it?"

"Got it," said Ali, smiling.

"I mean very fast!"

"Don't worry, I'll bring you up like a rocket!"

I wondered if he meant a well-manufactured, well-engineered space rocket, or a Fourth of July sky rocket, which explodes and disintegrates after traveling all of a hundred feet. I didn't press it.

Muhammad slipped a short piece of rope around my chest pinning the primary rope to my body, another "safety" measure.

"Ready?" Muhammad asked, snapping his fingers to Mara and Ali, signaling them to pick up their section of rope. He pulled back a little on the rope to make it taut. I felt my pulse quicken. I looked back at everyone and gave Yusef a quick smile, tightened my grip on the rope, took a deep breath, and stepped off the edge into the unknown. With my body weight supported by my foot in the loop and my hands firmly gripping the rope, they began lowering me slowly, in this standing position, into the well. I maintained eye-to-eye contact with Mara until I cleared the entrance. The opening to the well was just wide enough to allow my body to clear it. Mara was right, I couldn't have done it in a sitting position.

It was a scene straight from my nightmares: the pulley was the invisible hand lowering me in to the huge black cylinder. The cylinder in my dreams must have been some sort of combination of the cylinder that Yusef toted around and this, the Well of Souls. The only sound I could hear was the pounding of my heart in my chest.

Once my body cleared the entrance, I turned on the flashlight and shone it straight down into the depths of the well. All I could see was blackness. Lower and lower I went. The well didn't seem to be the epitome of engineering excellence. It was a simple construction with walls of flattened reddish rocks, probably sandstone, some covered with something like moss or lichen. The stones were piled, one on the other, in staggered brick-like fashion. The well, about five feet wide, afforded me a little latitude, but not much. The air was damp and the musty odor seemed to strengthen as I went deeper into the well. At first I gagged on the musky thickness of the air, but soon I got used to it.

An eerie, almost claustrophobic feeling washed over me as I descended farther. At one point I swore that I could hear the sound of my own heartbeat echoing off the walls and down into the darkness. Deeper and deeper I went, all the time searching the rocky walls for any sign, any message, anything that would give me a clue as to what I was looking for.

I must have been over a hundred feet down when I heard the faintly echoing voice of Yusef calling to me, "Trust in God, my boy, trust in God. For God and the Messiah!"

I didn't answer, I only looked up and gave a small groan. There I was being lowered into a bottomless well, one hundred, two hundred, three hundred feet down, my only real support being the loop of rope strapped around my foot. I felt like a Jewish worm on a hook being lowered into a barrel of starving anti-semitic piranha.

After a while I turned the flashlight up to see what was above me. All I saw was blackness. Blackness above me, and when I looked, nothing but blackness below me. It was like being buried alive. *Yusef's right, he is too old to do this himself.*

I found myself increasingly disoriented and weaker as I descended. It was as if the well itself was draining my strength. I became so weak that is was a struggle to simply hold the flashlight, let alone the rope.

I was just about to give up and have them pull me back to the surface when the light from my flashlight hit something shiny on an area of the well wall some thirty feet below me.

I tried to call up to everyone about my discovery, but my voice came out weak and airy, too feeble to make it to the surface. The impotent echoes of my own voice came back at me. Still, down I went. When I finally reached the source of the reflection, my mouth dropped open, half from weakness and half from disbelief. I quickly gave the signal rope two sharp tugs and the rope stopped. Suspended hundreds of feet down a well, I found myself staring at a series of Hebrew letters, which appeared to be solid gold, embedded in the rocky well. It was amazing. *It's all true!* I thought. Only King Solomon with all of his power, wealth, and wisdom could have been responsible for this. No one else could have thought of this, let alone actually have done it.

Fighting my growing weakness, I tucked the flashlight under my arm and took out the pad and pencil. This, of course, meant that I had to let go of the rope. My fingers eased their grip, and, to my relief, my cord to the outside world held. It wasn't easy directing the flashlight with my armpit but I was able to do it. My eyesight became weaker, everything that I saw seemed hazy and unsolid. With a shaking hand I copied down the letters as I saw them and put the pad and pencil back in my pocket.

There were thirteen letters altogether. A fortune in gold, enough to make a man reasonably wealthy. I took the flashlight out from under my arm, nearly losing it in the process, and shined it all around the rest of the well walls, behind me, above me, and below me. There were no other letters, and nothing unusual to be seen. Turning the light back to the letters glowing in front of me I noticed a small metal handle below one of the letters. It wasn't made of gold, instead it seemed to be made of iron.

No one was there to help me decide what to do about the handle. No instructions to follow. Throwing caution to the wind, I did the only logical thing I could do under the circumstances: I pulled it. In fact, as weak as I was, I still managed to pull the whole thing out of the wall. *Damn,* I thought, trying to focus on the long metal handle in my hand, *I hope I didn't break it.* I let it slip from my hand and watched it fall into the darkness below. I shook my head, trying to clear it, and looked around and waited for something to happen. How was I going to explain it to Yusef? What would I say? "I'm sorry I broke the handle, ruined your life, interfered with the training of the Messiah, condemned the world to darkness, and disappointed God?" Or I could just shift the blame to Solomon: "What do you expect, a 3,000-year warranty?"

In a way, I was relieved that nothing happened, I wanted to get out of there. I reached to the signal rope to pull on it three times, when, suddenly, the well began to quake. The thirteen gold letters in front of me fell away from the well wall as stones showered down around me. Everything plummeted into the blackness of the abyss. I covered my head and face with my folded arms, and finally the tremors subsided and the loose stones stopped falling from above. I took my arms down and found myself staring into a small compartment hewn into the wall of the well. I shined the flashlight into it and found, sitting in the center, a solid gold urn encrusted with diamonds, rubies, and sapphires. It stood approximately eleven inches high and about eight inches in diameter. Again, I thought, hazily, *Only King Solomon could have been responsible for this*. I reached over and took the urn. It was heavy and barely manageable in my almost delirious state. I was surprised to see that the lid wasn't sealed so I opened it. Inside was a small papyrus scroll written in Hebrew, which I couldn't read—my Hebrew was too poor and the writing too blurry. Yusef will have to decipher this. I replaced the scroll and lid, and tucked the urn in my shirt for safekeeping. I ran my hands along the walls of the compartment to see if I might have missed anything else.

Finding nothing, I was about to tug on the rope and have the crew haul me up when I heard something stirring below me. I couldn't tell what it was, but after a moment, though the sound was faint and distant, I realized that it was growling. I also heard an occasional stone crumbling off of the well wall surface, indicating that whatever it was was climbing up, breaking off loose stones along the way. To say that I didn't like it would have been the understatement of the century. This was the first time since I came down into the well that I wished I was alone. Now, something was in the well with me. Something that I didn't want to meet.

Reaching again to tug on the rope, I saw a small stone panel in the rear of the compartment spring open. Fighting unconsciousness, I shined my flashlight inside the compartment and found a gold medallion hanging from a hook in the back. I leaned over and tried to grab it but my reach just fell short. I shook my head to try to clear it and again tried to grab the medallion; still my reach fell short. I was wasting time, it wouldn't be too long before I was unconscious. I peered into the darkness below me, hoping that whatever it was that was climbing up the well wasn't close enough to see yet.

I knew that I couldn't leave without the medallion. Gathering all the strength I could, I tried again, this time managing to grab the outer edge of the compartment. I pulled myself closer to it. Too weak to even think, I felt my fingers graze the chain it hung on. I tightened my grip on it, and instantly felt a surge of energy travel through me like a lightning bolt. In seconds I felt myself returning to normal. My head cleared and my strength came back. "What is this thing?" I said aloud, holding the medallion up in front of the glow of the flashlight. As I admired it, a loud growl from below told me that I had to move. I shoved the medallion in my pants pocket and let go of the compartment edge.

I gave five sharp tugs on the rope; nothing happened. I tugged more violently, but still nothing happened. The growling was growing louder, closer. My palms and forehead were dripping with perspiration and my heart pounded in my chest. I tried the rope again. Suddenly, instead of moving up the well, the rope slackened and I was in a free fall.

"Wrong way, everyone," I yelled in vain. "The other way!" I had dropped another thirty feet or so when the rope suddenly went taut, stopping so abruptly that I lost my grip on it. All that kept me from falling into whatever was climbing up the well toward me was that little loop that held my foot and the small piece of rope Muhammad used to secure the main rope to my chest. I took a deep breath and grabbed for the line.

"Get me up, guys!" I yelled up the well. "Get me up! Now!"

The sound of the growling kept getting stronger—whatever was below me was closing in fast. I tugged on the rope again. Again, there was no response. The growling was very loud now. It wasn't an earthly growl—like a bear, or a lion, or even a wolf—it was something different, something unearthly and horrible. I turned my flashlight down the well and could just begin to make out its form some fifty feet below me. It was large, hairy, and practically filled the space of the well. I looked up.

"Get me out of this hole!" I yelled. "You better hurry, guys!"

I wasn't moving and I didn't know what to do. In desperation I threw the flashlight down the well, hoping to knock the creature back down into the abyss. I wanted to hear that thing lose its grip on the well walls and scream as it fell. But I heard nothing. I didn't even hear the thing react when the flashlight hit it—not a grunt, snort, or groan. It would have been nice if I had a samurai sword, flame-thrower, a bazooka, or even a baseball bat. I thought of throwing the urn down at it, but what would have been the sense in that? I tugged on the rope again and again nothing happened.

"What the hell are they doing up there?" I said, squinting down into the darkness to get a better look at the beast.

It was closer now, maybe twenty feet from me. I was just about to reach inside of my shirt, grab the urn, and drop it down on the beast when the rope suddenly jerked and I started traveling up the well toward the surface. To my surprise I was moving very fast, faster than a team of humans could pull me—at least the team up there. My body slammed against the sides of the well, but I didn't care, I just wanted to get away from that thing in the well with me. When I was about ten feet from the surface, the movement slowed to a more reasonable speed.

"Benjamin, are you all right? Is everything okay? Did you discover anything? Anything at all?" Yusef's voice was clear and distinct. I knew I was nearly out of the well.

Did I discover anything? I thought, *Yes, I discovered a number of things, the least of which was that I didn't really want to be in here.* I suddenly felt hands around my waist and chest pulling me out to safety. Finally, I was out. I hoped that whatever had been down there with me had given up the chase. It must have, or it would have been out already tearing all of us to little bloody pieces.

I stood staring at the hole in the ground while Ali and Mara untied me. Ali gave me a warm hug. Mara looked like she wanted to hug me, but she resisted the impulse. I wouldn't have minded if she'd let down her resistance for just a minute.

"What happened, Benjamin?" asked Ali. "Was there an emergency?"

"Well, sort of. There was something in the well with me."

"What?"

"Er . . . some sort of beast."

"Wow!" said Ali, looking toward the well. "A real beast?"

"Real enough for me! It was hairy and—"

"Benjamin, are you all right?" interrupted Yusef, as he stared at the large bulge under my shirt.

I checked myself over for any major injuries. I was banged up, but basically all right. "I'm okay, no problem."

"You must tell us all about this beast of yours, but first show me what you've found," said Yusef, in excited anticipation.

I took the notebook out of my pocket and handed it to him. He read the inscription I had copied from the wall. Raising an eyebrow, he slipped the notebook into his shirt pocket. I began telling him about the iron handle and the beast, but I could tell he wasn't paying attention to me. His eyes were glued to the bulge in my shirt. I figured that since he wasn't listening to me, there was no sense keeping him in suspense. I unbuttoned my shirt and produced the urn. Yusef's eyes lit up and he took the urn from me, turning it in his hands, inspecting every inch.

"Isn't it magnificent," he said, looking at the urn and then glancing at me. "Muhammad, come look what Benjamin found."

Muhammad, Mara, and Ali marveled at the urn. "It's a prize," said Muhammad. "It's marvelous!"

"Are those diamonds real?" asked Mara.

"Yes," said Yusef, looking at Mara and smiling, "they didn't have cubic zirconia in those days, although they did have colored glass. I believe that the diamonds are genuine and that the rubies and sapphires are real, too."

Everyone was so busy fawning over the urn that I felt ignored. Then I remembered the medallion.

"Oh, Yusef," I said, producing the medallion. "I found this hanging in a secret compartment behind the urn." I handed him the medallion.

"What kind of medallion is it?" asked Muhammad.

"I don't know," said Yusef, holding it up. "Give me some light."

Ali held his flashlight up illuminating the medallion.

"Interesting," said Yusef, turning the medallion over and examining both sides. "The Hebrew is easy. They are clearly names of God and the five letters are alefs." Yusef handed the medallion to Mara. "What do you think, Mara?"

"I've never seen anything like it," she said, turning it over in her hand. "It doesn't correlate with any of the ancient amulets that I had studied at college. The pentacle is clearly Solomon's symbol, his seal. It is definitely an amulet, and like most amulets, I would guess that it's for some sort of protection."

"Protection against what?" asked Ali.

"I don't know," replied Mara, handing the medallion back to Yusef. "My field is biblical archeology and we spent a lot of time on ancient amulets, but I don't recall seeing this type before. Yusef, what do you think?"

"I don't know," said Yusef. "Maybe the scrolls will tell us." He put the medallion in his pocket and turned his attention to the urn again.

I wanted to shake them all by their shirt collars and tell them that I hadn't been alone down there. Every time I tried to tell them about the beast, someone would mention something else about the urn and they would start chattering again. Then, just when I thought I was about to get through to them, Yusef removed the lid of the urn and produced the scroll.

"Give me more light," he said, unrolling the scroll. This time, Mara and Ali both held their flashlights over the scroll. Yusef began to read, muttering quietly to himself in Hebrew.

While Yusef was reading the scroll I thought that it would be a good time for me to bring the beast up again. "I wasn't alone down there," I said, trying to get everyone's attention. "Something alive, ferocious, and unearthly was in the well with me. I just thought I'd mention it."

"What?" said Muhammad, turning to face me. "A beast?"

"Yeah, Papa," said Ali, wide-eyed, "Benjamin said—"

"I know what Benjamin said, Ali."

"A beast," said Mara, sarcastically, "now really . . . ."

"I believe him," said Ali, nervously looking toward the well.

"You'd believe anything," snapped Mara.

I started to cough, trying to clear the dust from the well out of my throat.

"Here," said Mara, tossing me a canteen of water, "something to wash your fairy tale down with." Her arrogance angered me.

Yusef was so engrossed in reading the scroll that I wasn't sure he had heard me talking about the beast. *He must have heard,* I thought, *no one could be that engrossed in anything to ignore something like this unless, well, unless he knew about the beast before I even went down the well.*

"Yusef," I said, finally gaining his attention, "I wasn't alone down there! Something was—"

"You did very well, my son," he said, obviously changing the subject. "Don't you want to know what you copied off the wall?"

"What does it say? Was it written in code?" I said, realizing that I wasn't going to get anywhere with Yusef with my ferocious beast story.

"No, my boy, it wasn't written in code," he said, placing the scroll back into the urn and handing it to Muhammad. "It was a message to us from King Solomon. It was taken from Ecclesiastes, chapter three, verse six. It says, 'A time to cast away stones.' That was King Solomon's way of giving us a hint concerning the iron handle you mentioned you pulled out of the well wall. It was a time to cast the stones away. Clever, no?"

"Very."

Yusef smiled. "Come, everyone! Let's return to camp."

We left all of the gear just where it was and went back to the camp site. I was given water to wash with and then, after a fire was made, sat down to have tea and cake with Muhammad, Ali, and Mara. Yusef took the urn and disappeared into his tent.

Now that things had settled down, everyone wanted to hear about my escapade in the well. Naturally, I wanted to tell them, but first I wanted to know how they were able to bring me up to the surface so quickly.

"That was Mara's idea, Benjamin," said Muhammad, grinning. "I was blessed. I raised two clever children. Mara thought that it might be wise to run one end of the safety rope out to the van and tie it to the bumper. Clever, no?"

"Yes," I said, taking a sip of tea. "If you hadn't . . . ."

"Mara just thought that it would make it faster and easier to bring you up."

"You see? Just like a rocket!" Ali laughed.

Muhammad and I joined in, but Mara didn't. She just sat there stoically, tossing small stones in the fire. The three of us continued to laugh over this and that, and I told them the things that happened to me in the well, concentrating on the incident with the beast. They expressed their amazement over the beast, especially Ali who sat wide-eyed. From the look on Mara's face, she clearly didn't buy any of it. We spoke and laughed for a little over an hour when Yusef came out from his tent holding the scroll in his hands. Having experienced what I did while in the well, I now knew that this was all very real; what Yusef had told me about him being chosen to train the Messiah was true. When I thought about my part in all of this, that it was my task to help him by retrieving the holy objects hidden by King Solomon, I began to feel good . . . really good. Was this why I had to come to Israel? Was this the meaning of my dreams?

"So, what have you learned, Yusef?" Muhammad asked, interrupting my reverie.

"What have I learned? What I have learned!" said Yusef, beaming. He held the scroll over his head like some sort of victory banner. "I have learned that our great adventure is about to begin!"

About to begin? What was it he thought I was doing down that well? It certainly seemed like an adventure to me already. What does he call an adventure?

"What now, Yusef?" Muhammad asked.

"Now," said Yusef, still waving the scroll, "pack everything up, my friends, we're off for the ruins of Jericho!"

5

The Pact

"O LILITH, QUEEN OF THE UNIVERSE, MISTRESS OF THE DARK World, I have come as you have requested," Jamal Ha'id said, dropping to his knees and bowing deeply before an altar dedicated to the mother of demons. "I await your instructions."

Midnight fell dark over the old house on the outskirts of Be'er Sheba as he called to Lilith. A moment later, the air began to ionize and after several seconds of crackling electrical discharges, a form appeared in front of the altar. The winged demon, standing eight feet tall, had green, scaly skin and eyes that glowed red with a sinister fire.

"Do you know who I am?" said the demon.

"Yes, Master. You are Ababoath, the seventh born son of Lilith. You rule the southern quadrant of Malkuth Tachton, the Dark World."

"Did you not make a pact and strike a bargain with my mother that, in exchange for the wealth and power she has given you, you would fulfill a future demand?"

"Yes, Master. It is so."

"The time of that demand has come."

"Anything, Master! I will do anything that you ask," said Ha'id, nervously bowing again. "Your brother Adijan appeared before me the other night and—"

"Did my brother explain what needs to be done?"

"Yes, Master. He told me that I should hire someone to kill a group of infidels who are in possession of a special medallion, holy artifacts, and some scrolls that once belonged to King Solomon."

"Well?"

"I found the perfect man for the task, Master. He is an Algerian hiding from the authorities here in Israel. He is the bastard of a bastard, Master, and is no stranger to murder. His mother was a whore and his father was a French soldier. His name is Fu'ard. I gave him half of the money and promised him the other half when he delivers the medallion, relics, and scrolls. Your brother Adijan had given me information concerning their whereabouts, which Fu'ard is now in possession of. Even as we speak, Master, he and his men are pursuing the group. It will be done, Master."

"If they fail in this matter," said Ababoath, his great wings suddenly flaring, "you will pay a bitter price for it."

"Yes, Master," said Ha'id, shaking. "He will not fail. Master, may I ask about these things that you want Fu'ard to bring back? Please, Master."

"Very well. It would cause no harm to tell you since your future will depend on their being brought to us. The artifacts, Ha'id, are things of power once possessed by the prophets of the Hebrew god. They are instruments that have caused my people great harm in the past and if they fall into the wrong hands may yet do us great harm in the future. Once in our possession, they will be neutralized."

"I see," said Ha'id. "The scrolls, Master?"

"The scrolls I know little about. My mother commanded that they be brought to her. She wouldn't tell me why, she wouldn't tell anyone. Her command to do so was all that we needed to hear in the matter."

"And the medallion?"

"The medallion I know something of," said Ababoath, his eyes suddenly narrowing. "There is an ancient legend, well known among all demonkind, which speaks of the medallion. According to the legend, the medallion was given by the angel Ratziel to King Solomon so that the king would be protected from all demonic and negative psychical influences. It is said that it was a gift from his god."

"I see, Master."

"It is said that King Solomon would use the medallion to weaken a demon to the point where he was able to seal the demon up in vessels of brass. This is well known among us. My brother Adijan nearly suffered such a fate at the hands of the mighty Hebrew king."

"How so, Master?"

"One night, in the tenth year of Solomon's reign, my brother proceeded with a plan to do away with the king. Everything was in place. He had entered the sheath of a female human called Mila, the daughter of King Hiram of Tyre. She was one of King Solomon's favorite wives. My brother's plan was to kill Solomon and bring the medallion to Lilith."

"For a reward, Master?"

"For immortality, Ha'id."

"What happened, Master?"

"King Solomon had suspected that something was wrong and put forth a riddle to his wife Mila."

"And she, I mean your brother Adijan couldn't solve it, Master?" asked Ha'id nervously.

"Wrong! He did answer it."

"I don't understand, Master. If he answered it correctly then—"

"King Solomon asked him a riddle that he knew the woman Mila wouldn't be able to answer. That's how he knew it wasn't her."

"But, Master, how—"

"Suspecting that the woman Mila was possessed, he held his peace and had my brother turn around as if to massage his neck lovingly. When he did, King Solomon posed the riddle. When my brother answered the riddle, Solomon slipped the medallion around his neck.

Immediately, my brother weakened to the point where his only choice was to flee the woman's body or die. He left her and his plan to kill Solomon was thwarted. That Solomon was clever, Ha'id."

"Do you know the riddle, Master?" asked Ha'id.

"Yes, of course. Every demon since that time had learned it by heart. It serves to strengthen our resolve to procure the medallion and is a constant reminder of our hatred for the Hebrew king. It is so, Ha'id:

> *Of substance wrought by God's own will,*
> *empowered for His servant's sake.*
> *What is the object that thwarts the might*
> *of they, the gift of God would take?"*

"What was the answer to the riddle, Master?"

"The medallion, you fool!" spat Ababoath. "The answer was the medallion! As soon as my brother answered, Solomon slipped it around his neck. The king knew that the woman, Mila, would never have been in receipt of such knowledge."

"But . . . ."

"Ha'id, if that medallion is reproduced and distributed to humankind," growled Ababoath, "then we will no longer find human subjects to dominate and we will lose in our attempt to conquer the Light World. The wearer of that medallion or its copy will be protected from even the most powerful negative forces. No one, not even those casting the most potent of magical spells, can harm the wearer. More, the medallion, when worn on their person, displays for all to see their love and devotion for their god. It is an affront to my mother should such a thing occur, for even she would be powerless over that person. The original must be destroyed so that it cannot be duplicated in any fashion."

"I understand, Master. Fu'ard will find the group and kill them. He will not fail to bring back the objects of which you speak. You have my word, Master."

"He had better not fail, or you, Ha'id, will beg for death. You have my word!"

6

The Mossad

Jehuda ben Ari sipped his tea, reflecting on his career while writing his morning report. Twenty-two years of service with the Mossad had brought him little satisfaction, the problems of Israel's security were on-going. The epitome of the hard-nosed agent—tough, intelligent, and loyal—Israel's security took precedence over everything, including his own desires, which were many. The love that he had for his job and his country were the reasons that he never settled down, never married, though the opportunity had come up in his life several times. He knew that it would be unfair to a woman to have a part-time husband.

Ever since he'd become an agent for the Mossad, he'd always had a sharp eye for signs of potential trouble, like the time his sixth sense told him to have a suspicious Arab loitering around Ben Gurion Airport tailed. When they finally picked him up, the Arab had two hand grenades tucked neatly in a special pouch under his shirt. Then, there was the large group of French tourists traveling from Tel Aviv to Bethlehem. One of the members of the group didn't seem to fit in with the rest. Again his instincts had been right, the odd man turned out to be a Syrian agent sent to blow up several churches with the objective of destroying the Christian tourist trade.

Over the years, Jehuda's superiors, as well as the other experienced agents, learned to believe in his instincts. He was never wrong.

"Moshe," he said to his boss, seated at a desk opposite his, "there's something going on, something involving an American."

"How do you know?" said Moshe, propping his feet up on his desk and clasping his hands behind his head. "Is this one of those famous voodoo-hoodoo intuitions of yours, or do you have some hard facts this time?"

"You know I spent the whole night sitting in the lobby of the King David with Avram and Yitzak on that Russian thing."

"Yeah, so?"

"Well, at about a quarter to six I noticed this American sitting across from me. You can always tell Americans, they always have that 'important' look on their faces. Well, an Arab boy about fifteen or sixteen came up to him. They spoke briefly and then left the hotel together."

"So, what's the big deal?" said Moshe, turning his head and looking out of the window. "So, the American left the hotel with the Arab kid. What's suspicious about that? So?"

"So, the young Arab was twitchy, looking around like crazy. He was looking to see if anyone was watching them."

"That's not so strange in these times, you know. It's the 'in' thing," said Moshe, picking up a pencil and tapping it on his desk. "I call it political paranoia. Everyone is acting strangely these days."

"I know, but even so, I thought that there was a great deal more to it than just twentieth-century paranoia. This kid looked like he had a reason for it. When they left, I went to the front desk and asked about the American. He's nothing special, came from New York and checked in yesterday. He told the front desk that he was here on pleasure, just a tourist. He'd always wanted to see Jerusalem. I told the clerk at the front desk that I would be there all night, and if he noticed any strange activity going on with the American, he should signal me. The American's name is Stein. Benjamin Stein. I don't know any more about him, but—"

"But nothing! Get to it! What stirred up your interest in this thing? Just the kid twitching around? You said that the American was here on pleasure and wanted to see Jerusalem. The Arab could have been his tour guide for all you know, or—"

"Tour guide, hell!" said Jehuda, downing the rest of his tea. "If this kid was a tour guide, then I'm the freakin' king of France. Anyway, at around eleven o'clock the same Arab boy showed up at the hotel with an old man, looked like a Sabra. The two went right to the desk, spoke to the clerk and then went upstairs. The clerk signaled me and I went over. It seems that the old man and the Arab boy checked the American out of the hotel, left the hotel with all of his belongings. Strange, no? What the hell happened to the American?"

"Maybe nothing happened to him. Maybe he just changed hotels and the old man was his grandfather. Maybe . . . ."

"Get serious, Moshe! You know as well as I do that we can't have Americans disappearing around here. The people upstairs will go ballistic and come down on both of us if we ignore this. Our relationship with the United States is strained already, what with this peace initiative and all. Besides, this Russian surveillance thing you had us on is a big waste of time."

"Look, this 'Russian thing,' as you call it, wasn't my idea. The big shots wanted it done, so I had no choice. I'd like to retire with a pension. If they wanted us to sit in the King David and wait for an uncircumcised albino Martian double-agent to check in, that's all right with me too. I don't give a rat's ass! I just don't want to screw around with my pension, that's all."

"Yeah, well, the Russian thing's nothing, and this American business is something. That's how I see it!"

"That reminds me," said Moshe, walking over to a small table near the window and pouring himself a cup of tea. "Where are the Gold Dust twins?"

"When our two mystery visitors left the hotel, I sent Avram and Yitzak to tail them. I haven't heard from them yet, but I'll bet you a hundred shekels to a stale bagel that whatever's going on isn't kosher."

"Why the hell didn't you check with me first?"

"Very funny! Fat chance of checking with you on anything after six. When the sun goes down you go down with it."

"Well, from now on things are going to be different around here. Everyone has to put out a hundred percent."

Jehuda smiled. "Why, Moshe, what's crawled into your pajamas? You didn't suddenly get religion, did you?"

"It's the prime minister, he had me on the carpet yesterday. It wasn't too bad, but still—"

"I know, your pension. Just tell the PM if he calls that the Russian deal was a false alarm. Trust me on this American thing, all right?"

"You're a son of a bitch, Jehuda! If you screw this up, when I retire, and it'll probably be forced on me tomorrow, then I'm moving in with you. You're going to have me living with you for the rest of your life."

"Okay, okay, I get it!" laughed Jehuda, picking up some paper clips and shaking them in his hand. "Let's just see what Avram and Yitzak have to say, and then we'll make a decision, okay?"

"All right, but I think it's nothing," said Moshe, sitting back down at his desk and taking a sip of tea. "My pension will probably be nothing too!"

"What are you worried about? I'm telling you, it's something all right. I just don't know what. You may even get a commendation for this decision. You know me, Moshe, I'll find out what it is. If it's anything that's not in the best interest of Israel, then . . . ."

"Then, what?"

"Then, one way or the other, we'll eliminate the problem and collect our commendations at the Knesset."

"Jehuda, don't do anything rash. Handle it the right way or they won't be handing us commendations, they'll be handing us our walking papers."

"Don't worry, Moshe. I love this job and won't do anything to jeopardize it."

"Okay, do whatever it is you think you have to do."

7

Samuel's Oil

YUSEF WAS PORING OVER THE SCROLLS AS MUHAMMAD GUIDED THE
Land Rover over the bumpy terrain of our route to Jericho. I sat
in the back, trying to relax, knowing that whatever was coming
up at our next stop probably wouldn't be a walk in the park.
Looking out the large rear window, I saw Mara and Ali trailing
us in the van that carried our supplies. I hoped that for the next
adventure, I might be armed with something more than a pencil
and a flashlight.

From the Well of Souls we traveled south on a dirt road for a
short time, then headed west through a dry wadi for another
three kilometers. We continued our westward journey on a dry,
dust-filled weather track that proved to be an obstacle course
composed of potholes and stones of every size and shape. We
bumped along on this road for the next sixteen kilometers, until
we hit main highway 90, which we took south for the remaining
twenty-two kilometers of our journey. We were, at last, within
walking distance of the ancient ruins of Jericho.

It was early in the morning when we arrived and we made
camp about a half a kilometer from the ruins. Situated among a
few large boulders surrounded by a number of large-leafed date

palms, our compound was like an oasis without water. Never the rugged, outdoorsy, camping type, I adapted to these rustic conditions reasonably quickly.

Breakfast consisted of eggs, pan-fried toast with jam, tea with a dairy creamer, and light conversation. However, when the food was cleared, our conversation turned more serious as we planned our next move.

Yusef had deciphered the part of Solomon's scrolls responsible for bringing us to Jericho, and he wasted no time filling us in.

"Listen, everyone," he said, clamping both hands down on his knees, "according to King Solomon, there is a secret passage in one of the old houses abutting the eastern wall of the city. The secret passage is supposed to lead down to a chamber of some sort. In the chamber we should find a door made of iron that opens to a tunnel that leads down to a labyrinth below the city. King Solomon warns us that he placed his seal, a pentacle, a five-pointed star made of solid silver on that door, and that it is not to be removed or broken under any circumstances. Well, that is, not until we have retrieved the golden urn containing Samuel's Oil. He warns that to break his seal would mean a most horrible death for us all. Does everyone understand?"

It was a somber moment as we looked to each other, then nodded our understanding to Yusef. Everyone turned and looked at me, I knew something was up and I became more than a little uncomfortable. Had they all figured something out that I hadn't yet caught on to?

"Yusef, is there something special that I should know?" I said, feeling everyone's eyes boring into me.

"Well, you're the retriever, Benjamin, you know that already," he said, taking off his glasses and running his handkerchief over the lenses. "We will give you all the support we can."

"Do you mean that I'm going to have to do this all by myself?"

"Not exactly," Muhammad said. "We'll be with you up until we reach the iron door, and then . . . ."

"Then . . ." continued Yusef, "then, we will be with you in spirit."

"Fine. In spirit," I said, squirming.

I'd always hated the expression "we'll be with you in spirit." It always seemed to mean that the job ahead was really bad, that they would do it themselves if they had to, but since there was a choice, they'd rather let me do it. I was pretty sure that interpretation applied in this situation.

"We must do this after sundown," continued Yusef as he raised his empty cup toward Ali for more tea. "The creature that Solomon placed in the labyrinth to guard Samuel's Oil cannot be dealt with during the daylight hours."

"Creature? Did you say creature? Just what kind of creature are we talking about here?" I asked, hoping that Yusef would say that it was some kind of wild grain-eating hamster, or a deranged frog out to rid the world of annoying flies. But somehow I knew the creature Yusef was talking about was just a little more feral, a little more dangerous. King Solomon wouldn't have wasted his time with hamsters and frogs.

"Well, the creature is a . . . a demon," said Yusef peering over his glasses, looking for my response. "It's supposed to have fierce power. According to the scrolls, the great King had confined it to the labyrinth 3,000 years ago. The demon is supposed to protect the labyrinth from intruders."

"A demon? Come on, Yusef, do you expect me to buy that? It's the twentieth century. That's something that—"

"Benjamin, you really do need to keep an open mind. Twentieth century or not, demons exist. In fact, it's very well known that King Solomon had enormous power over demons. They feared Solomon with good reason because the power to control or destroy them was bestowed on him by God. No doubt that the demon that he had bound to his service in this case was handpicked for this task. In any event, you can be sure that it's a very nasty creature, and very good at what it does."

"But . . . ."

"Not to worry, Benjamin," said Yusef, nonchalantly taking a sip of tea. "I'm going to prepare you. There are some very ancient spiritual techniques that you should know how to perform in order for all of us to survive this ordeal. You have to trust me. It will be all right."

In a way, it didn't surprise me that I would now be facing an actual demon after what had gone on in the Well of Souls. After all, why not? All I would have to do is deal with a demon protecting an urn filled with the oil that Samuel used to anoint David, King of Israel, in a labyrinth under a city destroyed by God. The more I thought about it, the more I realized that I did not want to do it.

"Yusef," I said, "about this demon thing . . . ."

"What? Second thoughts, Benjamin?" said Yusef.

"All right, let's say that this demon really does exist, can't we find some way to lure it out into the open? Then we can all—"

"It can't be done that way," said Yusef. "The demon can't leave the labyrinth. You'll have to go in and—"

"But, Yusef," I interrupted, "I . . . ." A glare and smirk from Mara shut me up fast. Another fame or shame challenge—she had sunk me again, and she knew it.

"Besides, Benjamin," Yusef continued, "I have something for you that will protect you against the demon." He handed me the medallion that I'd found in the Well of Souls.

"What's it supposed to do?" I asked, glancing at Mara and then back at the medallion.

"It's supposed to protect you from any negative energies or unwarranted psychic influences that the demon might attempt to exert on you."

"And you're saying that I will be safe from the demon, right?"

"Well, safe from him psychically."

"What about physically?"

"Benjamin, I only know what King Solomon explained in the scrolls."

I saw Mara whisper something to Ali and then start to laugh. Another psychological, ego-destroying torpedo.

"All right, Yusef, it was just a thought." I said, exchanging pointed glances with Mara. "When do I have to do this?"

"In a few hours, my boy," he replied. "Put the medallion on and trust God. Now I would like to study the scrolls just a little longer. In the mean time just relax, there is a great deal for the rest of us to do." As I put the medallion around my neck and tucked it into my shirt Yusef smiled, turned, and departed for his tent.

As soon as Yusef disappeared I called Ali over to me. "What's your sister's problem?" I asked.

"What do you mean?" he said.

"I mean, she treats me like I'm some sort of . . . ."

"Oh, that. She likes you."

"What?"

"I said that she . . . ."

"I know what you said. What do you mean she likes me? How do you know?"

"She told me so last night."

"So, why all the wisecracks?"

"She's just testing you. When she was in college she had a love affair with some professor there who treated her badly. She didn't date after that for a long time. When she did, the few men that she dated she thought were jerks. Being a college professor was a strike against you at first, but she told me that she admired your bravery. She also told me that she really believed that there was a beast in the well when you told us about it, but—"

"But, she just wanted to see how I would react," I said, interrupting.

"Right! She wanted to see what would happen if you got angry at her. The other guy would hit her and . . . ."

"I understand," I said, suddenly seeing her in a different light.

"Women are crazy. I don't understand them," said Ali, shaking his head.

"Don't feel bad," I said, looking across the compound at Mara. "I don't understand them either, I never have. But I understand this. Thanks, Ali."

"It's all right," said Ali, walking toward his tent.

"Oh, by the way," I asked, "what did she do? Take a couple of archeology courses in junior college?"

"No," called Ali from inside his tent. "She got her doctorate last year in Biblical Archeology and has a Master's Degree in Ancient Semitic Languages."

"I've always underestimated women," I said under my breath. "I've got to stop doing that."

It was getting warmer as the sun rose higher in the cloudless sky over Jericho. I looked at Muhammad, Mara, and Ali, and noticed that the heat didn't seem to bother them. In fact, it seemed nothing really bothered them. Looking at them, I was certain that no matter how much trouble I'd encounter in the labyrinth, they'd be able to endure and survive it all.

The four of us were just about to discuss the possibilities concerning tonight's adventure when the flap to Yusef's tent opened and he called for me to come in. I excused myself and went to the tent.

"Sit down, my boy," he said, closing the tent flap. "Please, make yourself comfortable. I have some very important items to go over with you before tonight's adventure."

I sat on my bed roll and looked up at him. Even though it was my tent too, I still felt like a guest. Yusef sat on his cot.

"Son, from now on you are going to have to keep your wits about you. To help you do that, I'm going to teach you some techniques that very few men know about. One of those techniques is a very special meditation. Have you ever meditated before?"

"Yes, in the martial arts. My master stresses the importance of meditation."

"Hmm. Your master is a wise man, but what he taught was a different sort of meditation. The meditation that I have to teach you is really very special."

"Is it some sort of Jewish meditation?"

"Yes, Jewish meditation. It's only known to a privileged few, and it's truly very special. Legend has it that the great Archangel Cerviel taught this meditation to King David the morning that the king was to do battle with the Philistine Goliath. It served him very well, you know. It calmed his mind, giving him great concentration, and made him fearless in the bargain. I believe that they are all qualities that God would want you to have from now on, no?"

"I really hope so, Yusef."

"Fine, my boy! Now, if done correctly, this meditation can do for you what it did for King David. First, though, I have to teach you some things about the nature of the mind. It will help you understand the technique a little better. Please listen very carefully, Benjamin."

I nodded and sat up straight "Please, Yusef, continue," letting him know that he had my complete attention. He smiled.

"Benjamin, every human has in his possession two minds. One we call the Nefesh Na'moochk, the Lower Mind, and the second we call the Nefesh Ga'vo'ach, the Higher Mind. The Lower Mind is born with the body and dies with the body. It is the ordinary everyday mind that everyone is accustomed to using and listening to. It can be thought of as a sort of cassette tape recorder. From the time of conception it begins to record all of a person's life experiences. It is, in fact, the source of all of man's grief, all of man's misery. It is the reasoning, fearing, hoping, hating, loving, and conniving part of man that is responsible for filling his life with illusions, and prevents him from knowing not only his own true nature, but the true nature of the world around him. More, the Lower Mind has people believing in false concepts of existence that keep them from experiencing God. This keeps people from fulfilling their obligations to God. Now, some people have sixty-minute cassette tapes, some thirty-minute tapes, and some ninety-minute tapes. This accounts for their varying intellectual capacities. Do you understand, Benjamin?"

"Yes, Yusef, I do. Please go on."

"Good. Now, the Higher Mind, on the other hand, can be thought of as an infinite cassette tape. It has been recording since the beginning of time, and will continue to record forever. It has been recording throughout each of a person's many incarnations and is that person's personal link with God. The Higher Mind knows all things, Benjamin, past, present, and future. Fear, hatred, attachments, and so on are not to be found there. Unfortunately, with very few exceptions, man does not even know of the actuality of the Higher Mind. Because of this, he does not benefit as much as he could from its existence. Of all the people that ever lived, no one knew the Higher Mind better than King Solomon, who had been granted this very special wisdom by God. In fact, it was at God's command that the angel Ratziel taught these things to King Solomon. It was a blessing, a marvelous blessing, and it gave the great king a remarkable wisdom that no man had enjoyed before that time. In fact, it can be successfully argued that no man has had such remarkable wisdom since that time."

As Yusef spoke, his demeanor turned increasingly serious. It was clear that he was actually going to do what he said, that is, he was going to impart to me ancient secrets that were going to, somehow, help me get through all of this.

"Benjamin, in order to retrieve the holy artifacts, you must have a strong command over your Lower Mind. It's the only way that you will be able to access the great faculties hidden in your Higher Mind. You have to understand that if you rely solely on your Lower Mind under the conditions that you'll be facing tonight, you will fail. If you fail, it will, in all probability, result in all of our deaths. I don't think that any of us would be happy with that, correct?"

Yusef's demeanor was as grimly serious as the subject he was addressing. I had never seen this side of him. His eyes seemed to pierce my soul as he spoke, and there wasn't the slightest glimmer of a smile on his face.

"Please, go on," I said, trying to assure him that I didn't take the subject lightly, either.

"My son, in order to access the Higher Mind, the Lower Mind must be made quiet. There's no other way to do it. Understand that the average person's Lower Mind is constantly chattering away. It's like being forced to sit and listen to a radio that doesn't have an on-off switch, and one has no other choice but to listen to whatever it wants to play for them. It tells them things about the world, existence, themselves, other people, and God. Things that just aren't true. And, to make matters worse, it has them believing those things. The Lower Mind is the culprit responsible not only for man's ignorance, but, for the most part, his suffering as well.

With the flaps of the tent closed, it had become quite warm. I was sweating and Yusef, noticing my discomfort, handed me a canteen filled with water and went back to his lesson.

"Now, again," continued Yusef, "to access the Higher Mind and tap into its hidden resources, one must quiet the Lower Mind, and in order to do that, one must meditate. But before I go into that, I have to teach you how to gain an immediate control over your thoughts. You can call this an emergency technique. Are you with me, Benjamin?"

"Yes, Yusef, I am."

"Fine. You must understand that the activity of the Lower Mind and the activity of the breath are linked. That is, when the Lower Mind is disturbed, one's breathing is disturbed. A stressed Lower Mind is reflected in stressed breathing. When the Lower Mind experiences fear, for example, one's breathing becomes rapid and erratic. When one's breathing is irregular, one's thoughts become confused and irregular. I'm sure that you have experienced this, Benjamin. Remember back to what you experienced in the Well of Souls."

I closed my eyes, remembering the claustrophobic darkness, the beast nearing me quickly. "Yes, Yusef! I had that exact sensation in the Well of Souls. When the beast was climbing up the well after me, and I wanted to be brought back up, my breathing was so fast and irregular . . . my thoughts, they were just disjointed words, crazy, fractured images."

"Just so!"

"Please, go on." I was beginning to understand the importance of what he was saying to me. I needed to hear more.

"Try this, Benjamin," he said, suddenly straightening up. "Observe your thoughts for a minute or so, and notice how they flow. You will notice that they come and go as they want. Notice how you are breathing. Now, I want you to squeeze all the air out of your lungs and hold your breath for a few seconds. What happens to your thoughts?"

I did as Yusef instructed. "Yusef, when I stopped my breath, my thoughts stopped."

"That's right, my boy. When you stopped your breath, your thoughts stopped. This is very important, because you will need to do that in order to take an immediate control of your thoughts. There will be times when you'll need to do that or you will be lost, and that won't be good for any of us, right? Now, once you have stopped your thoughts, you must control your breathing. That is, you must make your breathing very smooth and regular, and you must breathe slowly. All breathing must be done through your nose and not your mouth. Once you've stopped your thoughts, you take a normal inhalation, but must make your exhalation much slower. Normal inhalations, slow exhalations. When you do this, you will find that all fear leaves you, and you will have access to the marvelous faculties of the Higher Mind. This ancient technique is called *Nefesh Hafsa'kah*†, mind-stoppage. Please, I want you to try it now."

I did as Yusef instructed. It was exactly as he described. All my thoughts had stopped and I felt extraordinarily calm. I was amazed by the results and wished I had known this technique when I was in the well. "Yusef, this is wonderful. Really, I wouldn't have—"

---

† See the *Nefesh Hafsa'kah* technique in the Appendix, page 375.

"Yes, Benjamin, it's all right," Yusef said, wiping the perspiration from his forehead with his handkerchief. "It's just one technique, I have many such techniques to teach you over the next few days. Some you will find even more marvelous. Let me give you one more for now. King Solomon, himself, prized this particular technique. It's a truly wonderful technique and is an instant meditation that will give you immediate focus and serenity. The great king called it the *Sha'ar Lev*††, or Heart Sephira technique."

I leaned in closer, not wanting to miss a single word or instruction.

"Know and understand that there are centers of great power hidden in the body. Such a center of power lies within the heart, or *Lev*, in the center of the chest. Through King Solomon's teachings we learn that there are ten such centers. Now, try this, Benjamin. Exhale all the air from your lungs and hold your breath for a few seconds. Then, inhale filling your lungs to their full capacity, and hold your breath for a few seconds. Now, place the palm of your right hand over your heart. Imagine that your arm is hollow, and imagine that, as you exhale, your breath is traveling down through your 'hollow' arm, out of the palm of your hand, and into your Heart Center. This need only be done once, but can be repeated, if necessary. You are not only stimulating the Heart Center when you do this, but actually injecting power into it."

I did what Yusef suggested and again was amazed at the results. It was instant meditation, all right. "It works!" I said, feeling a smile coming over my face. "I mean . . . ."

"Of course, Benjamin, King Solomon received his training directly from God," said Yusef, soberly. "When these ancient techniques are used, the loquacious Lower Mind will be quieted, and the knowledge and wisdom of the Higher Mind will come through. The Higher Mind will serve you well, but you must learn to trust it. Everything may depend on it. You understand, yes?"

---

†† See the *Sha'ar Lev* technique in the Appendix, page 376.

"I understand."

"Good! Now, please go outside and relax. Tell Muhammad that I want to see him."

I thanked Yusef and sent Muhammad in as I left the tent. I positioned myself close to the front of the tent so that I could hear everything that the two were discussing.

"Shalom, my good friend," I heard Yusef say, as he gave Muhammad a warm hug. "Please, Muhammad, sit down."

I heard Muhammad get settled as Yusef continued. "Everything seems to be going quite well, no?" Yusef said, walking over to the tent flap and closing it. "Our boy seems to be doing fine, but tonight may prove to be a major test for him."

"Yes, Yusef. I hope that he does well. He seems bright enough and is braver than he thinks he is."

"He does have chutzpah, even if it takes Mara to bring it out of him. Did you notice?"

"Yes, I noticed, Yusef," Muhammad said, and I heard him chuckle. "I think that something might be brewing between the two of them. I think that it's about time that she became interested in men again. I was beginning to worry about her. This is the first time in a long time that she had any sort of reaction to a man. We'll see."

"She's a good girl."

"Yes, she is, a fine daughter. Her mother would have been proud of her. Yusef, I think Benjamin will do well tonight."

"Yes, I have every confidence in him," said Yusef.

"Yusef, I know you didn't call me in here to discuss Benjamin and Mara. You have something for me to do?"

"Yes, Muhammad, there is something that I need you to do this afternoon. It's very important."

"Say it and it's done, my friend."

My mind raced—I knew it had something to do with tonight's mission.

"I need you and the children to locate the exact house that King Solomon mentions in his scrolls. Remember, it abuts the eastern wall of the city, that is, what's left of the eastern wall of the city. I hope it's still there."

"How will we know the house?" asked Muhammad.

"Solomon said that there is a vertical, rust-colored discoloration on the southern outer wall of the house. A pentacle about the size of your palm was scratched into the center of that discolored spot under King Solomon's direction. According to the scrolls, the house is near the eastern watch tower of the city."

"I understand, Yusef," said Muhammad.

"That's not all. Muhammad, it's very important that you go down into the lower chamber of the house to confirm the location. But don't, under any circumstances, disturb the silver pentacle on the iron door. And, whatever you do, if there are tourists or anyone at all around, don't let them see you."

"I understand," said Muhammad. "We'll go now. Is there anything else that I should know?"

"No, my friend, that's all."

"For God and the Messiah then."

"For God and the Messiah," returned Yusef.

8

The Labyrinth

WHEN MUHAMMAD, MARA, AND ALI RETURNED TO THE CAMPSITE, Yusef and I were sitting just outside of our tent talking. Judging by the looks on their faces, the errand Yusef had sent them on must have been successful. Muhammad was grinning and wasted no time pulling up a chair to join us.

"Salaam, Yusef," said Muhammad, brushing some dust out of his beard. "It was just as you said. We found the house and went downstairs into the lower chamber. There was no iron door that we could see, but I tapped the walls and found an area of the wall that sounded like it had something behind it. I figured that Solomon might have had the door mortared over to conceal it."

"Yes, Muhammad, it would be like Solomon to do something like that," said Yusef. "It makes sense, no?"

"Yes, of course," said Muhammad. He turned to Mara and Ali. "It will be dark in about two hours, why don't you two begin dinner preparations."

As the two left the tight circle, Yusef said, "I wouldn't worry, Muhammad. I think that Benjamin will do just fine. I only wish that I could go into the labyrinth with him. I think that it would be one of the greatest adventures of all time. Think of it,

Muhammad, entering a labyrinth sealed by Solomon himself almost 3,000 years ago."

"Yes," sighed Muhammad. "But, it's not to be. Benjamin has the great honor to do this by himself."

They stared at me as if they were waiting for some sort of response, but I had nothing to say. In that one moment I found myself suddenly wishing that what they said they wanted could be fulfilled. I wished that they could go, not just with me, but instead of me. I knew, though, that it was not possible. I was going in alone. My fate was sealed. I smiled weakly at the two men as they continued to look to me for some response.

"You're a lucky fellow, Benjamin, a very lucky fellow, indeed," said Muhammad, tapping my knee. "Soon, you'll discover King Solomon's cleverness. It is a great opportunity, you'll do wonderfully."

Muhammad looked at Yusef and raised an eyebrow. Yusef just stared back at him over his tea cup. *There's something they're not telling me,* I thought. My thoughts about this whole matter were suddenly interrupted by the spicy smell of dinner coming from a large pot suspended over the fire.

"It's done! Come and get it!" called Ali, stirring whatever Middle Eastern concoction was seething in the pot.

We gathered around the campfire and Ali dished out the meal. It was clear by the expression on his face that he was proud of his culinary accomplishment—a stew consisting of chunks of meat, potatoes, and mixed vegetables. I assumed that the meat was lamb, although, after tasting it I still wasn't sure. In any case, it tasted better than it smelled.

Ali pulled his chair close to me. "Benjamin, Yusef told me that you teach the martial arts. I always wanted to learn it. I knew a kid named Ahmed from Jordan who studied karate and he was able to handle himself pretty well. He showed me a few things, but he went back home before I learned the good stuff."

"Good stuff?" I asked.

"Yeah, you know, the secret stuff, like death touches, paralyzing stares, and things."

"Ali, it takes years of study and practice to—"

"Hiyaaah!" Ali suddenly screamed.

"Take it easy!" I said, looking around a little self-consciously.

"My friend told me that was the yell of power."

"Yes, some arts use that. We don't yell like that in my art."

"Benjamin, you look like a martial artist. You're in good shape, you look powerful."

"Well, the martial arts keep me in shape."

"I love Bruce Lee movies. He never lost a fight. Did you ever have to use it?"

"Yes, a couple of times, but real life isn't like the movies, Ali."

"Did you win?"

"Yes, but . . . ."

"I knew you won. You have to be good if you teach it."

"I'm all right."

"My sister was impressed when she heard about you being a martial arts teacher," Ali said, searching my face for a reaction.

"Really? What did she say?" I answered, trying to sound casual.

"Not much. Just that she thought that it required a lot of discipline, a lot of self-control."

"Speaking of your sister, did she mention anything about me lately?"

"I heard her ask my father his opinion of you."

"And?"

"And he said he liked you."

"So?"

"So, when my sister asks a question like that, it means watch out, Benjamin. Get it?"

"Thanks, Ali. Got it."

After dinner, everyone occupied themselves by preparing for our excursion into Jericho. Behind the van, Muhammad, Mara, and Ali were busy checking flashlights and packing knapsacks.

Yusef was in his tent praying. I just sat quietly, watching the last vestiges of sunlight disappear over the hilly horizon. It was night now—zero hour was fast approaching.

Just as the last ray of sunlight vanished, the tent flap popped open and Yusef came out, prayer book in one hand, Solomon's scrolls in the other, and a very serious look on his face. "Is everyone ready?" he asked, staring at me.

The old man said quite a bit with that stare, and I felt a sudden wave of nervous excitement wash over me. I stood up and gave Yusef a small smile. I was as ready as I'd be.

We gathered behind the Land Rover. Mara and Ali were wearing knapsacks and Mara was carrying a rock hammer. Muhammad was carrying a small sledge hammer and had an enormous coil of white nylon cord slung over his shoulder. He handed me a flashlight and an empty knapsack. "When you retrieve the urn containing Samuel's Oil, transport it in that," he instructed me. I slipped the flashlight in my belt and put the empty knapsack on. I was ready.

"Okay!" said Yusef, gesturing like a movie theater usher showing us the way to the balcony. "Shall we go?"

The walk to Jericho was not very difficult, only a half a kilometer over solid desert ground. We passed the crumbled mud-brick walls destroyed by Joshua and the Israelites during their historic siege as we entered the city. It was a strange feeling, almost as though we were making a second assault on the city. Like the first one, we were sanctioned by God, Himself. Muhammad led us directly to the house and I was overtaken by the sensation that we were being watched. I looked around, but saw no one. The way Yusef was looking around, I was sure that he felt the same thing.

On the outside, the house appeared to be built of ancient mud-brick. Surprisingly, it still had some spots of the original mud-mortar facing remaining. As well-preserved as it first seemed, it was still a ruin, and I imagined that the whole thing could collapse at any time, burying all of us forever. To make matters worse, I had the spooky feeling that the ghosts of the slaughtered soldiers of ancient Jericho still walked the streets and crumbling walls of the city.

The night was moonless and the only light came from the narrow yellow beams of our flashlights. We entered the house, and carefully, but quickly, made our way down a narrow stone stairway and into the lower chamber. Glancing around the ruins of the building as we made our way through, I looked for ancient shards of pottery, or anything at all that the ancient inhabitants may have left behind. I saw nothing, any relics that may have been left behind had probably long ago succumbed to ravages of time, thieves, tourists, ambitious archeologists, and an untold number of biblical historians.

The chamber was small, maybe twelve square feet and very dusty. We shined our flashlights all around the walls, searching for some clue as to the whereabouts of the secret door. Muhammad had been right, the iron door wasn't visible. Muhammad showed us where he believed the door to be by tapping on the wall with his knuckles. He tapped here, pounded there. Soon we heard an odd sound—not hollow like one might expect, but a dull, vibrating sound that seemed to echo through the dusty darkness of the room.

"Take it down," said Yusef, staring at the wall. "But, whatever you do, please be careful not to disturb the Seal. If you do, we may all be doomed."

It was clear that the demon, and whatever else existed beyond that iron door, was something that Yusef didn't want to encounter himself. If the demon was real, and somehow miraculously alive after being buried in the labyrinth for nearly three thousand years, then of course, he didn't want the seal broken. The Seal of Solomon was the only thing that kept the creature from escaping.

Muhammad, Mara, and Ali hammered and picked, and carefully removed bricks and veneer from the wall. Twenty minutes later, they had bared the entire iron door that Solomon had described in the scrolls. It wasn't huge—just marginally larger than the standard front door of a modern house. But it was a strange door, not so much in its appearance, but in the feeling that I got just looking at it. Maybe it was knowing that the door separated this world from another more sinister world. A world, I reminded myself, containing a demon.

The door was made of pitch black iron. Time had left it pitted and covered by large erose areas of reddish orange rust. Three iron bolts along the left side secured it and in the precise center of the door was a large silver pentacle, maybe a foot wide, inscribed in Hebrew. Even I recognized the words to be ancient and powerful names of God. Mara and Ali cleared away all the debris, and the five of us stood in silent wonder, staring at the door. I focused on the large silver pentacle, lost in my own thoughts, when suddenly a loud thud from above echoed in the chamber. With a quick nod from Muhammad, Mara and Ali each produced a gun and moved stealthily upstairs to investigate. Yusef, Muhammad, and I waited and listened. Yusef's tension and fear were palpable, my own heart was racing. I suddenly recalled the feeling that I'd had when we first entered the city, the feeling that we were being watched. *If we aren't alone,* I wondered, *are our spies living people, or ancient ghosts?*

Shortly, Mara and Ali returned. "We checked all around the house. There was nothing," Mara said. "No sign that anyone has been here."

"It was nothing more than a piece of crumbling wall finally coming down, I'm certain." Muhammad replied. "It happens in places like this, I suppose."

I didn't buy it. The feeling that we weren't alone stayed with me. I was startled by a hand on my shoulder. I turned around, only to find Yusef.

"Benjamin, remember the Nefesh Hafsa'kah Mind-Stoppage technique, and the Sha'ar Lev Heart Sephira technique." he said, squeezing my shoulder. "They will allow you to quiet your Lower Mind and give you access to the infinite wisdom of the

Higher Mind. Remember, the Higher Mind is your link with God, and nothing is hidden from God. You must remember this when you're in there."

"Yes, Yusef," I said, as I went over the particulars of the techniques in my mind. "I won't forget."

"Whatever happens inside the Labyrinth, whatever you encounter there," said Yusef, "you must remember to trust God, and trust in the wisdom of Solomon. If anything does go wrong, we cannot help you. You are on your own."

I knew that what Yusef was telling me was important, but it wasn't what I wanted to hear. I would have preferred to have heard the old rabbi say, "There's nothing to worry about, my boy." or "it's a cakewalk, no?" or "If you get into any sort of trouble we have the entire might of the Israeli Military standing by to rescue you." But, as Muhammad and Yusef had said in the tent, this was for God and the Messiah. I tried not to entertain second thoughts. I resolved to do whatever I had to do in order to get this done.

"Also," said Yusef, "don't forget that our thoughts will be with you."

"Got it."

"Good!" said Yusef, nodding to Muhammad. "It's time. Ali, secure the cord."

"What's this?" I asked as Ali tied the end of the thin white nylon cord around my waist. I felt like a convicted murderer being strapped into the electric chair. There was an air of finality around the proceedings in the small chamber.

"Do you remember the old Greek story of Ariadne and Theseus in the labyrinth of the Minotaur?" asked Ali, with a half-smile. "The way she spun a strand of silk so that he could find his way out of the minotaur's labyrinth? Well, this white cord will help you find your way back out of Solomon's labyrinth. It's also for your safety, so we can have you back with us again. Understand?"

I was so nervous that all I could do was nod, but there was some comfort in thinking that they planned to see me again.

Then again, it may have been their way of being able to drag my body back out without having to go into the labyrinth to retrieve it—like a team of commercial fishermen hauling in an over-sized tuna, pleased with themselves for finally landing it.

I turned to the door and noticed that Muhammad's hands were already positioned on the top bolt. My heart was racing, my palms were sweating, my mouth was dry, and my thoughts were unsettled. Then, with a nod from Yusef, Muhammad pulled on the bolt. At first it didn't budge, but with a little twisting action, Muhammad soon loosened it, and it slid open with a loud clang. The second bolt moved more easily, but still there was the clanking sound that sent shivers along my spine. Instinctively, my hand went to my chest. There I felt the medallion under my shirt, reminding me of what I had to do. Finally, he pulled the third bolt. Again, a loud clang. I couldn't help thinking that the opening of each of the bolts had sent their loud clangs not only through the house, but also through the passages of the labyrinth, giving whatever was in there a more than fair warning that I was coming.

"Benjamin," said Yusef, placing himself between me and the door, "according to Solomon, the key to finding your way through the labyrinth is to trust your heart. I take this to mean that you should trust in the Sha'ar Lev." Yusef paused. "Well, I hope that's what he meant. Are you ready? Remember, you are doing this for God and the Messiah."

I'm as ready as I'll ever be, I thought. *I have my flashlight in my belt, an empty knapsack on my back, and a thin white nylon cord tied around my waist. If that doesn't make me ready to face a 3,000-year-old demon, then I don't know what will.* Instead of giving my thoughts voice, I simply nodded.

"Wait a minute, Yusef," I said. "Shouldn't I have some sort of weapon? Maybe a gun, or a knife, or . . . or a couple of hand grenades . . . or . . . ."

"It wouldn't do you any good, Benjamin. Whatever is sealed up in the labyrinth has been there 3,000 years. If it's still alive, I can't imagine something as mundane as a gun harming it all that much. Don't worry so much, trust God."

Somehow, what Yusef said did make sense. The thing inside, if it was still alive, well, hell! "Okay," I said, taking a deep breath and a hard swallow, "I'm ready."

Yusef smiled and hugged me. He then turned and gave Muhammad a nod. Muhammad pushed on the door, nothing happened. He put his shoulder to the door and made a second attempt. Still nothing. He called for Ali and Mara to help him, and even with all three pushing there was still no movement. Muhammad turned to Yusef. "It won't budge."

"Try again," said Yusef, waving his open right hand toward the door. "Try again! It might be stuck from age."

They tried again and again, and still the large iron door wouldn't budge. Muhammad checked the door again for a fourth bolt that he may have missed somehow.

"Wait!" I yelled. "Yusef, remember what Solomon said about trusting your heart? What about the Sha'ar Lev? Maybe we need to use it just to get into this place. What do you think?"

"Try it," he said, looking at Muhammad who threw his hands up in frustration. "Try it. Do it correctly and the answer should come to you. If we can't get in, then we're finished. I'll never be able to train the Messiah. Do it, Benjamin. We have nothing to lose."

I moved closer to the door. My instincts told me that employing the Heart Sephira technique was the right thing to do. After all, Solomon said that, well, he said to trust your heart. I closed my eyes and stopped my thoughts using the Nefesh Hafsa'kah technique that Yusef had taught me. Then, I took in a long, deep breath, and applied the Sha'ar Lev, injecting that breath through my hollow arm, out of my palm, and into my heart center. It didn't take long, only a few seconds. I could see the door clearly in my mind. In fact, in that one moment, I miraculously knew everything there was to know about the door. I opened my eyes and looked at Yusef.

"Muhammad," I said, suddenly confident, "take your fist and strike the door in the upper right corner."

Muhammad looked at me. He was clearly puzzled and turned to Yusef for confirmation.

"Go ahead, Muhammad. Try it." Yusef said.

Muhammad turned and struck the corner of the door with a sharp blow of his right fist. Just as he struck the corner there was the loud, clanking sound of a metal bolt dropping on the other side and the door sprang ajar. Looking at Yusef in wonderment, Muhammad smiled and pushed the creaking iron door open enough for me to pass through. "Go!" he said, looking at me and jerking his head toward the now open door. "Go quickly!"

I looked back at my companions. I was overcome with the urge to give Mara a long, passionate kiss goodbye. I fought the urge, not knowing at all how she would respond to anything more than a handshake. Instead I gave her a parting glance, took a long deep breath, and stepped over the threshold into the darkness beyond. I immediately turned on my flashlight and found that I was in what seemed to be a tunnel. On closer inspection, it turned out to be a narrow corridor. I hadn't taken three steps when I heard the heavy iron door squealing closed behind me and the three iron bolts clanking back into place. I was locked in and not very happy about it. I checked the nylon cord around my waist, making sure that it was secure and gave it a tug to make sure that it would slide smoothly under the door as I traveled along.

I illuminated the corridor with my flashlight and looked around. It seemed well constructed—about seven or eight feet wide and seven feet or so high. The walls and ceiling were composed of glossy, sun-baked bricks that reflected the light from my flashlight in odd directions, making the length of the corridor seem very surreal. I could see no distinguishable markings or carvings on the walls, nothing to warn me about the creature that I was to face. I took one last look behind me at the iron door, then took a deep breath, turned, and started down the corridor. It sloped gently and was easy to walk. Each step echoed off the walls and ceiling, though, which made stealth nearly impossible. After about forty feet, the corridor ended and I found myself standing at the mouth of the labyrinth.

The labyrinth was much wider than the corridor, about twenty feet wide and fifteen feet high. The walls were the uneven rock walls typical of any cave. Angular black and gray rocks jutted out here and there, and the roof was also cave-like. The walls and ceiling offered an eerie, unearthly background for the fleeting black shadows cast by the beam of my flashlight. The air was heavy, stale, and laden with the musty, animal-like scent of something that I couldn't quite identify. I started to walk, stopping occasionally to check the white nylon cord, making sure that my "lifeline" was still intact. The only sounds I heard were the fall of my footsteps and the beating of my own heart.

After I'd traveled into the labyrinth about a hundred yards, the halls began to narrow. Now only about ten feet wide, my flashlight did little to illuminate the passageways. Surrounding me was a darkness greater than that I had experienced in the Well of Souls. I walked slowly until I came to a fork in my route—two narrow passageways diverged in opposite directions. To finish this mission, I would obviously have to choose one of them. I shined my flashlight into each, but could see nothing identifying about either. Then I remembered the Sha'ar Lev. I had no other option—I used it. Take the left one, my Higher Mind told me, the right one leads to death. The decision was made, I started down the passage to my left.

The corridor was very narrow and wound in a serpentine fashion—first to the right, then to the left, and then back to the right again. The air here was heavier with the same animal-like stench that permeated the larger section I'd just left. About thirty feet into the passageway, I heard something scratch along the rocky wall. I shined my light in a circle all around me, but couldn't see anything. Trying not to panic now that I knew I wasn't alone, I listened closely. I couldn't tell if scratching was coming from somewhere in front of me or from somewhere in the darkness behind me. Whatever it was making the noise seemed to be keeping its distance. If it was behind me, then it was between me and the exit. If it was in front of me, well, I didn't want to think about that. I only knew that I couldn't stay where I was, I had to push on. After a while, the sound of my own heartbeat seemed to drown out the sound of the scratching, and the smell of my own sweat replaced the musty stench. But nothing replaced the uneasiness in my stomach.

Finally, after another five or six minutes of walking, I entered a slightly wider section. It was similar to the first section that I had encountered, though it was much more foreboding. The animal-stench seemed even stronger here, and I couldn't escape the feeling that I had smelled something like it before. I took another ten steps and then it hit me. The odor that filled the labyrinth reminded me of the smell of the serpent house of the Bronx Zoo, where I'd often visited when I was a kid. I sniffed at the air again. Yes, that was the smell, all right. The serpent house. Recognizing the odor did nothing to calm me, instead, a greater unease crept over me.

I continued walking, periodically checking the nylon cord and stopping to listen for the scratching. Sometimes I thought I heard it, other times I was met with silence.

The further I ventured into the labyrinth, the more disorienting it became. It twisted left and right, right and left in a haphazard fashion, and at one point I could have sworn that it took a u-turn and I was walking, more or less, back in the direction from which I'd come. As I struggled to maintain my sense of direction, the scratching sounds occasionally echoed off of the labyrinth walls, reminding me that whatever it was was not only keeping up with me, but was intentionally keeping its distance. Whatever it was had some sort of intelligence. Was it watching me? Stalking me? Could it smell my nervousness and fear?

The labyrinth narrowed again and I had to make another choice of passageways. Now I was presented with three very narrow tunnels. I didn't waste any time, I used the Sha'ar Lev immediately. I was told to take the center passageway. This one proved to be less serpentine than the last, but it wasn't exactly straight, either. Only three feet wide, with a ceiling only six or seven inches over my head, it was like walking through a tomb. The musty animal smell strengthened with every step. It was clear that I was getting very close to the source of that smell, and I didn't like that one bit. The scratching sounds persisted, and still I couldn't tell if they were coming from somewhere up ahead of me, or from somewhere behind me.

I walked slowly along the narrow passageway, listening for any sign that would pinpoint the direction of the scratching when the passageway suddenly ended and I found myself facing a stone wall. The only way out was the way I had come in. Had the Sha'ar Lev technique failed me? Had I done something wrong? The stench was overpowering now—whatever was alive in the labyrinth was not only responsible for that odor but was very close. I was searching the wall in front of me with my flashlight for another exit, a doorway, passageway, anything that would allow me to go on when I heard a stirring behind me. My heart pounded in my chest. The source of the scratching was only a few feet from me.

I took a deep breath, mustered my courage, and turned. Before me, lit by my flashlight, was the creature I had dreaded running into. I was frozen in place; the creature was hideous. It stood a good seven feet tall, with a head somewhat human in appearance—except that its eyes glowed red and its face was sharply angular and covered with grotesque sores. Its body was extraordinarily muscular and he had a strangely regal stature. Covered with sparse patches of long black hair, it stood on two powerful legs that narrowed at the calves and culminated in large black cloven hooves. Its arms were also muscular, with large powerful hands that had nails as sharp as eagle talons. Its large, bat-like wings were folded and protruded outward and upward from its back.

If I was going to escape with my life, I would have to get past this creature. Entering into hand-to-hand combat with a demon was something that my martial arts training hadn't prepared me for. Neither of us moved, instead we stared at each other, his red penetrating eyes piercing my soul with spikes of icy fire. *I'm a dead man,* I thought, *doomed!* How would they retrieve my body? With all the twists and turns that I'd taken since I entered this place, I knew that there was no way that they would ever be able to drag my body out of here with a thin nylon cord. I figured that no one would ever see me, dead or alive, again.

The beast and I continued our stand-off. Certainly, this creature had the wherewithal to dispatch me to the next world with very little effort. I couldn't imagine what it was waiting for. I remained quiet and motionless, afraid to move or start something that I wouldn't be able to finish. My only choice was to see what it was going to do.

"Are you the one?" it said, surprising me with his deep, raspy voice that matched his gruesome appearance. "Are you the one that was promised?"

I was so startled that I couldn't answer right away. I was absolutely dumfounded. Not only did this creature speak, but it was clear to me that it had an intelligence that was totally incongruous with its appearance. Am I the one? The one what? Promised? The question made no sense to me and I didn't know how to answer.

"I . . . er . . ." I stammered, trying to gather my wits.

"Are you the one the Master spoke of?" it asked again.

The creature was clearly masculine in gender and not something that I would want to bring home with me. Yet, there was something in his voice, beneath the gruff tone, that told me that looks could be deceiving. In his voice was an incredible sadness, an unrelenting forlornness I had never encountered before.

He pointed a great taloned finger at me. "Stand where you are. Do not move."

I stood as still as a statue as I watched him turn and disappear in the darkness. Only seconds later I saw sparks and heard steel striking flint. He lit a torch in a brass holder fastened to the wall and then used it to carefully light a second, and then a third. Soon, five torches were burning brightly, the whole chamber was well lit.

Bathed in light, his gruesome appearance didn't improve. The only difference now was that I noticed that his ears came to points, and that he had a long serpentine tail, which also came to a point. And then, there were the horns and fangs. He had two horns, an inch or so long, placed slightly forward on top of his head.

Too short for either offense or defense, I observed, quite relieved. He had fangs—two over-sized canines—each about an inch and a quarter long that glistened in the light cast by the flaming torches. I took another look at his hands. Each hand had five fingers that bore razor-sharp talons that looked like they could shred a man's flesh and rip those shreds from his bones in seconds. But then I noticed that his hands bore something else: scars of assorted sizes and shapes. I guessed they were battle scars, and it was clear that this formidable looking creature had been put to the test before, probably many times, by someone or something. I shuddered to imagine what the losers looked like.

He stood in front of me like a general inspecting his troops, looking me up and down. "Who are you?" he asked, finally breaking the silence. He knew that I couldn't escape. "Are you the one that the Master promised me would come?"

"I . . . er . . . I am Benjamin Stein," I said, vaguely hoping that it might mean something to him. Of course, it didn't. I tried to figure out what master he was talking about. I knew that he couldn't be talking about my martial arts master—it must be someone else. The only name that came to mind was Solomon. "Was it King Solomon that—"

"You know the Master's name! Surely, you are the one. You must be the one," he said, clasping his hands in front of his chest in a gesture of hope.

Where I had sensed sadness in his voice, I now detected hope. A desire, or longing, which seemed to come from the very depths of his soul, that I was the "promised" one. His gestures, and the hope that I detected in his voice, made me believe that I might somehow survive this encounter.

"I am Benjamin Stein," I repeated, more confidently. "I am a descendant of the Great King, and I am here to retrieve the vessel containing the Oil of Samuel, the prophet. It was placed in your care, wasn't it?"

I didn't want him to sense too much arrogance in my voice, just enough to let him know that I wasn't afraid of him. It was all a bluff, of course, but it was my only card.

"On the day that I was imprisoned here," he said, relaxing his stance just a little bit, "I was told by King Solomon, my master, that one day a man would come into the labyrinth seeking the oil of the prophet Samuel. King Solomon said that if the seeker was the right one, then I should see to it that the urn is turned over to him. But, I was warned that I would be severely punished by the Master if I allowed the holy oil to fall into the wrong hands. To prevent that from happening the great king gave me three riddles to pose to those who would seek the oil. He told me that his riddles were devised by the wisdom given to him by God, and that they could only be solved by someone who had God's sanction. In other words, only the one chosen by God will be able to solve them. Those who cannot solve any one of the riddles, I am to kill. The great king told me that the deaths of the false seekers are to be made as painful as I can make them, or I, myself, will suffer greatly at the Master's own hands. Therefore, woe to you if you are not the one! Woe to you, indeed!"

When the creature finished, I glanced around the chamber for the signs of others who may have come to claim the holy oil. I saw no bodies—dismembered or otherwise—no bones, no blood stains on the floor or walls, nothing. There were no indications at all of anyone who had tried and failed to solve the riddles. "Am I the first to seek the holy oil? Were there any others?" I asked.

"You are the first," he said, folding his arms across his chest. "I have not seen anyone, human or demon, angel or devil, since the great king sealed me up alone in this labyrinth 3,000 years ago."

Despite his ferocious appearance, I began to sense that he was a creature of great compassion, one who had no wish to harm anyone. I felt better, at least until I thought about having to answer Solomon's riddles. If I missed even one, I was a dead man. Compassionate or not, it was clear that he would rather kill me than face King Solomon's punishment. I knew that I wouldn't have a second chance.

"I'm here to retrieve Samuel's Oil," I said, again trying to impress him with my confidence. "Ask me the riddles. I'm ready."

"I warn you," he said, his voice forceful. "If you fail to answer any one of the three riddles correctly, I will kill you at my leisure. You will not escape."

"Understood," I said, wearing my best poker face.

I watched as he paced back and forth several times, almost as if he wasn't sure how to ask the riddles. He finally stopped and turned to me with a very solemn look on his face.

"I warn you," he said, pointing his taloned index finger at me, "do not, under any circumstances, answer any one of them until you have heard all three. Once I've given you all three riddles I will repeat them one at a time. Only then will you answer. You will have until the sand runs out to ponder all three." He blew the dust off of a small hourglass on a stand near the wall. "When you answer, one failure and I will kill you. Do you understand this? Do you agree to it?"

"Yes, I understand and agree."

I surprised myself with my bravado. *If I could re-create this poker face when I get out of here,* I thought, *I'd make a fortune playing cards in Las Vegas.* But only, I reminded myself, after I'd collected all the items for Yusef and the Messiah.

"You are either truly the one, or you are a fool and impatient to die!" he said, turning the hourglass over.

Judging by the amount of sand in the hourglass and the rate at which it was falling, I had about three minutes to answer the riddles. If I failed, all hell would break loose and I would have to use my martial arts skill against a brand new type of opponent. It's what a fighter pilot would call "going down in flames."

"I hope for your sake that you are the one," he said, sternly.

"Me too," I said quietly to myself.

"Now, the first riddle:

> *Who is it that makes what he wants,*
> *loves what he makes,*
> *and, in the end, destroys what he loves*
> *out of the love he has for what he had made?*

And this is the second:

> *What is it that is small among the truly great;*
> *great among the truly small,*
> *and is the bane of both man and demon?*

And this is the third and final riddle:

> *What is it that made a king,*
> *who sired a king who bore a ring,*
> *whose powers bound me to this place?"*

"Now," the demon growled, "you have till the sands run out to ponder the riddles."

About three minutes! I spent the first minute praying that the next two minutes wouldn't be a waste of time and that by the end of the third minute I would have the answers to the riddles. During the second minute I stopped my thoughts using the Nefesh Hafsa'kah, and during the third I employed the Sha'ar Lev to access my Higher Mind. I came up with three answers with only a pinch of sand to spare. "I'm ready," I said, taking a deep breath and hoping that the answers I received were actually right, and not my imagination.

He looked me up and down with a critical eye and cast a glance at the last of the sand. "You remember the consequences of a mistake, don't you? Even just one and—"

"I know. I die," I responded.

He glanced at me again, grunted, and repeated his first riddle. "Who is it that makes what he wants, loves what he makes, and, in the end, destroys what he loves out of the love he has for what he had made?

"God," I answered, with confidence that even surprised me. "It's God!"

"Yes," he said, sounding surprised that I had answered it correctly.

"Go on."

"What is it that is small among the truly great; great among the truly small, and is the bane of both man and demon?"

"Greed!"

"Yes, greed! You are correct again, but remember answering the third riddle incorrectly will still mean your death."

"I understand."

"What is it that made a king, who sired a king that bore a ring, whose powers bound me to this place?"

"Samuel's Oil," I said, staring him right in his piercing red eyes. "It's Samuel's Oil!"

He stood in silence, staring at me. His demeanor hardened. His eyes narrowed, his nostrils flared and his mouth opened wide to reveal his fangs gleaming white and sharp in the torchlight. But his eyes welled up with tears, which confused me. I didn't know what that meant or what he was planning to do. Had I missed the last riddle? I slowly assumed a relaxed fighting stance and prepared myself for the fight of my life.

"You are surely the one!" he said, at last, bowing slowly and deeply. "You are the one that the great Master spoke of. Thank God! Thank God!"

As the demon finished speaking, his facial expression grew more sinister. His fiery red eyes narrowed and a sneer crossed his lips. He suddenly straightened and threw up his right hand with his taloned fingers extended in an ominous pose. I thought he would certainly kill me despite my answers to the riddles. Just as I ducked and dropped to the ground, an indigo-colored bolt of lightning burst from his palm and struck the wall directly behind me. The entire chamber shook and loose stones careened to the ground from the ceiling. I scrambled to cover my head. When the trembling stopped, I looked up and saw that part of the wall behind me had broken away to reveal a small compartment similar to the one hewn into the wall of the Well of Souls. There in the compartment stood a golden urn encrusted with diamonds and precious stones. I had no doubt that it contained Samuel's Oil.

"Take the urn," he said, making another small bow. "You are the one. There is no doubt of that. I thank God that you've come. You must take the urn."

I picked up the magnificent urn and examined it. It was sealed, but I could hear the oil splashing inside.

"Inside this urn," the Demon began, "was the actual oil that the prophet Samuel used to anoint the shepherd boy David, king of Israel."

I took off the knapsack and placed the urn safely inside for what I hoped would be a rapid journey back to the outside world. But I couldn't help wondering why the demon was so thankful. The whole thing was very odd; the demon just wasn't what I expected. He looked like one might expect of a demon, but he didn't have the demonic attitude of legend. There was something that made me feel sorry for him. After 3,000 years alone in the labyrinth guarding a treasure that would soon be gone, I wondered what would happen to him now.

"What happens now?" I asked, fixing the binding on the cover of my knapsack. I knew I'd never again have the chance to speak with an actual demon. I decided to take advantage of this opportunity.

"Now? Now you are to free me from the labyrinth," the demon said, tears streaming down his face. "The Master said that the one who answered the riddles would be the one who would have the power to free me from this vile place."

I had certainly been the one who answered the riddles, but I had no idea how to free him from the labyrinth. Perhaps it had something to do with the silver pentacle on the iron door. Anyway, I was sure that he knew what I would have to do to free him.

"I promise that I'll free you, but first I have a favor to ask of you."

"What is that?" he asked, slowly stretching his great wings. "If it's within my power to grant it to you, then you can consider it done."

"I know very little of demons. And I believe that much of the information that humans have about demons came from people who I don't think ever really met one. There are stories and legends, of course, but I don't know what's true and what's made up. I want to learn more about you, and about other demons. If you teach me, I promise that before the sun rises in the morning you'll be free. You have my word."

"What you ask is a serious business," he said, wiping the tears from his cheeks and folding back his wings, "but, since you will be doing me a great service by freeing me, I would be ungrateful if I did not do this for you. I'm sure that King Solomon would approve. Come, sit down and I will tell you how I came to be here. I will also teach you things that very few humans know about demons. I will tell you of demons great and small and you will leave here all the better for it."

9

A Demon Speaks of Demons

THE GREAT DEMON SAT DOWN ON A LARGE, FLAT STONE OPPOSITE me and stared at the ground. His sorrow was evident in his voice when he spoke. "I knew you were the one," he said, shifting his gaze to me. "I knew that you were the one that King Solomon said would free me from this labyrinth."

"How? How did you know?"

"When I heard the clanging of the opening door echoing through the labyrinth, I knew someone had entered. When I tried to apply my psychic powers to probe the mind of the intruder I was blocked. The chain that you wear around your neck, does it bear a medallion?"

"Yes, it does," I said, pulling the medallion out from my shirt and showing it to him.

"I thought so," said the demon, shaking his head. "That was the same medallion that King Solomon was wearing the day he sealed me in this labyrinth. I was unable to defend myself against its power."

"What would you have done if I hadn't worn it?"

"Psychically, I would have drained you of energy to the point that you would have been unable to move. You would have been helpless. Then I would have been able to deal with you on my own terms right then and there. Instead, I was forced to follow you and wait until I had you trapped in this chamber."

What he described sounded exactly like what I'd experienced in the Well of Souls. I wondered if I'd been the victim of a demonic energy drain. The weakness and exhaustion had stopped the moment I grabbed the medallion.

"I heard a scratching sound as I was walking. Was that you?"

"Yes, I was behind you in the shadows all the time."

"Why didn't you stop me then?"

"I thought it would be wiser to have you locate the chamber on your own. King Solomon had placed traps in the labyrinth to destroy you if—"

"Do you mean the false tunnels?" I interrupted.

"Yes. They would have led you to death. But each time that I saw you choose the correct tunnel, it gave me hope that you were the one."

"I see."

"You will free me, won't you?"

"As I promised," I said, slipping the medallion back into my shirt, "I'll free you before sunrise, but please, will you teach me? Do we have a bargain?"

"Yes, we have a bargain, as you say. Ask your questions and I will answer them truthfully."

I believed him and knew that he would give me honest answers. But I didn't know what to ask him. My mind reeled at the possibilities.

"Please don't be offended by my first question, but the truth is that human beings, for the most part, know very little about demons. I mean, most, if not all of us, have been taught to believe that demons are evil, vile creatures that come from hell and that Satan is their master. To tell you the truth, you have me confused. You seem friendly enough, and I can't detect any evil in you. How did demons come into existence? Are there different types of demons? Do demons know about God? Are demons—"

"Slow down, my friend! You have to give me time to answer. I will answer all of your questions, but you have to give me the chance."

"I'm sorry, but, this is so . . . ."

"I know," he said, cracking a small smile. "It's the same for me, and it's all right, I'm not offended."

I'd wager that I was probably the first human being since King Solomon to have had the opportunity to actually get to know a real demon. Up until tonight, I really hadn't believed that they existed at all. Even when Yusef mentioned them, I hadn't believed that they were real. But here I was, up close and personal with the genuine article. This demon was intelligent and had a sense of compassion, two attributes that would make him a good teacher.

"I think that I should begin by giving you a little history of demons," he said, resting his hands on his knees and readjusting his wings. "It will clear up many of the misconceptions that I think you have, and give you a good factual foundation with which to understand us."

I smiled and nodded. What could I say? He was the learned teacher and I was the willing student. I leaned forward to catch every word.

"Many of your kind," he said, looking me squarely in the eye, "have been taught that the Biblical Adam had only one wife, Eve. Well, this simply isn't true. Eve was not Adam's first wife, she was in fact his second wife. Back in the dim beginnings of time, before there was even a thought of an Eve, Adam had a first wife. Her name was Lilith. She had many names actually. Bat Zuge, Amezo, Abeko, Partashah, Gallu, Lamassu, and more. She was created of corrupted Darkness and was evil in the sight of God. Adam was created of the pure Light and had power, but Lilith's power was greater, and so Lilith looked to dominate him. It was the first instance of the corrupted Dark looking to over-power the Light. This was the beginning, and set the precedent for what was to follow in Ain Sof Aur, the physical universe. Do you understand?"

I nodded. "Please, continue."

"Now, Lilith despised her husband Adam and one day fled from his presence to hide deep within the Void of God. When God saw this, he became very angry and sent three great and powerful angels to bring her back. Their names were Samangaluf, Sansanvi, and Senoi.

"Did they bring her back?"

"Yes, they brought her back, but she fled a second time. This time she vowed never to return to Adam again. You have to understand, my friend, that Lilith represents the Dark Corrupted Powers of Creation, and Adam, the Pure Light Powers. This means that, at the beginning, the corrupted Dark dominated the pure Light. The Universe was in chaos and needed to be balanced. To do this God had to increase the Light Powers, so God created Eve and installed her as Adam's second wife.

"It was God's plan that their union would in time create more Light. However, Lilith despised Adam and his new wife Eve. More so, she despised God, for God sought to balance both the Light and Dark forces within the manifest Universe, and by so doing, limit her power. Remember, Lilith was corrupt and wanted to dominate creation. If the power of Light became her equal, her power would be thwarted and her domination curbed. To prevent this from happening Lilith made herself a vow, an evil oath, and swore to destroy as many of the offspring of Adam and Eve as she could. From that day on, whenever sons and daughters were born to the descendants of Adam and Eve, Lilith would try to kill them in infancy. The medallion that you wear thwarts all her attempts at such things. She would do anything to prevent that medallion from being duplicated and distributed among humankind. Do you understand?"

"Yes, please go on," I said.

"Now, you must understand that it was not enough for Lilith to randomly destroy human newborns, she wanted more! In order to prevent the Power of Light from achieving balance with her, she decided that if Adam and Eve could join in sexual union in order to bring more Light into the world, then she would copulate with their offspring and bring more corrupted Darkness into the world. So, with that in mind Lilith took every opportunity she could to enter into sexual union with man. The offspring resulting from her evilness were born neither pure corrupted Dark, like Lilith herself, nor pure Light like Adam, but came out as an evil corrupted gray. The children born of Lilith's illicit relationships with man were a race of beings that mankind calls *Shadim*, or demons. God, in His anger at Lilith's evilness, her interference with His Redemption, cursed all of her children and condemned them to a world of persistent twilight. That world is called the Dark Malkuth or Malkuth Tachton."

"I see," I said, wanting to know more. "So, that's where demons came from!"

"Yes, that's how we came into being. Now, the first generation of demons that sprang from Lilith's womb were the most powerful and most vile of demons. However, as time passed, her demonic children also copulated with members of the human race. As a result, myriad lesser demons were created. Lilith called her first born Sid. He is a truly evil demon king who rules over legion upon legion of lesser demons and over vast regions of the Dark Malkuth. Like his mother, he also hated mankind. At every turn, he would take the opportunity to kill their infant children. Among the other demon kings of that first generation were Belial, Ashmodai, Obizuth, Asmodeus, Ababaoth, Adijan, and Obandan. There were many others, of course. I am the great grandson of the demon king Belial. My name is Moloch. I was the demon who preyed on the enemies of the ancient Caananites, and so the Caananites thought that I was a god. They brought me all sorts of human sacrifices for my favors. Of course, I was not a god, nor had I ever claimed to be one, but they thought I was. It is very common, you know, for mankind to make the mistake of deifying demons. In fact, we've learned to count on humans doing that. It suits our purposes very well. Most of the peoples of your ancient world made gods of demons."

"Many ancient peoples deified demons?" I asked, truly curious. "And please, Moloch, call me Benjamin."

"Many, Benjamin, many," he said. "There was the demon Dagon, for example, who became the god of the ancient Phoenicians. He was the son of the demon Adijan and grandson of Lilith. He was their sea god. Through Dagon's machinations, the Phoenicians were protected on the sea and became great mariners. Then there was Baal, Dagon's half-brother, who also was deified by the Phoenicians. They made Baal their sun god. Of course Baal became the god of other nations in time. Baal and Dagon hated each other, there was great rivalry between them. One day, a great battle took place between them that lasted a full month. In that time they scarred each other to the point that they became hideous and disfigured. It was their father, Adijan, who finally put an end to it. It was the talk of the Dark Malkuth for ages. There were many, Benjamin, who became gods to the ancient peoples of your world."

"Didn't anyone try to oppose them?"

"Well . . . ."

"Do you mean to say that no one was able to oppose them?"

"I didn't say that, Benjamin. There were two that opposed them and came out victorious. The first was God's prophet Moses. Using the power of the One True God, he defeated them at every turn, but did not destroy them. Still, that was the beginning of the end for them as so-called deities. The one who was truly responsible for their demise was the Master, King Solomon. The ancient world was never the same after he finally destroyed them as gods. When those who had worshiped demons prayed from that time on, there was no one to answer their prayers, for they feared the mighty king. He was fierce in his dealings with them, Benjamin. The demons that humankind turned into gods were no more."

"What happened to them?"

"A few of the minor demons were sent back to the Dark Malkuth by King Solomon, but a great number of the others, the powerful ones . . . ." Moloch went silent.

"What happened to the others?" I asked, seeing Moloch's discomfort.

"King Solomon, well . . . he punished them severely for their evil doings."

"What did he do to them?"

"It's too horrible to talk about. Please . . . I . . . ."

I could tell by the expression on Moloch's face that the fate of the demons that King Solomon punished upset him. I wanted to know more, but decided to let it go.

"Moloch, could you tell me more about the Dark Malkuth?" I asked.

"Yes, Benjamin. As I said before, Malkuth Tachton is a foreboding world of eternal twilight. It exists between the two extremes, that of the pure Light and that of the pure Dark. Remember, Benjamin, that all the demon offspring of Lilith were condemned to that world. This, of course, caused them to hate and fear God all the more. Demons never feared man but hated him to the fullest extent of their beings.

"I understand why they hated God—because of Lilith. But why did they hate man? What did we do to earn their hate?"

"Mostly, because God loved man. That was reason enough for them."

"I see. Moloch, what is the Pure Dark? I was always taught that the beings of pure Darkness were in opposition to the beings of pure Light. How—"

"Benjamin, it's always been clear to my race that humans have had absolutely no understanding about the truth of the nature of things. What you were taught about the beings of Pure Darkness and the beings of Pure Light are perfect examples of this ignorance. For your sake, and for God's sake, I'll touch on the subject just enough so that you can learn the difference."

Moloch readjusted himself on the rock allowing him more space for his large wings.

"Understand, Benjamin, that there are basically six major types of beings in existence. There are beings or angels of the Pure Light, angels of the Pure Dark, corrupted angels of the Pure Light, corrupted angels of the Pure Dark, demons, and human beings. Those beings of the last four categories, namely corrupted angels of the Pure Light, corrupted angels of the Pure Dark, demons, and human beings are all steeped in varying degrees of impurity. That impurity came from the imbalance that existed at the time of creation. It continues to exist today. In time, all of these beings must be, and will be, cleansed of those impurities caused by the imbalance. When that occurs, they will be freed from their corruptions."

"Imbalance? Could you explain that to me?"

"I only know that the universe is imbalanced, an imbalance that had taken place between the masculine and feminine energies of God at the time of creation, and that God is seeking to rebalance it. The rebalancing is part of God's Redemption. It is very complicated."

"I see."

"My friend, you will need someone wiser than I to explain it to you."

"What about the Pure Dark and Evil? Isn't darkness evil?"

"No! No, Benjamin, you must understand that the Pure Dark is not the Pure Evil. The Pure Evil beings are those who intentionally oppose God's Redemption. They are insidious, vile, ill-natured beings who, whether born of the Dark or born of the Light are corrupted with thoughts and actions that center on their own person, their own welfare. They do not consider the welfare of God. The beings of the Pure Evil are known as the Fallen angels. On the other hand, the uncorrupted beings of the Pure Dark, like the beings of the uncorrupted Pure Light, seek only God's good, and do not think of their own personal welfare. In other words, Dark angels are not necessarily Evil angels. Do you understand?"

"Yes, I think so. What you're saying is that humans, on the whole, confuse Darkness with Evil. Because of that misunderstanding, they label Dark angels as Evil angels."

"Exactly!" said Moloch, lightly smiling. "It was your kind, Benjamin, who have never understood the difference, and so are chiefly responsible for perpetuating that ignorance among the more gullible members of your race. Just remember these things and you'll have some insight into the Truth.

"First, it is the impure who hate God, not the pure, whether they be of the pure Light or of the pure Dark. Second, eventually, everything will be purified and separated into the pure Dark and the pure Light. When that happens, then the pure Dark and the pure Light will unite into perfect union. Always remember that the corrupted, even if they are angels, fear God."

"Does Lilith fear God?"

"Yes, she does! She fears God more than any being in existence. She knows that, in time, God will confront her and will ultimately reabsorb her into his unmanifest being. Her interference with God's Redemption is her way of forestalling that."

"I see."

"Anyway, in being condemned to Malkuth Tachton, the demons were much too close to the power of the Beings of Pure Darkness. Understand, Benjamin, the Beings of Pure Darkness are not opposed to God's Redemption and so would, themselves, destroy the demons if they had the opportunity. Lilith was the only exception. She was a being of Corrupted Darkness who rebelled against the Word of God. Because the beings of Pure Darkness do not oppose God's Redemption, but are working with the beings of Pure Light for God's Purpose, the safest place for the demons to go is into the world inhabited by mankind, your world. This is because the Light Malkuth is as far away as they can get from both the beings of Pure Light and from the beings of Pure Darkness."

"Are there many demons in the Light Malkuth?" I asked.

"Yes, many! There are more demons in the world of man than you can imagine."

"Moloch, how can they exist in my world? I mean—"

"It isn't easy for them, Benjamin. To inhabit the Light Malkuth, the world of men, demons require two things. First, they require a sheath, an earthly 'form' to inhabit. It may be a human sheath, if they are fortunate; but demons can also inhabit a plant or animal sheath, some may even use the sheath of water or stone. Secondly, demons, like humans and all other living things, require energy in order to exist. This energy, we demons call Shatok Fen, the ancient Hebrews called it the M'retz Na'she, Feminine Energy. For your benefit, Benjamin, I will mostly use the terms that the ancient Hebrews used. When a demon enters into a human sheath, for example, many things take place that are detrimental to that person. The human loses control of his own body and the demon saps the M'retz Na'she from him, which leaves the human infirm. Often, that person ages very quickly and . . . ."

"And?"

"And eventually dies."

"Is that what we call 'possession'?"

"Yes, possession. I believe that's what humans call it. We call it Tartin Tetos, Proper Domination, the ancient Hebrews called it the Sh'letah Ra, the Evil Domination. Understand, Benjamin, it is an affirmation of demonic belief that it is our right to dominate mankind and his world."

"Do people help demons? I mean . . . ."

"Yes, Benjamin, I know what you mean. Because human beings fear us, or out of ignorance, some of them go to great lengths to see to it that demons are supplied with M'retz Na'she. For example, they make human and animal sacrifices for our benefit, thinking that we will serve them if they supply us with it. They are fools, because demons really only serve themselves. When a sacrifice is made, the dying human or animal gives up his M'retz Na'she and we assimilate the dying creature's energy. It strengthens us and allows us to survive the many rigors of life in your world. In the beginning, we demons did not require humans to make such sacrifices. But as time went on, we learned that mankind was weak. So, we began to demand that they enter into such rituals. It made it easier for us to acquire the necessary M'retz Na'she that we needed to sustain us. Before that, we had to gather it ourselves."

"Are there any other sources of the M'retz Na'she that demons can tap into?"

"Yes. From Lilith."

"Lilith?"

"Yes, Benjamin, from Lilith, herself. In some ways she is like any mother, making sure that her offspring are cared for. Eight times a year she dispenses M'retz Na'she to her demonic children. We call this Diaden Omry, Mother's Gift, the ancient Hebrews called it the Ha'Hay'zeen Ra, the Evil Nurturing. She sees to it that all of her offspring are well fed."

"When does she do this?"

"As I said, she does this eight times a year. Humankind even has special names for those times," said Moloch, with a half-smile. "You call them the Summer Solstice, Winter Solstice, Autumnal Equinox, Vernal Equinox, All Hollow's Eve, Rood-mas, Candlemas, and Michaelmas. The more learned among your race perform rites on those days that try to frustrate the Nurturing, but . . . ."

"But?"

"But it still goes on."

"Moloch, you've been imprisoned in the labyrinth for three thousand years. How long do demons live?"

"It varies on the sort of demon. At the very least, we live five thousand years or so. In my world, we have demons that are very nearly immortal by human standards."

"What happens when demons die?"

"Just like humankind, we go through the process of reincarnation and are reborn back into my world, the Dark Malkuth."

"Moloch, how can a human descend into your world?" I asked, leaning slightly forward.

"How, indeed," said Moloch, his voice seemingly just a little more cheerful now. "Do you know that you were very close to one of the entrances to Malkuth Tachton?"

"I was?" I asked, somewhat surprised. "When was that?"

"When you were down in the Well of Souls! Had you gone just a little farther down, maybe another hundred feet or so, you would have encountered a stone ledge. If you had stood on that ledge you would have seen the entrance of a tunnel that would have taken you to my world."

"How did you know I was in the well?

"As I mentioned, we demons have great psychic abilities, Benjamin. I picked up Ozimon's telepathic alarm—"

"Who?"

"Ozimon. He is one of the demons guarding the entrance to the Dark Malkuth, Benjamin. I believe that you had some sort of contact with him."

"I did. Sort of. I just made it out of the well in time."

"From what I understand, he was very close to killing you, or worse, taking you and binding your sheath to the Dark Malkuth. You'd reached the medallion just in time to break his psychic grip and restore your energy."

"Why didn't he follow me out of the well?"

"He couldn't."

"Why?"

"For two reasons. The first because he was bound to the well by the demon-king Sid. If he left his post, Sid would have killed him."

"And the second?"

"Because of the medallion. He had tried to destroy you psychically, but when he couldn't do it, he knew that you had the medallion. That left him only one choice, to try to get you physically before you left the well. You were very fortunate to have grabbed the medallion when you did. Once it was on your person, Ozimon was powerless over you. The rest you know."

"Was he trying to get the medallion?"

"Yes, even though touching it may have meant his death."

"How?"

"It would have started to drain him of energy. He would have had to hurry to bring it to Lilith."

"Why?"

"So that she could destroy it. She promised that she would bestow eternal life on the demon who brought her the medallion. For that reason and one other, he wanted to stop you from bringing it to the surface."

"What is the other reason."

"To prevent the wise among your people from duplicating it and disseminating it among humankind. Ozimon knew that if that happened, the Light World would remain forever out of reach."

"I see," I said, looking up at Moloch.

"Isn't that what you're going to do with it, Benjamin, have it reproduced?"

"It's not for me to decide."

"I understand," said Moloch, suddenly becoming very pensive. "So much death, so much grief, so much violence and misery."

"Do demons do that to each other? I mean—"

"Benjamin, in some ways demons and humans are very much alike. They look to dominate each other. Demons, like humans, are cruel to each other when it suits their purposes."

"Moloch, you mentioned your world. What is your world like?"

"My world? A human may not find it all that hospitable, but to me, it's home. It's filled with forests, mountains, valleys, lakes, rivers, and mist. It's been so long since I've been there . . . I miss it. Of course, you wouldn't find it nearly so beautiful. In fact, you would probably call it morbid and unfriendly."

Moloch suddenly started to laugh, a deep belly laugh. I couldn't help smiling.

"What?" I asked, almost laughing myself. "What, Moloch?"

"Many humans who actually experienced the Dark Malkuth thought that they were in Hell."

"But, it's not Hell, right?"

"Of course it's not Hell. I suppose for humans, it's what they imagine Hell to be like. But . . . ."

"But?"

"But, even so," said Moloch, his demeanor becoming more serious, "humans do wander into my world, some by accident, and some go there intentionally. They are fools. When their presence is discovered by the demons, the humans are either destroyed or imprisoned. Very few humans have ever escaped my world."

"Moloch, when you say imprisoned, what do you mean?" I asked, trying to imagine what he was alluding to.

"You can see the sheathed souls of the children of Adam and Eve chained to cave walls all throughout my world. There they remain in torment, constantly forced to give up their M'retz Na'she, their Feminine Energy, to us until . . ."

"Until?"

"Until, nothing. They're rarely released, and so they cannot go through the natural death process. If their physical bodies remain soulless, and are not inhabited by a demon, man calls them *dybiks*. We call them *ra'di*, empty vessels. Chaining the sheathed souls of men and women is a way to be able to inhabit their bodies in your world without having to share it with their soul. Of course, if there's no ra'di to enter, a demon would rather share a body than go without."

"How do demons bring this about? How can they enter my world?"

Moloch seemed to have a great deal of patience in fielding my questions. Maybe it was the 3,000 years or so that he spent in captivity here in the labyrinth—I don't know—but I was certainly thankful for it.

"My brothers and sisters enter your world through Vodeshi, what the ancient Hebrews called Sha'arim Pahtuch'im—open gates, or psychic channels created by ignorant humans who, for one reason or another, are too weak-minded to resist our psychic probing. They are unprotected individuals."

"Ignorant? Unprotected?"

"Yes, Benjamin, those whose ignorance has them not believing in God. They form no union with God, and therefore are not under God's protection in such matters. Of course, the medallion represents not only God's protection, but is a definitive declaration by the wearer of their love for God. The combination of the two seals the psychic channels from demonic violation. Do you understand, Benjamin?"

"Yes, I do."

"Good!" said Moloch, suddenly a lighter expression crossed his face. "It's really very funny, mankind even confuses demons with angels. That's how truly innocent they are in such matters!"

"I don't understand," I said. "What demons, with what angels?"

"Yes, Benjamin, they confuse demons with angels. I'll give you an example and you'll know exactly what I mean," he said, suddenly breaking into a broad smile and scratching his head. "Mankind had naively confused Sid, a king of demons, with God's loyal, loving, and obedient servant Satan."

"Wait a minute. Are you saying that Satan isn't evil? I've always been taught that—"

"That is exactly what I mean," interrupted Moloch, waving a taloned finger at me. "What you have been taught is wrong, my friend. Mankind is totally ignorant of these things, Benjamin. Mankind, through Lilith's evil machinations, began to believe that Satan, a loyal servant of God, was actually opposed to God. Humankind naively perpetuated that misunderstanding. It's a perfect example of the blind leading the blind. Satan is neither the foe of God nor the enemy of man."

"But, I've been taught that Satan is demonic and—"

"That's rubbish!" Moloch interjected. "It couldn't be further from the truth. In your own Holy Bible do you not have the story of the trials of Job? Wasn't Satan given permission by God to test Job? If Satan was operating independently of God, why would he need God's permission in order to do his work? In fact, God told Satan that he could test Job, but not to harm him physically. Satan obeyed God's wishes. All of this took place long after the rebellion of the angels. How could Satan have stood in God's presence if he was part of the rebellion? God would have punished Satan for his treason right then and there!"

"Hmm. That sounds right somehow! Please, Moloch, continue."

"Now, on the other hand, the demon king Sid, Lilith's first-born, has all of the attributes that man has ignorantly applied to the Archangel Satan. It is Sid, not Satan who is foremost among the enemies of both God and man. In fact, even the physical description that mankind has applied to Satan is actually a physical description of Sid. Sid is tall and lean, has featherless bat-like wings, and a pointed tail. Sid is the one with the horns of a ram and cloven hooves. Does it sound familiar to you?"

"Yes, it does. Do you mean to tell me that what people believe is Satan, and call the devil, is actually the demon king Sid?"

"Exactly!" Moloch said, leaning toward me. "The Archangel Satan is of a beautiful mien, gleaming white, and handsome. Yes, he is the 'Tempter,' but, as I said before, all the work that he does, he does for God. The idea that he was a fallen angel is absurd. It was created and propagated by ignorant and foolish men. Satan works only in God's best interest. Sid, on the other hand, works only for his own evil ends and those of his mother."

"But, what about all the stories about people selling their souls to the devil?"

"Yes, deals have been many over the years. But those deals weren't made with Satan, those deals were made with us. With our powers, we can grant humankind many of the things that they crave—power, wealth, companionship with the opposite sex. In exchange for those things, a man or woman commits or, in essence, sells their soul to us."

"But how does that work?"

"It's very simple, Benjamin. In making the deal, a psychic gate is opened between the demon and the human—a gate that the human is unable to close and seal. Through that gate we demons can draw that person's M'retz Na'she. When the time for full payment is due, the demon will draw so much M'retz Na'she from the person that the person's sheathed soul begins to separate from his or her body and is then taken to the Dark Malkuth and imprisoned. Once imprisoned, the demon can constantly draw the M'retz Na'she from that person. No, Benjamin, it isn't Satan who collects souls, it's the demons. Sid, by the way, has the largest collection of human souls that I know of. Understand that the collecting of human souls not only supplies demons with M'retz Na'she, but because those imprisoned souls cannot go through the natural process of spiritual evolution it interferes with God's Redemption. This, of course, is what Lilith wants. So, the devil as you call it isn't Satan, the devil happens to be one of us."

"Moloch, you didn't mention anything about Satan's wings. Are they like those of a demon, or feathered like a bird?"

"Wings?" said Moloch, bursting into a loud laugh. "Angels don't have wings!"

"But I thought that—"

"My friend, that is another thing that mankind has never really understood, not even the prophet Ezekiel. Angels do not have wings. What they do have are very powerful, almost plasmic auras surrounding their angelic forms that give them the appearance of having wings, but they're not wings. Often their auras pulsate, which give the impression that their 'wings' are flapping. I'm sorry for laughing, but I've always thought that mankind believing that angels had wings was very funny. Angels are special faces of God, Benjamin. Why would they need wings to get around? They only need to will themselves to where they want to be. Demons don't have that luxury and need wings to move them from place to place."

"I see. What is the relationship then between Satan and demons?"

"Demons fear Satan because he is such a stalwart servant of God. For this reason, demons try to stay out of Satan's way. Those that claim to be Satanists," said Moloch, breaking into almost uncontrollable laughter, "are really Demonists. Those who defile Satan are stupidly aiding the demons in their evil work."

"Moloch, you speak of evil. Clear this up for me, please. What exactly is good, and what's evil?"

"Evil, my friend, is easy to define. It is simply anything or anyone that opposes God's Redemption. There are bad men and bad demons, but they are not necessarily evil men or demons. For example, a man may kill, or steal, or lie, but these are acts that do not necessarily work against God's Redemption. They are merely the acts of bad men. Anyone who intentionally opens up the *vodeshi,* psychic gates, in order to allow demons to enter your world is to be considered evil. By doing this, they are interfering with God's Redemption. Also, anyone, demon or human, who harms God's servants in any way is to be considered evil. Good may simply be understood to be anyone or anything that aids in God's Redemption. It's not really very complicated. Be aware, Benjamin, that those who do not understand the difference between good and evil in this way are ignorant and foolish. They cannot claim to be true servants of God."

Moloch and I had talked long into the night, but I still hadn't asked him about his own situation. I knew that it must be nearly sunrise in the outside world, so I knew I had to be quick about it.

"How did you wind up here? I mean, why were you sealed up here in the labyrinth?" I asked.

Moloch sighed, and tears began to run down his face again as he began to speak.

"As I told you before, Benjamin, I was the great-grandson of the demon king Belial, and the great-great-grandson of the mother of all demons, Lilith. You could say that I was born to evil, and evil I was. I had a natural affinity for it, really. I was ignorant, Benjamin, and in those days I despised both God and man. Now, being the deity of choice of the Caananites, and hating God and man as I did, it was natural for me to make war on the ancient Hebrews and their God. This I did with relative impunity until King Solomon sat the throne of Israel. God, in His wisdom, granted the great king the knowledge and the power to not only control and rule over demons, but also the knowledge, power, and ability to destroy us. There wasn't a demon in existence that didn't fear King Solomon! In fact, even Lilith, herself, feared the mighty king."

"Why hasn't Lilith been destroyed?

"Lilith, the dark Mother, is not a demon, Benjamin. She is of the corrupted Darkness and is immortal. Her fate rests solely in the hands of God."

"I see. Please, go on."

"As I was saying, King Solomon had great power, the power of God. All the demons, including Sid, feared him. In fact, King Solomon was the one who punished my great grandfather, Belial, and even made him dance for the king's amusement. He was further punished by being cursed with flies so that he could no longer use stealth to plague man. King Solomon made it so that flies always preceded Belial, giving away his presence before he could do his nastiness. We demons did everything we could to avoid coming into contact with the nation of Israel while King Solomon lived. To us, going up against King Solomon was the same thing as going up against God, Himself. To do that, as far as we were concerned, would have been the greatest blunder of the ages."

"I see."

"Then, when King Solomon was sixty years of age," Moloch continued, "he knew that he wouldn't have much longer to live, and so he hid sacred relics of his heritage in various places around his kingdom. This labyrinth under the desolate city of Jericho was just such a place. Knowing of the hatred that demons had for God and mankind, and knowing of our longevity, he condemned me to serve him by sealing me in this labyrinth. I was threatened with great punishment if I allowed the prophet Samuel's Oil to fall into the wrong hands.

"Time has passed very slowly for me here. For the first thousand years of my internment I hated God, King Solomon, and all of humankind with a passion unequaled by any demon before or since. I swore in my anger and hatred that, if I were ever freed, I would carry on an eternal campaign to bring an end to them all. I fed off of that hatred. Then, during the second thousand years, I came to think about God and the nature of things. I started to understand things that I had never taken the time to try to understand before. Each new understanding, each new insight that I gained, changed me little by little. It was a kind of spiritual evolution, I suppose. During the third millennium I came to realize God's Truth, and I have repented my ways every day and night from the beginning of that period to the present time.

"Today, you see before you a genuine and humble servant of the One True God. The hate that I once had for God was born out of ignorance. Benjamin, I'm no longer ignorant. I love God with all of my heart and all of my soul, and I have sworn to God to do everything within my power to see to it that His Redemption is attained. To this end, I have done the unthinkable among my fellow demons. Benjamin, I have told you the truth of the things concerning us. I truly love God!"

"What caused you to change?" I asked. "I mean, why did you stop hating?"

"As I said, in my second thousand years I thought about life and God a great deal. I came to realize that hatred is born of fear, and fear is born of ignorance. In other words, I came to understand that demons, just like those of your race, hate the things that they fear, and fear the things that they do not understand. Spending thousands of years by yourself gives you plenty of time to think, and so I took the time to understand God, King Solomon, man, and myself. This understanding completely dispelled my fears, and so, no fears, no hatred. I would recommend this understanding to both demons and humankind alike."

I was both moved and impressed by Moloch's sincerity. I believed he was telling me the truth, that his tears were genuine. I had developed a great fondness for him during our hours together, and I thought that he had developed a great fondness for me as well. We'd become friends. Perhaps it was out of respect for the changes that he had made in his life, or the great love that he spoke of concerning God, or maybe it came from the great relief that I felt from not being mangled to death by him, I don't know. It could have been a combination of all of those things.

"Moloch, friend, the sun will be up soon, and as I promised I'm going to free you. We'll have to hurry, or you're going to turn me into a liar. We have to beat the sun."

Moloch smiled through his tears and said, "I won't make a liar of you, Benjamin. Remember, you must break the seal. I will never forget your kindness. Blessed be the God of Abraham. Come, I will guide you out."

I cut the nylon cord from my waist and followed Moloch through the maze to the beginning of the sloped entrance that first brought me into the labyrinth.

"Just through there," said Moloch. "Be well, Benjamin. May God be with you."

"God bless you, Moloch, my friend," I said, turning and walking up the inclined passageway. "God be with you!"

I was only a few feet from the iron door, and I turned to see Moloch one last time. We stood in silence, staring at each other waving a final farewell. Then, taking a deep breath, I turned and knocked twice on the iron door with my fist. A moment later, three iron bolts were thrown open on the other side and the heavy iron door was pushed open. I walked through the doorway and into the chamber where Yusef, Muhammad, Mara, and Ali were waiting. I handed Yusef my knapsack.

As Yusef began to open the knapsack, everyone, except Mara, rushed to me, telling me how worried they'd been. Mara stood silent, but I thought I detected genuine concern in her eyes. By the look on my face, I was sure it was no great secret that I was just as happy to see them. Once all the greetings and accolades had died down they started to asked me a thousand questions. I stopped them.

"I'll answer all of your questions in a minute," I said, holding up both hands, "but first I have to keep a promise that I made to a new friend."

I picked up the sledgehammer and walked to the iron door. I stared at the pentacle and thought about Moloch as I raised the hammer over my head. With one well-placed strike, I shattered Solomon's magical silver seal. The pentacle shattered into thousands of pieces, and before those thousands of pieces hit the floor, each burst into flame and burned a brilliant indigo. The pentacle was gone, not the slightest trace remained. A moment later something quite unexpected and remarkable happened. In front of our eyes, the reddish orange rust on the iron door began to spread as if it were a living organism. In a few seconds the entire door was covered. A few more seconds, and the rust had consumed all of the door's metal, and the door was reduced to nothing but a pile of rusted flakes on the chamber floor. I sighed and knew that Moloch was free.

We went back to the campsite, where I spent the next few hours discussing my encounter with Moloch with a group of enrapt listeners. Then, around noon, just after we finished eating, Yusef stood up.

"Our friend Benjamin did very well and, of course, we are all proud of him. But there is still much more to do," he announced. "I needn't remind all you that this is just the beginning! Collecting the rest of the holy articles may not be this easy. So, today and tonight we rest, everyone. Tomorrow morning, God willing, we leave for the south!"

10

The Decision

IT WAS NOON BY THE TIME JEHUDA BEN ARI REACHED HIS OFFICE AT Mossad Headquarters. His boss, Assistant Chief Mossad Coordinator Moshe Levy, had been there since eight o'clock.

"So nice of you to pay us a visit, Jehuda," said Moshe, looking at his watch and sipping his tea. "You look like hell."

"I didn't get much sleep." Jehuda rubbed his eyes.

"So tell me, did you hear from your men?" asked Moshe, as he leaned back in his chair and absently scratched food stains from his tie.

"Avram called in about an hour ago."

"Well?"

"Well, he said that my hunch was right. Something's up. He just doesn't know what the hell it is yet. He and Yitzak followed the old man and Arab boy from the King David north to a desolate spot just west of Shillo where they joined an older Arab, about fifty, an Arab girl, about twenty-six or so, and Stein, the American."

"The American? See, maybe it's nothing!" said Moshe, dropping his tie in disgust.

"I'm not so sure, Moshe. Just after dark our boys observed them lowering the American down some hole in the desert. Do you call that nothing?"

"Was he alive?"

"Yeah, but it was still strange. A little while later the American came up and handed the old man something metallic."

"Something metallic?"

"Yes, Avram said that it was some sort of metal cylinder."

"Interesting. Could it be some sort of electronic device?"

"Avram couldn't tell, he was too far away. He thought that the way everyone was fussing about it, that it was either something very valuable or something very dangerous."

"Maybe they're treasure hunters or archeologists? It's a possibility, no?"

"I don't think so. My gut feeling is—"

"Guts, schmuts," said Moshe, swallowing his last drop of tea. "I know your guts tell you a great deal, Jehuda, and I know that they're famous all over the Mideast, but what I want right now are some facts. Evidence! Before I start an international incident with the United States I want more information, something concrete. It's such a small thing to ask, Jehuda. You remember what evidence is, don't you?"

"All right . . . all right!" said Jehuda, holding his head, trying to fight off a throbbing headache. "Facts!"

"What about last night. Anything?" asked Moshe, making another attempt to scratch the stain off of his tie. "What did your man say about last night?"

"Last night?" said Jehuda, now rubbing his temples.

"Last night, man . . . last night! Come on, Jehuda, wake up!"

"All right! Don't push, my head is pounding. Okay, Avram tells me that yesterday they followed our little group through wadis and dry land tracks to Jericho, of all places. It was all they could do to keep from being spotted. He said that the group made camp about a half kilometer from the city."

"Hmm. That's interesting. Jericho, huh?" said Moshe, dropping his tie and giving up on the stain.

"Yeah, interesting. Last night our men almost blew it. They followed the group to an old house in the city. They heard banging and falling bricks like someone was hammering on the walls. Yitzak, well, you know Yitzak when he doesn't get much sleep. He tripped and got his foot wedged between two stones. He made a racket. Avram freed him just in time. Well, the noise that Yitzak made brought the young Arab and the girl up to investigate. They had guns. Our boys got to cover just in time."

"Guns, eh!" said Moshe, picking up a pencil and tapping it on his desk. "What would law abiding people be doing with guns?"

"Yeah, that's what I thought."

"There was no shooting or anything was there?"

"No, but our men had their guns out. We got lucky. But there was something else."

"What?"

"Avram said that he could swear that he saw someone else in the area."

"What do you mean, someone else?"

"I mean that everyone in the group was accounted for, they were all in the building. He and Yitzak swore that they saw someone dart from one building to the next across the way."

"Did they check it out?"

"Yeah, Yitzak did. He couldn't find anyone."

"Maybe we're not the only ones interested in our little group," said Moshe, tapping a pencil on his desk.

"That's what I was thinking. And please don't do that!" said Jehuda, holding his head. Moshe dropped the pencil on his desk.

"What else?"

"Avram said that the little group of ours was in the house until sunrise and then . . . ."

"And then? And then what?"

"And then they left and went back to their campsite. There is something else, though."

"What?" said Moshe.

"Avram said that the old man came out of the house in Jericho carrying a second metallic cylinder."

"You're kidding, another cylinder? So, what do you make of it?"

"I don't know what to make of it, but whatever these guys are I don't like it. Avram said that they're acting very strange. I think that Avram is right, they're trying to be too secretive to suit my tastes. We have to make some sort of decision here."

Moshe leaned forward in his seat. "If they're terrorists, if those damned cylinders are some sort of detonation devices, then we have to stay on them and stop them from using them. If those things are valuable relics of some kind, then we can't allow them to be taken out of the country. Either scenario is a bad one. What about a bug?"

"Avram and Yitzak don't have any with them. This was a spur of the moment thing."

"Right."

"What do you want me to do?"

"Have Avram and Yitzak stay with the group and we'll make our decisions based on their report. And have them watch out for anyone else tailing the group. Tell them to watch their backs. This sounds like it could get complicated."

"Avram and Yitzak have the know-how. If it does get sticky, they'll deal with it one way or another."

"If it does start to get complicated then I might have you join them, so keep yourself available."

"Right. Anything else?"

"Yes. My compliments to that gut feeling of yours."

Tonight I would attempt to retrieve Aaron's Rod. All I could think about as I tried to relax were the miracles that Moses and Aaron had performed with it. It had certainly been enough to impress the ancient Egyptians.

The shadows cast by the mountains lengthened and eventually enveloped us as the sun lowered in the western sky. As it sank, I knew that I would soon be on my way—either inside or outside—Yusef's mysterious mountain. With time drawing ever closer, I walked over to Yusef's tent. The flap was open, and I could see Muhammad pouring two glasses of water. He handed one to Yusef.

"L'chaim!" said Yusef, raising his glass.

"L'chaim, my good friend!" said Muhammad, also raising his glass.

Both men took a sip of water and then put their glasses down on a small brown folding table just inside the tent opening.

"Muhammad, according to the scrolls there is a golden box of some sort containing a very special shofar, a ram's horn, buried under a rectangular stone five paces from the base of the mountain. The scrolls say that the shofar will indicate the site of the entrance."

"How can a shofar do that?" said Muhammad, with a quizzical expression on his face.

"I'm not really sure. We have to trust King Solomon, my friend. Solomon doesn't lie. He's really quite clever. I'll admit he has a tendency to be a little cryptic, but I think that the circumstances require it, no?"

"I suppose," said Muhammad, scratching his chin. "So, we find the shofar, we find the entrance, then?"

"Yes, I have to stand in front of the western face of the mountain and blow the shofar three times."

"Well, then it's good that we're on the western side already. What's supposed to happen when you blow the ram's horn?" said Muhammad, taking another sip of water.

"I don't know, the scrolls don't say. Oh yes, there's something else. Mara asked me if she could accompany Benjamin tonight. I agreed. She's young and strong enough not to have problems, and besides she has an excellent working knowledge of Hebrew just in case it's needed, no?"

"Yes, of course, Yusef, I agree. If a knowledge of Hebrew is needed, Mara's Hebrew is excellent. She has that degree in ancient Semitic languages thanks to you."

"To me?" asked Yusef.

"Yes, you. You know that I make my living selling antiquities. Well, when we first met years ago and I saw the urn that you were carrying, it struck a chord in me that eventually got me involved in dealing in antiquities."

"Is that what got you involved in it? I have always wondered, my friend."

"Yes. My success made it possible to send her to college."

"You did well, Muhammad, she turned into a wonderful woman."

"If her skin weren't so dark, Mara would have no trouble passing for a Sabra. Yes, she's always been a good daughter to me," said Muhammad with pride. "And I must tell you, Yusef, I think that she is growing fonder of Benjamin minute by minute.

"Really? How do you know."

"She asked me how I felt about him," said Muhammad, smiling. "She only asks me how I feel about the men in her life who she is getting serious about. With all the trouble that men have given her, I'm relieved that she is breaking out of her cocoon. I was very worried about her."

"Not to worry, my friend, nature has a way of taking care of things," said Yusef. "It would be a good match, no?"

"Yes, I think so. He's a good man."

"Yes, a good man. Now, Muhammad," Yusef said, standing up and tightening his belt, "we have to find the shofar before we lose the sun, otherwise we're going to lose a day. There's too much at stake to do that. Besides, the way that Solomon explains it, we'll never be able to find it in the dark, so we have to move quickly."

Muhammad nodded and downed the rest of his water.

The two men left the tent, Muhammad with a shovel and Yusef with Solomon's scrolls in one hand and a small black note-book in the other.

"Benjamin," said Yusef, with a serious look on his face, as he noticed me standing near the tent, "you eat and rest, my boy. Muhammad and I are going to look for a shofar that Solomon buried. I'll explain later. We'll be back soon. Oh, by the way, Mara will be going with you tonight."

"Mara?" I said, pretending that I hadn't overheard his conversation with Muhammad.

"Yes, Mara. Not to worry, Benjamin."

I watched Yusef and Muhammad disappear from view in their pursuit of the shofar while the rest of us ate and rested. *Mara's coming with me,* I thought as I laid down on my sleeping bag. *I'm glad to have the company, but . . . .* I drifted off to sleep.

It was just after dark when I awoke. Yusef and Muhammad were just returning from their hunt, carrying a gold box between them. They put the box on the ground by the campfire and we all gathered around it for the grand opening. The box appeared to be made of solid gold and had three good-sized rubies on the front. While not as ornate as the two urns I'd retrieved, the lid of the box was engraved with the words "El Shaddai."

"What does it mean?" Ali asked Yusef.

"El Shaddai, God Almighty. This is the most aggressively protective face of God, Ali." Yusef explained. "The contents must be quite precious, indeed."

Yusef tried to open the box, but the lid wouldn't budge. After several unsuccessful attempts, I watched Yusef take two steps back. He closed his eyes and placed the palm of his hand on the center of his chest. I recognized that he was using the Sha'ar Lev.

A moment later he opened his eyes and dropped his hand. I could tell from the expression on his face that he now had the answer.

"It's the left ruby, then the right, and then the center ruby twice!" he said, smiling and bending down by the box.

He pressed the left ruby, the right ruby, and then the center ruby of the lid twice. The box popped open. A black pouch was cradled in the fine indigo linen that lined the box's interior. The pouch also bore the name of God, El Shaddai. Yusef said a small prayer blessing God and opened the leather pouch. Removing the shofar, he turned it over in his hands, carefully examining every inch of the horn. Nothing seemed special about this shofar—no engravings or markings of any kind. However, we all knew that King Solomon never did anything in an ordinary, unremarkable way. The shofar would show its true colors soon enough, I imagined.

"This shofar is the key that will get you and Mara into the mountain," said Yusef, looking at me and holding the ram's horn out for our inspection. "According to the scrolls I'm supposed to face the mountain and blow three loud blasts of the horn."

"What then? What's supposed to happen?" Mara asked.

"Well, I don't know exactly," said Yusef, with a smile, "but we're going to find out. Right now you know everything that I know. Oh, by the way, Mara, you are to take care of Benjamin tonight and see that nothing happens to him, okay?"

Mara smiled and nodded her okay. She glanced over at me, then looked to Ali and Muhammad.

"Remember, let nothing happen to him, Mara," said Muhammad sternly, and also showing a little pride on his face. "And let nothing happen to you either, or you'll . . . well, both of you come back safely."

"Yusef," I said, "inside or outside? What I mean is, are we going into the mountain, or are we going to have to scale it?"

"Inside, my boy, inside. At least I hope so. Soon we'll know for sure."

I looked at Mara and smiled. She caught my gaze and our eyes locked.

"Hey, pay attention, you two," said Yusef, his manner suddenly turning more serious. "There's something that you two should know that just might make things a little, well, sticky." Judging by the look on his face, that "little something" was not entirely inconsequential.

"What should we know?" I asked nervously.

"Well," said Yusef, locking my gaze with his, "it seems that there is a time limit."

"A time limit? What does that mean, a time limit?"

"Well, it seems," said Yusef, glancing at Muhammad and then back at me, "that the entrance will only remain open for three hours, so . . . ."

"So, we have to get Aaron's Rod and be out of there in three hours," I said, glancing at Mara. "What happens if we're not out in time?"

"Well," said Yusef, peering at me and Mara over his glasses. "You'll be sealed up inside that mountain forever. Do you understand, you two? Forever."

"I understand," I said, exchanging glances with Mara. We both knew what "forever" meant. It meant no more food, no more sunlight, no more walks on the beach, no more life.

Yusef handed Muhammad the shofar and then unrolled the scrolls.

"There's something else," said Yusef, pointing to a place in the scrolls. "King Solomon also added this passage. I'll translate it for you: 'For He will give His angels charge over thee, to keep thee in all thy ways. They shall bear thee upon their hands, lest thou dash thy foot against a stone.'"

"What does it mean, Yusef?" I asked.

"They are verses eleven and twelve of the ninety-first psalm," said Yusef, with a puzzled look on his face. "I don't know why he included it here, but I think that it would be a good idea if you remember it. I wrote it down for you. Remember, King Solomon didn't do anything without a good reason."

I took the piece of paper from Yusef, looked at it, and slipped it in my pocket.

"Now, we have an hour before we do this so I want both of you to stay here and relax." He stood and walked over to join Muhammad by the van. Clearly he wasn't going to give me the chance to ask anything else about what Mara and I were up against.

Mara was sitting across from me. She didn't say a word, in fact she seemed to avoid any sort of eye contact with me at all.

"Look," I said, getting her attention. "We don't have to be friends, but we don't have to be enemies either."

"I'm not your enemy," she snapped. "I just can't figure you out."

"You can't figure me out? That's a laugh. I can't figure you out!"

"There's nothing to figure out about me!"

"Look, your brother said that—"

"My brother is stupid and says too much."

"But—"

"But," she said, her voice suddenly softening as she looked up at the mountain, "but you're right. We're going to need each other tonight, so let's get along."

"Good," I said, extending my hand, "a truce then. Peace?"

She cracked a smile. "A truce." We shook hands.

Neither of us spoke much over the next hour. I was lost in my own thoughts about the mountain and what lay ahead for us that night. Occasionally, though, we exchanged glances that told me that the distance between us was narrowing quickly.

Suddenly, we heard Yusef's voice interrupting our musings. "Come on, you two, it's time."

A few minutes later the five of us, led by an anxious Mara, walked to the base of the mountain.

"Yusef," I said, not being able to help myself, "Did Solomon say anything else? Anything at all? Did he mention anything about the inside?"

"Nothing," Yusef replied. "He told us, I suppose, everything that he thought that we should know about the mountain. The rest you'll have to figure out as you go along. Are you ready?"

I nodded. Did I have a choice?

"Okay, everyone, stand back," said Yusef, waving everyone away. "We don't know what's going to happen and I don't want anyone getting hurt."

Everyone moved back to what we thought was a safe distance. Yusef took a step forward and said a short prayer in Hebrew. When he finished, we all gave an "amen" and watched him raise the ancient shofar to his lips. He blew three powerful blasts on the horn. We waited . . . five seconds . . . fifteen seconds . . . twenty seconds . . . nothing happened. Yusef looked back at us and shrugged.

"Try it again, Yusef," Muhammad urged. Yusef nodded and turned to the mountain. He lifted the shofar to his lips. As he filled his lungs with air for another powerful blast, there was a small, nearly imperceptible rumbling of the ground. At first, it wasn't much. Then its intensity increased and it was all we could do to keep our balance. Before our eyes a small section of rock-facing on the mountain gave way and crashed to the ground revealing a small compartment similar to those I had found in the Well of Souls and the labyrinth. As the tremors subsided, we dashed to the compartment.

In the very center of the compartment, glistening in the moon-light, was a solid gold, T-shaped lever. I looked at Yusef. "What should we do? What do the scrolls say?"

"You must be the one to pull it, Benjamin." said Yusef. "Go ahead, son, pull it."

I put my hand on the lever. "Stand back, way back. I have no idea what's going to happen when I pull this thing."

My companions stood back and I took a hard swallow, a deep breath, closed my eyes, and pulled the lever. Nothing happened. Nothing, except that the lever came off in my hand. I took a few steps back and looked up at the mountain. Nothing. I turned around and joined the group. Muhammad, Mara, and Ali didn't say a word, and I handed the lever to Yusef.

"Hmm," said Yusef, examining it. "Did we miss something?"

"I don't think so," I said, somehow feeling a little guilty. "Did I break it or was this the way Solomon's special handles worked, like the one in the Well of Souls? Maybe I was supposed to push it instead of pull it?"

"I don't know," said Yusef, looking up at the mountain. "Maybe you're right and this is the way it's supposed to work. I wish Solomon would have mentioned something about this."

"Maybe we have to . . ." began Muhammad.

"No!" said Yusef, his eyes narrowing as he continued to stare at the mountain. "Something's happening. Can you feel it?"

There it was, still faint, but I could tell it was slowly growing stronger. It reminded me of the subtle vibration I used to feel when I stood on a subway platform back in New York when the train was coming, but still far away. It was an exciting feeling, one that increased in tension as the train drew near—a low, muted rumbling that increased in intensity with every passing second.

"Yusef," I began, when I was suddenly interrupted by a tremendous cracking sound that echoed through the neighboring mountains. Then, a rumbling of nearly earthquake proportions shook the ground beneath us. Ali dropped to the ground followed by Muhammad and Yusef. Mara grabbed my arm, and we struggled to stay standing. The mountain shook violently for a good ten seconds and then, right in front of us, the entire red-rock facing of the mountain cracked, crumbled, and came crashing to the ground with a thunderous roar. After the dust settled and the rocks stopped falling, a dark, narrow portal just fifteen feet or so to the left of the center of the base of the mountain had been revealed.

"Quick, you two," yelled Yusef, waving us on, "that's your entry. Go! Go! You only have three hours. Go quickly!"

Mara and I ran to the entrance, turned on our flashlights, took a deep breath, and stepped into the darkness.

"God be with you!" called Muhammad. "God be with you both!"

Crossing the portal, Mara and I found ourselves standing in a small foyer. We could make out a dust-laden stairway ascending into, I guessed, the heart of the mountain. It seemed to be the only way up.

"Well, Mara, that seems to be our route," I said, staring at the very narrow, very steep sandstone stairs. "You follow me," I said. "Remember, we only have three hours, so let's move! Okay?" I began the climb with Mara close behind. Running my hands along the walls to keep balance, I found them rough and sandpapery. The ceiling hung low; I had a clearance of only about five inches for my six-foot frame. It was a claustrophobe's worst nightmare.

"It must have taken them quite a while to chisel this out," I mused aloud as I peered up the staircase into the darkness. "I would have preferred an escalator or elevator, but I guess the stairs will have to do." Mara only grunted her response as we climbed.

Moving cautiously at first, we gradually picked up both speed and confidence. The air was stale and musty, the product of three thousand years of stagnation. Every step we took raised little clouds of reddish gray dust, which only added to the pollution. Higher and higher we climbed, step by step, deep into the heart of the mountain. Along the way I checked my watch. Thirty-five minutes had passed already and we were still ascending. Mara started to cough.

"Mara, are you all right?"

"Yes." she said between coughs. "It's just all this dust."

There were no markings on the walls of the stairway, no signs, no engravings, nothing to indicate whether or not we would find Aaron's Rod at the end of our journey. Then, our path on the stairs turned sharply to the left. Then to the right. For reasons known only to him, King Solomon now had us zig-zagging to the heart of the mountain. Exacerbating our disorientation, there were no changes of scenery. One place along the stairway looked just like any other.

Time was passing very quickly in this nightmarish pursuit. I had no idea how high we had climbed or how far we had yet to go. All I knew for sure was that we were climbing higher and higher. Whether the stairway went left or right didn't really matter, we were climbing all the time. There was darkness in front of us and darkness behind us. The humidity in the air increased with every step making the sooty darkness almost palpable. My breathing become more labored and I could hear Mara panting behind me.

The sounds of our footsteps and the beating of our hearts seemed to echo up and down the stairwell. I couldn't help but remember the demon that had stalked me in the Well of Souls, and I found myself listening for the sounds of distant growling. Moloch had said that it was a demonic guard. *Could there be one in here?* I wondered. Well, if there was, then we were doomed. Where could we run?

Nearly an hour into our climb the narrow stairway took a sharp turn to the right and opened into a small corridor. It was only four feet wide, but after the steep, narrow stairs, it felt as wide as a football field. I turned to Mara, smiled and said, "Well, this is a little better."

Mara smiled back at me, pausing to catch her breath. Then, shining her light up ahead, I watched her smile slowly fade and disappear.

"What's up?" I said, turning around, flashlight in hand, to see what broke her smile. I felt my smile melt away, too. The corridor had ended and we now found ourselves facing what looked to be a twelve-foot-wide chasm. I walked to the edge and looked down. It was a sheer drop, probably to the bottom of the mountain, with no apparent way across. Twelve feet of nothingness stood between us and and the small ledge on the other side.

It may as well have been a hundred-foot gap, or a thousand-foot gap. There was no way that we could jump across it, no way for us to construct a bridge. We were trapped. What was I going to tell Yusef? "Excuse me, Yusef, but it wasn't our fault. Solomon should have told us about the gap."

"I don't like this," said Mara, staring down into the abyss.

"I don't understand it," I said, looking down into the abyss with her. "Damn! Why would Solomon have brought us all the way up here, only to have us fail?"

"Maybe we missed something along the way," Mara said, taking a quick look behind her. "Maybe King Solomon . . . ."

"No, we didn't miss anything. There was nothing to miss!"

I looked at my watch. Time was running out. I was just about to check the walls of the corridor for another hidden lever, or a sign of what to do next when I remembered the verses. "Solomon's verses, Mara! The answer has to be there!" I pulled the paper Yusef had given me from my pocket.

"What? What do you mean?" asked Mara.

"Sssh," I closed my eyes. "I'm trying to think."

I went over the verses again and again in my mind. Angels, stone, hands . . . damn it! I couldn't think straight. I had to clear my thoughts. I used the Nefesh Hafsa'kah, and then the Sha'ar Lev and went over the verses again. Suddenly, remarkably, the meaning of the verses crystallized in my Higher Mind.

"I have it!" I said, smiling and wiping the sweat from my forehead. "Let's go, but you have to trust me. Believe me, Mara, you're really going to have to trust me on this one. And, even more, both of us are going to have to trust God."

"What are you going to do, Benjamin?" said Mara, nervously rubbing her palms together. "You're not going to—"

"Quiet," I said, looking down into the blackness of the bowels of the mountain. "If this doesn't work then I'll be the first one down the mountain. I'll probably beat you to the bottom by forty-nine minutes."

Apparently, Mara didn't appreciate my gallows humor—she didn't smile back. All she did was drop a stone into the abyss and watch it disappear into the foreboding blackness below.

Slowly, I inched up to the edge of the abyss. I whispered a little prayer to tell God how much I trusted in Him, took a deep breath, and stepped off the ledge. To my amazement, I didn't fall. Something was there supporting me. I turned to Mara. She stood on the ledge, her mouth hanging open. She seemed as amazed as I was.

Step by careful step I made my way across the abyss and onto the small rocky ledge on the other side. It was nothing less than a miracle. "This is the genius of Solomon and the power of God!" I called to Mara. "Now you must cross. Just remember, trust in God . . . and don't look down!"

She ran her arm across her forehead to wipe away the sweat, closed her eyes, and took her first step. She, too, stood suspended over the chasm. Slowly, carefully, she took each step. "You're almost across," I called to her. Wide-eyed, she smiled to me. A moment later, she was standing next to me.

"How . . . er . . . " she stammered, putting her hand to her chest, and looking back at the gap she just crossed. "How . . . ."

"Do you remember the verses from Psalm 91 that Solomon put in his scrolls?"

"Yes, the ones that Yusef read."

"Right. Well, I knew that there must have been a reason for it. Solomon wasn't the type to waste words, but it wasn't until I used the Sha'ar Lev that I understood exactly what he was trying to say. I don't know, it came over me like a sort of revelation.

Listen to it again, Mara. 'For He will give His angels charge over thee, to keep thee in all thy ways. They shall bear thee upon their hands, lest thou dash thy foot against a stone.' Angels, get it? Real angels! They 'bore' us on their hands!"

"Angels?"

"Yes, angels! You're standing here, aren't you? How do you think we crossed the chasm?"

"God is great!" said Mara, looking at her feet planted firmly on the ledge, and then turning and looking back at the gap. "God is truly great!"

"Yes. Yes, he truly is." I paused for a second. "Now, come on, we have to move. The clock's ticking."

We turned and found a doorway that opened into a small room hewn into the core of the mountain. We stood at the entrance shining our flashlights into the darkness. It didn't help, we couldn't see anything.

"What do we do?" asked Mara, leaning in and moving her flashlight around. "I can't see anything, can you?"

"No, nothing. Well, that's good anyway!"

"How can that be good?" asked Mara, turning to me with a puzzled expression on her face. "What do you mean, 'that's good'?"

"Well, not being able to see anything means that from what we 'can' see, there's nothing bad in there, right?"

"So?"

"So, let's go in and take a closer look," I said, taking Mara's hand in mine. "What else do we have to do? We're not going to accomplish anything standing here. Besides, time is flying and I don't want to get trapped inside this mountain. Let's just go in, all right?"

Mara nervously nodded her agreement.

We stepped through the doorway and walked into the room. Everything seemed fine, but as soon as we reached the center of the room, there was a loud, grinding sound. Turning around, we were just in time to see a huge stone door slide out of the ceiling and crash to the floor. It had sealed our entrance—and our only exit. We rushed to the doorway and tried to lift the stone slab, but it was too heavy. We tried to push it, pull it, and hammer at it with our fists, it wouldn't budge. We were trapped.

"I don't like this," I said, shining my flashlight all over the door looking for some sort of lever or button. I ran my hands around the wall bordering the door. There was nothing.

"What now?" asked Mara, her eyes the size of half-dollars.

"Well, I guess we're stuck here. We may as well look around. Maybe while we're looking for Aaron's Rod, we can find another way out."

I shined my flashlight around the room and discovered there wasn't much to see. The floor and walls were made of some smooth polished black stone that reflected the light at all different angles. Five torches were set on the walls in brass holders—one each on three walls and two on the wall directly in front of us. However, there didn't seem to be any other doors or passage-ways. *This is it,* I thought, *our journey ends here.* I looked at my watch. It had taken us an hour to get up here, that meant an hour to get back. Unless we could get out of this room in less than an hour, Mara and I were finished—sealed up in here forever.

I fumbled in my pockets for the book of matches I'd grabbed from the lobby of the King David the night that my adventures had begun. We lit the five torches and the room became bright. In the glow of the torches, Mara and I searched every corner of the room, hoping to find Aaron's Rod lying on a table that we had missed, or propped against a wall just waiting for us to take it. No such luck! Aside from the torches, brass holders, and us, the room was completely empty.

I began running my hands along the walls, knocking here and there to see if there might be a secret panel hiding another door-way that might lead to another chamber. My hands slid across the walls, but the sounds my knuckles made were uniform wherever I knocked. My fingers caught on no seams where a panel might have been.

"Benjamin!" Mara interrupted my silent search. I turned to see what had captured her attention.

She was pointing to the wall in front of her. Set into it, between two torches, was a silver pentacle and an inscription in Hebrew, displayed in large gold letters. I must have been blind not to have spotted it first, but I guess I was too engrossed in the idea of finding a secret panel. Or perhaps it hadn't been there when I first looked at the wall.

"The whole thing just appeared out of nowhere! I mean, right in front of me," said Mara, not taking her eyes from the wall. "It just materialized. Just like . . . ."

"What does it say?" I asked, hoping, praying that Mara would be able to read it.

"It's written in verse," she said, walking closer to the wall. "It's some sort of riddle."

"A riddle?"

"Yes, at least I think it's a riddle . . . ."

"Translate it for me."

"Okay," she said, wiping the perspiration from her eyes and taking a deep breath. "It says:

> *Both cups erect and heart aligned*
> *stand firm upon the unseen line;*
> *If the staff you have, then the staff I'll give;*
> *If you fail to solve, you shall not live!"*

"It's a riddle!" I said, rubbing my nose, trying to keep from sneezing from the dust.

"Yes. I told you it was a riddle. I don't understand it, do you? What does it mean?"

"It means," I said, looking her squarely in the eye, "that we have less than an hour to solve this thing. If we don't, we're history! It means that if we don't find the answer to the riddle, your brother becomes an only child, Yusef never gets Aaron's Rod, the world gets an untrained Messiah . . . get it?"

We sat down against the wall with the inscription. Mara read the riddle to me over and over again. Cups? Heart? Line? I ran though everything that I knew of that related to cups . . . tea cups, coffee cups, oil cups, bra cups, hic-cups, athletic cups, cups this, cups that, cups the other, cups, cups, cups. I didn't get it! What kind of cups?

I looked over at Mara. She had her knees pulled up close to her chest and had her face buried in her folded arms. I took up the same pose. Time was running out and so were my ideas. Nothing came to me, so, quietly, I used the Sha'ar Lev. I closed my eyes and put my hand to my chest.

"Mara!" I said, jumping to my feet. "I've got it . . . hands!"

"What?" said Mara, looking up at me with a confused expression on her face. "Hands? I don't get it."

"Yes! Hands can form cups! Get it now?" I drew my hands together at chest level. "Heart aligned, it means that I cup my hands and bring them up to my chest, you know, at heart level, like this!"

"What about the 'unseen line'? What about that, Benjamin?"

"There must be a clue here somewhere. Maybe there's some sort of line drawn that we've missed."

Mara stood up and we searched the entire room for anything that resembled a line. We checked the walls, the floor, and even the ceiling. There was nothing that even remotely looked like a line. All the time, we both knew that time was running out. We sat down on the floor again and leaned against the wall.

"We're doomed," said Mara, turning her head down and covering it with her hands.

I didn't say anything, I just sat there searching the room for a sign of a line. I was drawn to the pentacle. There, right in the middle, in solid silver, was the image of a closed eye. I leapt to my feet and stood in front of it. I was sure that this had something to do with the line that Mara and I were searching for. I closed my eyes and used the Sha'ar Lev again. My Higher Mind responded immediately. "Mara!" I yelled. "Get up, I have the answer!"

"What?" said Mara, looking up at me. "You have the answer? You found the line?"

"Well, you're going to have to trust me again. Get up and stand directly behind me! Hurry!"

Mara came over and stood behind me. "Benjamin, I don't think that—"

"Sssh! Be quiet," I said, turning around and holding my index finger to my lips. "Just stand there and no matter what happens, no matter what you see or hear, or even feel, don't move! If you move from that spot we'll be trapped in here forever!"

Mara looked frightened. I watched her squeeze her eyes closed and cover her mouth with her hands. I turned back and stared at the closed eye in the middle of the silver pentacle, and then back at Mara. Everything was in place. "Remember, Mara, be still. Whatever you do, don't move!"

I took a deep breath and raised my cupped hands, bringing them into alignment with my heart. Then, with all my might, putting all my faith in God, I imagined that Aaron's Rod was already in my possession, that the great rod was already in my hands, and I waited for something to happen

Seconds later, countless specters of unimaginable terror came through the walls; grotesque images of grim demonic horrors, large images, small images, mixed images. It was a kaleidoscopic horror show. They assailed us from every direction. My shirt was soaking with perspiration, my heart raced, and my throat ached from lack of moisture, but I held my ground and affirmed my trust in God. Then, as quickly as it began, it was over. The whole grotesque display lasted only a minute, but it felt like an eternity. It had been difficult, but through it all I had continued to imagine Aaron's Rod in my hands. I refused to allow the bombarding images to break my concentration; instead they caused me to concentrate even harder. Still I continued visualizing Aaron's Rod in my hands. The minutes passed . . . one minute . . . two minutes . . . three minutes. As the third minute ticked past, I felt a heaviness in the palms of my hands, a woody girth. I opened my eyes. Aaron's Rod had miraculously materialized in my hands. It was real and it was solid, a six-foot staff of very old, and very real, wood. I felt its power vibrating in my hands.

"Mara!" I said. "It's all right! Open your eyes and see what I have."

Mara ran around and stood in front of me. I held the rod in my raised hands.

"Thank God!" Mara said, staring at the rod. "You have it, Benjamin. How on earth . . . ."

"I don't think that the earth had anything to do with it."

"How did you get the rod?"

"It was the eye," I said, nodding towards it. "It's closed!"

"So?"

"So, a closed eye can't see, right?"

"Right."

"I had you stand behind me, right?"

"Right."

"Well, you and I formed a line . . . an unseen line! The eye couldn't see the line we made! Get it?"

"Benjamin, you're a genius!" she said, a broad smile coming to her face. "But, what about the rest of it, you know, about having it or not having it, or something?"

"That's where the Sha'ar Lev came in. I used it, and just like that my Higher Mind brought me the words . . . 'Trust! You must believe!' At first I didn't know what it meant, but then it came to me. I realized that it meant that I had to believe that I already had the rod. So, I concentrated and began to believe with all of my heart that I already had it in my hands. Then, suddenly, well, we have the rod and that speaks for itself. What a world we live in, Mara."

"Yes! But, Benjamin, tell me what happened when I had my eyes closed," said Mara.

With her eyes closed, she had missed the horrific slideshow. "You didn't miss much. It was no big deal."

Mara stared at the rod.

"Is that really Aaron's Rod?" she asked, reaching out to touch it, but stopping short and pulling her hand back out of fear.

I looked at my watch. It was late. "Come on," I said. "We only have fifty minutes to make it out of here."

"But, the door?" said Mara, pointing to it.

"Right! I almost forgot about that."

"So?"

"Sssh! Let me think!"

I decided to let the Sha'ar Lev do the work for me again. I said a quick prayer and then sought the wisdom hidden in my Higher Mind. It came to me with very little effort. I walked to the door and touched the end of the rod to the center of the stone slab. A moment later, with a loud grinding noise, the slab started to rise.

"God is great," I said. "Who else but God could do something like this?"

The slab disappeared into the ceiling.

"Come on . . . let's go!" I said, nodding toward the exit. "Time's running out. We're going to have to run out too!"

We stepped out of the room and onto the ledge. Instinctively, I touched the end of the rod to the space over the abyss. A bright indigo-colored path flowed from the ledge and spanned the gap.

"Come on!" I said, looking at my watch. "We've got to hurry!"

I led as we ran over the indigo path bridging the abyss, scurried through the small foyer and started down the stairs. We ran down the narrow, dusty stairway as fast as we could go using our hands on the walls to steady us. It was precarious, the stairs were so dark and narrow, the walls we were using for balance uneven, and my hands were full with the rod and the flashlight. My heart was pounding in my chest, and at one point I thought I was going to pass out. The narrow staircase turned right, then left, then right again, then left. The tight curves of the zig-zagging stairs proved too steep for our speed. Mara tripped, falling into me from behind and down we went, bumping, bouncing, and rolling, ten feet, fifteen feet, twenty feet, down the stony stairway. My body didn't miss a step. When we finally stopped falling, I staggered to my feet. I had dropped the rod somewhere on the stairs behind us. We were now in darkness and coughing from all the dust we raised. I banged the flashlight against my hand; it was dead. But, light or no light, I had to go back for the rod.

"Mara, are you all right?" I called into the darkness.

"Yes, I'm okay," she answered, her voice disembodied in the pitch.

"Good! Now go! Run and I'll follow."

"Why? What happened?"

"I dropped the rod. I have to go back for it."

"No, I'm staying with you," she said, still coughing.

"Don't argue . . . go!"

"But . . . ."

"But, nothing. Go! And, don't kill yourself getting out of here. I'll be coming fast and I don't want to trip over you on my way out!"

I felt Mara's hands reach around my body giving me a hug and I felt her lips brush mine. I would have responded, I wanted to respond, but there wasn't time. I pushed her firmly from me. "Mara, please, run. You must get out of here."

"Benjamin, I . . . I," she said nervously.

"Whatever it is, it'll have to wait. Now go!" I said. She left. I could hear the sound of her feet running down the stairs and echoing off the walls. They grew more and more faint.

Damn it! I said to myself. *Where the hell is the rod?*

On my hands and knees I made my way back up the stairs searching for the rod. Five, ten, fifteen steps up, there was no rod. Step by step, wall to wall, I swept the darkness with my hand. Suddenly, my hand struck something. Then came the dull sound of wood striking stone. I felt around and finally grabbed the rod. I took a moment to run my hands along its surface, searching for damage. It seemed to be in good shape. Holding it tightly in my left hand, I turned and started back down the stairs as fast as my legs would carry me.

Down, down, down, I sped through the darkness, all the time knowing that I was running out of time. My heart was pounding in my chest and my lungs ached, but I knew that I couldn't stop to rest . . . I had to keep going. I hoped that Mara had made it out. I had no idea how much time I had left when I finally reached the main, nearly vertical stairway we had encountered at the beginning of our journey into the mountain. I stopped just long enough to light a match and check my watch. *Damn! Only seven minutes left,* I said to myself. *If I ever get out of here alive, I'll . . . I'll . . . well . . . shit!*

Just as I started down the final dark stairway, I began to hear a faint rumbling noise. A moment later the stairway started to quake beneath my feet.

"Damn it!" I tightened my grip on the rod and started to run again. My knuckles were raw and bleeding, but I was too filled with adrenaline to feel the pain. Everything was disintegrating all around me. I could hear great cracks splitting the walls and stone steps, and I could feel the steps quaking and crumbling beneath my feet.

"I don't like this!" I shouted out to the dark, almost tripping on an uneven step. Regaining my balance, I continued running as fast as I could. I heard the crashing of rocks on the stairway behind me, but I wasn't about to stop to look back.

"This mountain's coming down," I said to myself.

I could feel the blood from my skinned knuckles running down my fingers. I ignored it as I continued to use them, bloody or not, on the sandy walls to steady me. I was gasping for air now, it felt like my heart was going to burst. Below me I could see a splinter of light. The exit! I dashed for the light as stones of every size and shape fell all around me, one caught me on the shoulder sending a bolt of pain down my arm to the hand that held the rod. I almost dropped it again.

I knew there were only seconds left when I made it to the small foyer. I dove for the entrance only to look up and find myself just short of the goal. "Shit!" I said, as I turned my head and looked behind me. The entire inside of the mountain was coming down around me. *I'm a dead man,* I thought, tightening my grip on the rod. *I'm not going to make it out of here!*

I tried to get to my feet, but I couldn't do it. I was too weak to stand, let alone run. I was about to crawl when I felt two pairs of hands grab my shoulders and arms, yanking me out of the mountain. Just as my feet cleared the doorway there was a huge rumble and the rest of the inside of the mountain came down, sealing the entire length of the stairway and entrance foyer. I looked up to see Muhammad and Ali.

Braced between Ali and Muhammad, with Aaron's Rod firmly in my grasp, we hurried away from the entrance and turned around just in time to see the entire upper levels of the mountain come crashing to the ground raising huge clouds of dust and debris into the air. After the last of the rocks stopped falling and the dust settled, it was clear to all of us that it had been King Solomon's magical way of sealing the entrance to the mountain for all time. Awestruck, I stood staring at the rubble.

I was still panting and coughing when I heard Yusef call my name as he came up and joined us.

I turned to Yusef and handed him Aaron's Rod.

He smiled back at me. "God is great, no?" he said, looking at the rod with a great admiration and respect. "You and Mara are safe and that's good, very good, and you brought me the rod. You both did very well."

"It was close, no?" said Muhammad, taking out his handkerchief and wrapping it around my bruised and bloody knuckles. "When Mara came out and told us what happened, Ali and I decided to wait for you by the entrance."

"I'm glad you did," I said, finally catching my breath. "If it wasn't for you and Ali, I'd be, well, thanks."

"My sister feels very bad about what happened inside," said Ali, bending down to tie his shoe. "She really feels like it's her fault!"

"It wasn't your sister's fault at all. Where is she?"

"She's resting at the campsite, Benjamin, and that's where you should be right now!" said Muhammad, smiling. "Go to her, my boy."

Muhammad and Yusef exchanged glances. They always seemed to be carrying on some sort of clandestine conversation with their eyes.

"Come, everyone," said Muhammad, "let's go back to camp. I think we have some wounds to attend to. Ali, as soon as we get to camp prepare some food and tea. We have to celebrate the recovery of Aaron's Rod and toast our heroes!"

"And we have to hear of their exploits in the mountain," said Yusef, smiling and staring at Aaron's Rod, safe and secure in his hands.

As soon as we got to camp, Mara ran up to me and gave me a big hug. "Oh, Benjamin, I was so worried about you," she said, tears running down her cheeks. "I'd never have forgiven myself if . . . I feel like such a klutz."

"A klutz? Mara, I almost fell a dozen times. I couldn't have done this without you. You translated the writing on the wall. Without you we wouldn't have Aaron's Rod. You're a heroine!"

A smile spread across Mara's face. "Really?"

"Yes! Now, no more of this klutz nonsense, all right?"

"All right."

"Friends?"

"Friends," said she with a warm smile.

I was just about to throw my arms around her and kiss her. I lost my nerve at the last second, though, and stepped back. I think that I caught a look of disappointment in her face.

"Well," I said, feeling a little ashamed of my sudden cowardice. "Now . . . ."

"Now?"

"Now, let's join the others," I said, giving her a warm smile, "before they come looking for us." She nodded. I took her hand in mine and we joined the others around the campfire. Ali's Mideastern Stew Surprise was reheated, tea was on the boil, and we all settled back in our chairs around the fire.

12

Private Lessons

I DIDN'T GET UP UNTIL ALMOST NOON THE NEXT DAY. MY EXPLOITS in the mountain took more out of me than I was used to. Or maybe I was just getting old. I was a mess, my hands, elbows, and knees were torn up, but luckily, nothing that required stitches. I'd just woken up, and already I was sweating, too. The hot sun was beating down on the roof of the tent; it must've been a hundred and ten degrees. I kept looking at the tent flap, expecting Yusef to come bursting in to tell me that I had to go back into the mountain and dig my way up to the room to retrieve something that he had forgotten to tell me about last night. I sat on my sleeping bag and waited, but he didn't show up. Neither did Mara.

The tent soon filled with the aroma of food. Something wonderful—different than Ali's famous lamb stew—was being cooked outside. I was starving; I cleaned up and dressed in a hurry. Stepping out of the tent, I stopped dead in my tracks. To my surprise, I saw that Yusef was today's mystery chef. There he was, khaki everything, stooped over the fire, frying pan in hand, singing some Yiddish folk song. He wasn't a Pavarotti, but he wasn't that bad either. I could tell that he was a very happy man.

"Boker tov, Yusef!" I said, hoping that whatever he was cooking, he was cooking for the both of us.

"Boker tov, Benjamin," he said, splitting his attention between me and the frying pan. "You're up just in time for lunch. Well, breakfast for you."

"It smells good, really good. What is it?"

"I'm reheating Ali's lamb stew from yesterday," he said, smiling. "Have a seat, my boy, it's almost ready."

Yesterday I would rather have eaten reheated tree bark than any more of Ali's stew, but today, Ali's stew sounded great. *I must really be hungry,* I thought, breathing in the aroma of the stew and looking around the camp. Two director's chairs were in a shaded area next to the campfire. I walked over and sat down. A few minutes later, Yusef brought me my plate of stew and a cup of hot tea. Shortly, he joined me with his own lunch.

"Where is everyone?" I asked.

"Muhammad took Mara and Ali to Jerusalem to pick up some more supplies. They won't be back until late tonight. We'll have the whole day to talk."

I expected Yusef to mention something about Mara and me, but he didn't. I smiled and raised my tea cup. "A toast, Yusef! To good conversation, the Messiah, and God!"

He raised his cup, sipped his tea, and smiled. "Benjamin, how are you doing?" he asked, suddenly a little more serious. "Really, how are you doing?"

"Fine," I said, trying to balance the plate on my lap. "The scratches are nothing. I was in worse shape after last year's student-faculty football game. It's nothing."

"But beyond the scratches, Benjamin, how are you feeling?"

"Yusef," I began, "I'm feeling fine about everything."

"Yes, of course," said Yusef, scratching his nose. "You know, yesterday, God was just an idea to you, something much like a fairy tale character. Today, God is more of a reality, no?

"Yes, I guess He is."

"I thought that your experiences inside the mountain would change you a little. Change in this way is good, no?"

I nodded and sipped my tea.

"Benjamin, you must have a great many questions about what has happened so far. If you do, then this is the perfect time to ask them. When everyone returns from Jerusalem, we won't have the privacy."

I certainly did have questions, but I wasn't sure what to ask first. Some of the questions I didn't even know how to pose. So much had happened since I'd boarded the plane back in the States.

"Yusef," I began, "how will you know the Messiah?"

Yusef smiled. "God will let me know, Benjamin."

"How will God do that? I mean, will you receive word in a dream, or have some sort of revelation? Will the Messiah just walk up to you and tell you who he is?"

"I'm not sure, but God will let me know in His own time, and in His own way."

"Will it happen soon?" I asked. I was beginning to hope that I could somehow be there to meet the Messiah.

"I don't really know, but it can't be too far off. I'm too old to wait too long," he said, taking a forkful of stew.

"Were you told anything about me? I mean, did you know that I was coming to Israel or . . . ."

"No, not exactly. All I was told was that someone would be sent to me. This person would be the one to retrieve the holy objects. That was all. I didn't get much information."

I was a little disappointed with Yusef's answer. I wanted him to tell me that he knew all about me, long before he ever met me on the plane. I wanted Yusef to have been told by God, "I'm sending you a young man to assist you. His name is Benjamin Stein. He is six feet tall, one hundred eighty pounds, clean shaven, uncommonly handsome, radically intelligent, uncommonly bold, and has a small scar on his right middle finger from a mishap he had with a knife when he was a kid." Obviously, it hadn't happened that way.

"Yusef, what will the Messiah do when he comes?"

"The Messiah will be given a new Covenant by God which he will deliver to the world. It will be a wonderful Covenant that will be a sort of spiritual ark—like Noah's ark, but in a spiritual way—that will keep those who accept it safe from the storms of life that God will be creating in the world."

"Do you mean to say that God, Himself, will hand the Messiah the New Covenant?

"Yes, my boy, God, Himself. You know that it's written in the Bible that God promises to make a new covenant with the world. It is for all the people of the world. The Messiah will deliver that Covenant. It will be a wonderful event."

"I'm sure . . . ."

"I hope that the people will be ready for it," he continued, putting his empty teacup on the ground next to his chair. "Heaven knows that the time is right, the world is in trouble and is in need of salvation. But people are strange and do things that often aren't in their own best interest. When the Messiah offers the new covenant to the world, I hope that they accept it."

The answers that Yusef gave me seemed all right on the surface, but I couldn't help feeling that there were things that he wasn't telling me—a lot of important things.

"Benjamin, what's bothering you?" asked Yusef, finishing off the last of his stew.

"Well, I've been having dreams, strange dreams."

"You're under a great deal of pressure lately. I think—"

"No, it's not that. I've been having these dreams off and on since I was a kid. But lately they've been getting worse. Sometimes when they come, I can't tell whether I'm sleeping and really dreaming, or I'm awake and it's really happening. It's all very strange."

"Dreams can be strange," said Yusef, "but I wouldn't worry too much about them."

"I thought that maybe my dreams might be premonitions or visions. I've dreamt about a cylinder over and over again and then, there on the plane I saw the cylinder that you were carrying and I just had to find out more about it. I suppose that my behavior seemed a little odd to you?"

"Well, it did at first, but there was something very familiar about you. Besides, you seemed harmless enough and you struck a responsive chord in me that I couldn't ignore."

"It was the same for me. My martial arts master uses an expression that I suppose applied when I first saw the cylinder you were carrying. He says, 'Every once in a while a person, for whatever reason, swallows a flaming porcupine, something that gets stuck in your throat; you can't cough it up and you can't swallow it.' The black cylinder was my flaming porcupine. I couldn't totally accept the coincidence, yet I couldn't dismiss it either."

Yusef smiled. "I think that your martial arts master understands a great deal about life, Benjamin."

"Yes, he does. And so does Moloch."

"So I'm beginning to understand. Benjamin, what else did you and the demon Moloch talk about?"

"Moloch? Moloch mentioned reincarnation. He said that demons and humans both reincarnate. Do you know anything about it? I mean, do you believe in reincarnation?"

"Yes, of course I believe in it. Reincarnation is one of the basic truths of existence. In Hebrew it is called *T'cheyah*."

"It is? I thought Jews didn't believe in it."

"Most Jews don't believe in reincarnation," Yusef said, scratching his beard. "I think it's because most Jews haven't taken the time to investigate some of the deeper aspects of Judaism. They think that the subject is only relevant in other religions like Hinduism and Buddhism. Truth is truth, regardless of the source. If people took the time to understand reincarnation, they would understand a great deal more about not only Judaism, but about life, as well."

"How can I find out about my past lives? Is it truly possible?"

"Oh, yes. It's all recorded in the Higher Mind," Yusef said, tugging on his beard. "Remember, I told you that everything is recorded there. Well, all your past life experiences are also recorded there. If you want to find out who you were, that's where you would have to look."

"What do I have to do?"

"Meditate! You have to meditate and quiet your Lower Mind so that you can access your Higher Mind tape."

"How? Could you tell me how to do it?"

Yusef scratched his chin and peered at me over his glasses. "Are you sure you want to learn this?"

"Yes, very sure."

"Well, all right then, sit up and do as I tell you," he said, clapping his hands. "Close your eyes and rest your hands in your lap. Keep both feet flat on the floor."

I rearranged my body, letting my feet rest evenly on the desert floor.

"Good! Now, keep your back straight, but not rigid. Try to keep yourself physically balanced. Good! I want you to stop your thoughts using the Nefesh Hafsa'kah, you remember, the mind-stoppage technique that I taught you the other day.

"Okay! Now, begin to breathe slowly, very slowly. A slow inhalation through your nose, and an even slower exhalation. Do you understand?"

I nodded and slowed my breathing as Yusef had instructed.

"Good! Do that for a few minutes and don't expect anything to happen, just breathe."

I relaxed, emptying my thoughts and trying not to look for anything to happen. I felt a sudden release of tension in my body, and felt a serenity sweep over me that deepened with each passing breath.

"Now, you remember, of course, the Sha'ar Lev, the heart sephira technique. You used it last night, no?"

"Yes."

"Good. Now, when you're ready to exhale, take the middle finger of your right hand, touch it to the Daath Gate . . . ."

"The what?"

"It's a very special spiritual gate located between your eyebrows. Some believe that this gate is located in other areas of the body such as the heart or throat, but it is not so, as you will see. Now, have your breath flow through your hollow arm, out of your hollow palm, through your middle finger, and into that mystical gate. Tell me what you are experiencing. What do you see?"†

Suddenly, I felt my mind expand. I was swept up and moving deep into space. Not the type of space that has stars, planets, and galaxies, but some other type of space, a special transcendental space.

"I see darkness. Like deep space without stars," I said, softly.

"Yes, deep space without stars, exactly. That is the Void, Benjamin, the Void of God. There, nothing can harm you, nothing at all. There, your Ruach, your spirit, can detach from the mundane world of men and be free. Time doesn't exist there, only peace, and . . ." His words trailed off.

And, I thought, *and what?*

"Benjamin, there is dark irregular round patch suspended in the Void of God. Do you see it, Benjamin?"

"Yes. I see it."

"Good. That is the Sha'ar Z'man, the Gate of Time, and the doorway to your past. Will yourself through it, Benjamin."

I willed myself through the Sha'ar Z'man, and was immediately swept into a universe of images. Instinctively I knew that all of the images were mine. All of these people, places, and things—they all had something to do with me. All these images I knew to be from my past, my former lives. It was as if, with just a little practice, a little patience, I could get these images to settle down, and I would have access to them at will. As my breathing continued, slow and gentle, the vivid images slowed and I was able to view them as easily as if I were merely remembering people, places, and events from my present life. A great

---

† See time travel techniques using the Daath Gate in the Appendix, page 378.

number of the images were those that I had seen in my dreams and nightmares.

In one vision I saw myself astride a horse galloping through a pasture. On the far side of the pasture I could see a house with a thatched roof. I was sure that I had lived in that house; I felt I was coming home after being away a long time. In another, I was swimming naked in a lake. On the shore stood a woman whom I believed to have been my wife. We were having a picnic.

I was steeped in the visions of my past when I heard Yusef's voice calling to me. "Benjamin, release all your visions, let them go."

I allowed myself to relax even more. A moment later, all the dreams that I had been having, all the nightmares that I had been suffering, appeared in front of me as a huge, diaphanous collage.

"Now, will them to dissolve, Benjamin. Will them to dissolve!" I heard Yusef's voice echoing softly through the void.

I willed them to dissolve. I watched as they slowly dissolved within the blackness until there was no trace of them left.

"Benjamin," Yusef said softly, "come back. Open your eyes, my son."

I opened my eyes and sat quietly, unable to speak. I felt wonderful, completely at peace. I didn't have to say anything. All I could do was look at Yusef and smile. He smiled back.

"Benjamin, that is what we call the Sha'ar Daath, or the Daath Gate," he said. "Using it, you can access a great deal of knowledge, knowledge that is hidden from the average person. Using it, a person is able to see the past, present, and even the future. Also, one can utilize the Sha'ar Daath to release many things that are suppressed in one's mind, things such as the dreams and nightmares that have plagued you. You are free of them now, Benjamin. They have served their purpose."

"What do you mean, Yusef," I said, still experiencing the peace, "that they have served their purpose?"

"You are here, aren't you?" said Yusef.

"Do you mean that . . . ."

"I mean that God works the way God works. If it took dreams and nightmares to do it, then . . . well, here you are."

"I understand," I said, feeling totally free of them, totally light for the first time in my life.

"Good. Now, what else would you like to know?"

"Yusef, what's it like to look into the future? There are psychics who do it all the time. How do they . . . ."

"Looking into the future, Benjamin, is a tricky business. Some psychics can do it, but most of them are mere amateurs."

"How so?"

"They know very little and their predictions are often wrong."

"Why? They make all sorts of great claims."

"Exactly, they make claims."

"Why are they amateurs?"

"Because they don't understand anything about the future . . . they don't understand the process. It would help if they had a special covenant with God."

"Covenant?"

"Yes, my boy, covenant. Understand that nothing is hidden from God, not the past, the present, or the future. A special covenant with God would allow that person to access God's information. The prophets had that special covenant. That's why their prophecies were always correct."

"Where do psychics make their mistake when they look into the future?"

"It's their understanding of time, free will, and just what constitutes the future."

"I don't understand. What do you mean, Yusef?"

"Well, when a person looks into the future, he is seeing the future based on the present circumstances. Those circumstances could change at any time."

"I don't understand, Yusef, I can't . . . ."

"It's very difficult to understand, Benjamin. It's people! Every person has free will and everyone creates futures based on the particular choices that they make. This makes looking into the future very uncertain, except if looking into the future is sanctioned by God. You could say that, at any one time, there are an infinite number of possibilities—an uncountable, unlimited number of futures. This is why people who profess psychic abilities and claim that they can see the future are often wrong. They are only seeing the future based on the present conditions, and in the present moment. But as conditions change, so do futures. In order for them to be more accurate, they would have to be constantly looking into the future, moment after moment. Of course, as in the case of the prophets, if God Himself shows them the future, then you can be sure that it will come to pass."

"I understand."

"Of course," said Yusef, "when it comes to certain individuals, their futures are directed by God. They still have a free will but God has His own way of causing people to make certain choices."

"Such as?"

"Such as the time that I discovered the scrolls. I could have taken many paths to visit my friends, but I happened to choose that one."

"Yes, but it could have been blind luck, right?"

"Not in this case."

"Why?"

"Because just before I entered the Negev I came to a fork in the road. I chose the left road and followed it for about three kilometers when I came to a ditch in the road that was impossible to get across and impossible to get around. This forced me to turn back and take the right side of the fork."

"But the ditch in the road was a natural phenomenon, so . . . ."

"Was it?"

"What do you mean?" I asked.

"How is it then, after I recovered and took Muhammad on a small ride to show him the sight of my discovery, that the fork in the road was gone and—"

"What?"

"The fork in the road was gone, it didn't exist. No fork existed on my map and, according to Muhammad, who knew the area quite well, there was never any fork in the road there."

"Are you saying that . . . ."

"I'm simply saying that if God wants you to be at a certain place and at a certain time, He has his own way of seeing to it that it happens."

"That's incredible, Yusef."

"Incredible? No, that's God, Benjamin. And, of course, there's something else. How is it that my jeep happened to get stuck there and not anywhere else? It was at the precise location of the scrolls. No, Benjamin, it wasn't a coincidence. It was God. God can do these things."

"I'm beginning to see what you mean, Yusef," I said, nodding.

"Think of this, Benjamin. You're here because of dreams and visions that you've been having since you were a child. Where would you be if you didn't have those dreams?"

"I'd be teaching summer school back in the States."

"Exactly. It's not impossible, you know, that God gave you those dreams just to get you here. And what about the plane? Was it a coincidence that we happened to be on the same plane together and that you kept running into me the way you did? No, Benjamin. When God wants something done, He sees to it that it is done regardless of our exercising our free will. He simply sees to it that our free will coincides with His will."

"You mean like pharaoh's daughter discovering Moses floating in a reed basket . . . ."

"Exactly, Benjamin, the Torah is full of such instances. With the Messiah coming, shouldn't it be that God makes certain arrangements to see to it that everything moves according to plan? It's my job to train the Messiah, and yours to make sure that I have the tools to do it with. Do you understand? Yes, of course you do."

"So, God works in mysterious ways."

"No, Benjamin. The ways are mysterious to those who simply don't have any answers. Understand God and the mysteries disappear. It's just that simple."

"I see."

"Good," said Yusef, looking at his watch. "Now, we have to discuss tomorrow."

"Tomorrow?" I asked, somehow thinking that we were going to have a few days to relax and recover. I should have known better.

"Tomorrow, we have to drive back up north. And . . . ." His voiced trailed off again, as if he was thinking about how he was going to phrase it.

"And?"

"And, you are going to have to go down into the Well of Souls again," he said, looking at his fingers as if for a hangnail. He peeked over at me briefly to see if I had any reaction.

He was a sly old fox, all right, and about as subtle as a wrecking ball slamming through a house of glass. Sure, I had a reaction, if not on the outside, then, at least on the inside. If he could truly see into my thoughts, then he would see a thousand things suddenly rushing through my mind, chief among them, the image of the demon that had climbed up after me in the well. Then again, this was for God and the Messiah. And I did have the medallion this time. My life wouldn't be worth very much if I didn't have God. He had me, that sly old man had me, and he knew it.

"Okay, Yusef, if it's back to the well, then it's back to the well," I said, even impressing myself with my surprising show of bravado. "It wouldn't have anything to do with the Dark Malkuth, would it?"

"Exactly," he said, apparently relieved at my reaction. "All you have to do is to go into the Dark Malkuth and retrieve King Solomon's ring."

Yusef made it sound like a romp in the park, a stroll down the beach. All I have to do is to go there and get the ring. He made it sound so easy, maybe too easy.

"Yusef, what makes King Solomon's ring so special? I mean, does it have some sort of power, or . . . ."

"It has great power, miraculous power, Benjamin. With that ring, the king was able to control demons, even the most powerful of demons. He was able to punish them and bring them to justice. You're going to have to go into the Dark Malkuth and bring it back. I'll need it. Remember, I have to train the Messiah. You'll be doing this for God."

"My friend Moloch told me how to access the Dark Malkuth through the Well of Souls, so I know that part. But what does the ring look like? Knowing King Solomon, as I'm beginning to, it must be solid gold and encrusted with precious gems."

"No!" said Yusef, shaking his head. "The ring is made mostly out of iron and brass, and has five interlaced letters on its face—the Hebrew letter alef. Five alefs seemed to have some special meaning to Solomon since they appear on the medallion also. It must be a very powerful combination, indeed, Benjamin."

"Yes," I said, touching the medallion. "It must be."

Yusef saw me touch the medallion and smiled.

"Yusef, iron and brass?" I said, wondering why the great king wouldn't have made it out of gold. "With all of King Solomon's wealth . . . I mean, he had everything made of gold, didn't he?"

"Yes," said Yusef, breaking into a little smile, "everything. He had armor shields of solid gold, plates, cups, spears, everything. But the ring had to be constructed of iron and brass."

"Why iron and brass?"

"Because demons find the element iron to be offensive. That's why Solomon had the door leading to the labyrinth constructed of iron. Demons are repelled by it. They hate the metal with a passion."

"Was that why the handle that I pulled in the Well of Souls, when I uncovered the urn and medallion, was made out of iron instead of gold?"

"Exactly. King Solomon knew that the demons wouldn't touch an iron handle. Clever, yes?"

"Yes."

Suddenly, I couldn't help thinking that the whole sequence was backwards. Why did Solomon, with all his wisdom, hide the ring there among the demons. Wouldn't it have been better to hide Aaron's Rod there, and the ring somewhere else? I should be going down into the Dark Malkuth with the ring, rather than going down there to find it and bring it back. If I'd had the ring first, then I could have used it against the demon that chased me in the well and against whatever other creatures I would find lurking in the Dark Malkuth.

"Yusef, am I going down into the Dark Malkuth alone?"

"Yes. It's much too dangerous for anyone to go with you."

Yusef was right, of course, I had to do this alone. Still, from what Moloch had told me about the Dark World, I wouldn't have minded having the combined might of the Israeli and United States Armies as company just the same.

"Where is it in the Dark Malkuth? In fact, where is anything in the Dark Malkuth?" I said, hoping that Yusef would pinpoint it for me right inside the entrance to the demonic world. "Did Solomon draw a map or anything?"

"No need to bother with that now," said Yusef, casually waving his hand. "I'll give you all the details tomorrow. Listen, Benjamin, in a little while I want to give you a small demonstration. I want to show you something of the tremendous power that God invested in Aaron's Rod. I think you'll be impressed."

"I'd like to see that."

"I thought you would. For the time being, however, I want you to relax for the rest of the day. You'll like that I think, no?"

"Yes, I think I would like that very much."

"Good then, today and tonight you rest and tomorrow we'll go north."

I knew I wouldn't be able to relax. My mind was filled with the prospect of going back down into the well the next day. Even if I survived the descent and got past the demon, Moloch had called him Ozimon, I'd only be running into his friends somewhere in the Dark Malkuth.

13

Strange Doings

THE PHONE RANG AND MOSHE BOLTED UP IN BED. "DAMN IT!" HE said, still half-asleep. Fumbling in the dark for the phone, he knocked over a half-filled glass of water. "Damn it!" he cursed again. He picked up the receiver. "Who is this?"

"Shalom, Moshe, boker tov!" He recognized Jehuda's voice right away.

"Damn it, Jehuda! It's four in the morning. This better be important." The agent growled.

"It is! I have Avram on the other line. They're not terrorists, they're something else . . . ."

"Who?" said Moshe, still not awake.

"The American thing. Come on Moshe, wake up!"

"Okay! Okay! Right! Well, if they're not terrorists, what the hell are they?"

"That's the thing. Avram and Yitzak followed the group down around the Mizpe-Shalem area. Avram says that there's something funny going on."

"Well?" Moshe said, sopping up the water with one of his socks. "What's funny?"

"Avram says that he and Yitzak saw the old man and this other Arab, you know, the older Arab, dig up some sort of box just before sunset. Then they brought the box back to camp. But . . . ."

"But what?"

"Well, Avram said that it took two of them to carry it. Avram thinks that the box was made out of gold. He said that the old man opened the box and took out a shofar."

"A what?" said Moshe, still sopping up the spilt water.

"A shofar. You know, a ram's horn."

"I know what a shofar is, damn it . . . what about it?"

"That's the thing. Last night Avram and Yitzak saw the old man stand in front of a mountain and blow the shofar three times. Just after he did, the front of the whole mountain gave way, and a door or something appeared."

"What?"

"I said that—"

"I know what you said."

"Avram said that Stein, the American, and the Arab girl went into the mountain and were gone about three hours. When they came out, one of them, I think he said Stein, had some sort of staff or pole or something. Well, the whole group got away from the mountain just as the whole thing collapsed."

"What collapsed?" Moshe asked, searching for his other sock.

"The whole damn mountain collapsed. It came down. Avram said the whole thing was very spooky, something like magic. Especially the shofar thing. Damn, what the hell do we have here? What should I tell Avram?"

"Tell him not to make contact with them, but if this group does anything that might be dangerous to anyone other than themselves, tell them to intervene."

"Moshe, I think we have something special here. If it's as spooky as Avram says it is, then I want to see it for myself. You never know. Things get strange here in the Holy Land. Avram said that it doesn't look like they plan on going anywhere today, so I'm going down there. Okay?"

"All right, but be careful. Stay with them as long as it takes. Oh, yeah, take a camera with you so you can capture these guys on film. Then, we'll be able to check them out. Maybe you'll be able to photograph a miracle or two."

"Very funny. I'll take a camera. You're going to miss me around the office, Moshe."

"You may be my top field agent, Jehuda, but you hate the office, so what are you talking about? You love this stuff! Now, if you don't mind, some of us 'normal' people have to get some sleep! Now go away!"

"I'm out of here. I'll keep you posted. Boker tov!"

"Boker tov? Boker tov, hell! Leila Tov . . . good night!"

JEHUDA TRAVELED THE TWENTY-TWO KILOMETERS DOWN TO MIZPE Shalem where Avram was waiting for him. It was early in the afternoon when he pulled into a small, paved rest area on the Dead Sea side of the road. Avram got out of his jeep and walked over to Jehuda's vehicle.

"Shalom, boss!" said Avram, taking his sunglasses off and wiping the sweat from his forehead.

"Shalom, Avram. Where are they?"

"Just a few kilometers west of here. They made camp in a dry wadi. The three Arabs left this morning, but I don't know where they went. We only had one vehicle, so I thought it best that we waited here."

"All right. They'll be back."

"Yeah. Well, only the old man and the American are here any- way. The last time I saw them they were sitting in front of the tent just eating and talking. Yitzak is up on a small rise keeping an eye on them."

"Do they suspect anything?"

"No, nothing. I don't think they're spies or terrorists, boss." said Avram, scratching his nose and turning to see if anyone else was around.

Jehuda stared out of his front window at the Dead Sea, stretching north and south just below the rise they were on. A small group of tourists was getting out of a bus near the shore.

"What do you think they are then, magicians?"

Avram didn't laugh. "If they're not, boss, then I wouldn't know what else to call them."

"Come on . . . ."

"No, boss, really, these guys are spooky."

"All right, settle down. Take me to the sight," said Jehuda, shaking his head.

Avram led Jehuda west, down the dry wadi, to the site. They left their vehicles in a secluded spot just east of the encampment and traveled on foot the rest of the way. They climbed a small rise of weather-beaten sandstone and found Yitzak observing the camp through his binoculars.

"What's up?" said Jehuda, wiping the sweat from his forehead and taking out his own binoculars.

"Not much," said Yitzak, not breaking his concentration on the campsite. "The two of them talked for a while. The American is still sitting there. The old man went into the tent on the left about twenty minutes ago. That's all. The three Arabs took off together, they're not back yet."

"Our whiz kid over here," said Jehuda, glancing at Avram, "thinks that they're magicians or sorcerers or something. I suppose you're going to tell me that you think they are too."

"I only know what I saw last night," Yitzak said, taking the binoculars away from his face, turning, and looking at Jehuda. "If that wasn't magic, then I don't know what the hell it was. Anyway, magic or not, it just wasn't normal."

"Hmm. I think this desert sun has fried both of your brains. Magic . . . ."

"Boss, I, er . . ." said Avram, shrugging his shoulders.

"Quiet! I'll be with you two until we decide what to do with these guys. If I see any one of them perform magic, I'll, well, never mind."

Jehuda handed Avram his camera. "I want pictures of these guys. If they perform anything that even remotely resembles magic, I want it on film. Got it?"

"Got it, boss," said Avram, taking the lens cap off the camera. "Hey, boss, I like the city espionage stuff better, it's too hot out here. I'm not built for this desert work."

"No one is built for this desert work, Avram. Go to my jeep and get the stuff. I brought a cooler full of soda and sandwiches. Take some pictures of their camp on the way."

"Be right back," said Avram, as he smiled and left for the vehicles.

"I guess that means we're going to be here all day, right?" said Yitzak stoically.

"All night, if we have to."

"Wait a minute. Something's going on!" said Yitzak, holding the binoculars to his eyes. "The old man is signaling the American to come into the tent."

"I wish we had that tent bugged," said Jehuda.

"We didn't have any with us," said Yitzak.

"I know. I brought one, but the damn thing doesn't work," said Jehuda, taking it from his pocket and tossing it to Avram.

"Boss, where did you get this?" said Avram.

"From the office."

"Where?"

"It was in a box in the back room."

"Did the box have blue tape on it?"

"Yeah, why?"

"Those bugs were all bad, Boss."

"Great. Now we have to do this the hard way."

"Hey! They're coming out," said Yitzak, refocusing his binoculars. "The old man's carrying the stick from last night."

"That's a stick all right. At least you guys got that right," said Jehuda, training his binoculars on the suspects. "The old man is pointing to something over on the right. Looks like he's pointing to the boulder, the one by the shaded area. Can you see it?"

"Yeah. What are they doing?" asked Yitzak.

"The old man is taking the stick or staff, or whatever it is, and pointing it at the boulder. Wait!"

Down below, Yusef pointed Aaron's Rod at the boulder. A moment later, an indigo-colored bolt of lightning burst from the end of the rod and pulverized the boulder. Then he turned around and decimated another boulder.

"God, did you see that?" said Jehuda, lowering his binoculars and turning to Yitzak.

"I saw it without the binoculars," said Yitzak. "Damn! Was it some sort of laser device?"

"No, it came from the stick. It looked like lightning, not a laser beam. A laser would have drilled a hole through the boulder, not atomized it. Look, Stein's going over to look at the rubble."

Avram returned with the camera and cooler full of soda and sandwiches. "Did I miss anything? I thought I heard some kind of explosion, maybe two. What the hell was it?"

"Magic," said Jehuda, shaking his head. "You guys are right, they're not your ordinary 'people next door.' I wish I had pictures of that."

"Maybe they'll do it again." said Yitzak, raising his eyebrows as he continued to watch the scene below. "No, now they're going into the tent."

"Damn! I would've liked to have seen that." said Avram, staring at the soda and sandwiches.

"Well, whatever that stick was, magic or not, it's not a run-of-the-mill piece of wood. If it's not a magic wand, then it's some sort of new weapon," said Jehuda soberly. "If it's a weapon, then we're going to have to get our hands on it, right?"

Yitzak and Avram both nodded.

"Okay," said Jehuda, "As long as we keep our eye on them we'll know where that thing is. We'll stay with them, follow them wherever they go. Maybe they have these things buried all around the country. We'll have to wait and find out. We'd better get settled, it's going to be a long night."

14

The Dark Malkuth

WE FINALLY REACHED THE WELL OF SOULS LATE IN THE AFTERNOON. As we unloaded the supplies, Mara and Ali got to work setting up camp. When they had finished, it was in the same configuration as the original one—in an odd way, it was almost like coming home. After dinner, Yusef called a meeting to go over the details of the night's descent into the well. All of the equipment—the pulley device, the rope coils, everything—had been set up and we were ready to go.

The sun had long since disappeared and the campsite was bathed in various combinations of moonlight and shadow as our meeting began. The moonlight seemed to make an already chilly night just a little chillier, and everyone pulled their chair a little closer, to the fire. Ali refilled my tea cup and smiled, which I took not only to mean "good luck tonight," but also "I'm glad that it's you going down the well and not me."

"Tonight, as everyone knows," Yusef began, "Benjamin is going to retrieve King Solomon's ring," Yusef said, motioning toward me, almost as if he planned on having me stand up to take a bow. "Benjamin, as you know, you're going to have to go into the well alone. The demon Moloch told you how to enter the Dark Malkuth from the well, but there are a few things that Solomon wrote about that world that I'm going to have to explain to you. First of all, it is a dismal world of eternal twilight, which I think you have already learned from Moloch. Next, well, if you get caught in the Dark Malkuth by any demons, they will certainly try to kill you. More, they will make sure that your death is slow and painful. You must exercise a great deal of stealth in order to retrieve the ring."

"Will I have any sort of weapon with me?" I asked, hoping that Yusef would tell me I'd be armed with Aaron's Rod—if not the latest in modern hand grenades, or a small portable nuclear device.

"No. No weapons, Benjamin, but you will have the medallion," said Yusef, glancing over at Muhammad and raising his eyebrows. "Of course, the medallion will protect you psychically from the demons but, well, you'll have to rely on your stealth for your physical safety."

Fine! All I have to do is sneak around a place that I have no map for, populated by myriad demons who'll want nothing more than to kill me if they find me. As bad as that sounded, the look on Yusef's face told me that the worst was yet to come. But I couldn't imagine what it might be. Yusef's sudden silence was deafening, and I didn't care for the way he glanced over to Muhammad and raised his eyebrows.

"Also," Yusef continued, turning to me and forcing a small smile, "according to King Solomon, the demons will have two ways of detecting your presence when you're down there. First, humans give off an odor that is easily detected by demons. They're very sensitive to it. Second, because you are from the Light Malkuth and are descending into the Dark Malkuth, you will have around you a small . . . er . . . ."

"A small what?" I asked, sharply.

"Well . . ." he stammered.

"Well?"

"Well, you'll have a small glow."

"A small glow! What do you mean, a small glow?"

"Yes, my boy, remember you're entering a dark world, a world that is not just dark in the normal sense, but dark in the spiritual sense. This means that—"

"I know! This means I'll glow like some sort of light bulb."

"Well, sort of." said Yusef, squirming in his seat.

My pulse had suddenly quickened and my mouth went dry. I'll be like some glowing piece of Japanese incense, giving off light and fumes. This hardly sounded like the ideal situation when you're trying to be stealthy.

"Okay!" said Yusef, suddenly taking on the stalwart attributes of a Green Beret squad leader. "Now, Solomon's only instruction concerning the location of the ring is given, as he was apparently fond to do, in verse. I'd like to tell you that I understand it, but to tell you the truth, I'm not quite sure at all what the entire verse means. You're going to have to use your instincts to decipher its meaning. Hopefully, it won't be a problem and will resolve itself when you're down there. That's all I know. I translated the verse and wrote it down for you, Benjamin. You'll read it, yes?"

"Yes, of course," I said, taking the piece of paper from him. It read:

> *Hail! O seeker free of sin*
> *within the light world reared,*
> *The ring you seek is resting in*
> *a tree upon the sleeper's beard.*
>
> *Upon a stone that you should find*
> *within entwining boughs,*
> *The sleeper shall by moon appear*
> *as through the void you browse.*
>
> *First, you must secure a gift;*
> *a helpful magic balm,*
> *Beneath an object you can't lift,*
> *shall keep you safe from harm.*

Within the moonlight, smooth as glass
that object hides the vial,
Can only keep you safe, my son,
for but a little while.

Upon its surface you can't lean
you'll learn the reason why,
It's hidden well, but can be seen
within the opposing sky.

Near the edge, it finds its rest
it can be felt, but not be spied,
The pointing finger marks its place
where all the elements collide.

I read the verses. They were an absolute mystery to me, but I was hoping, as Yusef had suggested, that they would make more sense to me when I was down there. Down there? I was going down, probably four hundred feet, into a well where I had narrowly escaped at three hundred feet. What about the hairy thing that was chasing me? My friend Moloch said it was some sort of demon-guard named Ozimon. I couldn't believe that I was going to give that thing a second shot at me.

"Yusef," I said, clearing my throat, "I don't want to be a killjoy, but what about that demon that was down the well with me? I don't think that . . . ."

"Don't worry, Benjamin." he answered, cutting me off.   "I'll take care of anything that's in the shaft of the well. I'll clear the well and you should be able to make it to the ledge that Moloch told you about without any trouble. You'll have to trust me on this."

Yusef's confidence was reassuring, though he hadn't told me how he was going to do it. I imagined myself being lowered right into the beast's gaping mouth. And just as I was being torn to a million tiny little pieces, I would hear Yusef's voice echoing down into the darkness, "Benjamin, are you all right? Did it work? Is the shaft clear?" It was something I chose not to think about.

"Is everyone ready?" asked Yusef.

"The pulley is all set and ready to go," said Muhammad. "There's plenty of rope and I checked everything for any problems."

"Me too!" said Ali, proudly. "I checked the emergency line and everything is good!"

"Yes, everything is ready," Mara said softly.

Scratching his beard, Yusef gave everyone another glance. "Are there any final questions?" he asked.

"I have one," I said, leaning slightly forward in my seat. "Yusef, are you sure that you translated all of it? I mean, was there anything else? Maybe a map or—"

"Nothing, Benjamin, just the verses. Whatever the verses mean, King Solomon thought that it would be enough to get the seeker to the ring. You're going to have to trust God, King Solomon, and yourself."

He was right. I had gotten through some bizarre situations these past few days, this is just one more. But, what if . . . .

"Benjamin," Yusef interrupted my thoughts, "you are going to do fine, no?"

I nodded and forced a smile back at him.

Holding his teacup at eye level, Yusef stood and proposed a toast. "To God and the Messiah!"

Everyone stood and raised their cups and answered in unison, "To God and the Messiah!"

"It's time," said Yusef, putting his teacup down and then lightly clapping his hands. "Everyone go ahead to the well. I'll be along in a few minutes." He gave me a quick smile, turned, and disappeared into his tent.

Throughout the meeting, I'd clutched the paper with the verses on it in my hand, almost as if I were trying to break the code subconsciously or absorb it through osmosis. Of course, it hadn't worked—I hadn't really thought that it would. I read the verses again, shook my head, folded the paper and put it safely in my shirt pocket.

We walked to the well together. Muhammad and Mara went right to the pulley device to check it over for any last minute adjustments that would have to be made. As Ali rechecked the safety line, I took out the verses and read them again. A few minutes later, Yusef showed up carrying Aaron's Rod.

"Ali, Muhammad, attach the safety line to Benjamin. Benjamin, it's nearly time. Are you ready?"

I stepped to the opening of the well and slipped my foot into the loop of rope as Ali attached the safety line around my waist. Muhammad gave me a little slack on the line.

"You must all stand back now," Yusef directed. "I am going to prepare the well for Benjamin."

We all stepped back and Yusef centered himself over the mouth of the well. Holding the rod tightly with both hands, he pointed one end into the murky blackness. He looked like something out of Melville's *Moby Dick*: a brave harpooner poised to plunge his razor-sharp instrument of death deep into the heart of the great white whale.

Poised and ready, he looked up into the starry night sky and spoke a few words in Hebrew. Then, he turned his gaze downward and stared into the abyss. A few seconds later, a great bolt of indigo-colored lightning shot from the end of the staff with a mighty crack and fired down the shaft of the well. The sonic boom that came from the bolt of lightning was so powerful that it shook the ground. Nothing, human or otherwise, would be able to survive that, I thought. Surely, if the well really was bottomless, what had come from the rod would have been able to travel through the space without obstruction. I suddenly felt a lot better.

"As I promised, no?" said Yusef, turning to me. "God is truly wonderful!"

"Yes, more than wonderful!" I said, a great deal more confident now. "I'm ready, let's do it!"

"Don't forget, Benjamin," said Mara, "one tug to go, two tugs to stop, three to bring you up and . . . . "

"Got it! More than three, and you guys better bring me up fast. Right?"

"Right!" said Mara, her smile fading to a look of concern. "Benjamin, come back to me, to us, safe." She stepped forward and gave me a hug, turning her head and resting her cheek on my shoulder.

"I'll be back," I whispered. "We have things to talk about, right?"

She looked up at me and smiled. "Right." She kissed me lightly on the lips and stepped back.

"Benjamin," called Yusef.

"I'm ready," I replied, my eyes locked with Mara's. "I'm ready."

I stepped back to the edge of the well and looked around at everybody. I could feel their tension. Muhammad made the line taut as everyone wished me *mazel*, good luck, and, with flashlight in hand, I went back down the well.

The darkness that I was traveling through was familiar to me, but the musty odor that I had encountered on my first descent had been replaced by the nauseating aroma of charred flesh. I took that odor to mean that something alive had been in the well when Yusef discharged the rod. Now, with the stench filling my nostrils, I was reasonably sure that I was alone. On the way down I noticed that even the lichen and fungus lining the walls were blackened and smoldering—nothing seemed to have survived the blast.

Deeper and deeper I went, past the compartment that had held the urn and the medallion. My heart was pounding, the repulsive, permeating odor caused my eyes to tear.

I kept the flashlight focused on the well walls as I descended into virgin territory. I had no idea how deep I was when I finally saw a faint light shining into the well below me. I gave a hard tug on the safety line and my descent stopped. I listened for any sound that might indicate that I wasn't alone. There were none. I brought the back of my hand holding the flashlight to my chest to reassure myself that the medallion was still there. It was. I looked up into the darkness, gave two tugs, and my journey continued.

As I neared the light, I saw the ledge that Moloch had mentioned. It wasn't a natural ledge, but was made of thick, flat stones that had been intentionally embedded into the well wall. When I reached it I gave the line a tug and I stopped my descent. I shined my flashlight down into the bowels of the well—all I saw was darkness. Again, I listened for any unwelcome sounds of life coming from below and again, there were none, not a growl, not a peep. I said a small prayer as I prepared for the next leg of my journey.

The opening to the tunnel, composed of an extremely smooth rock, that would lead me into the Dark Malkuth, was directly in front of me. It was an easy step onto the ledge, which looked strong enough to support me. I tested it, slowly easing my full weight onto it, before I released myself from the rope lines that controlled my downward voyage. A few loose rocks crumbled, but the ledge itself held. I took one last look up the well, took a deep breath, then turned my attention back to the tunnel. I could see no signs of life, no movement at all. In my mind, that seemed like a good thing. I slipped my foot out of the loop and untied the safety line.

"Well, this is it," I said quietly. "I have to trust God." I stepped into the tunnel, stopping just inside to inspect myself for that glow. I was all right, no glowing yet. The tunnel wasn't very long, maybe only fifteen yards or so. It was fifteen feet wide without a single deviation from beginning to end. I reached out to touch the strange stone and found the walls of the tunnel were nothing like I'd expected. They weren't the cave-like, jutting rock-type walls of the labyrinth below Jericho, but just the opposite. These walls were smooth and seamless, composed entirely of fused stone. There was a curious lack of debris and loose stones on the tunnel floor—it was as if someone had taken a giant laser and bored a hole right through solid rock. I thought, *Could Solomon have been responsible for this? He did have the use of Aaron's Rod.*

As I journeyed farther into the tunnel, the stench of charred flesh from the well dissipated. The air seemed fresher—not the sort of "fresh" air that I was used to, but it was still a thousand times better than the air in the well.

I came to the mouth of the tunnel and carefully peeked out— it was my first glimpse of Malkuth Tachton. I stepped out and found myself on a rocky ledge that extended about ten feet from the mountain wall. It appeared to wind down the side of the mountain to the valley floor some five hundred feet below. As I inspected my surroundings, I determined that there were no signs of life on the ledge, I was alone—at least up here. I looked out over the valley and what I saw took my breath away. From my perch, I could overlook an entire world filled with stark mountains looming black against an iridescent gray sky sprinkled with billowy dark gray thunderheads. A full moon cast a morbidly orange glow over the landscape.

To say that it was a primitive world would be an understatement; it was positively primordial. My heart raced; there had been nothing like this in the Light World, at least not for the last hundred million years. From my vantage point, I could see a river of dark murky water flowing through a canyon of reddish shale-like rock, and far to my right was a plain of grayish sand dotted with lifeless trees with barren limbs reaching upward in frozen supplication, as if praying to some unheeding deity for mercy. Bordering the plain, cloaked in a low-lying mist of grayish white, was a dense primeval forest that filled the rest of the valley floor and ran to the left as far as the eye could see. Scattered across the valley floor, small steam geysers lent unearthly, surrealistic accents to the already dismal topography.

Already, from my position on the ledge, I could tell that the forest below was a dreary, foreboding place filled with both visible and unseen dangers. Just beyond the forest there was a mist-covered lake that seemed to separate the forest below from the equally obscured base of a small expanse of grim mountains just across the valley floor.

Up in the sky, a large bird with pointed wings was silhouetted as it glided gracefully through the peculiar sky. Shrill, animal-like cries echoed through the valley, and in the distant mountains, and at various places on the plain and in the forest, I could see the bright glow of fires. I knew that I would no longer be alone.

I reached into my shirt pocket to take out Solomon's verses and realized that I was glowing. It was a low, faint glow—not as bright as I had imagined or feared—but I didn't like it. I was glowing right through my clothes. Dim or not, I knew that it made me conspicuous. I moved behind a small escarpment of jagged rocks for temporary concealment.

I looked at the verses. "The sleeper's beard"? "Entwining boughs"? "First must secure a gift"? The verses were a total mystery to me but they were all I had to go on. I read them again, and it came to me. The "gift,'" that's where I have to start. But where? "Beneath an object you can't lift." Looking out over the valley I realized that there were many things out there that I couldn't lift. "Within the moonlight, smooth as glass." I went over what I knew in my mind. It's glass-like, I can't lift it, and I can't lean on it. Now, what about the "Opposing sky"? I looked up at the sky just as an enormous bird passed behind a dark gray thunderhead. "Opposing sky." A sky facing a sky. Right, but what the hell does it mean? I took another peek at the valley floor and took a quick inventory: mountains, sky, forest, trees, lake . . . lake! That was it! I can't lift it! I can't lean on it! It's often as calm as glass and you can see the sky reflected in it. Solomon's gift is hidden in the lake. It's a vial. But what about the pointing finger, felt, not spied, and colliding elements? Who knows? I hoped I would figure it out when I got to the lake, if I got there at all.

I looked down over the lake. Was this the lake of the verses, or could there be other lakes on the other side of the mountains? No, this had to be the lake. I looked at the mountains across the valley and knew that there was no way I could get to the other side of them. I began to develop my plan. All I had to do was go through the forest to the lake, get the vial, and then go back into the forest to figure out the rest of it. Easy? Sure! So, I glow a little bit, so what? So . . . hell!

I started down the mountain, carefully walking the ledge, keeping a watchful eye for loose rocks, and staying as close as I could to the mountain wall. As I walked, I imagined the denizens of this foreboding place staring up in wonderment at this strange glowing object slowly descending into their world. I also imagined them licking their lips and coming over in great hordes to investigate this curious phenomenon.

My descent continued until I came to a cave opening in the mountain wall. I peeked inside and saw, just as Moloch had described, the spirits of fellow members of the Light World chained to the walls like glowing Chinese lanterns, their cries of agony echoing throughout the cave. There were so many of them, so many captured souls never going back to the Light Malkuth again. I felt for them, but there was nothing I could do, I had to go on. Two demons stood with their backs to the cave entrance. Except for their color, a rusty orange, they were similar in appearance to Moloch. One turned around and began to sniff the air. *Damn it, I forgot about the odor.* I pressed myself against the mountain wall and tried to settle my nerves.

If the demons came out there wouldn't be anywhere for me to run, I would have to fight them. I took the flashlight out of my belt, it was the only weapon I had, besides my hands and feet. I raised it over my head like a sword and waited for the worst. I figured that if they came out I could nail the first one with the flashlight and multiple kicks and then . . . and then? Well, if I die, then I die for God and the Messiah.

A minute passed, then another, and no one came out. I peeked in and saw both demons torturing some of the chained sheaths. I hesitated, held my breath, and darted past the opening as quickly and as silently as I could. I waited on the other side of the entrance, my flashlight poised for action, just in case they had seen me. Nothing! I had passed unnoticed. Slipping the flashlight back into my belt, I continued down the ledge to the base of the mountain. When I finally reached the bottom, I took cover behind a small grouping of angular boulders that, no doubt, came from the upper parts of the mountain ages ago. The forest spread out before me and the lake just beyond that.

I examined my hands and arms, I was still glowing like a piece of white-hot steel. I looked back up the ledge for any signs of life and saw that it was clear. So far, so good, but I knew that I couldn't stay here. I was too exposed standing on the ledge. If one of those demons from the cave came out for any reason, I'd be a dead Kosher duck. I took another quick look around, took a deep breath and ran across a small stretch of barren terrain and into the forest.

The forest was unlike any other I'd ever seen. It was the forest from Hell. It was bad enough from a distance, but close up it was even more foreboding, more sinister than I had anticipated. The tree branches twisted out in odd directions, reaching out for a nonexistent sun, and their trunks were covered on all sides with black moss and rust-colored fungus.

An opaque gray mist covered the ground and engulfed my ankles. It prevented me from seeing what mysteries lay hidden on the forest floor—though I was sure that it concealed numerous creeping things whose presence and forms were best left unseen. But the mist also meant that I couldn't see any path to follow. All I knew for sure was that I had to get to the other side of the forest as quickly as I could. I looked behind me to make sure that there was nothing coming up on me, and then I started to walk. Every step I took was an adventure. I had no way of knowing what I would be stepping on or into. I tried not to think of the possibilities.

I made my way deeper and deeper into the forest, climbing over occasional logs that protruded out of the mist, and maneuvering around dead tree stumps. I don't know how long I had been walking when I spotted a branch dangling low enough from one of the trees for me to reach. I needed a walking stick, some sort of staff to poke at the ground in front of me, anything to keep me from falling into some hidden ditch or bottomless pit on my way to the lake. I looked at the branch again. It was an odd shape, but would do fine for a walking stick once I trimmed it a bit. I grabbed the branch with both hands and started to twist it, hoping to break it off. As soon as I started to twist it, the tree it belonged to gave out a high ear-piercing scream that seemed to echo through the entire valley. The scream from the tree caused the other trees in the forest to follow suit, and together it became a cacophony of horrible, high-pitched shrieking sounds. I covered my ears and dropped to my knees in pain.

After a minute or so the screams died down to whispers. All through the forest, the trees seemed to be whispering to each other, their slender twisted leafless limbs slowly moving in odd directions as they spoke.

"What kind of place is this," I said aloud, standing up again and shaking my head to clear it. The trees here had a consciousness, a sense of being, a life unknown to trees in the Light World. Here, the trees were actually talking to each other, communicating in an uncanny jumble of muted speech. I couldn't understand what they were saying, but I had the uncomfortable feeling that they were talking about me. I moved on, hoping that the shrieking of the trees hadn't alerted some kind of demonic forest ranger or a group of dangerously demented demonic boy scouts. In any event, it was clear that I wouldn't find a walking stick.

As I walked, the moon played hide and seek with the clouds and produced strange discolored shadows that shifted in odd directions, which made it difficult to keep my bearings. Even so, I kept walking. I feared that if I stopped, I would become prey for whatever creatures might be lurking beneath the mist. I tried to determine how long I'd been walking and figured that, if I wasn't walking in circles, I was nearly halfway to the lake.

Up ahead, just past the remnant of a tree that looked like it had been split by lightning eons ago, I could see a small clearing containing a small circular mound of earth that peeked out of the mist about two feet. In the center of the mound was a large black boulder with a flattened top, about three feet high and five feet across. Could this be the stone that King Solomon mentions in his verses?

As soon as I entered the clearing I went straight for the stone. The flattened top wasn't natural—chisel marks on its surface told me that some intelligent hand was responsible for it, giving me hope that I was in the right place. I climbed on top of the stone and looked around. All around me I could see the twisted tree branches reaching for each other in a seemingly eternal wanting. There were, however, two trees whose long spindly branches managed to intertwine to form a very dense mesh, in the middle of which was an opening. Now I was certain that this was the stone, and that this opening was the "void within the entwining boughs" that Solomon wanted me to find. I looked through the opening, hoping to see something spectacular, but all I saw was darkness. I looked for another opening among the numerous other branches around the clearing, but this was the only one.

I took out the verses and read them again, hoping that I hadn't missed anything. I found I didn't need the flashlight, the glow from my body was enough to illuminate them. I read them over and over, each time stopping to survey the clearing. Then I looked up in the sky, and it struck me. The moon! That has to be it. "The sleeper shall by moon appear!" I looked up and saw that the moon was hidden behind a large gray cloud. I waited several minutes until, finally, the moon left the cover of the cloud and bathed the valley in moonlight. Miraculously, as I peered through the opening in the branches, a large mountain appeared. It looked like a man lying on his back. Long, dark vertical striations gave it a beard-like appearance. That's where I had to go.

Just as I was about to step off of the stone I heard a loud rustling about twenty yards behind me and realized that I wasn't alone. Something large and heavy was moving through the brush. I jumped from the stone and pushed my way through the trees at the far side of the clearing. I had no time to be cautious about where I was stepping, whatever was coming up behind me was getting closer. I began to run, certain that it was attracted to my glow. The faster I ran, the faster the creature moved. It was gaining on me, there was nothing I could do about it. I could hear its labored grunts and snorts as I ran for my life. In the distance, I could now make out the vague image of the lake peeking through the outer edge of the forest. I had to make it to the lake before the beast caught up to me—maybe I could get to the vial in time. I ran another ten yards, skirting dead tree stumps and large stones, and took a quick peek over my shoulder. Suddenly, I was down, in pain, and couldn't get up. I'd fallen over something on the misty forest floor. I could only lie there.

The ground quaked as the beast drew near. Though the pain in my body subsided, the beast was too close for me to take off running again. I lay motionless, half-buried in the mist, and prayed. Without warning, the thundering stopped. The beast had found me. I played dead, a tactic I'd heard worked on bears. As I lay in the mist, I could feel its hot breath on my face, neck, and arms. I cautiously opened one eye and was staring directly into its dead eyes—large black pupils circled by black irises. Its gaze burned like a laser into my soul. The beast stared and snorted at me, its breath stirring the mist around me. Moloch had never mentioned that creatures like this existed down here. I didn't think it was a demon, but was something else, something animal-like and prehistoric. It was as large as a Sherman tank and walked on four legs as thick as tree trunks. Moloch hadn't mentioned this type of creature, and I'd never seen anything like it in any paleontology book. It had twin horns, each a foot in length and arcing forward from its forehead. It nudged me with its long, square snout and sniffed at my neck. Its breath was rancid and nauseating; I had to fight the urge to wretch. The great beast turned its head down and then nudged me again, now with its horns. I didn't move, fearing that it could hear my heart pounding in my chest and know that I was alive.

Finally, it grunted and reared its large head high into the air, roaring lion-like up into the leafless forest canopy. It did this three more times, each time louder. I didn't know whether it meant that it was seeking a mate, or that it was proclaiming a warning to all the residents of the forest and valley that the prey that it had found belonged to it. I just didn't know. Lowering its head again, its flaring nostrils were close to my face. It glared at me, hesitated, and then issued another ground-shaking roar high into the air. Then, turning back to me it clawed at the ground by my head, its front legs missing me by only inches. A moment later it stopped, turned, and took half a dozen steps away from me. It turned, looked at me again, and gave a final snort. A moment later it was out of sight, the ground still quaking as it traveled deep into the forest, the tremors diminishing as the distance between us increased. Whether it thought I was dead and it didn't eat dead things, or had merely confronted me out of curiosity, the fact was that it was gone. That was good enough for me.

I stood up, brushed myself off, and tried to regain my bearings. I could still see the lake vaguely peeking through the trees, and I knew that the "sleeper's beard" was just beyond that. I knew where I was—sort of. I made my way through the remainder of the forest without incident. Where were the demons? Where had the beast gone? I had no answers, and I wasn't complaining.

Within ten minutes, I was standing at the edge of the lake. I looked around for any signs of life—the beast, demons, anything. All I saw was that large dark bird making lazy circles over the forest, like a buzzard circling in the sky over carrion. If I believed in omens then I might have turned around and gone right back home. *But this is a special mission,* I reminded myself, *a holy mission.* I brought my attention back to the matter at hand.

I walked along the edge of the lake looking for what King Solomon called the "pointing finger." The lake was motionless and as smooth as glass. The water was clear and I could see bottom without any difficulty, and saw nothing in the lake itself that fit the description of the pointing finger. But, as I scanned the shoreline I noticed the branch of a nearby tree that pointed "finger-like" to a spot on the lake. I went over and stood under it. Looking up, I followed the length of the branch to determine the exact spot on the lake that it seemed to indicate—a site only about four feet from the shore. I looked and could see the sky clearly reflected in the water. This had to be the "opposing sky" that Solomon spoke of. I scanned the bottom from where I stood and saw nothing. Wondering if I had the right lake, I looked around again. Not wanting to believe that I stood on the shore of the wrong lake, I began to wonder if someone had already taken the vial. I wondered if Solomon could have made a mistake.

I dipped a finger into water. It seemed safe enough. I took off my shoes and socks, rolled my pant legs up, and waded into the lake. The spot indicated by "the pointing finger" was very shallow. I looked down, searched the bottom and saw nothing. I looked over and over again—always the same result, nothing. Meanwhile, I was still glowing and every second that passed meant the possibility of being detected. I had to hurry.

"Hell!" In frustration I dropped to my knees and searched the sandy bottom with both hands. I searched to the left, and then to the right and then to the left again. That's when I felt it—a small bottle. I picked it up, a clear bottle filled with a clear liquid. *So, that's why I couldn't see it,* I thought. *Very clever of King Solomon!* I waded back to shore and sat down on caked ground.

The bottle was corked with a glass stopper and was sealed, almost welded shut, with a yellowish metal I guessed to be brass. There were no instructions with the bottle, though it didn't matter. Any instructions would've been written in ancient Hebrew, and I wouldn't have been able to read it with my rusty Hebrew. I tried pulling on the glass stopper. It wouldn't budge, so I picked up a small stone and broke off the neck of the bottle. Now that it was open, I had another problem. I didn't know whether I had to drink it, rub it on, ignite it, or throw it at demons. For all I knew, I was supposed to spread it on bread.

I poured a few drops on the ground and waited; nothing happened. Drink it? No, at least not before I touched it. I stared at the bottle and hoped it wasn't some sort of acid. I touched my right index finger to a small drop slowly making its way down the side of the bottle. It didn't feel like acid. To my amazement and relief the tip of my finger stopped glowing. Now I understood. Solomon knew that a man from the Light World would glow down here, so he hid a potion that would counteract that glow. I poured a little into the palms of my hands and rubbed the potion on my hands and arms. The glow disappeared. But my clothes didn't stop the glow. I stripped and rubbed it all over my body, including all the unseen personal places. I emptied the contents of the vial as I covered my body with the liquid and dressed quickly. Tossing the empty vial into the lake, I remembered that Yusef had said that Solomon warned that the effects of the potion would only last a little while. I had to hurry or I'd be aglow again.

I made my way quickly along the left bank of the lake to the base of the Sleeper's Beard. Somewhere on a ledge high above me was a tree that held Solomon's ring. I looked up to a ledge wrapping around the face of the mountain, but I couldn't see a tree. I had to get up there. I had a little confidence now that the glowing had stopped, and as I searched the base of the mountain, I discovered a narrow, stony trail leading to the ledge. I followed the trail, skirting around various rocks and boulders along the way until I made it up to the ledge.

This ledge was similar to the one I had taken when I first entered the valley. I walked quickly, knocking loose stones down to the valley floor below as I went. It wasn't a very stealthy approach, but at least I didn't glow. I was about three hundred feet above the valley floor when I spotted a single tree growing where the mountain wall met the ledge. Its limbs were leafless, crooked, and didn't extend past the ledge, which explains why I hadn't seen it from down below. I walked toward it, looking around me for any signs of danger. So far so good.

As I approached, the more certain I became that this was the tree Solomon had mentioned in his verses. I was only thirty feet from the tree when I heard the clopping of hooved feet running up the ledge below me. I had to hurry. I ran along the ledge, clinging to the mountain wall, and stood in front of the tree, which filled the ledge and prevented me from going farther. I'd made it to the tree, but now I was trapped. *If I'm going to die here,* I thought, *then at least I am going to see the ring.* I hadn't come this far not to at least get to see the ring, and I was determined not to give up until I did. Quickly, I searched the base of the tree and found a hole just large enough to pass my hand through.

The sound of approaching hooves was louder now. Looking down onto the valley floor I could see a dozen large groups of wingless demons moving quickly toward the base of the mountain. In the sky, off in the distance, I could see several large groups of winged demons making their way toward me, but they were so far off that the demons on the ledge would get me first. I had to hurry. I searched the hollow compartment of the tree with my hand and felt a small wooden knob off to the right. I pulled it and a small door popped open at the base of the tree. I removed my hand from the hole and looked into the compartment. There, on a small tripod of solid gold, was Solomon's ring. I picked it up and looked at it. It was just as Yusef had described it—brass and iron, with five silver alefs interlaced on its face. It was large and heavy by modern standards, but it was Solomon's magical ring of power and I was holding it in my hands.

When I turned and looked down the ledge, I saw them—a half dozen wingless demons, scaly, horned, and orangey-gray in the moonlight. They were only fifteen yards from me, their eyes glowing red, and their talons glistening and poised for battle. I had no weapon and nowhere to run. I was trapped, facing six vicious demons ready to shred me to pieces. And if that wasn't enough, Solomon's magic formula had started to wear off and I was glowing like a beacon. *I'm a dead man!* I thought, staring at the approaching band of demons.

"There," bellowed the lead demon, pointing at me with a razor sharp finger, "there is the one of the legend, come into our world to steal the ring of the ancient Master. Let us end this legend, brothers, and let us destroy Solomon's ring of power for all time."

I was no match for any one of them, let alone all six, and all I had to defend myself with was my bare hands, feet, and the flashlight, which was a poor weapon in the best of circumstances.

Even so, I pulled it out of my belt and raised it high above my head. I tried to steady myself, stilled my thoughts with the Nefesh Hafsa'kah, and executed the Sha'ar Lev. I was as ready as I was ever going to be. An odd calm swept over me as I stood, poised to do battle and die. My martial arts master taught me that when one is outnumbered by the enemy, the best thing to do is attack. I had never been in a hand-to-hand combat situation with a demon before but it seemed like the right thing to do. It was better than dying without putting up a fight.

I said a quick prayer and prepared myself for combat. I was just about to charge at them, when, sweeping down on flaring wings toward the marauding band of demons was Moloch. He swooped down on my assailants, striking, slashing, cutting, and ripping at their flesh with his silvery talons. One fell to his death off the mountain ledge immediately. A moment later, another fell. It was then that I realized that the bird that I had seen soaring high above me, darting between the clouds since I'd first entered the Dark Malkuth, wasn't a bird at all—it had been Moloch watching over me. He was my demonic protector, my stalwart demon knight.

Moloch was magnificent, a ferocious demonic fighting machine. Soon a third demon fell to his death. Then, in the midst of battle, I saw a demon come up and, with a mighty slashing movement, cut ribbons of flesh from Moloch's body. A second demon began to slash away at Moloch, and then a third, but still Moloch fought on. I picked up some loose stones on the ledge and started pelting the attacking demons, striking one, and then another, hitting them hard but without any effect. I tried larger stones and moved closer. I struck one demon in the eye and he let out an ear-splitting howl. I quickly closed the distance between us and followed up with combination kicks to his body and multiple hand strikes to his face, all seemingly useless against him. I was just about to go in with a killing blow, when suddenly, I felt the back of a demonic hand strike me across the face. It threw me up against the mountain wall, and I felt the

ring drop from my hand. My head was reeling as I watched the
ring bounce toward the edge. Just as it was about to fall from
the ledge I saw a great taloned hand reach out and grab it. Looking up, I found it was Moloch's hand. I watched him fight on
with just one talon, guarding the ring with the other. He was
valiant, but the battle had taken its toll. Moloch was badly
wounded. He was lying on the ledge, leaning against the mountain wall and hardly moving. There was only one last demon
predator left on the ledge now. Moloch looked at the demon
coming, and then, weak and in pain, slowly turned his head to
me. He stretched out his arm and opened his hand.

"Take it," he said. "Take the ring!"

I reached out and he dropped Solomon's ring into my hand.

He could barely speak but managed to say, "The ring, my
friend . . . put the ring on. If you are the one, Benjamin, then it
will defend you. Hurry . . . please hurry!"

I put the ring on my ring finger and pointed it at the demon.
Nothing happened. I tried it again, and still nothing happened. I
didn't know what to do. I looked at Moloch for help.

"No," said Moloch, coughing and spitting up blood, "put it on
your right index finger . . . ." I switched the ring to my right index
finger just as the demon was poised to strike at Moloch. "Invoke
the name of God, El Shaddai, the defender," moaned Moloch.

"I am your servant, Lord, may El Shaddai, your protecting
face, defend me and mine," I heard myself say. The ring stirred
to life. A tremendous electrical charge was building up in the
ring as I pointed it at the demon, and then, with a mighty crack,
I saw an indigo thunderbolt leave the ring and strike the demon,
shattering its body into an infinite number of small pieces that
rained onto the valley floor below. The demon was destroyed.

"Now the others," said Moloch, "the others."

I turned toward the valley and held the ring up again and
invoked the name of God, El Shaddai. A moment later I could
feel the ring stirring back to life and I fought to steady my hand.
Suddenly, a dozen separate bolts of indigo lightning burst from

the ring, destroying the wingless demons on the valley floor. Then I raised the ring toward the sky and again invoked the mystical name of God. A moment later, three more great bolts of lightning sprang from the ring, striking each of the large squadrons of flying demons, sending their members burning onto the valley floor. It was done.

I ran over to Moloch, who was sprawled on his back on the ledge. "Oh, Moloch," I cried, dropping to my knees and cradling his head in my arms, pressing it ever so gently against my chest. "Oh, Moloch, my friend, I . . . ."

"Hush," he said, looking up at me, his blood beginning to soak my shirt. "There's no time now. Please . . . wear the ring. Don't remove it from your finger. It will protect you. You are my friend. Do not forget me in . . . in . . . your prayers tonight. I . . . I must go now to be with God . . ." Moloch smiled a final smile at me, and then quietly closed his eyes . . . he was gone.

I stayed on my knees and offered a prayer to God. "Lord, take into your bosom the soul of my dear friend Moloch. He was as true a servant to You as any in Your service. Love him, Lord, for he gave his life for his love of You. Amen."

I laid Moloch's head down and unsuccessfully fought back my tears. I had to leave. There was nothing that I could do for Moloch now. I stood and ran down the side of the mountain as quickly as I could. Then I sprinted around the lake to the edge of the forest, past the smoldering bodies of demons slain by the power of Solomon's ring. I couldn't help myself, I turned around to take one last look at Moloch resting on the ledge high above the valley floor. I could barely make out his dormant figure. I sighed and entered the forest. Whatever demons were still out there feared the power of the ring, and I knew that they knew that I had it. It gave me courage. No one bothered me as I passed through the forest and started up the winding ledge that would lead me to the tunnel, the well, and the Light World.

I reached the cave on the ledge that contained the chained spirits of those unfortunate enough to have been bound here. I decided that rather than trying to sneak by the entrance, I would stop by for a closer look. I stood squarely in the center of the cave entrance. There were four wingless demons standing guard with their backs to me. The agonized cries of those chained here reverberated off the walls of the cave. That there were untold numbers of caves like this one containing the chained spirits of unfortunate men and women whose fates brought them into demonic contact, forcing them to endure such agonies, was a sobering thought. I continued to stand my ground as the four guards turned to me. I raised my right hand and watched the four of them flee deep into the cave in utter fear of the ring. I started to go after them, but stopped, remembering that Yusef and the others were waiting for me in the Light World.

I stayed a moment, taking one last look at the chained spirits, hoping that one day I could help free them. I turned to walk the last yards to the opening of the tunnel. I took a final look back at the valley of demons, the Dark Malkuth. From where I stood, Moloch's body appeared as a tiny speck on the ledge across the valley. I had known him for a very short while, but we'd become very close—close enough for him to selflessly give up his life for me. Damon and Pythias? Well, in this case it was Demon and Pythias.

I passed through the tunnel to the small ledge, slipped my foot into the loop of rope and tugged on the safety line. I was swiftly brought to the surface. Morning had just broken with the first rays of sunlight slipping over the eastern slopes. *Real sunlight, in a real sky, a blue sky,* I thought. *I love it.*

Mara was the first one to welcome me back, throwing her arms around me and kissing me. A moment later, everyone else hugged me and immediately began asking questions. I handed Yusef the ring.

"My God," Mara said, looking at my blood-stained shirt. "What have you been through? Oh, Benjamin, you're hurt. Ali, run and get the first aid kit."

"No! Mara, I'm all right, really! The blood isn't mine. It belongs to Moloch."

Mara's hands went to her chest with a gesture of relief. "You scared me, Benjamin, but how . . . ."

"I'll explain everything," I said, between gulps of water from the canteen Muhammad had handed me. "It's all right."

"Okay, let's clean you up and you'll rest by the fire," said Yusef. "We have a great deal to discuss."

"So do we," said Mara.

"Ali will prepare breakfast," said Muhammad.

"Come, my boy," said Yusef, "you've learned some things, no? Clean yourself up and we'll speak."

I smiled at him and nodded, but I knew that he detected a great sadness in me. The diplomat in him chose, at least for the moment, to let it go.

15

The Nature of Things

BY THE TIME I HAD FINISHED CLEANING MYSELF UP, THE GOLDEN SUN burning in a cloudless sky had brought the temperature to nearly ninety degrees. I left my tent just in time for breakfast and took my seat alongside my four companions.

"Benjamin, my boy," said Yusef, clapping his hands together once, balancing his tin plate of eggs and potatoes on his lap. "I can't tell you how proud we are of you. Tell us what it was like, this Dark World. In my studies I have heard different descriptions of it. But you've been there, I have to bow to your experience."

I gave everyone a detailed description of the Dark Malkuth and told them of my experiences there, paying a great deal of attention to detail retelling the heroic exploits of Moloch—a story of heroism so compelling to the group that I found myself telling it over and over again.

"Yusef," I said, handing my empty plate to Ali, "is it possible for me to meet the Messiah when he comes? I mean, I would—"

"You're one of us, aren't you?" replied Yusef, nodding to the others. "After all, you're the one risking his life so that the Messiah could be trained by the things that you're collecting. I'm sure that he would want to meet you. I just don't know when he's going to make his appearance. It's all in God's hands."

"What will he do?" asked Mara.

"He'll deliver to the world the New Covenant and give the world a new understanding about God and the truth of existence."

"Yusef," I said, "I can see how the people of the world will change their ways when they learn that God is real, and that angels, demons, magic rings, dark worlds, bottomless wells, and miraculous staffs actually exist."

"I'm sure they would change their ways," said Yusef, raising an eyebrow, "but how could anyone else but the Messiah tell them about these things? If you, for example, told the average person about it, they would think that you were crazy. If you wrote a book about it, who would publish it? Of course . . . ."

Yusef stopped in mid-sentence.

"Of course . . . what, Yusef?" I asked, really curious.

"Well, you could write a novel."

"A novel?"

"Yes, you could make your exploits the basis of a novel. As long as the people thought that it was fiction, it would probably sell very well. Still, there may be some people who'll read it, and believe that it's based on truth. It's an outside possibility. You may even want to name it *The Truth of Existence*, or *My Journey Into The Unknown*, or even *The Lost Scrolls of King Solomon*. Yes, I like that . . . *The Lost Scrolls of King Solomon*!"

"Well, I'll consider it. Maybe someday I'll write it."

"Good, I think that you should. You never know."

"Right, you never know."

"Good, my boy," said Yusef. "I think that I wouldn't mind reading it myself."

"If they turn your novel into a movie," said Ali, smiling, "I want a very handsome actor to play me. The actress that plays my sister won't have to be so good-looking."

"Very funny," said Mara, making a face at Ali. "Very funny!"

I wanted to change the subject to something a little more serious. I had no plans for writing a novel. All I wanted to do was to live through all of this and meet the Messiah.

"Yusef," I asked, taking my breakfast plate from Ali, "what's wrong with people believing in all of this? I mean—"

"My boy," said Yusef, "mankind, for the most part, is much too involved in the material things of the world to concern themselves with spiritual matters. Yes, there are many people who love God, but their understanding of God is totally non-existent, and their beliefs are just based on faith. Faith is a wonderful thing to have, it's true, but experience is superior by far. That's exactly why the Messiah is coming. He will give mankind the experience of God, the Truth of God."

"Will he bring peace to the world?" asked Ali, handing me my cup of tea.

"He will bring the formula for peace," said Yusef.

"But, will the people accept it?" interjected Mara.

"People are, for the most part, ignorant," said Yusef. "Most walk paths in life that lead them nowhere . . . dead ends. Think about it. It's all really a question of choices."

"What do you mean, Yusef?" asked Mara, leaning slightly forward in her seat.

"Well, people are faced with choices every day of their lives. If they make the right choice, they have happiness; if they make the wrong choice, they have misery. More often than not, the choices that they make lead them into lives of frustration, fear, and misery. Why? Because the choices that they make are based on false information concerning the true nature of things. I think that God has run out of patience with mankind. I think that He will be issuing mankind a brand new set of rules of conduct, and will, from that time on, enforce those rules Himself."

I looked around the campfire. Everyone was deeply engrossed in the conversation. Even Ali ignored his breakfast and pulled his seat closer to us.

"The Messiah," continued Yusef, "will teach mankind that we are more than we ever imagined we were. He will teach us that there was never a time when we were separated from God. In fact, nothing is separate from God. He will teach us, for the first time since Moses wrote the Torah, how to contact God. Or, more specifically, how to allow God to contact us."

"Do you mean that God can't contact man?" asked Ali, a little puzzled.

"I mean that most people are so entrenched in the world, that they can't hear God speaking to them. It's like trying to speak to someone who is wearing earphones and listening to very loud music."

"I see," said Ali.

"Benjamin, if I were to ask you what you've learned so far, how would you answer?" Yusef asked, looking me squarely in the eye.

"Well," I said, leaning forward in my seat, "I've learned so much, Yusef, it's really hard to know where to start, but I'll try. One of the things that I've learned is that hatred is based on fear, and that fear is actually based on ignorance. People fear the things that are unfamiliar to them, things that are alien to them. Simply put, they fear the things that they don't understand. To them, everything that they don't understand is a potential threat."

"What about the hatred among people?" asked Mara.

"Exactly! Hatred, say, between races or cultures is based on ignorance and fear. As long as people refuse to take the time to understand other races and cultures they are going to fear them. No one likes to live in fear. So, what people do is attempt to get rid of the source of that fear through violence."

"How do you mean?" asked Ali.

"Well, fear of violence turns the fearful themselves into violent people. It's a paradox."

"Benjamin, are you saying that fear is the cause of all the world's problems?" asked Yusef, tugging on his beard.

"No, that's not what I'm saying. I think that fear is only a by-product of ignorance. The real culprit is happiness!"

Suddenly, a dead silence fell over the group. Everyone looked at each other with puzzled expressions on their faces. Mara was the first to speak. "No . . . are you saying that 'happiness' is responsible for the state of the world?"

"He's only kidding," said Ali, looking at Mara. "He doesn't mean that."

"Oh, yes I do," I said, glancing at Yusef and then turning my attention to Mara. "Think about it. There are almost six billion people in the world, and besides the necessities of having to eat and breathe, all six billion people have one thing in common, they all want to be happy. The problem is that people have different ideas of what will make them happy. The basis, though, is greed and attachment to the many things of the world."

Yusef raised an eyebrow and a smile broke out on his face. He looked over at Muhammad, and Muhammad winked at him. "Go on, Benjamin."

"Well, I was faced with my own mortality several times, and each time something seemed to change in me. "

"What changed?" asked Muhammad.

"My priorities changed."

"If you had to explain that to the people yourself, how would you do it?" asked Yusef, again exchanging glances with Muhammad.

"I would put it to them this way. Suppose that the doctors tell you that you only had three months to live, and that the disease that you have is incurable. What would you consider to be important in your life now? What would be really important? Would your priorities change? Would you consider a new car, new house, diamonds, rubies, gold, money, credit cards to be important? What would you worry about? Would you worry about the outcome of the next football Super Bowl? The cost of living index? Would you worry about your phone bill, rising taxes, next year's Oscars, or your car payment? No. Suddenly, under those conditions, your priorities would change."

"And?" said Muhammad, leaning forward in his chair. "This is most interesting."

"And, if they tell me that they are in good health and that what I suggest is only a theoretical exercise, I would say, 'Wrong!' At birth, when the doctor slaps your bottom to get you to breathe, that 'slap' is the doctor saying to you, 'I now pronounce you terminally ill.' You are going to die, and there is nothing that medical science or anyone can do about it. Now, little baby, what are you going to do with what's left of your life?"

Muhammad turned to Mara and Ali and with a serious look on his face said, "Listen to him, you two. This is wisdom."

"Go on," said Yusef.

"I would tell them to give up their attachment to things that are of no lasting value to them."

"What things?" asked Ali.

"The things of the world that they think will bring them happiness. It's all a product of their Lower Minds. At best, things can only bring about a short illusion of happiness. Ali, think back to when you were young. Did you ever ask for something that you thought would make you happy?"

"Er . . . sure," said Ali, looking at Muhammad. "I remember asking my father to get me a bicycle."

"Did you get it?"

"Yes."

"Did it make you happy?"

"Sure!"

"Well, does it still make you happy?"

"Not exactly," said Ali, looking directly at Muhammad. "I'd rather have a car."

"Forget it!" said Muhammad, giving Ali a stern smile.

"Okay! That's what I mean. Once people get whatever they think will make them happy, that thing is crossed off of their 'happiness' list and is replaced by the next item on the list. There's no end to the wanting. When a person doesn't get what they want, it makes them sad, miserable. It's all an illusion that has its genesis in a person's Lower Mind. Some people will go to great lengths to acquire the 'things' that they think would make them happy. Some people will cheat, lie, steal, and even kill to get what they want."

"Go on," said Yusef, crossing his legs and placing his folded hands in his lap.

"Their Lower Minds, not knowing of the reality of God, and His infinities, cling to a world of illusion. They make it their priority in life to collect things, to amass wealth, thinking that if they spend their time doing that, that their lives would have real meaning. They seek power over others, to control others. They can't even control themselves, or find a lasting happiness in their own lives, so how can they think that they know what's best for others? They're convinced that the only reality is what their senses tell them is real. If they knew the truth, they would live differently. Wars and hatred would cease to exist. Why? Because they would realize that it is all for nothing. I would teach them that ignorance is their true enemy, not their neighbor. Sooner or later they would have to realize that when their neighbor's wall is on fire, that it's 'their' problem too."

"Tell us more," said Mara, smiling at her father and moving her chair closer.

"I would tell them that their attachments and their ignorance makes them live their lives as if they were permanent residents here. Of course, they're not, but how they would change if they came to realize that. The unfortunate thing is that by the time most men and women realize that they are not permanent residents here, it's too late. Suddenly, they want to repent, but it's too late to do that also, and how they suffer when they realize that they've wasted their lives."

"Do you mean that a person should not have anything material?" asked Muhammad. "Should everyone live like a pauper?"

"Not at all. I didn't say that people couldn't have things, it's just that the things shouldn't have the people. In other words, you can have things, just don't be attached to those things."

"What about war?" asked Mara, scratching her nose. "I mean . . . ."

"War," I said, "is the consequence of principles."

"Principles?" asked Muhammad, with a puzzled look on his face.

"Yes . . . principles. In fact, every war that was ever fought, whether it was fought between countries, or individual people, was fought over principles. Principles are only ideas, and ideas are mind-created. Adolph Hitler, for example, had his army invade and take over Austria because of the 'principle' of German unification. Then, he invaded and conquered Poland, because of the 'principle' of having to defend the honor of Germany. You know the rest of the story . . . World War II. Principles of honor, revenge, superiority, and even taste, are only ideas that are created and perpetuated through the machinations of the Lower Mind. Countries, just like individuals, always have excuses for their aggressive behavior. They always have, in their own minds, justification for their violent acts."

"What about world peace?" asked Muhammad.

"There will never be peace between nations until the people that comprise those nations are themselves men and women of peace. World peace begins with the individual and not with groups or countries. Organizations like the United Nations simply can't do it. Moloch told me that there is a day coming when God will send the Messiah to teach the people of the world how to become peaceful people. He told me that God will deliver a formula for peace to the people of the world. He told me that he received that information in a prophetic dream."

"Did he tell you when the Messiah would be coming?" asked Mara.

"Or who the Messiah is?" asked Ali.

"No. He didn't have that information. I think that—"

"I see that the demon Moloch and all your recent experiences have taught you a great deal, Benjamin," interrupted Yusef. "What have you learned about good and evil?"

"I've learned that good and evil are everywhere. Not only in this world, but in other worlds as well. No race, no society, human or not, is immune from it. There are evil demons, like Sid, Asmodai, Obadan, Adijan, and Belial, and there are good demons like Moloch, and there are evil men and good men. Evil is anyone or, for that matter, anything, that opposes God's Redemption. Moloch taught me many things that night."

Yusef smiled. "Benjamin, you sound different, more informed."

"Do you really think so?" I asked.

"Of course, Benjamin. What do you think, Muhammad?"

Muhammad looked at me, smiled, and nodded.

"Benjamin, I'm very pleased with you," said Yusef, smiling, "very pleased, indeed. You are doing well for both God and the Messiah."

"Yusef," said Muhammad, giving Yusef a nod, "you have things to do, remember?"

"Okay," said Yusef, standing up and stretching, and nodding back at Muhammad. "Look, I have a great deal of work to do on the scrolls. I want everyone to enjoy the rest of the day and rest up. We're pulling out of here at sun-up tomorrow!"

"Where are we going?" I asked, wondering what was next on the agenda.

"South," said Yusef, turning and walking towards his tent. "South, my boy! South for Solomon's Treasure!"

Mara and I locked eyes.

"Now, why don't you two take a walk," said Yusef, seeing our exchange. "It will relax you. It will do you both some good." Clearly, Yusef was playing matchmaker and I didn't mind it one bit. I looked at Mara, smiled, and extended my hand. She took it. We walked just a short distance from camp and sat down on a large boulder.

"You know, I owe you an apology," I said, turning to her.

"An apology? Why?"

"Well, I thought you were a real bitch, a spoiled little girl who . . . ."

Mara started to laugh.

"What?" I asked, wondering what she found so funny.

"Then I guess I owe you an apology too."

"Why?"

"Because I thought you were just another macho-man who thought too much of himself. I was wrong to think that, I'm sorry." She extended her hand to me as if to bind her apology with a handshake—our eyes locked. I gently pulled her toward me and kissed her on the lips, tentatively as first. She responded and the kiss grew more passionate. We embraced and kissed again, even more passionately.

"I've wanted this since I first saw you," I whispered, holding her against me.

"I did too, but I was afraid. I've been through some . . . ."

"Sssh," I whispered, as I silenced her with another gentle kiss.

"I love you, Benjamin Stein," she said, looking up at me with tearful eyes.

"I love you, Mara," I said, cupping her face in my hands and looking deep into her eyes.

16

Solomon's Treasure

As the sun rose, we began the next leg of our journey by traveling south on Israeli road 80 past Ramallah. From there, we drove west on 31, south on 446, and then, leaving paved roads behind us, west again along a dry wadi that twisted through a series of well-weathered hills and sun-burned knolls that were typical of the primitive aspect of the larger portion of the Judean countryside. The wadi seemed endless, and took so many turns that I was certain, at one point, that we were traveling in circles. It wasn't until we entered a more rugged area of the wadi— where the rolling hills and knolls gave way to short intervals of vertical, canyon-like walls—that I realized that we were actually making progress. Even Muhammad, on more than a few occasions, would glance at Yusef for confirmation that he was driving in the right direction. Yusef didn't seem to respond, he remained silent as he ceaselessly pored over the scrolls and his map.

All through the trip, Yusef stayed aloof from any meaningful conversation. Several times along the way I tried to find out more about Solomon's Treasure, but each time I brought up the subject, Yusef would say things like, "We'll find out about that soon," or "We'll see, my boy, we'll see," or "How is your aunt in Phoenix?"

Eventually, it became clear to me that Yusef either didn't have much information about the treasure, or that he just didn't want me to know much about it. I began to speculate on the possibilities. I figured that it was either another urn or a small box of gold. Finally I let it go, knowing I'd find out soon enough.

We drove another fifteen minutes when Yusef broke his silence.

"We're close," he announced, looking up from his map and peering out of the window, "very close. I want everyone to keep their eyes peeled for a narrow vertical split in the canyon wall. It will be on the right."

Muhammad slowed down now that he knew what we were looking for. To me, all the vertical striations of the canyon walls were different and yet, somehow, all appeared to be the same. I didn't think we were ever going to find it. I was quickly proven wrong. We drove another five minutes when Muhammad stopped the Land Rover and pointed to what appeared to be the split that Yusef was talking about.

"Yes, that's it," said Yusef, smiling. "Take us closer."

Muhammad pulled to within ten feet of the split and Mara and Ali parked just to our right. Leaving the vehicles behind, we walked over to the crevice, which was barely wide enough for a man's body to pass through. I peeked in and saw that it ended about fifteen feet in.

"Yusef, are you sure this is it? I mean . . ."

"Relax, my boy," said Yusef, looking into the narrow fissure. "This is it."

"How do you know?" I asked.

"Well, first of all, it's on the map. That is, its location was explained by King Solomon, and it corresponds to this exact location. Besides, it's in King Solomon's verse."

"What verse?" I asked.

"Listen," said Yusef, opening the scrolls, and pointing to a particular passage.

THE LOST SCROLLS OF KING SOLOMON   201

Within the split, you'll find my friend,
a narrow path that seems to end,
Once you're in, then you shall see
it will take you where you need to be.

"The great king really loved his verse, didn't he?" said Muhammad, scratching his beard and looking into the crevice.

"What now?" I asked, not sure what the game plan was. "Do we make camp?"

"No. No need for camp," said Yusef, turning and looking down the wadi and then up at the cliffs as if he expected someone or something to be there. "Muhammad, I want everyone to have a flashlight. We're all going in."

"No time for tea?" asked Muhammad, curious at Yusef's rush to get this thing done.

"No time, my friend! We have to hurry. And don't forget the water," said Yusef with a renewed urgency in his voice.

"Mara, five flashlights! Ali, a five-gallon can of water! Yallah! Yallah!" said Muhammad, clapping his hands.

Mara and Ali dashed back to the van and quickly returned with the supplies. Yusef's order for the five flashlights told me that I wasn't going to be doing this alone, but I was puzzled by the demand for water. What were we looking for here?

Yusef seemed concerned as he looked up and down the cliffs, then down the wadi behind us. I followed his gaze, but saw nothing. As Yusef started toward the crevice, the rest of us followed. Stopping, he turned to me. "Benjamin, you lead the way. We will all follow."

I entered the crevice, followed by Yusef, Muhammad, Ali, and then Mara. Looking ahead, the path seemed to stop in a dead end, a wall of stone. But when I reached it, I saw that the crevice took a sharp turn to the left. The verse was right, it wasn't a dead end. Instead it was a very clever device to dissuade anyone from entering. Another ten feet in, the path veered to the right and opened into a large clearing surrounded on all sides by striated cliff walls rising a hundred feet above us. There was only one way in, and only one way out. In the center of the rectangular clearing, eleven gleaming white marble pillars—eight feet in diameter—stood thirty feet high in a perfect circle thirty feet across—it reminded me of Stonehenge, the Druid mystery of ancient England. This circular configuration of pillars was perched on a large square base of sparkling granite blocks—each must have weighed two or three tons apiece. In all, the base was eighty feet long on each side. The hot sun beating down on the granite base produced a harsh glare that was accented by vertical waves of distorted air like that found on very hot paved roads.

Admiring the structure, none of us seemed quite sure of what it was. If it was some sort of temple, Stonehenge not withstanding, it was a totally new design. Seven white marble steps that brought us up to the top of the base, and standing in the center of a circle, we saw a small structure not unlike a modern birdbath. The black marble bowl was supported by a white marble column. As we moved closer to examine it, Yusef pointed out a small hole, like a drain, in the middle of the basin. Running out from the base of the column were eleven narrow grooves, each fifteen feet long, carved into the granite foundation, and each running to one of the eleven pillars.

Standing by the bowl now, we could see portals hewn into each of the eleven marble pillars. Mara wandered over to one and was just about to step inside when Yusef noticed her. "Wait! Stop!" said Yusef, holding his hand up. "Don't go in there! We don't want to lose you!"

Mara stopped dead in her tracks, turned around with a frightened look on her face, and quickly rejoined us in the center of the platform.

"What's wrong, Yusef?" I asked, wondering just what the danger was.

"Listen to this verse," said Yusef, pointing to a particular place in the scrolls.

Eleven pillars standing tall
erected by a king,
In ten find death, in one find life;
the secret's in the ring.

"What was the secret that Solomon put into the ring?" I asked, annoyed that I hadn't examined the ring more closely.

"King Solomon put an inscription on the inside of the band of the ring," said Yusef, wiping some perspiration off his forehead with his handkerchief. "After I translated the verse last night, I reexamined the ring and found the inscription. It read: 'Water is treasure, but blue is true.' This is why we brought the water. I thought that we might be needing it."

"Water is, indeed, treasure out here," said Muhammad, looking at Yusef and then at me. "This is a cruel land, especially if you get caught out here without water."

"Yes, but I think that the king meant something else, no?" Yusef said with a smile. "Come, bring the water over here, Ali."

Ali brought the large water can over to the bowl.

"Pour it in the bowl and we'll see," said Yusef, pointing to the bowl and then folding his arms.

"All of it?" asked Ali, clutching the five-gallon can in his arms.

"Yes, all of it," said Yusef.

Ali nodded and then emptied all five gallons of water into the bowl. We all stood staring into the basin waiting for something to happen.

"What's wrong?" asked Mara after a minute had passed.

"Maybe it's clogged," said Ali, reaching down into the black bowl and swishing his hand around.

"Oh, yes, I almost forgot. How stupid of me!" said Yusef, shaking his head as he bent down and ran his hands along the sides of the pedestal.

It only took a moment. His hands stopped a few inches from the base of the pedestal. We watched as Yusef pressed the left side of the base and then slid a small rectangular panel down to reveal a small hole. He poked his finger in the hole and, a moment later, we heard a loud gurgling sound as the water slowly disappeared down the hole. The water streamed from the base of the pedestal and into each of the eleven grooves leading to each of the pillars. The water running down ten of the grooves was clear, but in one it ran a luminescent blue.

"Blue is true. That's the way in," said Yusef, smiling, and pointing to the entrance of the pillar indicated by the blue water. "Ali, we won't need the can anymore, so leave it out here. Okay, is everyone ready?"

Yusef took a final look up at the rim of the vertical walls surrounding us as if he still expected someone or something to be up there peering down at us. He shook his head. I looked, nothing was there. I had no idea what he was looking for.

"Follow me in," said Yusef, taking his flashlight out and turning toward the entrance. "Be careful, stay close together."

Yusef stepped through the doorway followed by me, Muhammad, Mara, and then Ali. There should have been light streaming in through the doorway, but the interior of the column was pitch black. Each of us turned on our flashlights as soon as we stepped in. What we found made our surroundings even stranger. The collective beams from our flashlights revealed a rectangular room at least twenty feet in length by fifteen feet in width. *How could this be?* I wondered. *The column itself is only eight feet in diameter and round, yet, here we are, just a few steps inside, standing in a rectangular room enormously larger than the diameter of the column.*

"A great illusion, no?" said Yusef, moving the beam of his flashlight around the room. "Leave it to King Solomon to do something like this!"

This truly was Solomon's world, one of magic and illusion a world where miracles were commonplace and things weren't always what they seemed. But this wasn't done with mirrors and smoke; this was real magic, the genuine article.

I looked around the room. The floors and walls all appeared to be made out of pure black marble. The room was bare; no objects, no furniture, no torches, no pentacles, and no spectacular gold letters on the walls. I was about to search the left side of the chamber when Muhammad's voice echoed off of the marble walls.

"Over here," called Muhammad, his flashlight focused on a large square hole in the floor on the far end of the room. "I think I've found the way down!"

The four of us joined Muhammad at the opening in the floor. Shining our flashlights into the hole, we found a spiral staircase that was carved into what appeared to be sandstone. We looked at each other for a moment, all at a loss for words.

"Shall we go down?" said Yusef, finally breaking the silence and stepping to the edge of the hole. "We've seen all there is to see up here." He turned and took the first step down into the unknown.

One by one, we followed Yusef down the stairway. There were no markings on the walls as we descended and, so far, no confirmation that this was not one of the pillars that would lead to death. I counted each of the one hundred and twenty steps on the long, dusty way down. Each footfall seemed to echo throughout the structure. The air was hot and as dry as the dust our footsteps raised on the staircase.

Finally reaching the bottom, we found ourselves in another rectangular room a little smaller than the room we'd just left and constructed of the same black marble. There were two doorways, one at either end of the long wall. Our flashlights revealed four torches in brass brackets mounted in the center of each of the walls, which we quickly lit. As the room became illuminated, we found, in solid gold letters on the wall in front of us, a message from the great King of Israel.

"What does it say, Yusef?" I asked, already expecting verse.

"Another verse," said Yusef, wiping the perspiration off his forehead with his handkerchief. He read the message on the wall. "Hmm. Very interesting. Very interesting, indeed!"

"Well?" said Muhammad in anxious anticipation. "What does it say? Don't keep us in suspense!"

"It says," said Yusef, rubbing his nose as he tried to fight off a sneeze,

> One door's right, the other not;
> one leads to death, the other gold,
> An older sun shall mark the door
> that shall my treasury unfold."

The five of us turned and stared at the two doorways. No one said anything, but we all knew that one would lead us to Solomon's Treasure. The other one would lead to certain death.

"Well, does anyone have any guesses?" said Ali, looking a little bewildered.

"We cannot afford to guess." said Yusef, looking back at the verse on the wall. "If we had to guess, would you want to be the first one through the door we pick?"

A frown came over Ali's face as he shook his head and took a couple of steps backward.

"Okay," I said, sliding my flashlight in my belt. "We know that one of these doors is the right door. The other one, well, leads somewhere else, right?"

Everyone nodded their agreement.

"Okay!" I said, now intrigued. "I think that the whole key has to lie in the term 'older sun.' That's what we have to concentrate on."

"And what's an older sun?" asked Muhammad, following suit and sliding his flashlight into his belt.

Several minutes of silence passed as everyone pondered the question. This time Yusef was the first to break the silence. "Muhammad, do you have your compass with you?"

"Yes," said Muhammad, taking his compass out of his shirt pocket and handing it to Yusef.

Yusef held the compass up, then turned to his left and then to his right, and then back to his left again. Everyone looked at him with great curiosity. He repeated his movements, then stood staring at the doorways and pulling at his beard. It was clear that he was on to something—but what was it?

"We take the doorway on the right," he said, with a small grin. "Yes, yes, the doorway on the right!"

"Why the right?" I asked, wanting to know how he figured it out. He seemed so sure of himself.

"Okay," said Yusef, turning to me, "Solomon said that an 'older sun' marks the door. Right?"

I nodded.

"Well, according to the compass, the left door is on the eastern end of the wall and the right door on the western end. Since the sun travels from east to west, it means that when the sun reaches the west, it is older than it was in the east. Clever of Solomon, no?"

The four of us looked at each other and then at Yusef, laughing with relief. Like always, Yusef's logic seemed to be impeccable.

"Shall we go, then?" said Yusef, beaming.

Again, he led the way. We took two of the torches off of the walls and brought them with us. In single file, we entered a narrow black marble-lined corridor that led to a long white marble ramp, which deposited us in front of a set of large solid gold double doors. On the transom above the double doors was a large solid silver pentacle, similar to, but much larger than, the one we encountered on the iron door leading to the labyrinth in Jericho.

"This is it," said Yusef, taking the scrolls from the leather case. "Bring the torch over here, Mara."

Mara brought the torch closer to Yusef who unrolled the scrolls and began to read silently. He called me over and reached inside his pants pocket to produce the ring. "Put it on," he said, handing me the ring. "Right index finger."

Slipping it on my finger, I waited to find out what would happen next.

"Now," said Yusef, pointing to a specific passage of the scrolls, "Solomon's next two verses say this:

Only he who won the ring
can break the seal upon this door,
And only the power it can bring
can open wide my treasure store.

Upon thy index finger place
the magic ring of iron and brass,
Repeat my name but twice and find
that to my treasure you may pass.

"Do you understand, my son?" said Yusef. "You are the one who brought back the ring. You 'won' it, so you'll have to be the one to do this."

"I understand, Yusef. "I'll do whatever I have to do."

"Are you ready?"

"Yes."

"Okay, then," said Yusef, putting his arm on my shoulder. "For God and the Messiah. You must direct the ring to the pentacle and repeat Solomon's name twice."

"Got it, Yusef," I said, as I positioned myself in front of the great gold doors. "Everyone stand back, just in case."

I raised my right arm and aimed the ring toward the pentacle. "Solomon!" I said in my most austere voice. Nothing happened at all. "Solomon." I repeated, and still nothing happened. I tried it again, and again nothing happened. I didn't know what to do next. I raised my arm to try one last time when Yusef interrupted me.

"No! No! Wait!" said Yusef, coming over to me and placing his hand on my shoulder. "Benjamin, you must say his name in Hebrew, not English. In Hebrew his name is Shlomo. Do you understand? Shlomo!"

"Oh, yes! Of course, Yusef."

I repositioned my arm in front of the doors and redirected the ring towards the pentacle. "Shlomo!" I said, carefully aiming the ring. "Shlomo!" I repeated. No sooner had I said the name the second time when the ring started to vibrate on my finger, just like it had when I was on the ledge in the Dark Malkuth with the demons. A second later a blinding bolt of indigo lightning shot from the face of the ring and struck the silver pentacle. A low-pitched rumbling of the ground followed and the silver pentacle began to glow. It glowed brighter and brighter until it was very nearly blinding. Suddenly, the pentacle began to vibrate, and then, changing from a silver color to an iridescent indigo, it crumbled into a heap of rubble on the floor. The two heavy gold doors leading to Solomon's Treasure slowly opened to reveal a large dark vault.

We cautiously entered the vault. The light from our torches quickly revealed what was undoubtedly the greatest treasure trove in the history of the world. Everything in the room seemed to sparkle and shimmer under the flickering light of our torches. We stood speechless, staring at the fortune filling the room. Golden treasure chests, each the size of steamer trunks, were stacked ten high in three great rows stretching the entire length of the hundred-foot-long room. Each was overflowing with untold numbers of huge cut and uncut diamonds, sapphires, and rubies. Countless piles of gold necklaces and bracelets studded with precious stones, standing taller than a man, were piled all over, as were at least fifty columns of neatly arranged solid gold bars stacked twenty feet to the ceiling. Heaps of solid gold daggers, spears, and swords were scattered about the room and solid gold shields lined the walls.

Muhammad, Mara, and Ali began exploring the vault. They busied themselves looking there, poking around, picking up one treasure after the next.

"Yusef," I said, awed by the spectacle, "was all of this Solomon's? Was this his fabled treasure?"

"Yes, my boy," said Yusef, looking around the room, "this was all King Solomon's. This place must have been his secret stash, his private storehouse. It was never mentioned in any of the written tracts that I studied in Yeshiva, but there were a few oral legends that have come down to us over the ages. One says that King Solomon had so much gold that he decided to have swords, spears, and shields made of them to decorate his palace. Of course, gold was too heavy and soft to be used for fighting equipment, just decoration. It certainly must have impressed the foreign dignitaries that visited him. Clearly, the legend is true. Fabulous, isn't it!"

I could only nod. "A man who had only a tenth of the wealth in this room could probably buy himself all of Europe and maybe a small piece of Asia, as well," I mused. "It's truly phenomenal."

"Did you know that Solomon was the richest man that ever lived? Oh, course you know that!" said Yusef, turning to me. "But, did you know that his personal income, by today's standards, would run nearly six billion dollars a year?"

"Six billion dollars?" I said, picking up a small gold necklace that apparently had fallen out of one of the gold chests. Feeling the weight of the necklace, I did the calculations. "Let me see, six billion dollars a year . . . an eight hour day . . . five days a week . . . fifty weeks a year with two weeks of vacation time . . . that comes to three million dollars an hour, not including perks and overtime. Not bad, not bad at all."

"Yes, six billion dollars! A lot of money, no?" said Yusef, blowing his nose. "Oh yes Benjamin, there's something else," said Yusef, putting his hand on my shoulder. "I almost forgot."

"Something else?" I said, knowing that Yusef was such a stickler for detail that if he 'forgot' something, he did so on purpose. It meant only one thing to me, that whatever he had to tell me, I was probably not going to like.

"Yes, my boy, we have to find the map."

"Map?" I said, not quite sure what Yusef was talking about. "What map?"

"Yes, I'm sorry, I thought I'd told you. You see, Solomon had mines of all sorts located in various places throughout the known world. The king had drawn up a map that pinpointed the exact locations of those mines. The map is hidden somewhere in this complex. I wrote down the verses concerning the map. It has to be found because I'll need it to train the Messiah. Again, this is something that you'll have to do on your own. The rest of us will have to go up and wait for you outside. You understand, no?"

Yusef reached into his shirt pocket and handed me a small scrap of paper with the translated verses on it. It read:

> *Within the confines of my hoard*
> *beneath the lion's piercing stare,*
> *A flight of gold beneath a cord*
> *shall yield the map to my Ophir.*
>
> *But, be thee warned that only one*
> *may seek the map to all my store,*
> *For all who quest shall be undone*
> *if there be seekers two or more.*

"I understand, Yusef. I guess I have to be the one, right?"

"Right!" said Yusef. He called to the others that it was time to go. "We'll leave you now, my boy. Just follow the directions in the verses and you'll be all right."

Ali handed me his torch and smiled. Mara gave me a hug. "Be careful, Benjamin. I love you." She kissed me then left with Yusef and the others. I was now alone in the greatest treasury in the world. With only one torch, the room was shadowy and spooky. I could hear the footsteps of the group fade away as they left the structure. Alone now, the treasure lost its appeal for me. I had to find the map.

As I moved around the room, my torch cast grim, foreboding shadows. "All right," I said to no one, "the lion's stare? The very first thing I have to do is find that lion. I hope that it isn't a real lion! No, that's silly! How can a real lion live in here, or any-where for that matter, for three thousand years? But then again, Solomon with all of his magic. No, I must be going crazy!"

I looked everywhere, in every pile, every stack, and every row. I examined the etchings carved into the gold shields on the wall for anything that even resembled a lion. After two hours of endless walking and searching I'd found nothing. I sat down on a golden chest that stood alone, centered on the eastern wall. I couldn't find the lion or anything that even remotely looked like a cat of any kind. I held up the torch and looked around from my new perspective—and still saw no lion at all. I didn't want to admit to Yusef that I had failed to find the map. It would break his heart. And I didn't want to appear inept to Mara. I decided to keep looking.

I picked myself up and began to search the room all over again. I walked to the center of the room, and, holding the torch high over my head, I slowly turned in a circle and looked in all directions. Gold, silver, jewels, and shadows were all I saw and not a lion among them. Just as I was about to walk to the western wall of the room, I caught a glimpse of a very curious shadow near the northern wall directly in front of me. I stared at it and realized, whatever that shadow was—living or statue, man or demon—it was solid enough to cast a shadow of its own. It was nearly four feet high and six feet long and warranted further investigation. Cautiously, I approached it. The closer I came to it, the more it faded. When I finally got to the spot where the shadow stood, it had disappeared altogether. Was it an optical illusion, or just my mind—my Lower Mind—playing tricks on me? I didn't know, but I was determined to find out.

I moved away from the spot of Solomon's magic. Each time I approached the shadow it faded and disappeared, there was no logical explanation for it. Frustrated, I was just about to give up when I caught a reflection on the blade of a polished sword that was leaning against a low chest. I quickly looked back at the sword—something was definitely there. I grabbed the sword and, keeping my back turned to the shadow, used the blade like a mirror. The reflected image was that of a lion, a real lion, with a tawny coat, a full dark brown mane, and eyes like burning embers. It didn't move. It just stood there with a cold and penetrating stare. I tilted the sword slightly for a view of the floor under the lion. I pinpointed the area below the lion's head as well as I could and slowly backed over to it.

As soon as I drew near, the light from my torch caused the shadowy lion to disappear. I looked at the floor and saw nothing but a small, round-cut ruby about the size of a nickel. I bent to pick it up and discovered that it was attached to a golden cord threaded through a small hole in the floor. I pulled at the cord and a trap door in the floor popped open. I looked around to make sure that I was alone, raised the trap door, and held my torch over the entrance.

A short flight of stairs, no more than ten steps long, built of what seemed to be solid gold, led me down to a small room. There, on top of a golden pedestal in the center of the room, lay an ancient scroll. Carefully, I unrolled the scroll. To my relief, it was a map, hand-drawn, and annotated in Hebrew. This was it, King Solomon's treasure map showing the location of all of his mines—the sources of all of his treasure—and I had it. This was probably the greatest find, the most valuable item in all of his treasury. Who knows how much more wealth was still down in those mines? I looked around the small room, there was nothing else.

I was just about to leave the small chamber when I heard the unmistakable roar of a lion echoing through the room above me. At first, I thought it was just my imagination. Then a second roar ricocheted off the walls. I had been all over that room and all I had found was Solomon's illusion. My throat suddenly went dry. Was there a real lion in that room that I could have missed? No, it was impossible. That left only one other reason for the roaring. Could Solomon's lion have somehow come to life?

I tried to gather my wits about me by performing the Nefesh Hafsa'kah and the Sha'ar Lev. Now I was calm, but I still had to face the lion. The only way out of the small chamber was the staircase, and if the lion came down here, I was a dead man. I knew that I had to get upstairs and make it through the treasury room without confronting the lion. *At least I have the torch,* I told myself, *it might be an effective weapon.* As soon as the thought crossed my mind, the torch flickered out. I was left in the darkness holding nothing more than a smoldering piece of wood.

"Great!" I muttered. "What next?"

I took my matches out and tried to reignite the torch. It wouldn't relight. I had no choice. I tucked the map in my shirt and left the room, using the torch as a cane, poking it here, tapping it there, swinging it there.

I retraced my steps the best I could and quickly found myself in the main treasury room. I couldn't see a thing, but I could sense the lion lurking somewhere in the darkness. Suddenly, there was another roar, then another, and yet another. I couldn't tell where it was coming from; sometimes it was coming from my left, sometimes from my right, and sometimes from somewhere in front of me. I refused to believe that King Solomon would have let me find the map, only to let me be mauled to death by a lion who hadn't been fed in three thousand years. Perspiration dripped off of my chin as I swung the unlit torch out in front of me and gradually made my way toward the open gold doors. My heart was beating like a drum, but not loud enough to drown out the sound of the roaring.

I was only a few feet from the doors when I heard the one sound that I really didn't want to hear . . . the sound of gold and silver crashing to the floor. The lion had located me and was on its way in a hurry. I tried to run, but after only four or five steps I slipped; crashing to the floor, the torch flew from my hands. I felt along the floor beside me, but I couldn't find it. The roars were louder now, the lion was only a couple of yards away. I lit a match, hoping against hope that its small flame would frighten the lion away. I had made it through the gold doors, but I still had a long way to go. I turned and held the flickering flame in front of me and saw the white marble ramp. I knew that there was no way that I could outrun that thing.

I heard another roar and turned around in time to see the lion, claws extended and jaws poised for the kill, spring at me from just inside the treasury room entrance. Instinctively, I jerked my left arm up just above my head as a defense. I braced myself for the attack. The lion, in mid-air, suddenly disappeared as it reached the golden doors that set the boundary of the great room. It was gone. Stunned and breathless, all I could do was sit on the floor, struggling to regain my composure, or at least enough of it to get to my feet. I checked my shirt, and was relieved to find that I still had the map.

"Solomon," I called out in the darkness, "you and your damned magic! Why can't you give a guy a break!"

I turned, walked up that ramp, through the small room, up the stairs, through the anteroom, and stepped out of the pillar. It took me some time, but I had made it. Treasure or not, it was good to be out in the sunlight, breathing fresh air.

Exiting the pillar I was disappointed to find that no one—not Yusef, not Mara, nobody—was waiting for me. I had expected all four of them to rush over to hug me and ask to hear all my adventures and how I was able to locate the map. But instead I was alone in the circle of columns. I started my route out of the crevice.

When I reached where we'd parked, I found only the Land Rover. The van was gone, along with Muhammed, Mara, Ali, and Yusef. I was alone, abandoned, and I didn't like it. I walked over to the Land Rover and noticed that they had left the keys in the ignition, but hadn't bothered to leave a note. I had found the greatest treasure trove in history, and a map that could lead me to more, much more, and everyone had disappeared on me. I was alone and that made the possibilities staggering. I could become, with just a little backpacking and dragging, the richest man on the planet. I could disappear with the map and find the mines and become rich that way. But, what good would that be? To become the richest man on earth, and lose God in the process was a bargain that I wasn't about to strike. I fell asleep sitting in the Land Rover waiting for Yusef and the others to show up.

I woke the next morning to the sound of tapping on the window of the Land Rover. I looked up, rubbing the sleep from my eyes, only to see Yusef's face beaming down at me. I sat up, stretched, and rolled down the window. "Good morning, Yusef, boker tov. I thought everyone had abandoned me."

"Abandon you, my son? How could we abandon a man, who faced with all of this wealth, couldn't find it in himself to abandon God?"

I thought Yusef would break my neck, the way he reached in and pulled my forehead to his lips. He kissed me on the forehead and said, "Come, my son, let's have some tea and something to eat. You have something for me, no?"

I stepped out of the Land Rover and handed Yusef the map. He hugged me again. Then, Mara threw her arms around me and kissed me as the ground began to rumble. We held on to each other to steady ourselves. A moment later, a bolt of gleaming white lightning came out of a clear blue sky and struck the cliffs by the crevice, causing the crevice to fill with boulders and rocky debris. Then, the seam of the two opposing sides of the narrow passageway was fused together for all time by a second powerful bolt of lightning. There was absolutely no sign of the crevice left.

"Benjamin, what . . ." began Mara.

"I don't know . . . ."

"Come, you two," Yusef said, matter-of-factly, "let's have something to eat. Ali has the fire started. Benjamin, you'll need your strength, you know. Tomorrow you're going to pay Satan a little visit and retrieve his Veil."

17

The Intervention

ON A MODERATE RISE ACROSS FROM THE NARROW CREVICE LEADING
to the treasure of Solomon, the three Mossad agents kept their
vigil on Yusef and the group.

"They're just standing around talking, boss," said Avram,
prone with binoculars pressed to his eyes. "Not much happening."

"All right," said Jehuda, raising the visor of his baseball cap.
"Just keep your eye on them."

"Damn!" said Yitzak, wiping the sweat from his forehead
with his forearm.

"What?" asked Jehuda.

"I was supposed to drop off my ex-wife's alimony check
today. She'll be looking for me, that's for sure."

"Well, she'll never find you out here," said Jehuda, grinning.

Yitzak smiled. "You're right. You know, the desert isn't that
bad after all. I could get used to it out here. I wanted to . . . ."

"Hey, boss. We've got company," said Avram, turning his
binoculars away from Yusef and the group, and training them
on a small rise on the other side of the wadi.

Jehuda and Yitzak crawled over to Avram and raised their binoculars.

"What company? Where?" said Jehuda, scanning the other side of the wadi with his binoculars. "I don't see anyone."

"The small rise over on the left. Do you see them?"

"Got 'em," said Jehuda, his mouth dropping to a sneer. "It's that murdering bastard Fu'ard and his band of cutthroats. Looks like six of them."

"Who?" asked Yitzak.

"You know, Fu'ard, the Algerian that the army has been hunting for over two years," said Jehuda, the binoculars still pressed against his eyes. "The word is that he came here fleeing the Algerian government for committing a couple of political assassinations. Since he's been here, he and his bunch have been preying on small groups of archeologists, rock hunters, and lost tourists. They cut up their victims and bury them in the desert. Then they take everything and disappear. He's an assassin."

"The guy's bad news. He never leaves witnesses," interjected Avram. "He and his men are like ghosts."

"Well, our 'ghosts' are watching our friends down there," said Jehuda. "I think they're getting ready to do their thing."

"Boss, remember I told you that we thought we saw someone dart from building to building when we were watching the group in Jericho."

"Yes."

"Maybe it was one of Fu'ard's men. Maybe they were tailing these guys all the time."

"It could be," said Jehuda.

"This is getting complicated," said Avram.

"What do we do now?" asked Yitzak.

"If we don't do something, boss, they'll kill the old man, the Arabs, and the American, and take off with all that stuff," said Avram, turning to Jehuda. "What do you want us to do? We have to do something."

"Okay! Okay! Listen, the way I see it, we have three choices," said Jehuda, putting his binoculars down and turning around. "One, we can ignore them. If we do, we're going to have some dead men on our hands and maybe an incident with the United States when his relatives want to know what happened to him. Two, we could shoot it out with these bastards, but all we have are our Birettas; they have Uzis, Ak-47s, and bandoleers with plenty of ammo. Third . . . we can . . . well . . . ."

"Well, what?" said Yitzak, exchanging glances with Avram.

"Well, we can take them out quietly."

"We do that, boss," said Avram, retraining his binoculars on the bandits, "then we're killing two birds with one stone. We can continue following our guys, and at the same time do the army's work for them and end Fu'ard's career once and for all. It sounds like a plan to me. Let's take 'em out."

"Yitzak?"

"Take them out! Why not?" said Yitzak, shrugging his shoulders. "I never really thought that I was going to live long enough to be pensioned off anyway."

"Okay! We're all agreed then, right?" said Jehuda, looking at his watch. "Yitzak, go to the jeep and bring me the long black case under the green blanket in the back. I brought a few things that I thought we'd be able to use just in case anything unforeseen happened."

Yitzak left for the jeep.

"Damn! I'd rather do this at night," said Avram, turning and spitting on the ground.

"You'd better save that spit of yours. You might need it before we're done out here," said Jehuda, readjusting the brim on his cap to keep the sun out of his eyes.

Avram smiled. "Right, boss."

"All right, keep your eye on all of them and let me know what's happening." Jehuda crept back to the shade and his sandwich as Yitzak showed up carrying the black case. He set the case down in front of Jehuda.

"What's in it?" asked Yitzak, taking a sip of water from his canteen. "It's heavy."

"This," said Jehuda, smiling and throwing back the three clasps on the case, "is my Just-In-Case."

"Your what?" asked Yitzak, really curious.

"My Just-In-Case. Do you remember when I went for that special training in the United States two years ago? You know, the training that the Mossad brass made their field leaders take."

"Yeah, I remember," said Avram, still concentrating on the two groups.

"Me, too," said Yitzak. "I remember."

"Well, I underwent training in a Japanese martial art called Torishimaru Aiki Jutsu. This is one hell of a deadly art. Well, one night the Grand Master of the art pulled out a black case just like this one. When he opened it, my eyes lit up. He had it all in there, all the quiet stuff. Get this! In the case was a compound bow, two dozen razor-tipped hunting arrows, a quiver, a long sword, a short sword, six throwing knives, a dozen poison-grooved star darts, a couple of piano wire garrotes, and assorted vials filled with deadly chemicals and poisons and a whole bunch of other stuff that I couldn't even identify. The Master's case was a quiet killer's dream. When I asked him what his case was for, he just smiled and called it his 'Just-In-Case.' He said that he keeps it handy 'just in case' he needs it. His philosophy is totally non-violent, but let me tell you, he is without a doubt one of the deadliest men on the planet." Jehuda opened the case.

"Where's the kitchen sink?" Yitzak asked, with a big grin on his face.

"Couldn't fit it in."

"This is really something," said Yitzak, staring at all the weapons.

"That's why you two are working for me," said Jehuda, "and not the other way around. The bow and the short sword are mine. Take anything else you want, you've been trained with most of these things."

Yitzak took a piano-wire garrote and a curve-bladed assassination knife. Avram took a piano-wire garrote and a couple of the throwing knives.

"What are they up to, Avram?" asked Jehuda as he kneeled in front of the case and took out four small jars.

"Our group down below looks like they're ready to move into the crevice. Fu'ard looks like he's giving instructions to his men."

"Let me know what's going on," said Jehuda, opening the four jars and placing them on the ground. Then, he took a small plastic bag out of the case.

"What's that, Jehuda?" asked Yitzak, staring at the jars.

"This? This is a surprise for Fu'ard and his band of cutthroats. It's a little trick that the master taught me. The purple crystals are potassium permanganate, the little pieces of metal are iron filings. The liquid is glycerine. I take the potassium permanganate and mix them with the iron filings. The squeeze bottle is filled with glue. I take the glue and spread it on the first third of the shaft of the arrow and cover it with a nice coating of potassium permanganate and iron filings like this. Now it's ready. It's that simple."

"What's ready? Ready for what?" asked Yitzak, picking up the arrow and looking at the strange concoction.

"Well, when the time comes, all I have to do is spray the mixture on the arrow with the glycerine, and . . . ."

"And, what?"

"And, presto-change-o, we have instant fireworks. Okay, let me explain. After I apply the glycerine, it takes a minute or so for it to kick in. When it does, a chemical reaction causes the iron filings to become white hot and they'll shoot off in every direction. Put one of these in someone and, well, it's not pretty. It's like shooting them with a flare."

"Are you sure that this master of yours is non-violent? I mean . . . ."

Jehuda smiled. "Very sure. This guy . . ."

"Hey, boss," said Avram, "they're moving! Our group just went into the crevice. I think that the old man might suspect something. He kept looking around before they went in. Like he felt us here, or maybe Fu'ard. I don't know. I guess it's too late for it to even matter now. Fu'ard and his cronies are splitting up."

"What's Fu'ard doing? How are they making the split?"

"It looks like they're leaving two men on top as look-outs. The others are climbing down over on the left."

"All right, here's the drill, you two," said Jehuda, lifting his black baseball cap and wiping the sweat from his forehead. "Yitzak, you start making your way down below. Do you see the three boulders off on the right near the vehicles? That's where I want you. Avram, I want you to make your way down to the wadi from the left. "

"Boss," said Avram, peeking over his shoulder, "three of the bastards slipped into the crevice. They left one guy down below. He's checking out the vehicles."

"What's he packing?" asked Jehuda, closing the black case.

"An AK-47 and a sidearm, looks like a .357 magnum."

"Yitzak, you'll take out the one checking out the vehicles."

"Right!"

"Avram, you wait down there on the left until I clear these two guys on top. Then come to the vehicles. Got it?"

"Got it, boss."

"One more thing. After we take everyone out, we have to get rid of the evidence. We don't want our group to suspect anything, right?

"Right."

"Right."

"Okay, take off, but wait for my signal."

"What signal?" asked Yitzak, stopping in his tracks and turning to Jehuda.

"When you see me stand up and fire my arrows at the two shmucks on the rise, I want you to say to yourself, 'Yitzak, that's the freakin' signal I was waiting for.' You'll have to take your man out right away, and don't screw up like you did at the airport at Entebbe. You remember what happened, don't you?"

"Yeah, but that could have happened to anyone."

"Yeah, right," said Jehuda, with a sarcastic smile. "You were about to take out that guard by the entrance, but when you spun him around he looked so much like Idi Amin that you froze and just stood there with your mouth open. Avram almost had to step in and finish the job for you. You snapped out of it just in time. What a matzoh ball! What the hell were you trying to do? Did you want to have your picture taken with him? Now take off, you two, and stay alert."

"I hope that guy down there doesn't look like anyone famous, boss," said Avram, with a smile. "Yitzak'll probably ask him for his autograph."

"Very funny," said Yitzak, turning and starting out.

"All right, let's do this thing, you two characters . . . no foul-ups."

"Right, boss! We're gone!"

Jehuda prepared himself to take out the two men standing guard on top of the rise. He took a good look at the black aluminum shafted arrows with black plastic fletching, each with a four-bladed hunting tip on it. *Perfect for bear,* he thought, as he picked up the compound hunting bow and got into position, *It's overkill for a man, but things are tough all over. They can sue me from hell if it bothers them that much.*

Jehuda looked down into the wadi and saw that both of his men were in place. He could see Fu'ard's man rifling the van, his back to Yitzak. *I'd better do this thing now or that bastard'll move away,* he thought, picking up two arrows, putting one in his belt, and nocking the other. As he wiped the sweat from his upper lip with his shoulder, a deep resolve came to his spirit. He looked once more at his two men down in the wadi and then up at his two targets on the rise. It was time. He stood, took a deep breath, drew the arrow back, aimed, and let the arrow fly. The arrow found its mark, striking the first guard in the center of his chest. The other guard spun around as his comrade fell. Just as he turned, Jehuda's second arrow found its mark and the second guard fell to the ground with an arrow in his chest.

When Yitzak saw Jehuda stand and fire, he came up behind his target and, cupping his right hand over his victim's nose and mouth, brought the blade of the curved assassin's knife swiftly across his prey's throat, severing both of the man's carotid arteries and both of his jugular veins. The man was dead before he hit the ground.

Jehuda picked up the quiver of arrows and scurried down below to join Avram and Yitzak.

"Okay," said Jehuda in a low voice, "Avram, you come into the crevice with me. Yitzak, get rid of this guy. Drag him somewhere out of sight and we'll take care of the body later. Be quick about it! I want you to cover the entrance to this thing and watch our backs."

Yitzak nodded, as he grabbed the dead man by his hair and started to drag him away.

"Avram, we're going in. I wish I knew where this thing was going to take us. The two up on top won't be seen by our group, so we'll just leave them where they are for now. Questions?"

"No."

"No? All right, let's do it."

"Hey, let me go in first, boss, okay?" asked Avram, with a mischievous smile on his face.

"Okay, if you insist!" said Jehuda, making a small bow and a sweeping motion with his hand towards the entrance to the crevice. "After you!"

Avram entered the crevice with Jehuda close behind. They turned left at the wall, and then right. Avram peeked out of the opening and saw two of Fu'ard's men, one standing by the crevice with his back to them, and one up on the square just in front of the entrance to the pillar. Both men had Uzi machine guns in their hands.

"Careful," whispered Jehuda. "If they fire one shot, we're sunk. You take this character by the entrance here, and I'll take the one on the square by the column. It's got to be timed right. I've got to fire my shot when you make your play, Avram, so move this guy out of the way . . . right?" Jehuda nocked his arrow.

"Gotcha, boss," said Avram, slipping a long strand of piano wire out from under his belt. "This is great, boss! It's just like the time—"

"Sssh! We'll trip down memory lane later. Now get ready!" Jehuda whispered, drawing back the bow. It's three and go . . . one . . . two . . . three . . . go!"

Avram slid out of the cave like a cat seasoned to the wild, slipping the noose of piano wire deftly and silently around the throat of his man, as Jehuda stepped out, planted, and fired his arrow. The arrow found its mark, striking the target in the center of his back just as Avram snapped the piano wire. Both men were dead.

"That's five," said Jehuda.

"Hey, boss, you're pretty good with that thing. You've got to teach me how—"

"Sssh!" said Jehuda. "Let's go!"

Jehuda and Avram dashed across the clearing, up the stairs and over to the entrance to the pillar.

"None of these guys are Fu'ard," whispered Avram. "Where the hell is he?"

Just as Avram stopped talking, Jehuda caught the fleeting image of a man running along the wall and darting into the crevice.

"Shit! Let's go! The bastard's on his way out of here."

"But—"

"Let's go!"

Jehuda and Avram ran to the crevice and made it through just in time to see Yitzak wiping the bloody blade of his knife on the runner's body. "Shalom," said Yitzak. "Everything go well inside?"

"Turn him over," said Jehuda, looking at the body and then at Avram.

Yitzak bent down and turned the body over.

"I thought so!" said Jehuda, slapping the side of his thigh. "Damn it!"

"What?" said Yitzak, putting his knife back in the scabbard. "Isn't this Fu'ard?"

"No, it's one of his cronies. This means that Fu'ard's still around here somewhere, so watch your backs."

Jehuda, Yitzak, and Avram looked at each other and then at the body on the ground.

"Yitzak, were you by the entrance all the time we were inside?" asked Jehuda, wiping the perspiration from his forehead.

"Yes."

"Okay, then that leaves only one possibility."

"What, boss?" asked Avram, threading the piano-wire garrote back under his belt.

"It means that Fu'ard is still lurking somewhere."

"But, if he was, wouldn't he have found the two guys you nailed with your bow by now?" asked Yitzak, pulling at the front of his sweat-soaked shirt to try to cool off.

"I hope not," said Jehuda, stepping out and looking up at the rise. "I didn't see any vehicles up there. They're probably parked just on the other side of the rise. I hope that means Fu'ard is hanging back with the vehicles and didn't see anything. I'll bet a week's salary that the bastard doesn't even know what's going on."

"Boss, we have to hurry or the old man, Stein, and the others will be out and we'll get busted."

"Avram's right," said Yitzak, now blowing down the front of his shirt.

"All right," said Jehuda, turning to them, "here's the game plan, so listen up. I don't want any arguments, right?"

Yitzak and Avram nodded their agreement.

"Okay, you two guys dispose of the bodies," said Jehuda, slinging the bow on his shoulder. "I'm going up the hill to pay our friend Fu'ard a personal call."

"Wait a minute, boss, I want—"

"I said no arguments. Oh yeah, make sure you do a good job getting rid of the bodies while I'm gone. I don't want our friends to . . . ."

"Gotcha, boss!"

"Okay, take care of this guy and the two inside. Get rid of them. Better do it fast, who knows when our little group will be coming out. I'll see you guys back up on the hill after you finish here."

Avram and Yitzak nodded and stepped into the crevice.

Jehuda left his two comrades and made his way along the wadi to the left of the crevice until he came to a break in the wadi wall that allowed him to make his way up the hill to where he suspected the thieves left their vehicles. He made his way up the rise and through a small field of large boulders, finally coming to a flattened area on the downside of the hill.

From his vantage point, Jehuda could see a late-model van and two ex-military hard-top jeeps parked some fifty yards down at the bottom of the hill. He took out his binoculars and scanned the vehicles. He didn't see Fu'ard. In fact, he didn't see anyone.

"Damn it! Where the hell is he?" he said. Then came the unsettling feeling that Fu'ard may have gone up the hill to check on his men. If he did, then everything was blown.

Just as he was about to make his way over to the two dead guards, he saw Fu'ard running down the hill toward the vehicles. "Damn it," said Jehuda, as he quickly took the bow off his shoulder and reached for an arrow. It was too late, Fu'ard had made it to one of the jeeps. A moment later Jehuda heard the jeep start. "The bastard's leaving!" said Jehuda. "He's not even waiting around to see what happened to his other men. What a leader. Well, I have a surprise for him!"

Jehuda dropped his regular hunting arrow to the ground and pulled out a coated arrow from the quiver. He removed a small squeeze bottle of glycerine from his pocket and sprayed the arrow. Satisfied with its preparation, Jehuda placed the arrow in his bow, drew it back, and aimed his arrow for the ten-gallon gas can attached to the rear of the jeep. He knew five gallons of gasoline had the explosive power of seventeen sticks of dynamite. Ten gallons would equal thirty-four sticks—more than enough to do the job. Just as he was going to fire the arrow, Fu'ard took off in the jeep, kicking up huge clouds of dust and sand.

Jehuda waited until the jeep cleared the dust clouds. "You didn't even say goodbye you murdering son of a bitch," said Jehuda, tracing the moving vehicle with his bow. "I dedicate this explosion to all the poor bastards that have chased you around the country for the last two years." Jehuda held his breath and fired the arrow. The steel-tipped arrow found its mark and penetrated the gas can. Jehuda watched Fu'ard drive down the hill, across a small depression, and then up another hill. He waited, knowing that it would take about sixty seconds for the mixture on the arrow to work its deadly magic.

"Come on, do your stuff," he said, his attention jumping from his watch to Fu'ard's vehicle. The sixty-second mark came and went . . . seventy seconds . . . eighty seconds. "Damn!" said Jehuda, thinking that either the gas can was empty or that something had happened to the mixture on the arrow. As Fu'ard's jeep reached the top of the hill, a huge pillar of flame exploded high into the cloudless Israeli sky. A moment later, a second explosion tore the jeep and its occupant into a million tiny pieces. "I've got to get a new watch," he said, and tapped his watch with his index finger as he descended the hill and returned to the original observation site across from the crevice to wait for Avram and Yitzak.

Within ten minutes, Avram and Yitzak joined Jehuda. "Welcome back, you two. How did it go? What did you do with the bodies?"

"Boss," said Avram, taking off his baseball cap, bending, and pouring water from his canteen over his head, "I figured that our group went into the pillar that Fu'ard's man was guarding, so I thought I'd check out the other pillars. I went over to one pillar and peeked in. All I saw was black. I tossed a stone in and never heard a sound. Then I realized that there was a huge hole just after the entrance. I dropped another stone into the hole. Boss, it never hit bottom. So, I figured, why not? We dragged the others in there and dropped all of them down the hole. We never heard them hit bottom."

"It was the strangest thing," said Yitzak, raising his eyebrows. "Avram was right, they never hit bottom. They must still be falling! What about Fu'ard? What do you want us to do with the two on top?"

"Screw them!" said Jehuda, taking another swig of water. "It's too hot! Let nature have them."

"Jehuda, we heard an explosion. Was that—"

"That was just Fu'ard saying goodbye. He had the sudden urge to visit Jordan, Lebanon, Iraq, Egypt, Syria, and the Mediterranean, all at the same time. All I did was help him. You could call me his personal travel agent."

"Boss, your clients must love the personal service."

"Well, no one's ever complained. But, then again, no one's asked for a second trip either."

Yitzak and Avram laughed.

"All right, you two, back to what we're here to do! The fun and games are over. Yitzak, take a break. Avram, keep an eye on the entrance and let me know when our little group comes out."

"Check," said Avram, lying down and picking up his binoculars.

"Okay, all we can do now is wait, so let's relax."

The hours passed slowly as the three Mossad agents kept their vigil. The only respite from the hot sun was the sparse shade afforded them by the various deviations in the hill just above them.

"Hey, boss," said Avram, adjusting the focus on his binoculars, "our little group is coming out."

"It's about time! Is everyone accounted for?" Jehuda bolted to attention. "Are they carrying anything, like another one of those rods, or another metal cylinder?"

"I count four of them. I don't see Stein," said Avram, scratching his upper lip. "No one's carrying anything but flashlights. Maybe the American—"

"What are they doing?"

"The old man and the older Arab are talking by the entrance, the two kids are sitting on the back bumper of the van."

Jehuda leaned back against the wall of the cliff and re-adjusted his baseball cap. He glanced over at Yitzak fast asleep beside him. Jehuda's body craved sleep, but he knew that at least two of them needed to stay awake. At least for now. "What are they doing now?" he asked, stretching his legs out.

"Boss, they're all getting into the van."

"What about the American? Did he come out yet?"

"No, he didn't come out. What do you think, boss?"

"Damn! Nothing better have happened to him. As it is, I don't know exactly how I'm going to write all of this up. Moshe is such an old hen when it comes to written reports. That's what you become when they pull you out of the field and make you a desk jockey . . . an old hen."

"They're leaving now," said Avram, turning to Jehuda and then turning back to the group.

"What do you mean, leaving?"

"They're taking off."

"Are you telling me that the old man, the Arab, and the two kids are leaving without the American?"

"Right, but they're taking only one vehicle."

"Damn! We may have a problem here."

"Yeah, boss," said Avram, taking the binoculars away from his eyes and turning to look at Jehuda. "What does it mean?"

"Well, if they're taking only one vehicle, let's hope it means they're leaving the other one for the American. It must mean that the American is all right . . . I hope."

"What do you want to do?"

"We'll stay with the American. Maybe . . ."

"They're gone, boss."

"Okay, we'll just have to sit here and wait for the American to come out. That is, if he comes out. By the way, my complements to both of you. You guys covered your tracks pretty well."

"Right," said Avram, spitting down onto the wadi floor. "The Arab and the kids didn't suspect a thing, but I'm not so sure about the old man. The way that he was looking around, it's like he knew something was up. He's a strange one. He'd probably make a good agent."

"Well, whether he suspected anything or not, he's gone. Let's hope that the old man isn't an agent already, a foreign agent. Anyway, we're going to have to wait the American out."

"Boss, I don't mind being out here," said Avram, sitting up and pulling at his sweat-soaked shirt. "But I'd rather be in the bar of the Ambassador Hotel in Tel Aviv with an ice-cold piña colada and a beautiful woman, staring out over the sailboats on the Mediterranean."

"Avram, I would too, but this is what we've got. Now stop daydreaming and just let me know when you spot the American!"

SEVERAL HOURS PASSED AND THE LATE AFTERNOON SUN BEGAN TO descend over the western ridge. Lengthening shadows covered most of the dry wadi. The temperature was dropping quickly to an almost bearable level.

"There he is, boss," said Avram, watching as Benjamin exited the crevice. "It's been more than two hours. I think that . . . ."

"Is he all right?" asked Jehuda, lifting up the brim of his hat and looking at the still sleeping Yitzak.

"Yeah, but it looks like the other guys didn't tell him they were going."

"What do you mean?"

"Well, he's looking around like he expected to see them when he came out."

"That's interesting. At least he's alive and in one piece. Is he carrying anything?"

"He has a roll of paper, that's all. He doesn't have one of those sticks, or a gun, or anything if that's what you want to know."

"All right. What's he doing?"

"He's getting into the Land Rover, boss, but I don't think he's going to pull out. He's just sitting there."

"How do you know?" asked Jehuda, opening a bottle of warm soda. "What makes you so sure that he's not going to pull out?"

"I think that he's surprised that he's alone. He's probably sitting there trying to figure out where his buddies went."

"You're probably right, that's what I would do."

"I'd do it too," said Avram, looking over at Yitzak sleeping in the shade of a small boulder. "Hey, boss, maybe you should hold a mirror under Yitzak's nose. He looks like he hasn't moved in two hours."

"No, he's alive, all right. I can hear him snoring," said Jehuda, looking at Yitzak. "Better just let him sleep."

"Why?"

"Because, he's replacing you in an hour, and he's going to work the glasses the rest of the night."

"Right, boss. You know, I don't think the American is going anywhere tonight."

"Maybe. Maybe not."

"Hey boss, do you remember the time that Yitzak fell in love with that blonde Russian broad with the short black skirt and the long tan legs? The one we were tailing down by the docks in Haifa about three years ago?"

Jehuda sat up, looked at the sleeping Yitzak and started to laugh. "Yes, I remember. How could anyone forget that?"

"From the first time he laid eyes on her, all he talked about was how he'd like to bring her to the first motel he could find, and give her . . . ."

"Right!" said Jehuda, breaking into a big smile.

"Boss, is a guy in drag a double agent or a triple agent?" asked Avram, laughing hysterically.

"It depends on his legs," laughed Jehuda. "I think that you were taken in by him, too."

Avram's laugh suddenly disappeared and his smile turned to just a sliver of a grin. "Well, it was dark that night, and I couldn't . . . ."

"Sure . . . dark!"

"Hey, I'm hungry. You?" said Avram, quickly changing the subject.

"I could eat," said Jehuda, looking at his watch. "In fact, wake up the sleeping Jew over there. Screw the hour. He has to eat too. I've gotta take a leak. I'll be right back."

Avram stretched out and tapped the sole of Yitzak's foot with his foot. "Hey, wake up, sleeping beauty, it's your turn to watch the American."

Yitzak stirred to life and slowly sat up. "What's up?" he said, slowly stretching his arms.

"Everyone took off except the American. He's in the Land Rover. I think he's going to spend the night in that thing. Anyway, it's your turn to watch him."

"Okay," said Yitzak crawling over to Avram. "Eat and get some rest. Where's Jehuda?"

"He's pissing behind the boulders," said Avram, moving away. "Damn, to hell with food . . . I've got to get some sleep. Wake me if anything happens."

"JEHUDA, AVRAM, GET UP, THE OTHERS ARE BACK," YITZAK whispered, tossing small stones at the pair of sleeping agents.

Both men stirred, slowly stretched the sleep from their bodies, and slowly crept over to Yitzak. All three men sat on the rise, binoculars pressed to their eyes, watching the activity of the men below.

"The old man's by the Land Rover talking to the American. They showed up a few minutes ago," said Yitzak.

"Did we miss anything?" asked Jehuda, yawning and rubbing the sleep from his eyes.

"No, not much. The old man found the American asleep in the Land Rover. He tapped on the window and woke the American up. They talked and then, believe it or not, the old man kissed the American on the forehead."

"Interesting," said Avram, shaking his head. "Maybe the old man's a relative, a grandfather, or maybe an uncle."

"Now the American's out of the Land Rover kissing the girl."

Suddenly, the earth began to rumble and quake, and a bolt of lightning struck the top of the cliffs facing them.

"Damn! What was that?" yelled Avram, pulling the binoculars from his face and rubbing his eyes. "Shit!"

"Lightning," said Yitzak, rubbing his eyes also.

"It struck the crevice," said Jehuda, looking through his binoculars and pointing to the crevice.

"But there are no clouds. Where the hell did it come from?" said Yitzak, turning and staring Jehuda squarely in the face. "You can't have lightning without clouds! I don't . . . ."

A second bolt of lightening interrupted Yitzak. It struck the outer face of the crevice.

"Hey, I don't like this, boss," said Avram. "I really don't like this! This is spooky!"

"You're right, I don't like it either," said Jehuda, shaking his head in an attempt to get his hearing back.

"Boss, there's no sign of the crevice. I mean it's like it was never there."

All three men trained their binoculars on the face of the cliff across the wadi. Nowhere could they detect any trace of the crevice.

"What's going on?" asked Yitzak, still trying to find signs of the crevice.

"I don't know," said Jehuda. "All I know is that we're dealing with something special here. I don't think that these guys are terrorists or Arab agents. I think our friends are something special."

"Special?" asked Yitzak, still looking for signs of the crevice. "Do you mean like space aliens or something? C'mon, you've got to be kidding!"

"No, not space aliens, you dummy! I mean—"

"What, boss?" asked Avram, his vision just returning to normal.

"Well, do you guys believe in God?" asked Jehuda, pulling the binoculars away from his face and turning to them.

"I do, you know that," said Yitzak, "but . . . ."

"But what?" asked Jehuda.

"Boss, are you saying that God did this?" said Avram, raising both eyebrows. "Are you trying to tell us that the lightning came from heaven or something?"

"Well, if it didn't, where did it come from then? Japan? I don't see a cloud in the sky and if you two geniuses don't have a better explanation then, well, I don't know."

All three men stared at each other, and then, in unison, turned their gaze skyward.

"What are we into, boss?" asked Avram, still looking up at the cloudless sky.

"I think we've witnessed something miraculous," said Jehuda, looking around. "I don't know what else to call it. Don't you guys remember the stick or staff the old man was wielding? Maybe it wasn't a weapon at all. You know what the staffs in the Bible were able to do. They turned water to blood, brought water out of solid rock, well, you know."

Again, the three men stared silently at each other.

"What will you tell Moshe about this, boss?" asked Avram, slowly looking heavenward.

"I don't know. Nothing yet. All I know is that we have to finish this thing. We have to play it out."

18

Satan's Veil

As the morning sun rose fresh in a cloudless sky, we were already headed south. When we reached the town of Telem, just five kilometers or so northwest of Hebron, we pulled off the highway and drove north for about two kilometers on a dirt road. The terrain was rugged and sun beaten, typical of the hilly Judean countryside. Throughout our trip, Yusef had been poring over the scrolls, occasionally looking over to Muhammad who would then peek into his rear- and side-view mirrors. Each time this happened Muhammad would simply look over at Yusef and shake his head.

"It's near here. We're very close now," said Yusef, as he looked at the scrolls and then out of the window. "There, stop!" he directed, pointing to two conical spires of twisted brown and tan rock over on the right. The first spire stood only three feet high, the second, three feet away, was a bit larger at approximately four feet high. "Those are the pointers! I'm sure of it."

Muhammad pulled the Land Rover to within a few feet of the rocky spires. Yusef left the vehicle, walked over to them and began to carefully examine their alignment. He bent down as if he were looking through a telescope, turned to us, pointed, and smiled. He was indicating a small opening between two moderately sized hills about two kilometers from us. He returned to the Land Rover, climbed in, and gestured with his hand to Muhammad to drive ahead.

The dry land track that we were following was full of potholes, ruts, and rocks, making the two-kilometer trip very slow and very uncomfortable, but through it all Yusef's demeanor didn't change. He had a determined but serene look on his face that assured me that good things were in store.

Finally, we passed through a narrow gap between the two hills. It opened to reveal a small range of rugged mountains worn almost smooth by the ever-present Mideastern sun and punishing semi-desert winds. We drove up to the top of a small hill overlooking our destination. It was a shallow valley containing a singular stout mountain surrounded by a fifty-foot-high semi-circular ridge that lay open to the south.

Yusef glanced at the scrolls. "Muhammad, let's drive around the mountain. Do you see the hollow crescent formed by the ridge? We'll take that."

Muhammad nodded, and we drove down into the valley, followed by Mara and Ali in the van. We entered the tract between the mountain and the ridge on the right side and traveled over rocks and furrowed ground until, at last, Yusef told Muhammad to pull over. We were on the north side of the mountain.

"This is the place. Everyone out," said Yusef, folding the map.

Mara pulled up and parked to our right. We all gathered behind the vehicles.

Yusef pointed to a dark area on the mountain wall. "That must be the entrance. Yes, I'm sure that's the entrance."

I saw nothing that indicated any sort of entrance, only a solid wall of stone. However, after my experiences of the last few days, I had no doubt that there was an entrance there somewhere.

"Do you want us to make camp?" Mara asked.

"No," said Yusef, staring at the mountain, "just set out the chairs, we're not going to be here that long."

Mara nodded, and went to the van for the chairs.

"Benjamin, we have to talk," said Yusef, turning to me. "Come, let's take a walk."

We walked to a small group of boulders about twenty yards away. "Sit, my boy." said Yusef, pointing to a suitable boulder.

I sat and waited for Yusef to begin.

"Benjamin, I know that you have had a trying few days, no?"

"Well, it's had its moments," I said smiling. I wanted to tell him that it had been easy, but I found myself unable to say it.

"My son, I have to tell you that you have done very well. Very well, indeed. I'm sure that you will do just as well now, but . . ." Yusef stopped in mid-sentence and turned his head to look at the mountain again. "Now you must retrieve Satan's Veil."

"Do you mean from Satan himself?" I said, hardly believing what I was hearing.

"Yes," said Yusef sternly. "Satan. If you fail to secure his veil, all we've accomplished is for nothing. You must understand that all of the items must be collected to complete the Messiah's education. Failure to collect any one of them would be a tragedy. I know that you wouldn't want to see that happen."

"No, of course not."

"Good. You're going to have to deal with Satan, and I have to warn you that if you fail you may not come back. That will make all of us quite sad, you know."

"It wouldn't exactly make me happy either," I said, trying to make light of a bad possibility. "Will I be doing this alone?"

"Yes, it has to be that way. It will require a great trust in God, my boy!"

"I do trust God," I said, giving Yusef a little smile. "I'll do whatever I have to do to bring the veil back to you. I know what's at stake."

"I know, my boy, I know," he said, coming over to me and putting his hands on my shoulders. "We are all depending on you."

Yusef had a way of putting things that made me feel simultaneously good and not so good. Every time I started to feel comfortable with what I was doing, Yusef would bring me back to a state of edginess by dropping the future of humankind on my shoulders. Somehow, I still couldn't believe that the training of the Messiah—the Savior of the world—depended on me. If I failed, the Messiah wouldn't be able to save the world. It was mind-boggling. "What do you want me to do?" I asked Yusef. "How do I get Satan's Veil? What does it look like?" I needed as many details as I could get before I started this adventure.

Yusef turned away from me, seemingly lost in thought. When he turned back he gave me the one answer that I had expected, but didn't want to hear. "I don't know," he said. "King Solomon wrote a small piece of verse about it, but I don't know what it means. We're going to have to figure it out. I think that you better memorize it, no?"

Yusef produced the scrolls from the black leather cylinder he kept at his side. He unrolled them carefully on top of a flattened boulder. "Come, look, Benjamin," he said, pointing to a particular place in the scrolls. "Now listen and memorize it. Solomon wrote:

> *Throughout one's life the veil is viewed*
> *'neath starry nights and sunny skies,*
> *Its wearer's often misconstrued;*
> *for truth is often veiled in lies.*
>
> *The grasping mind cannot hold still*
> *before the power of the veil,*
> *And he who seeks, but lacks the will*
> *is doomed eternally to fail.*

"I'm not sure what it means either," I said, "but I've learned to trust in Solomon's wisdom. I mean, he hasn't let us down yet, right?"

Yusef nodded and we started back to the others. Yusef seemed uneasy. He kept looking up at the ridge, just as he had done back at the crevice.

When we rejoined the others, Muhammad, Mara, and Ali were sitting in the chairs talking to each other in Arabic. We sat down.

"How will he get in?" asked Muhammad, leaning back in his chair and crossing his legs. "While you were gone, Mara, Ali, and I went over the face of the mountain. We couldn't find any way into it. What do the scrolls say, my friend?"

"Solomon gives instruction, but, as always, we have to figure it out," said Yusef, again removing the scrolls from the cylinder, unrolling them across his lap. "Here," he said, pointing to a section of the scroll. "Solomon is actually quoting himself. It's from the book of Proverbs. Chapter fifteen, verse twenty-one. It reads:

Folly is joy to him that lacketh understanding;
but a man of discernment walketh straightforwards."

Mara leaned forward in her chair. "What does it mean, Yusef?"

Yusef sat back in his chair and stared at the mountain, now dotted with shadow, and shook his head. "I can't be sure, but I have an idea." He looked at Mara and then at me.

"What's your idea, Yusef?" I asked.

"Come, my boy, it's time anyway," he said, standing up. "In a minute we'll know if I'm right."

We followed Yusef to a dark stony patch on the wall of the mountain.

"This is where you go in," he said.

I looked at the patch and wasn't very confident that this was an entrance to anywhere at all. I picked up a small stone and threw it at the patch. I wasn't surprised when the stone bounced off the solid rock surface of the patch and fell to the ground.

"Is there a secret entrance?" asked Ali, tossing another stone at the dark patch.

"Well, sort of," said Yusef.

Muhammad went over to the dark patch and looked for a seam or a crack. "This mountain is solid," he said, picking up a stone and tapping various places of the patch with it. "There's no entrance here."

"There is," said Yusef, looking up from the scrolls and turning to me. "Benjamin, before you go in, I must remind you that you are going to meet Satan, so be on your guard. You must bring me back Satan's Veil, or we are all lost and the Messiah could never be properly trained. Do you understand what's at stake?"

Yusef certainly knew how to apply pressure. If I were to fail, the world would lose the messiah and God loses the world. And what happens to me? I didn't even want to guess.

"Will I need to take anything with me? I mean, anything special?" I asked, hoping that Yusef would tell me that any of the treasures that we had collected already could help me through this task.

"You can't take anything with you," said Yusef, rolling up the scrolls and putting them back into the case.

"Okay, then how do I get in? Have you figured it out?"

"We'll know in a minute," said Yusef, staring at the dark patch and then at me. "Are you ready to try it, Benjamin?"

"Yes, Yusef. I suppose I am, but—"

"Good, very good," he said, positioning me directly in front of the patch. "Now, trust me on this, Benjamin. There's no other way. First, settle yourself down and clear your mind. Use the Sha'ar Lev. It will quiet your Lower Mind and bring the Higher Mind forward. Then . . . er . . . then . . . ."

"Then?" I asked. His hesitation concerned me.

"Then," said Yusef, looking me right in the eye, "you'll have to walk straight into the patch. Easy, no? Just walk."

"What? Yusef, are you saying that I have to walk into solid rock?"

"Well, yes. Benjamin, it will be easy."

Sure, it'll be easy! I thought. *He's not the one who has to do it. But who is going to pick me up and carry me to the Land Rover after I hit the mountain?*

"Maybe I should explain how I arrived at this answer," said Yusef, seeing my discomfort with the idea of walking into stone.

"I would really appreciate it, Yusef," I said.

"Okay," said Yusef, putting his hand on my shoulder. "Try to stay with me on this, Benjamin. The first line states that 'Folly is joy to him that lacketh understanding.' When I thought about who lacks understanding I thought of children, morons, the mentally ill, politicians. Well, one of the things that children who lack understanding do is to play with matches. I dismissed children, because when they get burned, they're hardly joyful. Then, I thought of the mentally ill. Well, the dangerous ones are put into padded cells so that they don't hurt themselves. The walls are padded because these people run into the walls. Why? Because they 'lacketh understanding.' In fact, they've been known to exhibit great joy doing it. For whatever reason, it makes them happy. Now, 'a man of discernment walketh straightforwards.' I take this to mean that a sane man, a man of wisdom, one who is able to discern what he is doing, should walk straight, straight into the patch. Does it make any sense to you, Benjamin?"

It did make some sense to me. "Okay," I said, staring at the patch and then looking at Yusef. "I'll give it a try, but I'm not promising you anything."

"Don't worry, Benjamin, I'm sure I'm right. If you falter or hesitate when you walk, it won't work. You must walk straight into the patch with confidence."

I nodded.

"Remember, I don't know what you're going to find when—"

"I know, Yusef," I said. I could feel my pulse start to quicken. "Whatever I find in there, I find in there. I'll deal with it. Don't worry."

Yusef gave me a hug and stepped back. Muhammad and Ali wished me mazel and quietly moved off to the side. Mara kissed me. "Come back safely," she whispered.

With all good wishes said, I put my hand over my heart and closed my eyes. Immediately, the Sha'ar Lev settled me down. I took a deep, slow breath and walked toward the patch.

My journey through the face of the mountain lasted only seconds. I'd somehow, miraculously, walked through solid stone. As I gathered my thoughts, I realized I was standing in a magnificently ornate room. It wasn't quite what I expected. I had imagined that I'd end up inside a fiery furnace somewhere in the bowels of hell with fire and brimstone all around me—after all, I was on my way to meet Satan. What I found instead was not Dante's *Inferno*, but rather *The Arabian Nights*. Silken throw pillows of the most intense colors were strewn everywhere and low, flawlessly lacquered black tables were placed about the extraordinary chamber. The floor and walls gleamed with an unearthly iridescence, surely made of the finest white marble. On either side of the room, large arches led to more rooms, and through glassless windows I saw the purest, blackest night I'd ever seen, it was like deep space without stars. I turned around to look at the stony entrance I had passed through to get here, but saw only another gleaming white wall.

When I turned back to face the room again, an old man dressed in a bright silk robe, soft Persian slippers on his feet, stood in front of me. I hadn't heard him enter.

He bowed slowly and deeply to me. "Are you here to see the Master?" he asked.

I didn't know whether to bow in return or shake his hand. I did neither, instead I answered, "Yes, if Satan is your Master then I am here to see him."

"Yes, oh, yes," the old man said, "Satan is my Master . . . my Master, indeed."

"Well, is your Master in?"

"I regret, sir, that the Master is not in residence at the moment. He is expected to return tomorrow."

"But . . . ."

"Please stay and wait for him, sir. He will be very upset if you do not stay and will be cross with me for not having seen to his guest properly. There is a great deal of pleasure here, sir. Please stay."

I had no choice; leaving would surely mean failure.

"Yes, of course, I'll stay," I said, knowing I had no choice. "I wouldn't want to see you punished on my account. I hope that . . . ."

"Oh, good, sir, very good. Please, sir," the old man said, pointing across the room to a large gold colored silk pillow. "Please sit and make yourself comfortable. I will return momentarily."

I crossed the room, sat down, and waited. After a few minutes, the old man returned, followed closely by three beautiful women in diaphanous red gowns. As soon as he reached me, he clapped his hands. The women placed the large silver trays they'd carried in on the black lacquer table in front of me. Then, each of the women bowed deeply and left the room.

I looked at the trays and found an incredible variety of exotic-looking foods: pheasant under glass, roast leg of lamb, veal steaks, assorted caviars, and much more. The aroma stirred my appetite, but I couldn't help being suspicious. I wondered how it could have been so quickly prepared. I could only think of three reasons. The first, that the food was prepared for someone else but had been diverted to me. The second, that they knew I was coming and prepared the food ahead of time. And finally, that the food didn't really exist, it was some kind of illusion. If the third reason was true—and the aroma was part of that illusion—then the whole thing was an amazing trick.

"Please, sir, eat!" said the old man. "It really is delicious. Eat all you want."

The food was certainly enticing, but somehow I didn't trust it. Maybe it was because it was just too convenient, or the old man was just too polite. All I knew was that I didn't want any part of it.

At the clap of his hands, a fourth woman entered. She carried a silver ewer filled with wine and an ornate silver goblet. Placing them on the table, she smiled, bowed, and quickly left.

"Please enjoy our humble offering . . . I will return soon," he said with a smile. He then turned and left me alone.

I had to think fast. There was no way that I could eat this food. Instead, I pushed the food together on the trays to give the impression that I had eaten something. I dipped my finger into the wine and touched it to my tongue. It tasted sweet, but I wasn't about to drink it either.

Thirty minutes passed before the old man returned. Following him into the room were four men dressed in silken robes and carrying strange-looking musical instruments. The musicians sat on pillows in the far corner of the room and began to play music that was exotic, soothingly intoxicating, almost hypnotic. It wasn't the sort of music that made me tap my feet or jump up and start dancing, but it was pleasant and relaxing.

The old man clapped his hands again and seven veiled and scantily clad dancing girls entered the room shaking tambourines, whirling, spinning, leaping, and moving seductively. They swirled around me for nearly an hour when the old man clapped his hands and the dancing girls stopped their dancing, bowed, and left. This left me, the old man, and the musicians, who continued to play softly in the background. The old man approached me.

"Are you pleased, sir?" he said. "They are wonderful dancers, are they not?'

"Yes," I said, "they were very talented."

"If you like, they will continue dancing for you. I will arrange it, if you so desire."

"No, thank you," I said, hoping that I wouldn't insult him. "They've danced so well. I don't want to impose on them."

"Are you tired? Would you like to rest?"

"Yes, please," I said, strangely tired. "If you don't mind, I would . . ."

"Very well, sir! I will show you to your room! Please," he said with a smile and a hand gesture indicating that I should follow him. "I will bring you to your room. I'm sure it will please you very much."

I followed him through an archway and a second room similar to the one that I had just left until we stopped before ornately
carved mahogany double doors. He clapped his hands and the
doors swung open. "Please, sir," he said, ushering me into the
room with the sweep of his hand.

It was smaller than the other rooms but seemed cozier and
more comfortable. There was a single arched window offering
the same view of dark starless space. The same sort of colored
silk pillows littered the floor, along with a low black-lacquered
table, which held a large gold bowl filled with jewels and coins—
large diamonds cut and polished, emeralds, rubies and sapphires—a fortune in gems. The coins were mixed, sixteenth
century Spanish doubloons, a few golden ducats minted by the
Medicis, and gold coins from the time of Tiberius Caesar. I was
accustomed to a host putting out large bowls of potato chips and
French onion dip or candies. Here, they put out a bowl of precious treasures.

The old man pointed to the tray and said with a smile, "For
you, sir. A gift from my Master for the inconvenience of having
to wait. Please, you take what you want. Take it all, if it
pleases you."

"I, er . . . ."

"Perhaps you want rest, sir," he said pointing to a large velvet
couch. "Please, make yourself comfortable. If you require anything, just ring the bell by the couch."

The old man smiled, bowed, and left the room, closing the
doors behind him.

I picked up a ruby and a couple of large diamonds from the
bowl. They seemed genuine, but I wasn't interested. I was here
to get the veil and nothing else. I tossed the gems back in the
bowl and sat down on the couch. I pulled a satin pillow under
my head and fell asleep wondering what the old man's Master
was really like.

I awoke to the sound of a gentle knock. "Come in," I said as I
sat up and rubbed the sleep from my eyes. When the double

doors opened, Mara walked in dressed in a sheer pink robe and a thin pink veil that did little to obscure her perfect features. I was stunned and felt more than a little self-conscious. Her beauty was mesmerizing. I stood up, but nearly lost my balance; I felt drugged. She ran to me and threw her arms around me.

"Benjamin, I love you," she said, lifting the bottom of her veil and kissing me deeply.

I gently pushed her away. I was still so groggy. "Mara, how did you get here?" I asked.

"Sssh." she pressed her fingers to my lips. "Do you love me, Benjamin?"

"Yes, you know I do but—"

"Sssh. We're alone now," she said, looking deep into my eyes. "Make love to me, Benjamin. Make love to me now." She pushed me back onto the couch and leaned over me. Lifting the bottom of her veil, she kissed me again. Straightening up, she slowly untied the ribbon that secured her robe. Staring into my eyes, she shrugged the robe from her shoulders and it fell to the ground. She stood naked before me, only the veil remained. "Make love to me, Benjamin," she whispered.

Everything was hazy around her. Only she stood out clearly in the room. She was beautiful, a vision within a vision. She came close once again and took my hand in hers, guiding it until it rested on her breast. As I began to caress her, she closed her eyes and a soft moan rose in her throat. I stood up, held her against me and kissed her. She pressed closer against me and my arousal grew.

Mara broke our kiss. "I love you, Benjamin," she whispered as she closed her eyes and gently pressed my shoulders down. Slowly, I began to drop to my knees, kissing and caressing her soft skin—her lips, neck, breasts, belly, lower. She moaned softly. She bent down and lifted my chin with her fingers. "Benjamin," she said softly, interrupting my kisses, "I have a message from Yusef. He sent me after you, Benjamin, he wants you to return to camp."

"What?" I said, looking up at her through the haze.

"Yusef wants you to come back. It's all over, the plans have changed."

"What? Plans changed?" I felt stoned, my mind was reeling.

"Benjamin, if you end this pursuit, Satan will offer you wealth and eternal life."

I slipped away from her fingers and began to unbutton my shirt. "But, we have to make love."

"Don't unbutton your shirt," she cried, reaching out with her hand to stop me. It was too late. I was down to the third button when I felt the medallion. My mind immediately cleared. I remembered my mission and the verses Yusef had given me:

> Throughout one's life the veil is viewed
> 'neath starry nights and sunny skies,
> Its wearer's often misconstrued;
> for truth is often veiled in lies.
>
> The grasping mind cannot hold still
> before the power of the veil,
> And he who seeks, but lacks the will
> is doomed eternally to fail.

"You're not Mara," I said, looking up at her, finally understanding what King Solomon was telling me with the verses. It wasn't merely instructions, it was a warning!

"I am . . . I am Mara," she insisted.

"No, you're not," I said, looking her squarely in the eye. I stood up and I reached out, grabbing her veil and tearing it from her face. Suddenly, a blinding beam of pure white light burst from her face, filling the entire room. I covered my eyes.

When I peeked out from behind my hands, I saw that I was not in the room anymore, but was standing instead in a void— deep space without stars. A gleaming white apparition stood before me. It was of such enormous proportions that I could barely see the top of it. I froze.

There was a second blinding flash of light. As I again uncovered my eyes, I saw that the entity had reduced in size to about ten feet. I could now see that this being was male and incredibly handsome, with facial features that were perfectly symmetrical and magnificently flawless. His eyes were like the bluest of sapphires and as deep as the void that we were standing in. He still glowed a brilliant white. The glow gave the impression of great wings against the darkness as he looked down at me with a stern gentility. Around his neck he wore a silver chain bearing a silver medallion that rested on the center of his chest, an inscription of Hebrew letters burned with flames of bright indigo.

"Be at peace, my son," the being said, in a voice that was both forceful and soothing. "Do not be afraid. I am the Archangel Satan, a grateful servant of the One True God. I wish you no harm."

My mind was reeling. Moloch was right. Satan wasn't a pitch-fork-bearing, pointy-tailed, horned, demon-like, winged creature, at all. He was serene, gentle, and handsome.

"I am Benjamin, also a servant of the One True God," I heard myself say as I dropped to one knee and looked down.

"Stand up, Benjamin," said Satan, gesturing with his hand. "Do not bend your knee to me. Worship only God, and not His servants."

I looked up at him and rose to my feet. Then I looked in my hand and realized that the veil that I had taken from the woman, or whatever she had been, was gone. My disappointment showed in my face.

"Why are you so sad?" he asked, his voice showing sincere concern.

"I failed. I was supposed to return the veil to my friend Yusef, and now . . . well, I don't have it."

Satan smiled gently. "Don't worry," he said, raising both of his hands, his palms facing outward, and lowering them again. "You have not failed, my son. You have indeed removed my veil and its removal is now deep within you."

I was confused. "How . . . ."

"Yusef will understand. Know, Benjamin, that I am instructed by God to teach you the truth of things for the sake of His servant Yusef, so that he may train the coming Messiah in His work. If you have questions, then I will answer them truly and without deceit. I will teach you and you will learn of the mysteries of things that very few men have been privileged to learn. In fact, I shall show you things that no man has been allowed to see before. This is the will of God."

Questions? I had so many questions to ask, I didn't know where to begin. I was dumfounded as I realized that I was standing somewhere in space, speaking with the Archangel Satan, himself. Even more amazing was that he was ordered by God to answer all of my questions.

"Where are we?" I asked, struggling to regain my composure.

"We are deep within the Void of God, deep within the core of God's Being, my son," his voice resonated through the void.

"Are you telling me that you are a servant of God?"

"Yes, Benjamin, I am a true and loyal servant of the One True God. See this medallion that I wear? It bears the name of God, Yahweh, a very powerful face of God. Each of God's angelic servants, if they are truly servants of His, bear a similar medallion given to them by God. Each angel is responsible to certain faces of God, and thus has different names engraved on their medallions. These medallions mark us to his service and are a link to His infinities. But, in all this, I must remind you that, though God has an infinity of faces, He is in truth, One God. You will learn more of these things later."

"Why is it that humankind has always thought of you as God's opponent? I mean, to most people in the world you are the arch fiend, the sworn enemy of God."

"This is so, Benjamin," said Satan gently, in a saddened voice. "It is because mankind, in their ignorance, has mistaken me for the vile and contemptible demon Sid, son of the loathsome Lilith. Didn't Moloch explain this to you?"

"Yes, he did, but . . . I . . . . Wait, you knew about Moloch?"

"Nothing is hidden from God, Benjamin, nothing."

I nodded my understanding.

"Listen well, Benjamin, and I will explain the nature of things, so that you may know where mankind has erred in understanding. Hearken to me and know, now and forever, that nothing lies outside of the infinity of the One True God; neither angel nor demon, neither humankind nor the myriad creatures that walk, or crawl, or fly. Know further that nothing whatsoever, be it sentient or non-sentient, lies outside the being of God. This is the truth of the matter. It is in the book."

"What book?" I asked.

"The first of five books that God had given his servant Moses."

"The Torah?"

"Yes, the Torah."

"But I don't remember reading that in Genesis. I'd read, and was taught, that man was created in God's image and that—"

"That understanding is wrong," Satan interrupted. "In truth, that sentence reads: 'Let us make man within our image, within our likeness' not 'Let us make man in our image, in our likeness.'

"But why had we always been taught that we were made 'in' God's image?"

"That interpretation is a false one. It is based on the misinterpretation of the Hebrew particle 'beht,' which should have been read as 'within' and not 'in.' Because of that misinterpretation, humankind has always thought of themselves as beings separate and apart from God. The coming Messiah will clear up the matter for humankind and set them on a proper course."

His words began to fill me with a new understanding, washing away a defilement and ignorance in me that I didn't even know was there. I found myself wanting to know so much that, out of sequence or not, I posed another question. "Satan, what are angels?"

Satan smiled. "Angels are but minor faces of God, my son, and each serves God in a very particular way. That is, each angel has his special function."

"What is your function?" I asked, hoping to finally dispel any semblance of my misunderstanding of him.

"My function is to serve God by testing the strength, character, and resolve of those who claim to be in his service. I am neither the opponent of God, nor a destroyer of humankind. You may know me as the 'Tempter,' but the temptations that I present to humankind are devised by God, Himself. It is for the sake of God that I hope mankind will shed his ignorance once and for all time, and in so doing avoid the pits, snares, and gins of my machinations. I do these things not in hate of God, but truly, for my eternal love of Him."

What Moloch had told me about Satan and man's confusion concerning the demon king Sid was suddenly becoming clear to me. Satan was no hater of God. On the contrary, I was convinced that he was truly a loyal, loving, and obedient servant of God.

"Have I not plied my trade against you?" he said, his smile turning to a narrow grin. "Have you not felt of my power, my prowess, my expertise?"

"Me?" I asked, not understanding what he meant.

"Yes, you, Benjamin, you! The palace that you were just in was an illusion, a fiction, a lie, a play of both mind and time. I offered you the woman you are in love with, riches and luxuries beyond the ordinary, and you turned them down for your mission's sake, and for your love of God. I have even offered you eternal life, and you turned that down. Remember the secret treasury of King Solomon? It, too, was an illusion. No such treasury ever existed! It was as real as the lion you fled from in the darkness. You were left with the means to cart the whole of it off unopposed, but instead you waited for your friends so that you might continue in the service of God. This pleased me very much, for it pleased God. Do you understand?"

"Yes," I said, suddenly struck by the idea that God was aware of what I was doing and that everything was actually being monitored. The whole thing was an illusion, and that included the lion. "Satan, are there different kinds of angels?"

"Benjamin, there are angels of the Order of the Seraphim, such as myself. And there are Cherubim, Malachim, Hashmalim, Kadishim, well, many kinds of angels, but what you must know is simply that angels are minor faces of God, they are not separate entities. They just appear to be."

"Satan, why is it that mankind is such easy prey for you?"

"Because man in his folly lives his life believing that he is the center of all of existence. He lives foolishly believing that he is a permanent resident of the earth. This gives him a false sense of his importance and causes him to attach to things of naught—things that he believes will serve his stay in each of his incarnations. His ignorance is displayed in his prayers, Benjamin, for his prayers are requests for things that serve only himself, to further his own ends. He prays for wealth, health, long life, women, victory in battle, and vengeance against those who have wronged him. God does not abide such prayers, for those who pray for these things do not work in God's service. Their leaders erect great houses of worship and teach false doctrines to their flocks. They make me the enemy of God because it serves their purpose. They understand nothing of angels, demons, Lilith, the Heavens, the Hells, good, bad, and evil. So long as their spiritual leaders continue to teach their false doctrines and cause their flocks to cling to things of the world, they are to be counted among the opponents of God, for they neither understand God's Redemption, nor do they seek to understand it."

"What exactly is God's Redemption?" I asked, hoping that the question wouldn't reveal my own ignorance. "And, what about man's redemption? Some religions speak of man's redemption. What about—"

"Those religions that speak of man's redemption understand nothing!" he said, his expression suddenly turning fierce. "Those who look for man's redemption understand God's Redemption the least, for they are caught up in their own self-importance. It is out of attachment and ignorance that they seek their own redemption. They do not understand that God's Redemption is, in fact, their redemption. It will be the Messiah's mission to bring to the world, once and for all, the meaning of God's Redemption and to teach all of mankind how to serve in its cause. It will mean peace and unity for the entire world."

"I see."

"Benjamin, to understand God's Redemption you must first understand the Creation, and to understand the Creation you must first come to understand something of the nature of God, Himself. To begin, know that God is infinite, and within that infinity all things reside. God is infinitely this, and infinitely that; infinitely not this, and infinitely not that. He is everything that ever was, and everything that ever will be; everything that never was, and everything that never will be. Do you understand, Benjamin?"

Having the nature of God and the means to God's Redemption explained by Satan, himself, was a great deal to take in. "Yes," I said, "please go on."

"Understand," continued Satan, "that God is all things, all things existent, and all things non-existent! God is both infinitely perfect and infinitely imperfect. Know, Benjamin, that the Universe that man has found himself in is the result of one of the infinite imperfections of God. In other words, its existence is the result of a mistake within the very being of God. Let me explain. Within the unmanifest body of God exists an infinite number of individual 'flashings.' Each 'flashing' is a virtual spewing of the Great Indigo, which is composed of the masculine and feminine energies of God. We call the masculine energy of God the M'retz Za'char, and the feminine energy of God the M'retz Na'she.

"Normally, when a flashing occurs, the Great Indigo goes out from the unmanifest being of God, and the masculine and feminine energies that comprise it divide one from the other in perfect balance. The unmanifest being of God we call Ain Sof. Then, as quickly as they divide, the masculine and feminine energies recombine in perfect unity, perfect harmony, becoming the Great Indigo once again, and are reabsorbed into Ain Sof. But, because of God's infinity, and His nature being both perfect and imperfect, mistakes occur. If an imbalance between the masculine and feminine energies exist when the Great Indigo leaves Ain Sof—the unmanifest nature of God—and divides into the masculine and feminine energies then recombining to become the Great Indigo once again is not immediately possible. It is the imbalanced recombination of the M'retz Za'char and the M'retz Na'she that is responsible for the creation of the manifest Universe—it is responsible for the creation of matter. We called the manifest Universe Ain Sof Aur. The Redemption of God is the successful separation of the masculine and feminine energies of God that comprise matter, followed by their subsequent rebalancing, so that they can recombine with equanimity, and dissolve back into perfect union with God as part of His unmanifested nature, Ain Sof.

"Benjamin, all of the manifest Universe, all of Ain Sof Aur, must be dissolved in this way. But before this can occur, man must leave. Mankind is not to be present at the time of total dissolution. Here is the problem! Mankind has become corrupt with evil attachments to the many things of the world, not understanding that it is all an illusion, and that all of his strivings, be they good and noble, or evil and ignoble, are ultimately for nothing. As King Solomon has written, 'They are all a vanity . . . a striving after wind!' It is man's attachments that cause him to reincarnate. And, as long as he does so, as long as he clings to the multitudinous things of the world, he is working against God's Redemption. It is a great and serious matter. Do you understand this, Benjamin?"

"Yes, Satan," I said, struggling to absorb as much of his wisdom as I could. "Is this what the Messiah will teach?"

"Yes! The Messiah, God's Chosen One, will bring to mankind a new and complete understanding of the nature of God and creation. It will be his task to serve God, in His

Redemption, by ridding the world of ignorance and leading mankind to a path that will bring them into final union with God. The Messiah will teach man what true wisdom actually is."

"What is true wisdom and how can a person achieve it?" I asked, hoping that he might recognize some of it in me.

"First," he said, "man must receive all of the proper knowledge. This knowledge will concern the nature of God and existence. Then, he must endeavor to understand that knowledge, for without understanding, knowledge is for naught. Finally, he must take the understanding that he has gained and employ it, for understanding without action is also for naught. It is only when understanding turns kinetic, when it is in use, does it turn into wisdom. Therefore, with true wisdom, man is to turn away from his attachments to the world and the things in it, and apply his new knowledge and understanding toward God's Purposes and God's Redemption. To do otherwise would be pure foolishness and humankind will suffer greatly for it."

"I understand," I said, now understanding this great Archangel in a new way. "There are so many religions in the world. Each claims to be true. Which one is? I mean . . . ."

"None of them is the true religion, Benjamin. None of them!"

"None of them?" I said.

"No, none of them, Benjamin, though many do earnestly try to serve God. Each of the world's religions is based on only a very partial understanding of the truth of God and existence. Even those religions that teach detachment from the things of the world fall short because of their lack of understanding of the whole of God's nature. It will be the Messiah who will teach the truth of things both eternal and ephemeral, and it will be through the Messiah and his wisdom that all of humankind will be united into one great religion—the True Religion. The True Religion will give humankind the experience of God."

"What will happen to the other religions? I mean, won't they oppose the word brought to them by the Messiah if it means the end of their religion?"

"They will learn, Benjamin, they will learn!"

"Satan, some religions teach reincarnation, others don't. I know you mentioned it. Does reincarnation really exist? If it does, then what is the process of reincarnation and what happens to man when he dies? Some people believe that nothing exists for man after death. I guess what I really want to know is . . . ."

"I understand, my son," said Satan, smiling broadly and beckoning me with his hand. "Come, Benjamin! Travel with me, and I will show you some of the wonders of Heaven and Hell, so that you may know the truth of the matter. You shall see for yourself. It is God's Will that you are shown these wonders so that you can relay what you see and learn to the one who is to train the Messiah."

19

The Seven Divisions of Hell

IT WAS A STRANGE JOURNEY. WE SEEMED TO TRAVEL WITHOUT traveling—there were no markers, no mileposts, no scenery, nothing at all to indicate that we were actually moving at all. Yet, we seemed to be propelled through the Void at an incredible rate that seemed to dwarf even that of the speed of light— we were traveling at the speed of God. Deeper and deeper into the Void of God we went, still I saw nothing. We finally stopped and Satan pointed to a dim patch of gray in the distance. "Can you see it, my son? Those are the gates of Hell!"

I looked, but was able to make out very little detail—just a tiny spot of mist in an eternal sea of nothingness. The idea that I was about to explore Hell with the Archangel Satan as my tour guide was fantastic. Then again, this was not the ominous, soul-stealing, anti-God Satan depicted by those whose understanding of him was intricately entwined and confused with the nefarious attributes of the arch-demon Sid. This was the Archangel Satan, servant of God.

"Come, Benjamin," said Satan, his gleaming aura gently pulsating, giving him the appearance of having great angelic wings.

We began to travel again and were soon standing before the very gates of Hell. My heart raced with excitement as we stood before an untold number of bright, narrow pillars of pure blue fire stretching to the left and the right, above us and below us, as far as the eye could see.

Four angels of enormous stature, paired on either side of the entrance, greeted us. Between them a seemingly impenetrable flaming curtain of bright indigo sealed the gate. Each angel clutched a double-edged silver sword inscribed with the holy name of God, Shaddai Tzabaoth. Around their necks they, like Satan, also wore silver medallions bearing that same name of God. Their demeanors were fierce, almost grotesque, with eyes that glowed like white-hot steel rivets. Their only movement was the occasional pulsating of their auras. They were the ultimate guardians, each staring deep into the Void of God as if seeing to the very limits of it.

"These, Benjamin, are the great, mighty, and fearsome angelic guardians of the gates of Hell. They are the great and powerful angelic servants who protect the sanctity of Hell from corruption and violation. They are truly formidable defenders, Benjamin. My two brethren on the left are the angels Kinor and Kipod. On the right are the angels Nasragiel and Nairyo Sangha. Benjamin, it was the angel Nasragiel, who, at God's command, guided Moses through this place of tears and sorrows. Moses was taught a great many things here. The angel Kinor is the very same angel who punished the demons Algongol, Ramahan, and Fengalin when they attempted to break into Hell to learn its secrets. Do not be afraid, my son, these angels serve God and will do you no harm."

I couldn't come up with a single understandable reason that anyone would want to break into Hell. Looking at the four imposing angelic guards, I couldn't imagine anyone or anything getting by them. It was clear that anyone gaining entrance to Hell was either sent here for punishment—or was granted permission by God.

"Satan, what possible reason would anyone have for trying to break into Hell?" I asked.

"Ignorance . . . pure ignorance, Benjamin. They search for knowledge of things that they believe will give them power. All they gain is sorrow."

"I understand," I said, nodding.

Satan smiled. "Now, come, my son, and let us enter so that you may learn the truth of the secrets of Hell. There are great secrets here hidden from the common man."

Satan held the open palm of his right hand toward the rectangular entrance and the curtain of flames magically parted. Crossing the threshold, we entered a hallway of pure darkness, which led us to a room constructed of pure white marble, much like Satan's palace. *Yet another illusion,* I thought as spectacular images of innumerable angelic personages lining the walls of the great chamber held my gaze.

"These are just a few of the myriad angels of punishment," said Satan. "Here reside the angels Baruel, Amnixiel, Amudiel, Bludon, Rezazel, Pa'arhiel, Amnodiel, Caridon, Lentatiel; there are far too many to name. They all serve under the leadership of the Archangel Zaphiel. This is a place of Divine Justice, not a place of punishment merely for punishment's sake. Know that the punishments issued here are not eternal, for God is a loving and just God. He condemns neither man nor demon to eternal punishment for He knows that they act out of ignorance. For Him to do so would be to work against His own Redemption. Like a loving parent who chastises a child out of love, God chastises and corrects those whom He loves. This is the place of such correction. Know too, Benjamin, that even Heaven and Hell will be dissolved in the Ha'masah, the End Time, when all of the manifest aspects of God are once again reunited in perfect union with God. There are seven divisions of Hell, Benjamin, and each has its particular purpose. Come, let's go on."

I nodded, eager to see what lay beyond the confines of this great room. We crossed the floor to pass through a mist-covered doorway that led us to an area of such great dimensions that I saw no end in any direction. It was filled with tables of dark marble, all surrounded by a blanket of gray fog. Spectral beings rested atop each table and angels, swords in hand and medallions around their necks, stood silent vigil throughout this misty realm.

This vista wasn't nearly what I'd imagined Hell would look like. I'd expected great caverns filled with billowy pillars of fire and brimstone, the horrible cries of torment from agonized souls echoing through the realm. I'd expected souls writhing in unrelenting agony in great pits of fire—I expected Dante's *Inferno*! It was clear to me that Dante had never been to Hell; what he had written was pure fiction. Fire? Brimstone? There was none of that here, only the seeming bliss of souls who appeared to be resting in peace.

"Where are we?" I asked.

"Benjamin, at the end of each incarnation, each person and demon must endure the rigors of this place before they go on to one of the Heavens. Each human and every demon must come to one of the seven Gehennom, or divisions of Hell, to pay for what they have done in life. We now stand in one of those seven Gehennom. It is Gehenna Ba'arut, the Hell of the Ignorant.

"The forms lying on the tables are the sheath-encased souls of those who, in life, did not have knowledge of an existing covenant with God and have caused injury to others of their kind because of this ignorance. In this division, the ignorant suffer and learn. They must experience the anguish, fears, pains, and torments that they had intentionally caused others to suffer. Remember, Benjamin, God is just in His dealings with man and is fair in his punishment. The souls that you see here may have the appearance of being in a state of serenity, but that is just an illusion, for they suffer much indeed."

As I looked out over the sea of souls lying in torment before me, I suddenly felt a great compassion. When I turned to Satan, I saw that he, too, was compassionate toward these souls.

"Who are these angels and what do they do here?" I asked, pointing into the distance.

"The great angels stationed here are charged with the responsibility of seeing that these souls remain undisturbed in their punishments. Further, they make sure that the punishments are correctly and fairly administered. Overseeing this first division, Gehenna Ba'arut, is the Archangel Dumah. He is a mighty angel, Benjamin. Do you see that angel?" he said, pointing to a particularly bright angel in the distance. "That is the angel Malach Memune. He is one of Dumah's chief assistants."

Just as I was about to ask Satan another question, a great angel gripping a flaming sword appeared in front of us. "I am called Dumah," he announced. "I welcome you both and wish you the peace of the One True God."

"I see the compassion that you have for these souls, Benjamin. It is in your face," said Dumah with a warm smile. "Do not be dismayed at their plight. They are reaping the growths of their own gardens, the fruits of their own labor. They are here in Gehenna Ba'arut to learn of the wickedness they have committed in life so that they may be all the better for it. It is God's chastisement and is neither to be delayed nor avoided. As my brother, Satan, has told you already, God chastises and corrects all whom He loves, all whom are dear to Him, and so be at peace for their sakes, my son. I am here to teach you of the nature of certain things, Benjamin, so that you may pass it on to he who will train the Messiah. Please, if you have questions, then voice them, and do not fear."

As with Moloch and Satan, I had many questions. And again I was at a loss as to where to begin. "Satan referred to the forms that lie here as 'sheaths.' What exactly is a sheath?"

The great Archangel Dumah smiled. "The sheath, my son, is the ethereal body within which the soul resides. It is called the Ta'ar. The human sheath is called the Ta'ar Adam and the demonic sheath is the Ta'ar Shadim. It protects the souls and allows man to undergo the various rigors of life in the world of men, and demons to do the same in Malkuth Tachton, the Dark World. It is all very natural. You may also think of the sheath as the blueprint of a man's body. Notice, Benjamin, how fine the features of each sheath are. Each sheath is as unique in death as it was in life. But, as you can see, unlike in life, each sheath here is pristine, flawless, and without blemish."

I looked around me at the sea of sheaths. From where I stood, the sheaths that I could see did appear flawless. Each had an individualistic face—no doubt the same one as in life—but without any sort of disfiguration or flaw.

"Nothing can exist within Ain Sof Aur, the manifest Universe, Benjamin, without a sheath," said Dumah. "Even demons and angels must be sheathed in order to exist in the manifest world. Regardless of what happens to a man's body during his lifetime, the sheath remains intact, inviolate. Naturally, many of those that you see here have been scarred through accidents and disease. Some had even lost limbs during their last incarnation. But as you can see, disease and injuries that affected their physical bodies then do not have any effect whatsoever on their sheaths."

"Does a person's sheath remain the same throughout each of his or her incarnations?" I asked, looking first at Satan and then at Dumah. "I mean, does—"

"No, Benjamin," said Dumah, interrupting me. "Before a person reincarnates, that person's sheath is destroyed and they enter into a new sheath that, in combination with genes from the parents, is responsible for the characteristics of the person's new body. Do you understand these things, Benjamin?"

I nodded.

"Come over here," said Dumah, pointing to a sheath reclining on a table just a step from him. "This is the sheath containing the soul of a man who was considered great in the eyes of humankind. Come and look at him."

I walked over to the table and stared down at him. The sheath looked so calm, so at peace. It was hard to imagine that he was going through any agony at all.

"Now, take your right hand and place your palm upon his forehead," said Dumah. "It will tell you the fortune of the man."

I placed my palm on the sheath and was immediately swept into the man's life's experiences. Great flashings of images of the man's former life came to view; I wasn't just seeing his life before me, but saw glimpses of my own, as well. I saw the tears he had caused others to shed collect into small swirling pools of warm, briny liquid. These pools boiled and churned and overflowed, uniting one with the next to become rushing streams. These streams, in turn, quickly merged to a single great raging river. It was horrendous! My own pulse raced as I saw that there, in the center of that raging river, bound helpless before the relentless torrent of tears, was this man whose only hope for salvation lay in his own tears. They ran down his cheeks and fell drop by drop, one by one, to merge with his victim's tears. I pulled my hand away from the ghostly form and looked at Dumah.

"Do you understand, my son?" said Dumah. "That this man in life was only great in his own eyes, and in the eyes of the ignorant who flocked around him. To God, he was just a man, that's all; a man that sought greatness in life by hurting those that, in his greed, he thought stood in the way of that attainment. He was a man fraught with many attachments to earthly things, my son."

Sadly, I nodded.

"Come and learn more," said Dumah, pointing to a form on the next table. "Go see the torment of that woman."

I moved to the next table and placed my right palm on the woman's forehead and immediately saw images of great poverty, of starvation and deprivation, and the anguish of losing control over one's possessions. I saw that she was bound hand and foot and was forced to watch as others picked through her most cherished possessions and carted them away. I took my hand from her forehead.

"In life, she was a vain woman who had great attachment to her possessions, to things of naught. Here, she is experiencing the loss of those possessions. It is an anguish to her that can only be extinguished when she returns again to life and takes a new path, one that leads to freedom from such attachments. Do you understand, Benjamin?" said Dumah, raising his left hand. "Attachment to the things of the world not only causes a person enormous grief during their lives, but torment afterward, as well. Do not grieve over them, they are still loved by God and will be brought into harmony through this process. Eventually, they will live in eternal union with God."

"Will they remember being here when they reincarnate?" I asked.

Dumah smiled gently. "Their experiences here will be recorded in their Higher Minds. The memories of the lessons that they learn here will be, in part, their feelings of guilt and remorse in their next life. Those feelings will act as guides and teachers for them. It is their conscience. If they fail to heed those feelings and opt to continue their foolishness, then, when their life in the world of men ends, they will return to a deeper, more severe division of Hell. There, their agonies will be all the more arduous. It will take them many incarnations to bring their lives into harmony with the Truth of Existence, but it will happen. Of course, there are those who learn more quickly than others. The more spiritual a person is, the more quickly that individual learns not to harm others and not to have attachments to the things of the world. You will see that they are rewarded by God for it."

"So, that's where a person's conscience comes from," I said quietly. "We bring that conscience with us every life."

"Mankind has choices, Benjamin," said the Archangel Dumah, raising his left hand again and looking momentarily upward, "and those choices are to listen to the Divine Instruction recorded in their Higher Minds, or to succumb to the blind reason of attachment generated and perpetuated by their Lower Minds. There are no other choices for man; holiness for God, or insurrection. This, Benjamin, is the teaching. It is time."

I took that to mean that Dumah's instruction was over. The great angel nodded and smiled to Satan and to me, indicating that it was time to move on.

"Come, Benjamin," said Satan, nodding to Dumah, "it is time for us to descend into other, darker, regions."

With a wave of Satan's hand, we left Gehenna Ba'arut and immediately entered a new realm, slightly darker than the first, but otherwise seemingly very much the same. An endless sea of glowing sheaths lay before us in what appeared to be serene repose, with brilliantly glowing angelic guards standing vigil.

"This," said Satan, pointing to the profusion of sheaths before us, "is the second division of Hell. It is called Gehenna Tachton, or the Dark Gehenna. Those who, having learned of the terms of God's Covenant given to man through His servant Moses, never accepted those terms and refused to make Covenant are assigned here. They chose to worship idols, prophets, angels, and demons. Some here have even offered up prayers to me, believing that I was an enemy of God and would reward them for their prayers and sacrifices. How foolish to think that I would dare to disobey God. Well, their reward is here in the Dark Gehenna. Yes, they who lie here have sinned in life, Benjamin, for they did not offer their prayers directly to God. As we speak, they are learning the foolishness of their ways."

I looked over the sheaths of those who dared to place God second to other beings. "Their torturous existence here must be more burdensome than those in the first division," I said. "How could they have been so foolish? They should have known better."

As we were looking out over the great ocean of sheaths, an angel appeared before us, his eyes sparkling with flames of red fire. Like the angel Dumah, he was also clothed in pure white and like all of the other angels that I'd encountered, had a brilliant, wing-like aura.

"I am the Archangel Lahatiel," the angel said, nodding his greeting to Satan. "I am the 'Flaming One of God' who oversees Gehenna Tachton, the second division of Hell."

I smiled and nodded my greeting to him.

"I have come here to teach you and to answer your questions so that you may pass on the instruction to the one who will train the Messiah. If you have questions, Benjamin, do not hesitate to send them on."

I looked at Satan. "Go ahead, Benjamin. Please take advantage of the benevolence and wisdom of Archangel Lahatiel," he instructed.

"I was told by Satan that those who are here have sinned against God by offering their prayers up to others, to false gods. Is there any comfort for those that thought they were not doing evil, but were doing right by God?"

"What man thinks often has nothing to do with the truth of things, Benjamin," said Lahatiel, his aura pulsating. "Their thoughts in their last life were guided primarily by their foolish fears and ignorant self-interests. With those things in mind, they chose to offer their prayers to beings other than God. They did this because they knew that God would not bend to their desires. So, in their foolishness and pride, they created gods of God's servants and had even bent their knees in supplication to statues of plaster, wood, and stone. Further, they foolishly sought forgiveness from man for the sins that they have perpetrated against God. Blasphemy! Mankind has no such authority to forgive man of their sins against God. It would be like thieves forgiving thieves for robbery, or murderers pardoning murderers for the taking of life. Those who take it upon themselves to forgive the miscreants for the sins that they have committed against God go to an even deeper level of Hell, for in their own way, they are interfering with God's Redemption. All who repose here, Benjamin, are learning of the errors of their ways, and are paying a bitter price for it."

"I understand," I said, turning to look at the sheaths lying in state. "Will they really learn?"

"They are learning as they lie there," he said, his expression turning very serious. "But their stay here is limited, for they must eventually enter into one of the heavens and then be returned to the world of matter. What they learn here shall be recorded in their Higher Minds. If they do not change their ways when they reincarnate, and instead continue to offer their prayers and services to false gods, then their lives will be fraught with misery. Those angels stationed here will see to it that their lives become an unrelenting extension of this dreary place. They will find no rest from it at all until they repent their sins against God and change their ways. They will then learn during their earthly existence that the gods they have worshiped are false. Not only that, but they will learn that the false gods that they sought succor from have, in the end, become the cause of many of their earthly sufferings."

"What about those who have made covenant with God and have broken that covenant and turned to other gods?" I asked.

"Those who have had covenant with God, and have broken that covenant, are punished in a much deeper division, Benjamin. Their sins are greater and their punishments are longer and harsher. Walk among these souls and learn of their crimes and torments."

I walked among them, placing my hand on their foreheads as I had with the sheaths in the first division. One soul was enduring the hardship of bearing the weight of a statue on his chest. It was the statue that he had used to pray to while he was alive. Under its great weight he was forced to listen over and over to the sound of all the prayers that he had ever offered to that statue. Another, a woman, was forced to relive the sins that she had committed in life that were forgiven by man, but not by God. I experienced the grief and suffering of many inhabitants of Gehenna Tachton and learned a great deal from their trials.

"Benjamin, in all of this, know that God loves them all and will show that love when they turn only to Him in their prayers. There is forgiveness here for them, my son, as soon as they repent their disobedient ways. Then, they shall be released from this place and move on all the more swiftly."

As we spoke, a second great angel appeared at Lahatiel's side.

"This is the angel Babaniel, Benjamin," said Lahatiel. "He is charged with overseeing the punishment of those who have spread the ideas of mankind bending their knees in supplication and prayer to false gods. Babaniel sees to it that they are also made to suffer the punishments of those that they have led away from God. Their stay here is much longer than the others."

I looked at the angel Babaniel. The fire of God was in his eyes. This great angel was more than suited to this purpose.

"We must move on, Benjamin," said Satan, exchanging parting glances with Lahatiel and Babaniel. "Our stay in each of the divisions of Hell must be short, for there is much to see and learn. We must move on, my son."

With a wave of his hand Satan swept us deeper into Hell.

The third division of Hell was even darker than the first two. It was bathed in eternal twilight; the oppressive gray pallor of this realm seemed to make the angels here glow more vibrantly than those in the first two divisions.

"This is the third division of Hell, Benjamin," said Satan, looking out among the endless sea of sheaths. "This division is Gehenna Chara'tah Gadol, the Hell of Great Remorse. You will learn much here, my son. Are you ready?"

"Yes, Satan. I am."

"Then go to that great angel clad in white," he said, pointing to an angel about thirty yards from us. "He awaits you, Benjamin. Go and have no fear."

I made my way past row after row of reclining sheaths until I stood directly in front of the great angel. As I approached, it looked like he was wearing a white robe, but as I neared, I saw that it was, in fact, the solid aspect of his aura.

"I am the Archangel Shaftiel," he said, raising both of his hands. "I am overlord of the shadow of death in Gehenna Chara'tah, this third division of Hell. You are here to bring back instruction for the teacher of the Messiah."

"Yes. I am Benjamin," I said.

"The sheaths before us, Benjamin, are the sheaths of those who have entered into Covenant with God, but have broken that Covenant. Also residing here are those instrumental in having others break their Covenants. The stays of those residing here are longer than those of the first two divisions and their punishments more severe, for they should have known better than to make Covenant with God and then not fulfill the terms of that Covenant. Come, place your hand upon their foreheads and learn of their sins."

I went to one of the sheaths and placed the palm of my right hand on his forehead. Immediately I experienced the transgression of this sinner who had made Covenant with God during a particular period of crisis in his life, but turned away from God when times had gotten better. I learned that his punisher was the great angel Tumetriel, and that this man was being made to experience what would have occurred if God had not intervened in his crisis, reliving those horrible consequences over and over again.

I went to the next sheath, a woman who had made a personal covenant with God, but soon after had turned away from God and offered up prayers to various servants of God. Her punishment was to relive myriad agonies at the hands of the angel Hudariel, an angel of Divine Punishment.

I went to a third, another woman, who had sworn to God during a marriage ceremony that she would not commit adultery. This promise, this oath that she had taken before God, she had broken throughout the course of her marriage. Her punisher was the angel Iodiel.

I went to yet another sheath, a man who had made Covenant with God and had promised God that he would change his ways and repent his sins. He had promised God that he would not commit a particular sin again. He broke his promise time and time again. It was his fate to suffer at the hands of the punishing angel Podoliel, who had the man experience what it is like to be on the receiving end of his own sins.

Finally, I turned to Shaftiel.

"I see that you have some questions, Benjamin. Do not hesitate, send them on, for your time here is short."

"Is there forgiveness for these souls?" I asked.

"Their stay in this division, Benjamin, is shorter than the stay of those below, and longer than the stay of those above. God forgives all, for He knows that change in all sentient life takes time. The Lord God is a forgiving God, but still chastisement and correction must be made. Man must know that God will hold him responsible for any promises made and not kept."

The great Archangel Shaftiel turned to his left and pointed to a group of sheaths that were separated from the others. "See those, Benjamin?"

I turned to look at these sheaths surrounded by countless grim-faced angelic guards.

"Those are the sheathed souls of those God had freed from their captivity in Egypt. Under the leadership of the prophet Moses they had made Covenant with God. But at the foot of Mount Sinai, God's Holy Mountain, they turned away from God to bow and pray to the golden calf that they had constructed to honor the loathsome demon Baal. Among them are Dathan, Yellan, Targem, Minna, and Syllusem. These five, Benjamin, were chiefly responsible for the construction of the golden calf and were instrumental in turning the people away from God. Their stay here shall be longer than all the others, for they have seen God's might with their own eyes and have received God's mercy so that they would not perish on the way to the land that God had promised them. Further, in that time they had constantly put God to the test and did not believe, though God had proven Himself to them over and over again. I have placed the punishing angel Abdagdiel to oversee the horrors that they are now enduring. Woe to them for their vileness. Woe to them, indeed."

"Will they eventually be freed from this place?" I asked.

"Yes, in time even they will be freed from here so that they may enter one of the Heavens, and then be returned to the world of men."

As we were talking, Satan came over to us and thanked the Archangel Shaftiel. Then, he turned to me and said, "Come, Benjamin, we must move on."

After Satan and I said goodbye to the Archangel Shaftiel, he waved his hand and we materialized in the fourth division. This division was quite different than the previous three. Not only was it much darker, but there were no sheaths laid out. In fact, I saw no sheaths at all, only countless brass urns nearly obscured by the dim gray mist. On the side of each urn, I could see a small silver pentacle similar to those on the iron door leading to the labyrinth and the doors to King Solomon's treasury.

As I was looking out over the sea of urns, an angel with eyes of the deepest blue appeared in front of us, a grim, foreboding expression on his face.

"This is the fourth division of Hell, Benjamin," Satan said, casting a quick glance at the angel and then turning back to me. "It is called Gehenna Shadim, the Hell of the Demons. This great angel before us is the Archangel Makatiel, the overseer in this dreadful realm."

I looked at the Archangel Makatiel and trembled as his eyes bore into my soul. He didn't smile like the other angels I had met in the upper divisions. His demeanor wasn't offensive, but it was very stern. "This division, the Gehenna Shadim, to which I attend, is a special division of Hell," he said, pointing toward the horizon and sweeping his arm wide. "This realm was given by God to his servant King Solomon so that the king might use it for the good of God's Redemption and condemn evil demons to suffer here. This cursed place is not for the soul of man, my son. If you have questions for me, Benjamin, please voice them."

"Why are all the urns made of brass?" I asked. I knew that our stay here wouldn't be long, so I began with what seemed to be the most natural question.

"They are made of brass because the great king, in his wisdom, chose a metal that would not fall prey to the elements of the Light Malkuth. Within each of these sealed vessels is a second vessel made of the element iron, and within that vessel are imprisoned the Ta'arim Shadim, the sheathed souls of the demons that King Solomon had punished in his duty and love for God."

I remembered, then, that Moloch had told me that the demons feared King Solomon. Looking out over the sea of demon-filled urns, it was clear why. "What crimes did these demons commit to cause them to be condemned to this place?" I asked.

"Hearken well," the Archangel Makatiel said, raising his right hand just above his head and piercing my soul again with his stare. "Here is imprisoned the demon Agares," he said pointing to an urn by his side. "There lies the demon Marbas. There lies the demon Malphas. There lies the demon Ryastas. There the demon Ungardia. There the demon Kuipe . . . ." The Archangel Makatiel went on and on, naming demon after demon. He pointed to other urns and spoke of demons with names such as Marax, Orobas, Valefor, Stolas, Dantalion, and Eligos. All of them were condemned to this division of Hell by King Solomon. Then, the great angel pointed to his right and cited other demonic names such as Andromalius, Berith, Gamigin, Sallos, Raum, Shax, and Vepar. He told me of the heinous crimes that these and other demons had committed against both God and man, that they would shed the blood of man and commit great acts that interfered with God's Redemption.

He told me how the demon Hephias had tried to interfere with the construction of Solomon's Temple by attempting to weaken the resolve of the woodcutters in Lebanon, who were responsible for the supply of cedar for the House of God. When the angel Cerviel told King Solomon what great mischief the demon Hephias was committing, the King became angry and sent the angel Baruel to bring the demon before him. King Solomon then condemned the sheathed soul of the demon Hephias to remain in Gehenna Shadim until the Messiah comes to free him, converting him to obedience and service to God.

Next he told me the story of the nasty demon Thagus, condemned to Gehenna Shadim by King Solomon for attempting to give the Caananites information concerning the strength and disposition of Solomon's troops. Makatiel also told me about the demons Shax and Vepar conspiring with the vile demon Rahab to thwart the parting of the Red Sea by Moses. He told me that some of the ancient peoples believed that Rahab was blessed for his efforts by the demon mother Lilith, and he was placed in the sky by her and became the constellation of Orion. Of course, Rahab's real fate wasn't nearly so noble, he had been condemned to suffer here."

The Archangel Makatiel told stories of the Babylonian demon gods, the Assyrian demon gods, the Phoenician demon gods, the Edomite demon gods, and how they all met the same fate for their crimes against both God and man. When Makatiel finished, he stood silently looking out on his dismal domain. Finally, he spoke.

"Do you have questions, Benjamin?" he asked.

"Yes. What are the fates of all these demons? How long will these demons be in Gehenna Shadim?"

"They are fated to remain in this place of punishment for periods determined by the great king. Some have been here for three thousand years, others for less."

"What then?"

"In time, or when needed, they shall be released and sent back to the Dark Malkuth, or even to the Light Malkuth. However, they will not be free, but will be in special service to the great king and the Workers of Light. Never again will they be able to ply their evil trades in either world and interfere with the great work at hand. They suffer greatly here, my son, and would not want to return."

"Are you saying that some of these demons will actually be allowed to enter the Light Malkuth?"

"Yes, but only a few," said Makatiel. "They are used by the Workers of Light to combat those people and organizations that oppose the Tikkun, God's Redemption."

"Was King Solomon also reincarnated throughout the centuries like other men?" I asked.

"King Solomon has reincarnated many, many times since he sat on the throne in the land that God had given to His people. It is King Solomon who, simultaneously, sits on the throne in the Temple of God deep within the Void of God, and who reincarnates to gather his Workers of Light together so that they may collectively work on behalf of God's Redemption. He is the one that God has chosen to oversee the Tikkun."

"Is he the Messiah?" I asked.

"The Messiah? Perhaps." said Makatiel, turning away from me and once again looking out over his domain.

Just as I was about to ask Makatiel more about King Solomon and the Messiah, Satan appeared. "Come, Benjamin," he said, as he raised his hand, "we must go! It is time."

We said goodbye to Makatiel and Satan swept us out of Gehenna Shadim with a wave of his hand. We descended instantly to the fifth division of Hell.

This division was the dreariest yet, and the angels stationed here glowed even brighter in that darkness. Here, the sheaths of both humans and demons seemed to float atop the omnipresent gray mist.

"This, Benjamin, is the fifth division of Hell. It is called Gehenna G'mul, the Hell of Retribution. Humans and demons who, in life, have caused harm to God's servants are condemned to this dreary place. God will not tolerate those who harm any of His servants."

I scanned the morbid sea of sheaths and saw that their repose did not seem as serene as those in the other divisions. Each writhed in the presence of some outwardly undefined agony; their discomfort made it obvious that they were suffering greatly. Satan and I were greeted by a great angel of terrifying demeanor—his eyes burned like fiery rubies and his aura was brilliant in the darkness. His power and ferocity were awesome—as he spoke, I felt my body vibrate.

"I am the Archangel Hutriel," he said, holding up his right hand, palm facing me. "I am a servant of the One True God, and I welcome you both in peace to Gehenna G'mul, the fifth division of Hell."

Satan and I nodded, respectfully acknowledging his greeting.

"The great Archangel Hutriel," said Satan, turning to me, "is called The Rod of God. He will teach you much, Benjamin."

Looking at this angel, I hadn't the slightest doubt that he was an expert at divine punishment.

"The sheaths you see here," said Hutriel, spreading both arms, "are those who have tried to interfere with God's Redemption by causing God's servants to suffer at their hands. Whether they have caused physical or mental injury to God's servants, here they lie in agony. Ask your questions and I will answer you truly, Benjamin."

"How long do the souls of these beings remain here?" I asked.

"Century upon century, millennium upon millennium," Hutriel's voice boomed through the darkness, his eyes flashing with fire. "It depends upon their crime."

I glanced back at Satan to assure that my question was acceptable; he nodded his approval.

"There," said the Archangel Hutriel, pointing to a human sheath squirming and pulsing in agony, "is the sheathed soul of Ahab, king of Israel. For well over two thousand years, he has been here in agony, and so shall he stay for that much more. He caused great harm to the Workers of Light while he reigned."

"Two thousand years of unrelenting agony," I quietly mused, "for what he has done in just a few years of life. But, then again, he was condemned to be here not so much for what he did, but for whom he did it to."

"There lies the female demon Atzmah, and there the female demon Enepsigos, and there lies the female demon Obizuth," he said, pointing to each. "Here in this place of tears and agony are such demons as Arioch, whose crime was to teach man evil arts; and the demon Abezithibod, son of Beelzeboul, who was condemned to this world for assisting the magicians of pharaoh when Moses and Aaron sought freedom for their people. There are many here that have caused harm to the servants of God, and their sufferings are great. But even they, in time, will be returned to their respective worlds, hopefully, never to sin again against the servants of God."

I walked over to the sheath of the demon Obizuth. She was a winged demon, and although her sheath was flawless and unscarred, she was by no means what I would call beautiful. She had angular features, horns, and a very pointed chin. Her face pulsated and contorted in agony.

"What was her crime?" I asked.

"The she-demon Obizuth looked to harm God's servant Noah. She did so by preventing the raven that he had sent out from the Ark from returning to him with signs that the waters were receding and that the appearance of dry land was imminent. Because of her interference, God sent the punishing angel Bazazath to slay her and condemn her soul to this realm of mist and agony."

I walked to the next sheath, a wingless male demon that seemed also steeped in the throes of agony.

"That," said Hutriel, in a stentorian voice, "is the demon Bardorf. It was he who sought to do harm to God's servant David by entering the sheath of a wolf and attacking David while he tended his flock. God saw this great evil and sent the angel Gidaijal to slay Bardorf and bring him for punishment to Gehenna G'mul."

"There are many here whom you may have heard of in your own time," said Satan, pointing to a human sheath writhing in the agony of his sins. "There lies the sheath of Adolf Hitler. He and his underlings who were responsible for the torture and annihilation of those who had covenant with God."

I looked around and learned that a great many of Hitler's cohorts were condemned to this fifth division of Hell. I saw the sheaths of Joseph Mengele, Adolph Eichmann, Rudolph Hess, and the rest of that vile lot.

"Also here," said Hutriel, pointing to his left, "are the sheaths of those who, through their religious policies, have tortured those in covenant with God, policies such as those that were responsible for the various inquisitions and pogroms of the middle ages. Their self-serving religions and their self-appointed saints could not save them from their just punishment for their crimes. Know that nothing that humankind does escapes the eye of God, and though they may find justification for their actions in their religions, and in their own minds, it is God who ultimately determines guilt. And so, here they lie in utter agony until the time of their release. None escape God's judgment!"

As we were speaking, a second angel appeared. "I am the angel Oniel," he said, nodding to Hutriel. "I oversee the agonies of this place as it relates to those who have prayed to false gods and have been a source of harm to God's servants. As you have seen, and as my brother Hutriel has told you, none escape God's justice. For the sake of the One True God, and for he who will train the Messiah, I will take you on a tour of this place of tears."

He led me deep into the heart of the fifth division. Strewn throughout this morbid realm were many of mankind's historically ignoble men and women lying in agony for their crimes against the servants of God. He showed me the famous and the infamous. There was Herod the First and Herod the Second, a father and son lying next to each other for the crimes that they committed against God by harming His servant Jesus. There was Absolom who rebelled against his father, David, and tried to steal the throne of Israel. The angel Oniel was right—no one escapes God's justice.

"Oniel," I said, "what are these souls actually experiencing?"

"They are experiencing the pains and griefs of their victims," he said, his great aura pulsating as he spoke. "They are experiencing the mental, physical, and spiritual pain that they caused their victims to face. It is a grave matter, my son."

"If they repent, will they be released from here?"

"This is not a place for repentance, Benjamin. This is a place of punishment. The time for repentance was before they were condemned here. Once they are committed to this place it is too late for such things. In time, they will be returned to life. Any repentance that they have, if it is true, will then be reflected in their deeds."

"I understand."

"Good, now let us return to the others. You have other divisions to visit, my son."

I didn't know how long I had been with Oniel, but when we returned it was clear that Satan was ready to move on.

"Come, Benjamin," said Satan, bowing to the angels Hutriel and Oniel, "it's time to descend to the sixth division."

I thanked the angels, left Gehenna G'mul, and promptly materialized in the sixth division. It was so dark that the sheaths of those condemned there seemed to glow with a sort of brilliance and the angels stationed here glowed like absolute beacons.

Before us stood an angel of such fierceness, such power, that it was difficult for me to look at him without beginning to shake.

"Be at peace, Benjamin," the great angel said, obviously aware of my discomfort. I am the overseer of the sixth division of Hell, Gehenna Aysh, the Hell of Fiery Damnation. I am called Pusiel. I am known as the Fire of God, for I burn into the souls that are condemned here the fire of God's displeasure, and how bitterly they who lie here suffer for it."

Pusiel's manner and words calmed me. Then, as had become custom on this odyssey, we all exchanged nods. I looked over at Satan and he smiled at me.

I wondered if this was the fiery hell that was spoken about by the sages. If it was, then it was clear that they had never visited this place. They probably had learned of the name of this hell, and had made assumptions about it that gave rise to ideas of fire and brimstone, and, of course, to Dante's tale.

"In my division," began Pusiel, "the most heinous of all human and demonic beings are punished because they opposed God's Redemption. This is the place of ultimate punishment for both human and demon. There are no deeper divisions to which they are assigned."

I thought of Pusiel's words. It was incredible that anyone or anything could oppose God's Redemption. How could they ever hope to prevail against God? I looked to Satan.

"Benjamin," said Satan, "you seem surprised that there are those who would dare to oppose God. There are those among humankind and among the demons who look to their own needs and refuse to even believe in the existence of God."

"What do they do to oppose God's Redemption?" I asked.

"They commit many evil acts," said Satan, turning toward me. "Men, for example, make unholy pacts with demons and so bring into the world of men these vile demons who are bent on destroying God's work so that they may survive to take over the Light Malkuth. It was too late for them when they learned that nothing is ever hidden from God—neither goodness, nor evil—and how bitterly they who lie here are suffering for it."

"What my brother Satan says is so!" said Pusiel, his eyes suddenly flashing a deeper brighter fiery white. "My brother Satan is correct, indeed. They sinned, Benjamin."

Questions began to form in my mind as Pusiel continued.

"God will not tolerate those who oppose His Redemption in any way, they will remain here longer than any others in any of the divisions of Gehenna, that is, except those beings condemned to the seventh division."

"What other crimes against God's Redemption have those condemned here committed?" I asked.

"Many," said Pusiel, raising his right hand. "Chief among them is the propagation of philosophies and religions that encouraged mankind to cling to the things of the world; philosophies and religions that caused mankind to attach themselves to a world that God had set for dissolution at the very time of its creation."

"Do you mean that attachment to the things of the world is working against God's Redemption?"

"Yes, Benjamin," said Pusiel. "The world cannot be dissolved as long as man reincarnates into it. It is man's attachments that keep him returning, my son. Those lying here are learning the error of their ways, even as we speak."

"Suppose that they return to their evil ways when they leave here?"

"Then," said Pusiel, glancing briefly at Satan, "then, they shall return to this place for a longer stay, before . . . ."

Pusiel suddenly stopped speaking, turned, and walked away.

"You must excuse Pusiel," said Satan, seeming to know what had caused Pusiel's dejection. "He was going to say that those who cannot be taught to change their ways will be condemned to the seventh division of Hell. That, my son, is the worst fate of all. It is no small matter, as you will see. Come, let us go."

I watched the angel Pusiel walk away in great sadness as Satan waved his hand and brought us into the seventh and final division of Hell. It was totally devoid of any sort of light, ethereal or otherwise. Even the angels assigned to stand in vigil over this place were black as pitch and invisible. It was a domain of utter darkness, the kind of darkness that only God, Himself, could create.

"Tell me about this place, Satan," I said, unable to see him.

"Forgive me, Benjamin," said Satan, his voice noticeably laden with sorrow, "this is the most horrible place of all, the most horrible place in all of creation. Those that are assigned here, all of them, have been completely cut off from God. Here, they lie until the Ha'masah, the End-Time, in the utter darkness, a darkness wrought from the very fabric of their own evil deeds. They are totally cut off from God's mercy, Benjamin. Yes, this place and those resident here are still part of God, but they are as a void, an utter and dismal void within the deepest part of the void of God. This is the most desolate place in all of existence, my son."

I heard Satan sigh deeply and I knew that even he feared this place. "Who is the angel that oversees the seventh division?" I asked, looking out into the darkness and seeing nothing.

"The angel who oversees this division," Satan said, "is the great angel Rogziel, but we cannot speak to him, for he will not speak. He is known to all of us as the Wrath of God. I must be the one to tell you about this place, Benjamin. The seventh division of Hell is called Gehenna Tachton Gadol, the Hell of the Great Darkness. It is also called Gehenna Mavet Gadol, the Hell of the Great Death, but only by the True Workers of Light."

Here, for the first time, I couldn't even see the fire in Satan's eyes. He had told me that God had decreed that no light whatsoever will ever be seen here. I had never experienced this type of darkness before and it frightened me. Here I felt totally separated from all of existence. It was as though Satan and I were nothing more than two disincarnate voices groping in the darkness for companionship.

"Here, in utter darkness," said Satan, "lie those foolish angels who have rebelled against God. Here lie angels such as Araziel, Gressil, Gadreel, Hakael, Semyaza, Tumael, Yonyael, Turael, and many, many others. We call these angels the Sar'im Ra'im, the evil angels. Their punishment is to be separated from the Spirit of God until the End-Time when all else in existence is taken care of."

"Why until the End-Time?" I asked, my voice sounding strange in the darkness.

"It must be this way, my son, so that these evil angels cannot interfere with God's Redemption any longer."

"What have they done to deserve this?" I asked, turning in the direction of Satan's voice.

"They have committed many forbidden acts, Benjamin, acts that have interfered with God's Redemption. Had it not been for these rebellious angels, God's Redemption would have taken place already. All of the manifest universe must suffer because of what they have done."

"I understand," I said, wishing that I could see them.

"The rebellious angel Araziel had corrupted the women of the world by instructing them in the evil ways of Lilith."

"Lilith?"

"Yes, the evil angel Araziel taught women to be rebellious and to sin against their husbands by defiling the marriage bed. The angel Semyaza revealed the Explicit Name of God to a woman named Ishtahar. This corrupted her and caused her to delve into secret matters, and resulted in great problems for mankind. Then, there is the angel Gadreel whom mankind had confused with me. Benjamin, it was the evil angel Gadreel, not I, who corrupted Eve, Adam's second wife, into the eating of the forbidden fruit in the Garden of Eden."

When Satan explained Gadreel's sin everything suddenly crystallized in my mind. *Satan is innocent!* I had increasingly begun to believe this since Moloch had explained it to me, but now, for the first time, it all suddenly came together. When I thought of all the religions of the world that have made Satan their arch villain and God's chief adversary, it became simple to see why those religions cannot possibly assist in the holy task of bringing about God's Redemption. That's why one of the missions that the Messiah must accomplish is to enlighten those religions once and for all, not only concerning Satan, but of the many things that they have never had the correct knowledge of before.

"Satan, are the Sar'im Ra'im the fallen angels?"

"Yes, they are the fallen angels. Fallen from the Grace of God."

"Many people of the world believe that you were the one who led the rebellion against God."

"I know, Benjamin, I know," said Satan, his voice growing a little sterner. "It was not I, but the evil Lilith who incited the angels to rebel against God. We angels call that rebellion the Z'man Shel Tza'ar Gadol, the Time of the Great Sorrow. It was the vile and loathsome Lilith who falsely named me as God's enemy and spread those lies among mankind. Her lies were further perpetuated by her evil offspring, the demons, chief among them is Sid, her eldest. It was her way of striking back at God for the indignities that she imagined that she had suffered at God's Hand."

"But why you?" I asked, knowing that she could have chosen any of myriad angels to spread lies about.

"She chose me out of revenge, Benjamin, for it was I who was the one that first uncovered her rebelliousness, her disloyalty to God. I was sent by God to test her loyalty to Him, and since that time she has hated me for it. To avenge herself, she sought to make me seem like God's opponent and the leader of the Rebellion. She and her evil offspring sowed those lies among the children of men so that she would remain blameless in their eyes, and I would be branded as the evil traitor. So it was, Benjamin, that I became a Sar Ra, an evil angel, in the eyes of those who could not see the truth of the matter."

Suddenly, all of the pieces fell into place. It made a great deal of sense, and confirmed what I was told by Moloch. Lilith and her vile offspring were the culprits in all of this, and humankind fell for their lies.

"Satan," I said, "will these angels ever be saved? I mean—"

"Understand, Benjamin, that in truth, nothing is ever separated from God, not even these evil angels. Everything is irrevocably one with God. In the End-Time, even these evil angels, being all minor faces of God, will be reabsorbed back into God's unmanifest nature, and shall by then have been cleansed of their inglorious defilements. This is the way of things, my son. Come, we must leave. I cannot bear this place any longer."

We were promptly transported out of the seventh division and materialized back in front of the Gates of Flame, the entrance to Hell.

"Benjamin," said Satan, once again gleaming white and beautiful in front of me, "do you understand what you have seen in this place? Do you understand the sins that men, demons, and angels have committed to condemn them to the various Divisions here?"

"I understand," I said.

"Good! Very good, indeed!" he said, his mouth gently sweeping into a gracious smile. "Now, we must go to the Heavens, and I must teach you of the secrets of what is there. There are many there, you know!"

I felt the impulse to begin asking him questions about Heaven, but resisted, knowing that everything would be explained to me in time. My mind was still trying to absorb all that I'd learned in Hell. Before this very moment, I could never have imagined that Satan would even have been allowed entrance into Heaven. How wrong all of these religions were to have been taken in by Lilith's evil machinations. How wrong to have misunderstood this great servant of God.

Satan smiled. "Come, my son, we must leave."

Then, with a nod of his head and a wave of his hand we were traveling once again—this time deeper and deeper into the void of God toward Heaven.

20

The Lower Heavens

MIRACULOUSLY MOVING AT THE SPEED OF GOD, WE RUSHED DEEP into the Void of God. The gates that protected Hell from intrusion had disappeared into the eternal Void behind us. And then, suddenly, we stopped. I looked around us and saw only the endless Void stretching around us on all sides. Where were the gates of Heaven? I looked at Satan who stood with his eyes closed, as if he had suddenly fallen into a deep, mystical trance. After a few moments he broke our silence.

"Listen, Benjamin!" he said, with a gentle smile spreading across his face. "Do you hear what comes to us through the Void of God?"

I closed my eyes and listened, but wasn't sure that I heard anything except my own heartbeat.

"Quiet your Lower Mind, my son," he said, opening his eyes, looking at me, and holding his index finger up to his lips.

I performed the Sha'ar Lev and listened again. When Satan saw my mouth drop open and tears well up in my eyes, he knew that I had heard.

"What is it?" I asked, wiping the tears from my cheeks. "It's so beautiful!"

"Benjamin, what you hear is the mystical sound of the Kadishim. They are glorious angels who reside in the Tenth Heaven and praise God unceasingly with transcendental hymns of love and adoration. At the same time, Benjamin, these great angels proclaim God's glory and God's love to all of existence. All that one has to do is to listen, my son. If the world of men would only take the time to listen, by God's grace they would hear His holy angels singing, their sweet voices radiating throughout the Void of God. Then, my son, mankind would truly know that God is among them. Hearing the Kadishim, the Angelic Choir, is just one way for mankind to experience the reality of God."

"Are you saying that everyone has the ability to hear the angelic choir?"

"Yes, Benjamin, they have the ability, but not the technique."

"What is the technique?" I asked, hoping that when I returned to the Light World I would be able to continue to hear the Kadishim.

Satan smiled. "It's really very simple, you already have part of it, Benjamin."

"I do?"

"Yes. There are five necessary elements that will allow one to hear the voices of the Kadishim. Collectively, the five elements are called the Tebul Tov, the Good Immersion.† It is one of the techniques that will be taught to the world by the Messiah. It is first necessary in the Tebul Tov that the individual have both an abiding love for God and an uncompromising trust in His Word. Second, the individual should be in quiet surroundings, a location free from noisy distractions. Third, the individual should quiet the Lower Mind with the Sha'ar Lev. Fourth, the individual should unite both the Void of God and the Light Malkuth with the Nefesh Kafdan, to breathe in both worlds and unite the two within one's self. This is accomplished by breathing through the Sha'ar Ha'ar, the mystical gate located in the lower abdomen

---

† See the *Tebul Tov* techniques in the Appendix, page 382.

just below the navel. Inhaling the external Light Malkuth, sending that breath through the Sha'ar Ha'ar and deep into the Void of God, and then exhaling from deep within the Void of God and out into the Light Malkuth. The Sha'ar Ha'ar unites both worlds. Finally, the individual should enter into the silence and peace brought about by the Nefesh Kafdan and turn his or her spirit over to God. Should a person employ all five elements of the Tebul Tov, then they will experience the Kadishim, the great transcendental Angelic Choir. They will experience something of the reality of God. Do you understand, Benjamin?"

"Yes, I understand, but why isn't it possible for people to experience the Kadishim without having to resort to Tebul Tov?"

"Humankind and demon-kind alike, Benjamin, are much too engrossed in the affairs of their respective worlds. Their lower minds are much too cluttered with idle chatter to be able to hear the Kadishim sing their hymns. This is part of the mission of the Messiah, to help the world lay down their foolish notions of existence and to teach them how to listen to and experience the reality of God. To those who listen to his teachings, the Kadishim will pervade their lives and bring them, in song, the eternal love of God."

"That would be wonderful," I said, "I mean for those who—"

"It will happen! You must trust God, Benjamin. It will happen. Now close your eyes and quiet your mind. Let the Kadishim lead you to your destination."

The quieter my mind became, the louder and sweeter the melodious voices of the Kadishim singing their praises to God became. Soon, I had no thoughts of myself, no thoughts of Satan, Hell, Heaven, Yusef, angels, demons, or of anything—all that existed was the sweet, mystical sound of the celestial choir. I was lost in their sweet singing when I suddenly felt myself being whisked deeper into the Void of God.

A moment later, I opened my eyes and saw that I was standing before a gate not much different than the gate that we had encountered when we reached the entrance to Hell. Instead of narrow pillars of blue fire, there were narrow pillars of golden fire stretching as far as the eye could see—the fabled Gates of Gold referred to in religious folklore, I assumed. Somehow, I'd expected to find a gate of solid gold sparkling in the glorious rays of a golden sun. It wasn't that at all, but the brilliantly glowing golden fire of the Gate of Heaven didn't disappoint me in the least and I wished that Yusef, Muhammad, Mara, and Ali could have been with me to experience this.

Directly in front of us was a curtain of brilliantly glowing indigo flames, which I guessed concealed an opening. On either side of the curtain, for as far as the eye could see, stood enormous angels with fierce demeanors standing shoulder to shoulder. Each angel bore a great silver medallion engraved with flames of indigo fire with the holy name of God, El Shaddai, God Almighty, and held great gold swords against their chests. Not a single one acknowledged our presence, they only continued their solemn vigil, staring with eyes of red fire, seemingly to the very end of the Void of God.

"The angels that stand before us, Benjamin, are of the Order of the Cherubim," said Satan. "They are fierce in their countenance and fiercer in their fighting for their love of God."

I looked at them standing constant against the enemies of Heaven, against those who would take it upon themselves to defile the austere sanctity of Heaven. I had always thought that Cherubs were the sweet, baby-like angels of love that the great painter Raphael had introduced in so many of his works. These were no innocent-looking beings!

"Come, Benjamin," said Satan. "Time is fleeting. Let us enter."

With a wave of his hand, the flaming indigo curtain parted and we passed through a short, well-lit corridor of black and white marble into a huge room lined with more fierce Cherubim. The floor of the room seemed to be the purest black onyx, and the walls the purest white marble. Everything shimmered and sparkled. Directly across from us were the only doors that I could see in the room. They must have stood forty feet high and seemed to be made of ruby. I looked to Satan for an explanation about the nature of the room, but he stood silent, staring at a large square of blue sapphire in the center of the chamber.

After a moment, a magnificent angel clad in a flowing white robe appeared in the center of the sapphire square. At first, the angel stood motionless, staring back at us. It was unsettling. Finally, he raised his right hand, smiled, and spoke. "Greetings, brothers," he said. "I wish you both peace in the name of the One True God."

The angel stared deep into my eyes and announced, "My name is Deheborym, I am an aide to the Archangel Gabriel, chief angelic resident of the first Heaven. I was sent by Gabriel to greet you. My brother Satan will be your guide through our Heavens, but at each level you will be greeted by one or more such as I." He turned and addressed Satan. "If you are ready, then please enter." The angel Deheborym dissolved and disappeared.

"Ready, Benjamin?" said Satan, turning to me, poised to wave his hand.

I took a deep breath and one more look around the great angel-filled room. "Yes," I said, "I'm ready."

With a wave of his hand we left the great room and instantly found ourselves in the town square of what appeared to be a city. Small Tudor-style shops lined the cobblestone streets that ran in almost all directions, very much like the spokes of a bicycle wheel. People—or at least the images of people—were gathered in the square and walking through the streets. They were, in fact, ethereal forms, diaphanous grayish white sheaths. The whole spectacle reminded me of what the city of London might have looked like during the seventeenth century.

"Is this the first Heaven?" I asked, noticing that Satan seemed to glow a little brighter here.

"Yes, Benjamin," he said, turning to me, "this is the first Heaven—a very tiny bit of it. It goes on forever in every direction."

"Forever?"

"Yes, forever. Understand that God is infinite in all things and that the Heavens, as well as the Hells, are infinite and cater to an infinite number of possibilities. Those divisions of Hell that you've seen were only a sampling of the endless possibilities. The same applies to the Heavens."

"I see."

We walked down a narrow street, passing people and shops, and came to another, slightly different square. It was circular, with a large, ornate fountain in the center, which spewed brilliant indigo water. The people, or rather sheathed souls, who milled about seemed happy.

Satan smiled. "Are you surprised, Benjamin?"

Images of the various Hells ran through my mind. This appeared to be more normal, much easier to comprehend. "It's much different here than . . . ."

"Yes, my son, much different. As I told you, after their Hell experiences, the sheathed souls are sent to one of the Heavens. The first Heaven is the lowest, and meanest, of all the Heavens. It is called Shamayim Ahfel, the Dark Heaven."

"The Dark Heaven?"

"Yes, the Dark Heaven," said Satan with a smile. "It is the lowest of all the Heavens and farthest from the light of God. So it is considered to be dark. Those who are sent here have led lives of great attachment. Their stay here is minimal depending on the magnitude of their attachments. The greater their attachments, the shorter their stay will be. Some stay only days, others years, or even centuries. Of course, when you realize that time is meaningless here, it all comes out the same as far as they're concerned. What you see here, Benjamin, is what these individuals were used to in life. There are, of course, an infinity of lifestyles present in this Heaven. It all depends on the century and circumstances of their particular lives. Remember, there are infinite possibilities within the infinity of God, my son. This is just one sample."

Aside from the fact that they were flawless sheaths, everyone appeared to look somewhat natural here, doing what I supposed they did, more or less, when they were alive. "Are they really happy here?" I asked.

"They enjoy only the merest of happinesses here," he said. "Their stay here will be short, for their attachment to the things of the world beckons them to life again. Here in Shamayim Ahfel they meet others of similar nature, even some whom they may have known in life—friends, relatives, teachers, even enemies. Of course, there is no violence here. It is just a momentary place to spend some time before returning to the world of men. Here in Shamayim Ahfel they consume the illusion of fine foods, fine drink, and so on. Although there is no real hunger or thirst here, their memories of hunger and thirst—born of great earthly attachments—warrant certain illusory indulgences."

I supposed it made little difference whether their hunger and thirst were real or imagined. The souls that I saw populating this place did seem to be happy.

"Benjamin, come, we must move on."

Satan raised his hand and transported us to a vast misty area. This place had none of the illusions of a city, town, or anything else. Standing before us in the mist, a short distance away, was an angel gleaming white in the Void of God. I could hardly see his face. "I am Gabriel, servant of the One True God," he said, in a great thundering voice. "I greet you, and wish you both peace in the name of the One True God."

Satan turned to me and then to Gabriel. "This is Benjamin, brother," he said, gesturing to me. "He is on a mission of great importance for the One True God we both love and adore."

"I know, brother" said Gabriel, his expression slowly changing from stern to gentle. "You are sent here to learn about this place, are you not? To learn so you can inform he who is to train the Messiah in its mysteries?"

"Yes," I said. I didn't want to say too much, fearing that I would somehow insult him.

Gabriel smiled more broadly. "Very well then! I will tell you what you should know, so listen well and learn, my son! Know that the Lord God, blessed be His name, has placed me in the First Heaven to oversee its workings. I am charged with the responsibility of seeing to the needs of those whose fates and lifestyles have placed them here. Yes, this is heaven, but only to those unfortunates who have not learned to end their clinging to things of naught in the world of matter. Do you understand?"

"Yes, Satan's told me."

"Good," he said, nodding to Satan. "I see that you have a question, my son."

After all I'd experienced so far, I wasn't the least bit surprised that Gabriel knew that I had a question. It was simply another confirmation of the fact that nothing is hidden from God. As I began to speak, Gabriel stated my question for me.

"You are wondering, Benjamin, how mankind can divest himself of his attachments and achieve for himself the grace of God, and so eventually be granted entrance into one of the Higher Heavens?"

"Yes," I said. "What can man do to further his knowledge and to let him know that there is more to existence than his vain attachments? Is there some way during his lifetime that he can actually experience the Void of God?" I looked at Satan. His expression told me that I had asked the right question.

Gabriel held his open palm up and I immediately felt an enormous heat pass through my body.† He looked upward, deep into the Void for a few seconds, and then, looking back at me, said, "You have asked well, my son! I will teach you a way that it may be shown to the sons of men that they may know some of the truth of things. My brother Satan has touched on it when he taught you how one may come to experience the Kadishim. I will explain it further. Listen well, Benjamin! Know

---

† This is an example of projecting the *M'retz Na'she*, or Feminine Energy. For instructions, see Appendix, page 378.

that within the body of each individual, there lies a special gate called the Sha'ar Ha'ar, the Gate of Glory. It is a mystical gate or entrance leading to the very Void of God. The Sha'ar Ha'ar connects the two worlds—the Light Malkuth and the Void.[†] The key to this mystical gate lies in the breath. It is attained with this technique: Have the person of faith who wants to experience the Void of God sit quietly in a candle-lit room that is neither too dark, nor too light. Instruct that person to sit erect with folded legs on a cushion firm enough to support their weight. Then, have that person sway gently, to and fro like a pendulum in a small arc, slowly coming to stop in the center. This will cause that person to find the center of his or her balance. The spine should be straight, but not rigid. The Sha'ar Ha'ar is located within the hollow of the body just below the navel. The eyes may be closed, or they may be slightly lowered. Instruct that person to breathe in and follow that breath with their mind deep into the void within their body. When they do, they will find that their breath exits their bodily void and enters the Void of God. When they exhale, have them follow their breath, which now originates deep within the Void of God, through their bodily void, and outward to the external world. As this process continues, they will come to realize that they, themselves, are a living connection between the worlds. In time, and with practice, they will be able to merge both voids and both worlds. They will come to realize that all of the manifest Universe is part of the eternal Void of God. This is the way of the Sha'ar Ha'ar and the Tebul Tov, the Good Immersion. Do you understand, Benjamin?"

"Yes, I understand the technique of the Tebul Tov," I said clearly, "but, are you saying that the entire physical universe is actually part of the Void of God, and that a man or woman of faith can actually experience that? Are you saying that—"

---

†See the *Nefesh Kafdan* technique in the Appendix, page 381.

"Benjamin," said Gabriel, holding up his right hand, "it is God's wish to bring mankind into the experience of true spirituality so that they will, once and for all, end their foolish ways, and sever their vain attachments. It is His hope that mankind, once he experiences the truth of the nature of things, will repent of his foolishness and work for His salvation. For this reason, the secret of the Sha'ar Ha'ar and the Tebul Tov are to be introduced to all of mankind through the Messiah. Once man realizes that he can connect the two worlds within himself, he will come to realize that God awaits him. Then, all of humankind will know that they truly exist within God's being. It is the sincere hope of the angels residing in all the Heavens and all the Hells that experiencing of the Sha'ar Ha'ar and the Tebul Tov will incite humankind to enter into Holy Covenant with the God, and serve Him in His Redemption. I see you understand, Benjamin."

"Yes," I said, glancing at Satan and then looking back at Gabriel. "It's wonderful that the teaching of the Tebul Tov will be part of the work of the Messiah. I mean, it will get humankind to experience the Void of God and—"

"Yes, my son," said Gabriel, a broad smile coming to his face, "the Messiah will dissolve disbelief in God by teaching how to experience God. This is what God wants."

"I understand," I said. "I think that it'll be wonderful. Why hasn't the Tebul Tov been shown before?"

"It wasn't time, Benjamin," said Gabriel. "Humankind wasn't ready to learn of such things."

"But suppose the people of the world refuse to accept the Messiah? Suppose they reject him?"

Gabriel's face suddenly turned dark and ominous. "They will learn, Benjamin, they will learn."

Just as the Archangel Gabriel finished speaking, six great angels appeared beside him—three to his left, and three to his right.

"I am summoned, my son," said Gabriel, nodding to Satan.

"And you must move on. May the God we adore grant you both peace!" With those words, Gabriel and his angelic attendants dissolved and disappeared.

Satan and I stood there in silence. Then Satan turned to me. "I see that you have questions, Benjamin. Ask and I shall answer."

"Could you tell me more about Gabriel? I've heard his name before, but I don't know much about him."

"Gabriel's name means God is my strength. Besides being in charge of the first Heaven, he is a great angel of destruction. When God is angered by the ways of sinful cities, it is Gabriel that is sent to destroy them. In fact, it was Gabriel that God sent to destroy the sinful cities of Sodom and Gomorrah. He is a prince of God's justice and dispenses that justice at God's command. He was the angel God sent to rescue Hananiah, Mishael, and Azariah from the fiery furnace. He is a great Archangel, Benjamin, a great face of God."

"What about the angels that just appeared? Who were they?"

"They are among the myriad angels that are resident here in the first Heaven," he said. "Their names were Ashrulyu, Padael, Hizkiel, Hubaiel, Jekusiel, and Sheviel. They are great angels serving in the first Heaven under the Archangel Gabriel.

"Do they have special functions?"

"Yes," said Satan, folding his arms. "The angel Ashrulyu was the angel that was on the far left of Gabriel. He was one of the angels that God sent to aid the prophet Moses in writing the Holy Torah. He taught Moses the true nature of creation. Next to him was the angel Padael, who was sent to Manoah's wife to instill in her unborn child the strength of God. That child's name was Samson. Next to Padael was the warrior angel Hizkiel who often assists Gabriel when the great angel is engaged in battle with members of the Sar'im Ra'im—those evil angels who have rebelled and turned away from God. On the far right was the angel Hubaiel, one of Moses' teachers and guides when he toured the first Heaven. Next to him stood the angel Jekusiel, an angelic guard, one of myriad angelic guards stationed here in the first Heaven to protect its sanctity from intrusion. Finally, there was the angel Sheviel. He is Gabriel's message bearer. He transports any necessary angelic information from the first Heaven to the Upper Heavens on Gabriel's behalf. Every angel has a function, Benjamin."

"Come now, Benjamin, we must go. There is still much to see and learn." With a wave of his hand, Satan brought us into the second Heaven, which he identified as Shamayim Sigsug, the Heaven of Growth. Brighter than the first Heaven, it looked otherwise similar. This time we materialized on a grass-covered knoll overlooking a large rural city set among rolling hills, gently flowing streams, and a placid lake of indigo-colored water. Three great angels stood before us, their dense auras pulsating like great ethereal wings.

"Greetings and peace be upon you both, brothers," said the center angel. "I am called Raziel, my companions are the angels Sehaltiel and Sakriel. We were told by the One True God to meet you here that we may be of service."

This time Satan and I nodded to our hosts simultaneously. I noticed that all three lacked the golden swords that I had become accustomed to seeing since I entered the Heavens. Each was clothed in white robes, and had stern but kindly expressions on their faces.

"Raziel," said Satan, "is the great Archangel that God ordered to instruct Moses in the use of certain mystical powers. His name means the Secret of God. He is the angel who bestows knowledge of the mysteries of the workings of God. It was through Raziel's instruction that Moses was able to bring about the Ten Plagues in Egypt and the deliverance of God's Chosen People. He is a powerful angel, Benjamin, a very powerful angel, indeed."

"And the others?"

"The angel on Raziel's right is the angel Sehaltiel. King Solomon used him to capture and control the demon Moloch, the same demon Moloch you met in the labyrinth beneath the city of Jericho."

The three great angels stood silent as Satan continued to explain.

"Now, the angel on Raziel's left is the great angel Sakriel. Sakriel assisted King Solomon in his dealings with the demon Dendares, the evil twin brother of Moloch. When Moloch was captured and sealed in the labyrinth, Dendares swore to destroy King Solomon. Upon learning of Dendares' vile oath, King Solomon sent Sakriel to destroy the demon and seal him in a brass urn. Even today that brass urn is among the sea of urns in Gehenna Shadim."

Having finished speaking, Satan and I turned to our three hosts.

"You are wondering about the nature of those who are sent to the second Heaven," said Raziel, reading my thoughts.

"Yes, I am."

Raziel smiled. "Those who are resident here are those who, in life, remained relatively harmless and blameless in most things. Their understandings of the nature of things prompted them to do no harm to their fellow man. By human standards they were good people. Their stay here is short, however, for they must return to life in the world of men. They still suffer greatly from earthly attachments. Still, their stay here is more pleasant than those temporarily resident in the first Heaven."

The angel Raziel glanced at his two angelic companions, and then looked at me. "When I was teacher to God's servant Moses," he said, "I taught him many important things—esoteric, mystical things. Armed with the knowledge that I had imparted to him, he was able to thwart the powers of pharaoh's evil magicians. By so doing, he freed God's chosen people from their captivity. I will give you the key to such knowledge, Benjamin, for this I am instructed to do by God. You will pass this knowledge on to he who is to train the Messiah."

I glanced at Satan. He smiled and then nodded, indicating that I should pay close attention to Raziel's instruction.

"Know, my son," began Raziel, "that all of the matter in the manifest Universe is composed solely of the powerful Masculine and Feminine Energies of God. The Masculine Energy is called the M'retz Za'char and the Feminine Energy is called the M'retz Na'she. Even your body is composed of this, Benjamin. To experience the proof of this, place your hands in front of you, positioned palm to palm, with four inches of space between them."†

I did as Raziel instructed, holding my hands, palm to palm, in front of my chest.

"Now," said Raziel, "pump your palms toward and away from each other slightly and tell me what you feel."

"I feel pressure, a resistance between the palms of my hands," I said. It was very much like the pressure that one would feel doing the same thing with two magnets by pumping the like poles back and forth.

"Just so," said Raziel, with a smile spreading across his face. "What you feel, Benjamin, is the magen, or shield, that exists around all matter both animate and inanimate. It is generated by the imbalanced union of the masculine and feminine energies of God. The magen is what some refer to as the aura. Always remember that all of the matter in Ain Sof Aur, the manifest Universe, contains an imbalance that produces the magen. If you keep this in mind, then many areas of mystical learning will open before you."

"What areas?" I asked.

"With your magen, Benjamin, you will be able to influence the magen of other people and objects, even at great distances. You will not only be able to move objects, but actually break down the structure of physical matter. You will be able to transfer or withdraw energies from matter. I see that you

---

† For instructions on experiencing your magen, see Appendix, page 377.

understand, Benjamin? I can see that you understand what the possibilities are."

I nodded.

"Most excellent," said Raziel, raising his left palm towards me. "Now raise your left palm as I do."

I raised my hand and waited for the next instructions.

"Clear your mind, Benjamin, and perform the Tebul Tov. On exhalation, have that breath flow upwards from the great Void of God and travel through your arm, and then out from your palm so that I can feel the energy in the palm of my hand."

I felt my breath come up from deep within the Void of God, through the Sha'ar Ha'ar, through my arm, and out of my palm.

"Most excellent, indeed," said Raziel, obviously feeling something in the palm of his raised hand. "This is how to send forth the power of the M'retz Na'she, the Feminine Energy of God. You are doing well, indeed. The power of the M'retz Na'she may be directed through your right hand, or, with practice, through any other part of your body. Even your eyes. This practice is the basis of great power. It is not to be abused."

A wave of pride swept over me. I'd actually done it, but at the same time, I knew that I shouldn't cling to that prideful feeling. I felt myself let go of the pride.

"I have introduced you to the acquisition of the power of the M'retz Na'she," said Raziel sternly. "You will be instructed in the many uses of that great power by other ministers before Satan brings you back to the world of matter, the Light Malkuth."

"I understand, Raziel," I said, bowing humbly.

"Good! Then, I will bid you and my brother Satan farewell, for thee both have much to do." Raziel and the three great angels dissolved, leaving Satan and me alone on the knoll.

"It's time," said Satan, waving his hand. "You are doing well, my son." We left the second Heaven for the third.

The third Heaven was much the same as the first two. It consisted of sheath-filled cities, farms, valleys, mountains, and islands placed at various historical periods. Just like the first and second Heavens, there was an infinity of possibilities, an infinity of combinations. It all seemed very personal, yet paradoxically impersonal. A great cosmic illusion.

We materialized on a tropical island paradise surrounded by a golden beach that stretched from the edge of the water up to forests of date palms and citrus trees. The azure sky was dotted with fluffy white clouds and gentle waves of indigo water swept rhythmically from the sea to caress the shoreline. The sun was warm and set high in the sky. It was very pretty and I imagine the idea of heaven to a great many people.

"This is just one of the infinite possibilities in the third Heaven," said Satan, gazing to the horizon, seemingly looking for something to appear. "The third Heaven is called Shamayim Man, the Manna Heaven." Judging by the expectant look on his face, I knew that whatever was to come over the horizon would be worth waiting for.

"Those receiving entrance to the third Heaven," he said, "are those who have made covenant with God but have not freed themselves from their attachments to worldly things. Their stay in the third Heaven is much longer than the stay of those in the second and first Heavens. Still, they too will be returned to the world of men when their Heavenly period is over."

"Who are some of the angels here?"

"There are many, many angels resident in this Heaven," said Satan, staring again toward the horizon. "Rachmiel, Penac, Kyniel, Corat, Famiel, Ohazia, Rabaciel, Malashiel . . . many angels."

"What are their functions?"

"Malashiel was the prophet Elijah's teacher. He delivered the mystical visions to Elijah, thus allowing him to serve God. Malashiel taught him about many of the mysteries of creation. Now, Rachmiel is a great angel of mercy. He dispensed the Manna from the third Heaven for the Israelites led by Moses on their journey through the wilderness. Kyniel, Corat, Ohazia, Penac, and

Famiel are five of the angelic attendants serving here. It is their function to see to the needs of the souls that are sent here."

"I see."

"The Archangel Peniel, though, is the angel that we are waiting for, Benjamin. He was the angel that wrestled with Jacob."

I was sure that Satan would have been able to name all of the angels in all of the Heavens if we'd had the time. He seemed to know all of them personally. "Do you know what I am going to learn here?" I asked.

"Patience, my son," he said, with a broad smile. "You will learn much that . . ." Satan stopped in mid-sentence.

"Is something wrong?" I asked.

"Peniel is here."

Before us materialized an angel of fierce demeanor. He was awesome. I wondered how Jacob could have ever defeated him.

"I bring you greetings from on high," he said. "Is this the one who is to bring the teachings back to he who is to train the Messiah, brother?" Peniel raised his right hand and pointed to me with a slightly curved index finger.

"He is, brother," said Satan, with a nod. "He is here for your instruction."

"Your name is Benjamin, is it not?" asked Peniel sternly.

"It is."

"Then listen closely to me and I shall instruct you in what you should know."

"Listen well, my son," said Satan, "and my brother Peniel will teach you an invaluable secret."

Peniel raised both of his hands, palms facing me. "Benjamin, he who knows the Breath of the Tebul Tov and can control the M'retz Na'she can perform many wonderful things—especially in the world of men. Do you see me standing here before you?"

I nodded.

"Listen well. I want you to perform the Tebul Tov. Then take your left hand and hold it up at your right side, palm facing outward."

I did as Peniel instructed.

"Now, stop your breath and move your hand in a slow sweeping movement in front of you toward your left side. Tell me what you experience."

I performed the Breath of the Tebul Tov and placed my left hand, palm facing out, across my body to my right side. Then, I stopped my breath and began to slowly move my hand in a semicircle toward my left side. I didn't notice anything at all until my hand was in front of Peniel. It was then that I noticed a great amount of heat in my palm. When my hand passed him, my palm cooled. When I reversed the process and brought my hand back the other way, I again felt heat in the palm of my hand when it came to the place that Peniel was standing.

"I felt heat in the palm of my hand when my hand reached you, but when my hand passed you, my hand became cool again," I said, a small grin on my face.

"Just so, my son," said Peniel. "What you felt in the palm of your hand is the M'retz Na'she, the Feminine Energies radiated by my magen. This technique is called He'stakail Gadol, the Great Scanning.† You can locate humankind, demonkind, and even angels with this technique. In fact, you may use the He'stakail Gadol to scan for men, demons, and animals hidden behind walls, be they stone walls, wooden walls, or anything else. Remember to center yourself between the two worlds so that you are more sensitive to it. You may also, if you like, locate any sentient life form with this technique, even at great distances. Now close your eyes and I will change my position. When Satan tells you, with your eyes closed, perform the technique you have just learned."

I closed my eyes and performed the Breath of the Sha'ar Ha'ar. I was centered very quickly. Then, when Satan told me to, I brought my left hand across my body, held my breath, and began to slowly sweep my hand towards my left side using the

---

†See the *He'stakail Gadol* technique in the Appendix, page 384.

He'stakail Gadol. I continued until I felt heat in the palm of my hand. When my hand moved a little farther it cooled again and I knew that I passed him. When I brought my hand back, once again I felt heat in my palm. I moved my hand to the right, and then zeroed in on it.

"Point, Benjamin, when you think you have found Peniel," said Satan.

When I finished zeroing in, I pointed.

"Open your eyes, my son," said Peniel.

I opened my eyes and found that I had located his exact position.

"Good!" said Peniel. "Very good! Now you know one more use of the mystical Tebul Tov. It will serve you well when you return to the world of men. Show it to he who is to train the Messiah. Other ministers shall show you more. Now I must go. I bid you both peace in the Name of the One True God." The angel Peniel's stern face broke into the vaguest of smiles as he disappeared. Satan and I were alone.

"You are learning well, Benjamin," said Satan. "Let's move on."

21

The Middle Heavens

IN THE BLINK OF AN EYE WE WERE IN THE FOURTH Heaven, BUT instead of finding another wonderful rural or urban scene reminiscent of life on earth, we were standing in the middle of a galaxy of sheathed souls suspended like stars in the Void of God. It was absolutely breathtaking. Sheaths floated peacefully in place in every direction.

"This is the fourth Heaven, Benjamin," said Satan, stretching his arms out. "It is called Shamayim Ne'dar, the Wonderful Heaven. The souls here are blessed, indeed. They have freed themselves from a great deal of their mundane attachments and have entered into covenant with God. They have practiced non-violence toward mankind during their lives and have spread the doctrine of non-violence among those with whom they had contact. They are beings of peace. Because of the great strides they have made during their lives in the Light World, they are each suspended in a wonderful bliss state here. That is why this is called the Wonderful Heaven. Each soul, Benjamin, being closer to the light of God than those of the Lower Heavens is experiencing even more blissful peace within the infinity of God. It is wonderful, indeed."

As Satan spoke, two angels of great brilliance and staggering size appeared in front of us. Both angels shone a gleaming white against the black of the Void of God.

"I welcome you both to Shamayim Ne'dar, the fourth Heaven," said the smaller of the two angels. "I am the Archangel Michael. I am Prince of the Holy Presence and am by God's Grace the Overseer of God's Holy Covenant." The larger angel remained silent.

"Greetings to you both," replied Satan.

"Yes," I said. "Greetings to you both."

"Your charge is growing bolder," said Michael. His beauty was surpassed only by that of my companion and guide Satan.

"He is not what he was," said Satan, glancing at me and then back at Michael.

"I am here to teach you, Benjamin," Michael began, "of the covenants made with man that please God and of those covenants that do not. Know that God has in the past, and will in the future, only abide covenants made with Him that fulfill His purposes. God has never entered into covenant with man if that covenant ignores the requirements of the Tikkun. Be aware that God will not enter into a Covenant with man if the fulfillment of that Covenant will perpetually maintain man's presence in Ain Sof Aur. Be forewarned that those who claim to have covenant with God, but have lifestyles that are fraught with attachments to the world of matter, are making false claims. Their claims of such covenants are false, for they truly do not understand the nature of things, they do not understand the Tikkun. Their beliefs and so-called covenants are purely of their own design, based on their own wants and desires, with no basis in Truth. If they are the shepherds of flocks, then they grievously sin against the God that they claim to serve, for they make their flocks to follow in the same calamitous philosophy. Woe to them! Woe to them, indeed!"

Michael's brilliant magen began to pulsate with what could only be described as some sort of great angelic agitation. Fortunately that annoyance was short-lived. After a few moments of silence the pulsations stopped and the great angel regained his composure.

"There," he said, his magen once again brilliant and even, "I have told you what I had to teach you. Now I see that you have questions."

"Suppose," I said, in my firmest voice, "that there are those who really believe that they have a special covenant with God and that they believe that what they're doing is right. They preach love and the spreading of brotherhood, and—"

"Know," interrupted Michael, "that though their hearts be good, and they preach love and brotherhood among mankind, they do nothing to help cut off attachments from their followers. That is not good, my son."

"I understand, but how will people know whether or not the covenants that their leaders say that they have with God are real?"

"They will know that their covenants are false when their prayers are not answered, and their lives are filled with suffering. They will know, also, that their self-created covenants are false when the Messiah enters their world, for he will bring with him a new Covenant, and will offer it to all the peoples of the earth. The peoples of the world will hear the terms of that new Covenant from the Messiah, and will love God for it. The new Covenant that the Messiah will deliver to the world will be, in truth, the Word of God!"

"What if the people don't accept the terms? I mean, many people may not even accept the Messiah as the Messiah. So many people are locked into their religions and won't accept anyone or anything that lies outside of their doctrines. What will happen then?"

The Archangel Michael's smile disappeared and his voice deepened. "They will learn, my son, they will learn."

Michael's words made me think of all the sheathed souls that I had seen in utter torment for the mistakes that they committed during their lives—and that those who've sinned against God suffered the most.

"But . . . ."

"The terms of the new Covenant that will be brought to man through the Messiah will be clear enough for them to understand," said Michael. "Further, the Lord God, the One True God, will enter into that New Covenant with a relentless vigor that has not been seen, even in the days of your ancestors. It will be God, Himself, that will make the people of the world accept the word of His servant, the Messiah. Do not worry about this, Benjamin."

"What are the terms of the new Covenant that the Messiah will deliver to mankind?" I asked.

"That is for God to tell the Messiah and the Messiah to tell the world. I must leave now, for I am summoned elsewhere," said Michael. "My brother will speak now. I wish you both peace in the Name of the One True God." With those words, the Archangel Michael faded into the blackness of the Void, leaving us with the great angel that he called his brother.

Satan and I waited for the angel to speak.

"I am the Archangel Sandalphon," he said, in a thunderous voice. "I am the angel of prayer. I determine which prayers are worthy to be sent on to God. I was sent here to tell you of the nature of prayer so that you may learn those prayers that are pleasing to God. Also, I shall instruct you in the manner of acceptable prayer so that you may tell it to others."

"Listen well then," said Sandalphon. "I will be brief. Prayers that request material things, things of naught, that will bind a man or a woman to the Light World, the physical world, are prayers I will not permit to enter into God's presence. Those prayers, if answered, will work against the Tikkun, God's Redemption."

"I understand."

"Now understand that prayer is to be a conversation between man and God. The prayers that are best are the prayers that come from one's heart. The Messiah will explain proper prayer to the people. Further, know that God is not bored with prayer, and the one who offers up his or her prayer may speak at leisure. Better a very short prayer than no prayer. I see that you understand, Benjamin."

"I do."

"Good! Very good! Humankind must understand the nature of God's Redemption and adjust their prayers so what they request does not interfere with it. When this is considered, then all of his or her prayers will be heard. What I tell you, Benjamin, is the Word of God and cannot be debated or argued."

I was just about to ask the great angel Sandalphon a question when he suddenly left us.

"They are great angels," I said, looking squarely at Satan, "but I know so little about them. Could you tell me something more about them?"

"My brother Michael," Satan began, "is a great Archangel. His name means He who is as God. Besides being in charge of Shamayim Ne'dar, he is the angel that protects Israel, the country of your ancestors. Some believe that it was Michael who vanquished me from God's presence. This, of course, is a fallacy. For this, and other reasons, man's understanding of angels is sorely lacking. Michael's secret name is Sabbathiel."

"Why would an angel have a secret name?" I asked.

"Many angels have secret names. Those names are known to only those who are permitted to use the power of God in order to aid in the Tikkun. Both Moses and King Solomon were well versed in the secret names of angels."

"They were?"

"Yes, because both of them held special covenants with God, the secret knowledge of angelic names was imparted to them. They were taught those names by the angel Raziel."

"The Archangel Sandalphon, can you tell me something about him?"

"Sandalphon is a great angel who, besides being the angel of prayer, is the angel who assists Michael in dispensing and maintaining special Covenants between God and man."

"Like the new Covenant that the Messiah will be delivering to the world?"

"Yes, exactly. It will be the first time that such a covenant is offered to the world. It will be wonderful."

"I see," I said. "Satan, what other great angels reside in the fourth Heaven?"

"A great many, Benjamin! There is Charsiel, Kfial, Pachdiel, Almon, Hilfatei, Hubudiel, Margiviel, Bachiel, Agbas, Osael, Naromiel, Uslael, Vel Aquiel, and many, many others. It was the angel Pachdiel who placed the flaming sword in front of pharaoh's chariots to bar their way so that Moses could lead God's Chosen People safely across the parted Red Sea. In fact, it was the angels Naromiel and Bachiel, also of the fourth Heaven, who parted the Red Sea for Moses. It was the angel Agbas that guided the reed basket containing the child Moses safely into the hands of pharaoh's daughter. There are many angels here who have, at God's command, been involved in the affairs of men. But now the time has come for us to move on, Benjamin."

I took one last look around at the sheaths floating peaceably in the Void of God here in the Shamayim Ne'dar. I couldn't help feeling their contentment, it seemed to radiate from their blissful souls. "God is good in his mercy," I quietly said. "They are blessed to be here."

"Come, my son," said Satan. Then, with a wave of his hand, Satan and I materialized in the fifth Heaven.

It was magnificent. Again, sheathed souls were suspended like stars in the Void of God. There were, however, two noticeable differences between this Heaven and the Lower Heavens—the sense of bliss was far greater here, and this Heaven seemed a great deal less populated.

I saw the translucent gray sheaths of those assigned here floating in the darkness of the Void of God and turned to Satan. "These souls must really have been special to have ascended this far in the Heavens. How did they earn placement here?"

"These souls earned the bliss of the fifth Heaven by cleansing themselves even more thoroughly of the attachments that bind men to the world of matter. Like those of the fourth Heaven, they have also made proper covenant with God and were non-violent toward their fellow man. Further, they have obeyed the Ten Commandments given to them through Moses, God's prophet. Those in the fourth Heaven have also adhered to the Commandments, but have not striven to teach them to others as those resting here have. That is why the fifth Heaven is called Shamayim Ne'ehman, the Heaven of the Faithful. Still, understand that the time spent here is limited. Like all of those within the Heavens that we have seen, they will eventually return to the world of men to learn more of what they will need to know to evolve to the Higher Heavens and eventually to the Supreme State of Union with God. They will strive for the perfection required of them by God and will eventually evolve to the point where they will no longer reincarnate. That is when they find lasting union with God in the Highest Heaven."

"Is that what men have to do when they reincarnate? They evolve spiritually?"

"Yes, my son," said Satan, his voice becoming very serious. "Each person's life in the world is very short. While they live, they must learn the truth of the nature of things and apply what they've learned to benefit God. They must learn detachment within the world of matter. It is, of course, a long process, but the Messiah who God will place in the world will make that evolution easier for them."

I looked out over the sheaths floating in the Void of the fifth Heaven and noticed that among them were angels who glowed like beacons in the blackness. "What are the names of some of the angels that are assigned to the fifth Heaven?" I asked, thinking that they looked so beautiful.

Satan, looking out at the spectacular view, said, "Like the other Heavens, Benjamin, there are many angels residing here.

There are the angels Adiriel, Calzas, Gamrial, Sefriel, Techial, Shatqiel, Gehatsitsa, Paltrial, Erastiel, Janiel, Zaliel, Mathiel, Rahumel, Vianiel, and many others. Remember, my son, each angel has a special function. The angel Totraviel, for example, is a Seal Holder—it was through his offices that we were given special permission to enter this Heaven. His name actually means A Sign to Explore God. He serves with the angel Zahaftrii here. It is a Seal Holder's function to maintain the sanctity of each Heaven. The angel Sefriel was the angel that God sent to protect Hiram's ships so that they could safely deliver their cargoes of gold and precious stones to King Solomon. On your left is the angel Shatqiel. He was the angel that God sent to guide and protect Moses when he was exiled by pharaoh and sent out into the desert. Off in the distance to your right is the angel Janiel. It was the angel Janiel who explained to Joshua what he had to do in order to destroy Jericho. In all of this, Benjamin, you must remember that although angels appear as great beings, we are all just minor faces of the one true God."

Although Satan tried to remind me that angels were only minor faces of God, I still couldn't help being impressed by their awesome majesty.

"There!" said Satan, pointing to an angel in the process of materializing in front of us. "This is the one who is to meet us here."

The angel who appeared before us glowed brilliantly in the Void of the fifth Heaven. His demeanor was that of a warrior and he carried a golden double-edged sword.

"I am called Gadriel," he said in a robust voice that only furthered the impression of his warrior-like nature. "I am sent by the One True God to greet you and teach you. I wish you both peace."

"Greetings! May the peace of the Lord God be upon you, brother," said Satan, nodding.

"Greetings!" I said.

"Is this the one who is to bring back the teachings to the trainer of the Messiah?" asked Gadriel, pointing to me.

"This is the one," said Satan, nodding to Gadriel. "His name is Benjamin."

It wasn't the first time that I heard that question being asked. It made me feel very special.

"I am here to teach you something of the nature of angels, Benjamin," said Gadriel, "but I first must teach you the ways of detachment, and how a man or woman may find freedom and peace during their brief stay in the world of matter, so that they may ascend the Heavens and find eternal peace within the Paradise of God. Are you ready, my son, to learn these things?"

I looked at Satan and then back at Gadriel and nodded.

"Good! Very good!" said Gadriel, his voice growing sterner. "Know and remember, my son, that mankind is part of God, and as much as a part of God as we, his angelic servants. Understand that man's life within the world of matter is fraught with pain and suffering, each separated by only the merest fleeting periods of happiness. In many ways, the world of matter might rightly be considered to be a level of Gehenna, a division of Hell. In each incarnation man is doomed to suffer because his sufferings are the result of his multitudinous attachments to the things of the world. Man must come to realize that he owns nothing, and that whatever he calls his own is nothing but an illusion, a vanity. In his ignorance, mankind clings to notions of existence that are false ideas of permanence, impermanence, having, not having, truth, and lies. Although the idea of detachment is explained to them in the Book of Ecclesiastes, humankind misses the point, and goes on to suffer not only life after life in the world of matter, but also between his lives in the dark and torturous realms of Gehenna. If they would learn to let go of their attachments to the things of the world, then peace would reign among them. The hating, warring, and bloodshed would end. Remember these things, my son, when you return to the world of matter, for it will serve you if you do. Ah, I see that you have a question. Ask it and I shall answer."

"Yes," I said, looking up at the great angel. "Will the Messiah be teaching these things when he makes himself known to the world? Will his speaking of detachment become the means to bring about the necessary changes in man's life?"

"Only in part," said Gadriel. "Understand, Benjamin, that the patient is never cured by just hearing the medicine described to him. He must take that medicine! So it must be with the messages that will be presented to mankind by the Messiah. That is, hearing the message is fine, but they must be willing to apply the Messiah's teachings. Only then will they reap the benefit of having God's Chosen One among them."

"I understand." I said.

"Now," said Gadriel, "as to the nature of angels. Angels are, in truth, minor faces of God, not beings separate and apart from God. Each angel has a specific function to perform and that function is in the service of God. You may think of angels as masculine faces of God. We are called the Sarim. We are not independent of God as many believe. Like all other beings, we have to be empowered by the M'retz Na'she—we could not function otherwise. Man, in his ignorance, believes that our function is primarily to make his life easier, that we are his personal 'protective' angels, and more, that our function is to make the world of matter a paradise for him. We are even asked to do these things for him in his prayers. How ignorant mankind is of the truths of things." Gadriel shook his head and continued. "First, God does not even receive the prayers of those who are motivated by their own self-interests, so their pleas for angelic intervention are never entertained by God. Second, God will not authorize any angelic intervention in man's life, if by so doing it interferes with His Redemption. Any angelic action taken on the part of man that would ease man's pain would also cause man to further cling to the world by having him believe that God, indeed, would have the world a paradise."

"I understand. Please go on."

"Good. Only those who could be trusted by God not to abuse the use of His powers are given access to angels."

"How does someone earn the trust of God?"

"In order to be trusted with the use of angels and the powers of God, man must be free of attachment. If he is not rid of attachment then he would be controlled by his own desires. His judgment would be impaired and he would thus use the powers of God for his own selfish purposes and not for the good of God's Redemption. If a man or woman is under another person's control, then the receipt of that power would not be sanctioned, for they could not be trusted. This is because the person who controls them would make judgments for them concerning the uses of the powers of God. This will not be allowed. It is for this and other viable reasons, my son, that very few men living in the world of matter have actually been given such authorization. Do you have questions concerning this matter, Benjamin? I will give you answers."

"Yes. My question is this," I said, "how can mankind make the proper covenant with God?"

"The proper covenant with God will be both offered and explained to them by the Messiah, God's Chosen One. He will offer the world a new Covenant that will lead to the salvation of all of mankind. It is what many have been praying for."

"Are you saying that all former covenants will become null and void? There are so many religions in the world today claiming to be the correct and proper religion, claiming that all other religions are false. They call everyone outside of their religion pagans and infidels. What will happen to change all of this when the Messiah's presence in the world is known?"

Satan glanced over at me and smiled, I saw that he was pleased with my question.

"What I am saying, my son," said Gadriel, "is that a new Covenant will be offered to the world and that peace and deliverance can be theirs if they choose wisely."

"What if they don't? What if they don't accept the Messiah because they think that the Messiah is going to destroy their current beliefs?"

"Although they mean well in their current beliefs," said Gadriel, holding up both hands, "when the Messiah appears before them, they will voluntarily make the necessary changes, for through the Messiah they will come to know the Truth of God. They will see and believe."

The manner in which the angel Gadriel delivered his answers told me that this was very serious business.

"It is time! I must go now, Benjamin," said Gadriel, raising both of his hands and smiling gently. "I have taught you what you needed to know in this matter. You must move on to the sixth Heaven, where you may learn more. I wish you both peace in the Name of the One True God!"

Satan and I bowed as Gadriel faded into the Void.

"Come, Benjamin," said Satan, waving his arms, "the sixth Heaven awaits us."

The sixth Heaven, another galaxy of sheathed souls floating peaceably in the infinite Void of God, was much lighter and even less densely populated. It was clear that they were truly content to be here.

A moment after appearing in the sixth Heaven we were greeted by an angel whose demeanor was much more pleasant than the Archangel Gadriel's, but, as with most angels we had encountered, there was still a seriousness about him that announced the importance of his mission. He carried in his hand a large sapphire ball that radiated a brilliant indigo glow.

"I am the angel Rochel," he said, holding up one hand, the other hand turned palm up as the large sapphire ball slowly rose to hover above it. "I am a servant of the One True God, and I bid you both a gracious welcome in His Name."

"Thank you, brother," said Satan.

"This is Benjamin," said Satan, pointing to me.

"I know," said Rochel. "As you know full well, my brother, nothing is hidden from God. That is the lesson that I shall teach your charge."

Satan nodded and then looked to me.

"Benjamin," said Rochel, "I am the angel that retrieves that which is lost or hidden and would teach you the use of the power of the Sha'ar Ha'ar in such matters. Are you prepared to receive instruction, my son?"

I nodded and gave the angel Rochel my full attention.

"Fine! Fine, indeed!" he said, returning my nod. "Know, Benjamin, that nothing is hidden from God . . . nothing whatsoever! Through the use of the power of the Sha'ar Ha'ar you may be able to locate anything or anyone that is lost or hidden from sight. This is a most useful tool in the world of men."

He was right, it would be a very useful tool to have. My mind began to wander and I imagined all the things that I'd lost over the years that I would be able to find. Rochel's booming voice startled me out of my musings. I glanced at Satan, but he hadn't noticed my momentary lapse of concentration.

"Now," continued Rochel, "in order to locate lost or hidden things, first center yourself between the two worlds by using the Tebul Tov. Once you are centered and your mind is clear, close your eyes and picture in your mind the object you are looking for. For example, if you are seeking an article of jewelry, then have the picture of that article clearly formulated. If you are seeking a particular person, then picture that person's face clearly. Once it is done, take up your left hand and proceed to scan in a circle about you, just as you did under the tutelage of the Archangel Peniel. As you have experienced before, the heat in the palm of your hand will tell of the article or person's location. That heat is the M'retz Na'she generated by that object's Magen. This technique is called HaGe'lah, the Uncovering.[†] Do you understand this, my son?"

----

† See the *HaGe'lah*, the Uncovering, technique in the Appendix, page 388.

"Yes," I said, "I understand."

"I see that you have a question, though," said Rochel. "Send it on!"

"Rochel, the technique that you just described can be used for locating objects and people that are reasonably close. Would I be able to use this technique to locate hidden or missing people or objects that are very far away?"

"Of course," said Rochel, glancing toward Satan. "Distance is but an illusion. It is not a problem. I taught these things to King Solomon so that he could accurately locate the mines containing the wealth that the Lord God wanted him to have. Employing the HaGe'lah, he was able to locate great mines of gold in Ophir, Ramatan, and Selzidi, silver mines in Carnos, Velitan, and R'gaat, and diamond mines in Zinge, Met B'rin, Pol'hip, and Astira. He was also able to locate great deposits of emeralds, rubies, and sapphires. What I taught the king I will teach you, my son. With it you may find objects, hidden or lost, near or even at great distances. You may even locate people, living or dead, by its use, Benjamin."

It wasn't difficult to imagine all the uses for the HaGe'lah. The idea of using it to locate great sources of wealth didn't really appeal to me, but when I realized that it could be used to locate missing children or missing objects that might be of some use to the Messiah in his work—that definitely appealed to me!

"Now," continued Rochel, "to find lost or missing objects or people at great distances, Benjamin, get a large map. Then, perform the technique of HaGe'lah that I just described, but instead of passing your left hand about you in a circle, take your left hand and pass it in the air slowly over the map. The heat that appears in the palm of your hand will indicate the location. Remember, Benjamin, you must have the object of your search clearly in your mind. Do this and all will be well. This is the use of the HaGe'lah in the finding of things lost or hidden over great distances. A question, my son?"

"Yes, suppose that for some reason I'm not able to use the techniques that you just described? What would I . . . ."

"You should not have trouble with what I have just taught you. The Hage'lah will not fail. In any case, know that you may summon me in your moment of need and I shall find what you seek, for I serve those whom God has chosen to serve Him. I have taught you what I was instructed to, now I must go."

The angel Rochel wished us both well and faded from sight.

Though I was happy to have been instructed in the use of the HaGe'lah by the angel Rochel, I still wanted to know more about what the requirements were in order for a soul to ascend to the sixth Heaven. I also wanted to know what other angels served there. I knew that Satan could supply those answers.

"Satan," I said, turning to him, "what are the requirements for entrance into the sixth Heaven?"

Satan smiled. "The sixth Heaven is called Shamayim Berakhah, the Blessed Heaven. Those that have ascended to this Heaven have made their first true Covenant with God. That is, they had been instructed in the truth of the Ten Commandments and having acknowledged that they understood those Commandments, have sworn to God that they accepted those Commandments. This is known as the First Covenant. Those souls that you see here have lived the letter of their promise to God, and so, as a reward for their efforts have acceded to this blessed realm. Further, they have detached to a large extent from the things of the world and in so doing have furthered the cause of God's Redemption. They have spread among their fellow man the teachings of detachment, peace, and non-violence. God is gracious and giving, Benjamin, to those that further His Cause."

"Satan, you say that they've entered into the First Covenant. Are there other Covenants?"

"Yes, Benjamin, they will soon be explained to you."

"Suppose that a man or woman lived part or even most of their life without following the Commandments, but had a change of heart and decided to make Covenant, what then?

"If a man or woman has a change of heart and decides to enter into the First Covenant by accepting and implementing all ten of the Commandments, as well as living a life of detachment to the things of the world, spreading peace through non-violent means, then God, in his great mercy, shall forgive them of all their prior sins and they shall be as a newly born babe when they stand before him. This is God's promise to them, Benjamin. It will be a new beginning, a second chance. Further, the promises that God makes are set down in the Ninety-first Psalm. It's all there."

"I see. Then, there is always a chance for them to make Covenant with God."

"Yes, but only while they live. Repentance and acceptance must take place while they are incarnate in the world of matter. Once they enter one of the Hells, it is too late. They must wait until they enter the world of matter again before they can avail themselves of God's mercy. For this reason, mankind must take advantage of making the necessary adjustments to their philosophies while they live, and not fritter their lives away in vain and useless pursuit of things that will not ultimately be useful to them."

"Satan, what angels are resident in the sixth Heaven?" I asked.

"Many. The angels Zachiel, Asrasbarasbiel, Dirael, Gaghiel, Katzmiel, Zebul, Atufiel, Atsaftsaf, Bodiel, Caraniel, Parziel, Pesuker, and Tufriel are some of the residents here," he said.

"Have any of them done things that I might be familiar with?"

"Certainly," said Satan, smiling at me. "God sent the angel Gaghiel to punish pharaoh when pharaoh took Sarai, Abrahm's wife, as his own. Gaghiel struck the pharaoh with blindness and disease until the pharaoh returned Sarai to Abrahm. The angel Tufriel was sent by God to set the rainbow in the sky as the symbol of God's Covenant with Noah. It is a reminder to man that God will not destroy life on the earth in this way again. The angel Dirael was sent by God to punish the Amorites for the harm that they did against God's Chosen People Israel. The great angel Caraniel was the very same angel that God sent to punish the vile demons Rebek, Ornumas, and Dendarus for their participation in the destruction of the Second Temple. I have named only a few who are among the many angelic residents of this Heaven, Benjamin. Now, we must move on, my son."

I took one last look around at the sheathed souls finding bliss and blessing. A moment later, Satan and I departed the sixth Heaven.

22

The Upper Heavens

THE SEVENTH HEAVEN WAS A COMPLETE SURPRISE. IN A FABULOUS chamber of gleaming white marble, great angels stood silently among an untold number of sheathed souls who not only moved about the chamber, but were actually able to communicate with each other. A large indigo-colored curtain of flame hung just across the room from where we stood.

"This is wonderful!" I said, looking around the chamber.

"Yes, it is," said Satan with a smile on his face. "This is the seventh Heaven, my son. It is called Shamayim Na'ahleh, the Sublime Heaven."

"What angels are these?" I asked, looking at the angels scattered around the chamber.

"These are the angels who attend to those fortunate enough to receive sanctuary in this Heaven before being returned to life in the world of men. There are the angels Avriel, Gedudiel, Adiriah, Alat, Asamkis, Gehirael, Geroskesufael, and Labarfiel. They are all angelic guards. Avriel and Gehirael, the two angels on the far left, are the angels that God sent to capture the evil angel Araziel and bring him to the deepest level of Gehenna for punishment. The angel Alat was the angel that

God sent to protect King David when he fled from King Saul. Over there, standing in front of the curtain, are the great angels Boel and Kamiya. They are the two great Archangels who have the power to deny entry into the seventh Heaven."

"Are you saying that this isn't the seventh Heaven, but just a sort of ante-room?"

Satan nodded. "The seventh Heaven lies beyond that curtain of flame, Benjamin. If you are ready, then let us pass beyond the curtain."

We crossed the room and stood in front of the curtain of bright indigo flame. Both Boel and Kamiya nodded and bowed to us and then promptly parted the curtain with a wave of their hands. We passed into the realm of the seventh Heaven beyond.

"Satan, it's wonderful. No, it's absolutely magnificent!" I exclaimed as I took in the spectacle. Everything was gleaming white and the sheathed souls were completely mobile and inter-acted with each other in a very friendly and natural manner. It didn't have the scenery that the Lower Heavens had, but no one here seemed to mind.

"This is marvelous!" I said, turning again to Satan. "Everyone seems to be so happy here."

"You sense that, Benjamin? Well, they should be," said Satan, smiling. "It is a great blessing to be sent here. A very great bless-ing, indeed."

"What did they do to earn this?"

"Much, Benjamin, much. First, they maintained the barest of attachments to the things of the world. Second, they all have made and maintained their covenants with God. Third, they were all instrumental in the propagation of the truth of God's Redemption. That is, they helped spread the truth of the Tikkun among those in the world of matter that would listen. This made them God's servants, and God does not forget his servants, my son, not in life, and not in the life beyond life."

The words *not in life, and not in the life beyond life* suddenly awakened something unexpected in me. With Satan's words, I realized that death was just an illusion. Yes, of course we die, but only in a way. In truth, we continue to exist.

There is no real death! I thought, marveling at the sheathed souls before me, just a transition from one state to a slightly altered state, but it isn't death . . . it isn't the end to a person's existence.

I was just about to walk over to a small group of sheaths to my right when I heard a familiar voice calling my name. I turned, only to stare into the beaming face of my good friend Moloch, who stood not three feet from me in his sheathed form. It wasn't a human sheath, but a perfectly formed demonic sheath. There were no sores, no wounds, no blood, no scars, it was perfect.

"Moloch!" I cried, raising my hands in surprise. We moved toward each other and embraced like brothers reunited after years of separation.

"Benjamin, my good friend," Moloch said softly. "I . . . ."

I felt my eyes well up with tears. "Moloch, I never thought that I would see you again. I mean—"

"You mean, because you saw me die?" said Moloch, with a broad smile on his face. "My good friend, there is no death. There is just the changing of one's venue, that's all. I owe so much to God and King Solomon. If it weren't for them, I wouldn't be here. I'm so happy here."

All I could do was share Moloch's happiness. We embraced again. "So much has happened to me since that incident in the Dark Malkuth. You can't . . . ."

"I know! I know!" said Moloch, smiling. "Nothing is hidden from God, Benjamin. Listen, I have something to tell you, Benjamin, something wonderful!"

"What?" I asked, my curiosity piqued.

"Well . . . ."

"Come on . . . what?

"Well, I am to return to life as a Worker of Light. Can you believe it? I'll still be a demon, of course, and not human, but could you imagine, a real Worker of Light. I'm so happy."

"A Worker of Light?" I asked, not really knowing what a Worker of Light was.

"Yes, Benjamin," said Satan, standing next to us and smiling. "Moloch will, indeed, be a Worker of Light when he returns to life again. He has proven himself worthy of that status. He has pleased God very much."

I looked at Moloch and saw that he was all smiles. I turned back to Satan. "Satan, what exactly is a Worker of Light? I mean, I've heard people use that expression, but they never really explained it to me."

"Benjamin, there are many people in the world of matter who claim to be Workers of Light, but most offer false claims. A true Worker of Light is one who has entered into very special Covenants with God. They are called the Second and Third Covenants. Those that do not have these Covenants are not Workers of Light, they are misleading themselves and those who listen to them."

"What are the Second and Third Covenants?" I asked.

"Simply put, my son, they are Holy Promises, Holy Agreements. In the Second Covenant, one promises God to work for His Redemption throughout one's entire life. That is, one promises God to devote the rest of one's life to His service. In the making of the Third Covenant, one promises God to return to the work at hand, namely, His Redemption, throughout each and every future incarnation."

"Isn't it wonderful?" said Moloch, still beaming. "Benjamin, you . . . ."

"Oh, Moloch, I'm so happy for you!"

"Come, Benjamin, we must move on. You will see Moloch again, I promise!" said Satan. "Now, say your goodbyes."

"Really, Moloch," I said, almost unable to contain myself, "I'm so very happy for you. I want to thank . . . ."

"Come, Benjamin, we really must move on," said Satan again.

Moloch and I embraced again. "Bye, Benjamin, my friend. Be happy for me!"

"I am very happy. Goodbye, Moloch, I'll see you again."

I turned to look at Satan, and then turned to see Moloch again, but he was gone. When I thought of how he sacrificed his life for me in the Dark Malkuth, and how God rewarded him for it, I knew that the One True God was a just God, even in His dealings with demons. It was then that I really understood the truth; man or demon, God loves all of His servants.

"Come," said Satan, leading me over to an angel standing near us.

Right away I noticed that the angel wasn't as beautiful as the others I'd met, and certainly not as imposing either, but still this angel had a sort of majesty that made him seem quite overpowering. His magen was every bit as white and solid as all of the other angels, yet something was subtly different about him.

"This is the Archangel Halelviel, Benjamin," said Satan, nodding to the great angel. "He will speak to you of Death so that you may come to understand the mystery of it. Therefore, do as you have done before and be attentive to him. You will learn much."

I nodded to Satan and bowed to Halelviel, giving him my full attention.

"Benjamin," said Halelviel, raising his right hand, "I am instructed by God to teach you of death, so that you may know the truth of the matter."

I nodded.

"Know, my son," he said, "that life and death are, in the final understanding, not two different things. There is no end to the existence of your soul, of any soul. The physical body is nothing but an outer garment covering the sheathed soul. We call it the B'ged Ar'ee Shel Nefesh, the temporary garment of the soul. Just as a frayed and worn garment is discarded by a person, so is the body, the garment that clothes the soul, likewise discarded. This is the truth of the matter and cannot be disputed. Man is born with two sources of M'retz Na'she, which serve and sustain him throughout his life. Think of these sources of energy as wells.

The first source of M'retz Na'she is that source that needs to be replenished daily. It is called the B'ehr Ar'ehr, or the temporary well, and can be replenished from food, air, sun, sleep, and even from other incarnate beings. When this well needs refilling, the body becomes hungry and desires food, or becomes tired and requires sleep. You have a question, I see. Send it on, my son."

"Yes," I said, now accustomed to an angel's ability to read minds. "I understand that sleep, food, and the air are sources of the M'retz Na'she, but you also said that we can receive this energy from other incarnate beings? How does this—"

"Benjamin," said Halelviel, "everything in existence in the Light Malkuth has a magen composed of the M'retz Na'she. When one object or person comes into the vicinity of another object or person, an energy exchange takes place. The object or person with the least energy will have the tendency to draw the M'retz Na'she from the other object or person. This is a natural phenomenon, the world of matter seeking a balance. You have experienced this many times, Benjamin."

"I have?"

Halelviel smiled. "Yes! Have you not been around a person who makes you very tired, and you feel emotionally and physically exhausted after leaving them?"

"Yes."

"This is an example of that person draining the M'retz Na'she from you, from your B'ehr Ar'ehr, your temporary well. This type of person may be suffering from a temporary lack of energy, or may be constantly low on energy. If the latter is the case, then this person will drain M'retz Na'she from you at every meeting. Now, there are people who have an abundance of M'retz Na'she. These people are constantly radiating that energy and they draw many others to them, others that are aware of that abundance of energy and seek that person out so they can benefit from that energy by drawing it to themselves. They use that siphoned energy to recharge their own well, their own B'ehr Ar'ehr. The person with 'extra' M'retz Na'she normally becomes the central figure of a group. They become very popular and have many friends. Also, when people have pets, there is an exchange of M'retz Na'she between themselves and the animal. When a person is nervous or depressed, the pet exchanges its M'retz Na'she with that person, evening that person's energy out, thus producing a calming effect in that person. Do you understand these things?"

I nodded. Of course I understood everything that the Archangel Halelviel was speaking about. It was all true. Being around certain people had always left me drained, tired. I had always tried to avoid those people. On the other hand, people who had an excess of M'retz Na'she, I'd always seemed to be attracted to. Yusef is like that, so is my martial arts master.

"Good! Very good!" said Halelviel. "Now, the second source of energy, Benjamin, is a finite quantity of energy. You may think of it as a non-refillable well, a sort of permanent well. It is called B'ehr Shel Chai, the Well of Life. Everyone, Benjamin, is born with a certain amount of M'retz Na'she in this well. How much M'retz Na'she they have in their B'ehr Shel Chai determines the length of that person's life. As the finite M'retz Na'she of this well depletes, the body of man ages and withers. When there is no longer enough of the M'retz Na'she in the well to support one's life processes, then the body dies and is discarded by the sheathed soul. You have another question, Benjamin?"

"Yes. What of the sheath and the soul? What happens when the body dies?"

"The sheath is the ethereal body that contains the soul. We call this sheath the Nefesh C'lee Re'chev, the vehicle of the soul. At death, when the body is cast away, the Nefesh C'lee Re'chev, or sheath, leaves the body but is still attached to the body by the Ma'tah K'sef, the silver cord. It takes between forty-nine days and one year for total separation between the sheath and the physical body. At that time, the sheath containing the soul normally leaves the Light Malkuth and enters into a temporary world within the Void of God. There they wait to be assigned to one of the divisions of Hell in order to pay for their sins. After their Hell experiences, as you know, the soul then goes to one of the various Heavens for their rewards. Of course, one's Hell experiences, as well as one's Heaven experiences, are learning experiences. They are not places of permanent residence. Once completing their term in one of the Heavens, the sheathed soul enters the Guf, the Hall of Souls. There, the old sheath, the Nefesh C'lee Re'chev, is finally discarded. The soul enters a new sheath and awaits reincarnation."

"I see."

"The soul," he continued, "is now in its new Nefesh C'lee Re'chev. It is then placed in sperm and it enters into the world of matter through sexual union. The process of birth, growth, decay, and death begins again for that person. It is all really very simple."

"The sperm contains the soul?"

"Yes, Benjamin. The female egg contains the nutrients that will allow the growth of a new body based on the design of the new sheath, coupled with traits from both parents."

"I see. Halelviel, when a person dies, some say that they see a great light at the end of a long tunnel. Is this really what a dying person experiences?"

"Yes, Benjamin, it is true, but the light that they see is really nothing more than the differences between the two worlds. Malkuth, the manifest Universe, is a dark world compared to the world that the soul enters upon death. At death, the soul temporarily enters a place called Yesod. You can think of Yesod as a resting place, a depot. Being slightly closer to God, it is much brighter than Malkuth and so when the person first sees it, it appears as a light. Do you understand, Benjamin? It is a light only because of the darkness of Malkuth. In Yesod, a person may even see people they've known in life who may also be awaiting entrance into one of the Hells."

"Halelviel, you are teaching me so much. I can't begin to thank you for all of it. If you don't mind, I have only a few more questions."

"Of course, Benjamin. It has been most enjoyable to teach you. Please continue with your questions."

"Halelviel, what exactly is a ghost?"

Halelviel smiled. "A ghost, Benjamin, is nothing more than the Nefesh C'lee Re'chev, the sheathed soul separated either by death from the body, by a deep sleep, or by coma."

"A deep sleep? Coma? Death? What do you mean?"

"When a person enters into a deep sleep the sheathed soul may be seen hovering over his physical body. If one looks very carefully, one can see the silver cord that lies between them. In the case of a coma, the sheathed soul is locked out of the physical body and is unable to reenter. Because of the great attachments that person has had to the things of the world, the sheathed soul sometimes remains in the manifest world after death and is unable to leave to finish the death process. This causes their spiritual growth to be stilted. Of course, once the sheathed soul reaches total separation from its earthly existence and the silver cord is broken, they can no longer be seen as ghosts in the world of matter. If you understand these things, then you may ask one more question of me. I must leave you so that you might continue your journey."

"Yes," I said. I had a thousand more questions, but this was my final opportunity with Halelviel. "I understand and I thank you. There are many people who don't believe in reincarnation because they claim that if reincarnation really did exist they would be able to remember their past lives. Why can't people remember their former lives?"

"All of a person's past life experiences, Benjamin," said Halelviel, "are to be found recorded in their Higher Minds. But they cannot acquire that information because of their Lower Mind's interference. Their Lower Minds are simply too active, too loud for them to be able to access such memories. If they were trained properly, and their Lower Minds were made quiet, then they would be able to access the information stored in their

Higher Minds, the memories of their former existences. They would even be able to recall their Heaven and Hell experiences between those lives."

"I understand, thank you," I said, looking the great angel squarely in his bright indigo eyes. *Most people do have Lower Minds that are so loud that they couldn't possibly access their Higher Minds and remember their former lives. No wonder they would deny the existence of reincarnation,* I thought.

"The Messiah," interjected Satan, "will teach mankind how to quiet their Lower Minds so that the truth of such things may be known to them."

"Good, Benjamin," said Halelviel, "then I will leave you with this last thought. So long as humankind continues to quest after things of naught, relentlessly clinging to the things of the world, their grief in both life and the after-life shall continue. If humankind wants to be free of their fears, to be free of violence, and to attain the eternal bliss of Paradise, then they must accept the terms of the New Covenant to be offered to them by the Messiah. There will be no other way. Now, I bid you both peace in the Name of the One True God!" Halelviel smiled, raised his right hand, and then vanished.

"Halelviel is correct, you know," said Satan, turning to me. "Accepting God's New Covenant is the only way for humankind to become free. Come now, let us leave." Satan waved his hand and we left the seventh Heaven.

WE WERE IMMEDIATELY IN THE EIGHTH HEAVEN, IN A BRILLIANTLY lit great hall made of the clearest blue sapphire. Even the numerous columns around the chamber were of blue sapphire.

A great angel stood in the middle of the chamber. His very presence brought me a peace like I had never experienced before. He radiated that peace from the very center of his being. I looked at Satan, and wondered if he was experiencing the same peace.

"I am the Archangel Raphael," he said in a low, smooth, and melodic voice. "I greet you both in the Name of the One True god, and welcome you to Shamayim Zohar Gadol, the Heaven of the Great Splendor, the eighth Heaven." A broad but gentle smile appeared on Raphael's face. He raised both of his hands, palms upturned, and the chamber began to glow with a brilliance that forced me to close my eyes.

When I opened my eyes, I found that we had been transported into a realm of amazing splendor. Instead of the blackness of the Void of God, we were immersed in a clear sapphire light. All around us numerous angels hovered in the air. Below each angel were sheathed souls that glowed an extraordinary white. It appeared that each sheathed soul was guarded by its own angel. Looking around, I noticed that the population of this Heaven, the Shamayim Zohar Gadol, was much smaller than that of the seventh Heaven. The bliss of the sheathed souls residing here was more than apparent, it was astounding. Each sheath seemed to radiate bliss, and I knew that they must have been blessed during their lives in order to have been placed here.

"The sheaths that you see before you, Benjamin," said Raphael, "contain the souls of those who in life made a very special Covenant with God. They chose to commit their lives to the work that will ultimately lead to God's Redemption. They are blessed among most of mankind. The special Covenant that they had made with God is called The Second Covenant, or HaB'reet HaGadol, The Great Covenant. It is of the HaB'reet HaGadol that I speak, so that you may know it and its terms when you return to the world of men."

"Each of those that you see here have been assigned an angel to guard over them and instruct them in the true nature of things. This is God's reward for their work on His behalf. Their stay in the divisions of Hell were commuted, for they were blessed by God, Himself."

I looked at Satan and saw that he was pleased with what was happening here. The sight of the sheathed souls in the eighth Heaven seemed to make him very happy.

"Those here," continued Raphael, "have, in life, promised God to work for the benefit of God's Redemption. As part of their covenants, they have sworn before God to detach themselves from the mundane world and pursue the eternal. Under the direction of their teachers, these blessed souls performed selfless services for the Lord God. One of their duties was to assist their teachers in the correction of those who were either intentionally or unintentionally impeding God's Redemption. When the Messiah presents to the world God's New Covenant, the number of souls that reside here in the eighth Heaven will increase. You have questions, I see."

Of course I had questions, but the peace that I was experiencing here was so overwhelming that I had to struggle just to formulate them. "How did these people come to serve God?" I asked. "Were they chosen or—"

"Each of those here, my son, are spiritually evolved to the point where God, in His infinite Wisdom, saw to it that their paths crossed the path of one of the Bene haAur, the Children of Light. Once they had met a member of the Bene haAur, their spiritually developed Higher Minds told them of the path in life that they should take."

"The Bene haAur?"

"You will learn of the Bene haAur soon, Benjamin." said Raphael, abruptly interrupting me.

"What are the terms of the Covenant that these blessed people had made with God?"

"Again, the terms of their covenants were very simple," said Raphael, "but do not be fooled by that simplicity. It was God's wish to have them assist the Bene haAur, but in order to do that correctly they had to swear unto God not only their allegiance, but they had to learn each of the ten levels of the Ten Commandments of God as taught specifically by the Bene haAur, and they had to both accept and implement each one in their lives. Further, they had to turn their current lives over to God and work towards His Redemption. They had to learn to be in the world, but not of the world. Once they had committed to God's Redemption, they were held responsible for the fulfillment of those promises. In return, God promised to protect them and grant them His blessed peace, both in the world of matter, and in the Higher Heavens at the end of their incarnation. Each of them, at the time they made covenant, was assigned an angel to watch over them. The angels that you see here are the very same angels. They will remain with them even after they reincarnate back to the world of matter."

"What if they fail to keep their side of the Covenant?"

Raphael's face turned serious and his great magen began to pulsate. "If it isn't their fault, then God will understand and all will be well with them. But, if it is their fault, then God will punish them more severely than He would the ordinary person because it is better not to make promises to God, than to make those promises and not fulfill them. Once a Covenant is made their fate is sealed. They must learn from the Bene haAur how to live in the world of men, but to not be part of the world of men. This is the way of true spirituality. The only way truly meaningful to God!"

I wanted to know more about the Bene haAur. I looked at Satan and, with a smile, he encouraged me to continue my questioning.

"If those who reside here have devoted their entire last incarnation to working for God's Redemption, what will happen to them when they return to the world?"

"That is a matter for them to decide," said Raphael. "If they come into contact with members of the Bene haAur in their next lives, and they should, then they may once again be given the opportunity to enter into the Second Covenant with God. They would be given that choice. However, if they decide not to do so, then one of the Hells and a lesser Heaven would await them when they depart that life, just as it would the ordinary person."

I was about to ask another question when Satan interrupted. "It is time for Raphael to move on, Benjamin," he said, turning to me.

"Farewell, my son," said Raphael with a smile. The Archangel Raphael departed, disappearing in a blinding flash of indigo light.

"What other angels reside in the eighth Heaven?" I asked, turning to Satan.

"Many, Benjamin, many. Among them are the great angels Hefriel, Galeniel, Mephisiel, Todgadfiel, Khasdiel, Todatamael, and Ruhiel. The angel Hefriel was sent by God to warn King David of the plot against him by his son Absolom. Galeniel was the angel who brought the great famine to Egypt in the time of Joseph. King Solomon used the angel Mehpisiel to destroy the evil demons Meresin and Sallos when the great king learned of their plot to kill his good friend King Hiram of Tyre. Todatamael was sent by God to protect Isaac during his life, his guardian angel. The great angel Ruhiel serves under the Archangel Metatron and prevents unauthorized entreaties from reaching him. As I have said, my son, there are many great angels residing here. Now Come, Benjamin!" Satan said. "It's time."

With a wave of his hand we left Shamayim Zohar Gadol.

WE FOUND OURSELVES SUSPENDED IN THE MIDDLE OF A BRILLIANTLY lit indigo colored void of infinite dimensions. The atmosphere was more peaceful, more calming, more mystical than even that of the eighth Heaven. The peace was so intense that it was almost palpable. On this level, there were few sheathed souls, in fact I could actually count its inhabitants. Most of the brilliantly glowing sheaths were each attended by twenty powerful angels who surrounded their charge in every direction. There were twenty-six sheaths, however, that were separated from all the others. Each of those sheaths was surrounded by literally thousands of angelic attendants.

Each sheath and its attendant group of angels, including the twenty-six special sheaths, were surrounded by a transparent shield, like a bubble of iridescent indigo. The whole scene was utterly breathtaking. Satan even turned to me and started to laugh a little bit when he saw me standing there with my mouth open.

"Are you impressed with this, Benjamin?" he asked, smiling. "Know this to be Shamayim Osher Aharon, the Heaven of Ultimate Bliss; it is the ninth Heaven."

All I could do was stare at the wonderful spectacle before me. I couldn't even form a question. I knew that Satan understood my dilemma.

"You will become accustomed to this Heaven," said Satan, with a smile. "I know you have questions. They will be answered, please be at ease."

At ease? I don't think that I've ever felt more at ease in my life. There was so much peace there that I didn't want to leave, and I imagined myself having to be picked up and physically tossed out of there by angelic guards when the time came for us to go.

I finally gathered my thoughts and was about to respond to Satan when an angel of such magnificence, of such a peaceful demeanor and grace appeared before us. He was clad in white and glowed brilliantly against the mystical indigo background of the Void.

"I welcome you both, in the Name of the One True God, to Shamayim Osher Aharon, the ninth Heaven, the Heaven of Ultimate Bliss," the angel said, raising both arms with palms facing us. "I am the Archangel Uriel, servant of the One True God, and am sent to teach you, my son, about those who may attain unto this Heaven."

I looked around at the angels clustered about the sheathed souls. As was his habit, Satan remained politely silent.

"Those that you see here, my son, are of the Bene haAur," said Uriel, pointing in a wide arc around him. "Know that these great souls, who dwell in the Bliss of God, are the true Workers of Light. Know that while they exist here in the Shamayim

Osher Aharon, they also exist and function in the world of matter, the Light Malkuth. It is their task to perform God's will among mankind. They are the Blessed of God for they have entered into the HaB'reet HaAharon, the Third Covenant with Him. These blessed servants have promised God to devote every life, every incarnation, to work for His Redemption. Upon the ending of each incarnation they do not enter into a division of Hell for they are the Blessed of God. There is no greater task, Benjamin, than to do the work necessary for the fulfillment of God's Redemption."

I thought about what the Archangel Uriel was saying, imagining what it must be like to actually work for God each and every incarnation. I knew not only that it was a blessing, but that I would do it too, if I were offered the opportunity.

"The angels that you see surrounding each of the Bene haAur are their angelic households. Each angel is skilled in a particular function and is attendant upon the needs of that person to whom they are assigned. The Bene haAur are only allowed to have one attachment in the world of men, my son, and that attachment is to be to a mate who will balance them in life. That mate is a gift to them from God and is to share in both their lives and in the work at hand. I see that you understand."

"I do," I said.

"Good!" said Uriel, his great magen gently pulsating.

"Who are the Bene haAur? Are they—"

"The Bene haAur are those of the HaB'reet HaAharon, the Third Covenant. Their leaders are the former kings of God's Chosen People Israel. Solomon, David, and Asa are among their numbers. It is King Solomon whom God has chosen to take charge of the Bene haAur, for he has been appointed to oversee the Tikkun in the world of matter. The leadership of the Bene haAur numbers twenty-six in all."

"What will be the relationship between the Messiah and the Bene haAur when the Messiah appears?"

"The Bene haAur will be his support and work under his instruction. Together they will bring the Word of God to the peoples of the world and unite them into one great religion."

"What powers do the Bene haAur have that help them work for God's Redemption?" I asked, my curiosity about these great people growing.

"They have the ability to use the angelic powers of those in their households, Benjamin. This allows them not only the ability to heal mankind of physical diseases and other medical problems, but to be able to heal them psychologically and spiritually, as well. They can raise the dead by reuniting the separated sheath with the physical body. They can control the elements and bring about what humankind calls miracles. They can do much, my son, for they have the use of the powers of the angels of God. But, understand that anything they commit to do involving the use of those powers must be used for the benefit of the Tikkun and cannot be employed for any personal reasons. The use of the powers of God by the Bene haAur can and will, for example, be used to bring about a great many changes in people's lives in order to make them more spiritual. This is sanctioned by God because it is ultimately good for the Tikkun. Know further that they may even destroy or cause the death of individuals if, as a result of that action, the Tikkun is benefited."

"If the Bene haAur returns life after life to work the Tikkun, when will their reincarnations come to an end?"

"The Bene haAur will be the last to leave Ain Sof Aur, the manifest Universe, when the Ha'masah, the End-Time, comes. The Messiah, of course, will be the very last to leave. Know that—" Uriel suddenly stopped speaking.

I glanced at Satan, wondering why the Archangel Uriel had suddenly gone silent, and noticed that Satan was stepping back, creating a little distance between us. When I looked back at Uriel I saw that he had both hands raised and his palms facing me. He said nothing but remained in that position for a moment. Suddenly, two other angels appeared, one on either side of him. Later, I would learn that the angel to his right was the Archangel Pahadren and the angel to his left was the Archangel Boamiel. They stood side by side, their hands raised as if communing with God, Himself. After a few moments all three angels lowered their arms and gave me a small bow. I didn't know what they meant by the small bow, but assuming it to be courtesy, I returned the bow.

"I wish you both peace in the Name of the One True God," said Uriel, as he and the two angels at his side dissolved into the Void and a fourth angel appeared in their place.

The newly arrived angel stood silent among the sheaths of the ninth Heaven. I looked at Satan for some sort of explanation and he approached me.

"Benjamin, the great angel that stands before you is the Archangel Anael. He is very special, my son, only he can open the gates to the final Heaven, to Paradise. That he has appeared before you is a great event. It means that he will allow you entrance into the final Heaven. I must remain here."

"Aren't you going with me?" I asked, looking at the Archangel Anael and then back to Satan. "How can I go on without you?"

"No, my son," said Satan, with a very serious expression on his face. "I am not, nor are these other angels, permitted entrance to this final Heaven. Even the Archangel Anael, who has the power to pass you into the tenth Heaven, cannot enter that Heaven himself."

"But . . . ."

"Be happy, my son, for you have been blessed by God. Do not fear! You must trust God in this matter. I will wait here for your return. Now go and stand before that great angel so that he may grant you entrance."

23

Union With God

ANAEL STOOD SILENT, STARING AT ME WITH A STOIC EXPRESSION ON his face. I stood before him not knowing what to expect. It was the first time that I was going to travel without Satan, and I was nervous. His eyes seemed to look right through me as if I were transparent, which made our difference in stature seem even more significant. He finally diverted his eyes from me to cast a quick glance at Satan. Although they didn't speak, I was sure that in that one quick glance a great deal of information passed between them. The confidential exchange between the two great angels made me feel very uneasy.

After a moment, the Archangel Anael glanced at me again and then turned away from both of us and raised both of his arms, his palms facing outward. I didn't see anything happen. I glanced at Satan, who gestured that I should be patient. Another fifteen seconds elapsed and the Archangel Anael turned to me. "Enter now, Benjamin. It is time."

I looked but couldn't see anything there. I turned and gave Satan another questioning look, and he indicated that I should walk forward. I did as Satan told me, not quite sure that there was actually anything there or that anything was actually going to happen when I did. Then, as I took my fourth step, Archangel Anael and Satan suddenly disappeared. So did the Bene haAur and all of the ninth Heaven—it was all gone. With that fourth step, I had passed through some invisible portal and had entered a realm much different than any I had experienced before. It was like floating in the infinity of the Void of God—except that instead of the clear darkness, I was floating in the depths of an infinite ocean of the purest, warmest, whitest light. It was the brightest light that I had ever seen, yet it didn't seem to affect my vision. Pervading the light, coming from every direction, were the sweet voices of the Kadishim singing their eternal praises to God.

I looked around and realized that there was nothing to see—there were no shadows, no angels, only the clear white light. I floated in the light waiting, knowing that if I waited long enough, something would eventually happen. I felt my heart beating in my chest with so much force that I thought that I would pass out.

I don't know how long I'd been floating there when something began to happen to me. It was subtle at first, but gradually picked up momentum. It was as if my very being were starting to dissolve. I lost the feeling of my body. It was as if I were actually merging with the light and there was nothing that I could do about it. I felt helpless as my body seemed to merge with the light. I was the light. There was no "me," yet at the same time, there was a "me." It was the oddest, yet most pleasant sensation that I had ever experienced.

I had no sense of the passage of time, no conscious thoughts, yet somehow I was thinking. It was like thinking without thinking. Suddenly, the white light that I was immersed in turned to a deep, electric shade of indigo and began to pulsate, changing from indigo to white, and back to indigo over and over before finally turning back to a steady white again. I felt purified, as if every cell, every molecule, every atom, every electron, every meson of my body had just been cleansed of an eternity of collected defilement.

Suddenly, something else started to happen. I began to see visions, images of the Void of God, of the Great Flashing, of angels, of Creation. There were images of everything in existence, things familiar to me, and things unfamiliar. There were images of earth, the planets, the solar system, angels, demons, people, animals, supernovas, earthquakes, balmy tropical isles, frozen polar regions, trees, sand, skies, everything that existed and everything that didn't exist, it was all there. At first, the images came at me very slowly, but they gradually increased in speed until they became nothing more than great flashes of blinding color. I could do nothing as each image passed through me like myriad shadows passing through a shadow. But there was something else. Each time I felt an image pass through me I had the sensation of merging with it. Every image brought me into an infinite number of worlds, and each of those worlds was composed of an infinite number of other worlds. Still they came— images of lights, mountains, valleys, oceans, storms, sunlight, shadows, stars, galaxies, deaths, births, martyrs, temples, churches, mosques, and much more.

Sounds began to assail me from every direction, each abounding in infinite combinations of tonal possibilities—screams, laughter, crying, an infinite number of beating hearts, waves pounding against rocky shores. It seemed that all existence was bound within the infinity residing within each of those images and sounds. Faster and faster the images and sounds passed through me, until, at last, they subsided in a last blinding flash of light, leaving me alone and in total peace. I had no thoughts, no fear. All I had was the overwhelming feeling of peace, one I had never known before. I was suddenly in union with all of existence. I was that white light.

I was floating there, at peace with all existence, when I heard my name being called. "Benjamin," said the Voice, "Benjamin, open your eyes!"

I opened my eyes and I found myself surrounded by seventy-two masculine faces of seemingly infinite dimensions. Each of the seventy-two faces was composed of an infinite number of other faces turned and looking off in an infinite number of directions. Each had eyes of the deepest clearest indigo. I found myself peering into each and every set of eyes, and seeing within them infinite worlds within infinite worlds within infinite worlds. Every one of the infinity of faces that surrounded me had its own characteristics, and instinctively I knew that they all shared an incredible oneness that defied description.

I was spellbound in the presence of those images. I had no thoughts and still no feeling of my body, but I was there, whole and safe. Suddenly, the faces began to speak to me in unison—an infinite number of faces and voices simultaneously passing through me.

"Benjamin, I am the Lord your God," said the voices, "the source of all existence, and all non-existence. Everything that you have seen, that am I. Know that I am the beginning and the end of all that is, and all that is not; all that must be, and all that cannot be. Know that all that is exists within My being, for nothing can exist outside of Me. I am the Lord God of all beings, of all things, of all existence. In all the faces that you see before you, know that I, the Lord God, am One. Know, Benjamin, that there is but one purpose in all of creation, and that purpose is My Redemption. Benjamin, you shall be of great aid in its cause for you shall know My Face and you shall be of My Spirit. Now, close your eyes and raise your hands above your head and do not lower them until I tell you."

The very moment that I closed my eyes and raised my hands above my head, I felt the Spirit of God enter me. It entered through the palms of my hands, through the area between my eyebrows, through my Heart Sephira, and up from the Void of God through the Sha'ar Ha'ar, the Gate of Glory. My soul was filled with His Spirit.

"In you," said God, "I have poured My Spirit so that humankind and demon-kind all may know Me through you. Now, lower your hands and open your eyes!"

I opened my eyes and slowly lowered my hands to my side only to find that I was deep within the Void of God standing outside of the Gates of Heaven. Satan was standing in front of me. He bowed to me and looked at me with delight.

"Know that we are with you, Benjamin, the hosts of the Heavens and the hosts that serve the One True God throughout all of existence. What you need, we His angels, shall, in the Name of God, provide. Do you understand, Benjamin? Yes, I know that you do. Now, Benjamin, your friends await you. It is time for me to return you to the world of men so that you may finish your tasks for God."

"I . . . I . . . ."

"I know," said Satan, smiling. "I know, my son! Now, be happy. Turn around and take three steps forward. Do not look back."

I nodded, and just as I made my third step I found myself passing through the mountain wall through which I had first entered into this odyssey. It seemed so long ago. Standing there waiting for me were Yusef, Muhammad, Mara, and Ali. They were standing in almost the exact positions they had been in when I left. They all stood in silence, staring at me with their mouths agape. Looking at them in their abject stupor I knew that none of them would break the silence.

"Hello, everyone," I said, trying to get them to at least close their mouths, "I'm back. Hello . . . hello!"

Mara ran over to me. "Benjamin," she cried. She threw her arms around me and gave me a warm kiss. No one else seemed to be able to speak or move.

I expected Yusef to be the first of the group to break the silence; instead it was Muhammad. "Benjamin, my friend, are—"

"This is really great," I said, smiling at Muhammad and winking at Ali. "I finally came back after days of separation and you can't even find the word *hello* in your vocabulary. What's wrong?"

"I'm sorry," said Muhammad, "it's just that you've changed . . . er . . ."

"Changed?"

"Your hair! It's grayed a little, and your eyes, they're different too. And . . . and, there's something else different about you that I can't quite explain. And . . . ."

I did feel different. I felt the Spirit of God in me, and I suspected that it showed. I waited for Muhammad to finish his sentence, but he couldn't, all he did was stutter. "And what?" I said at last.

"And, well, you weren't gone for days or even hours, Benjamin." Muhammad said, covering his mouth with his hands. "You were only gone for six minutes."

"Six minutes? No. I—"

"Only six minutes," said Mara, looking at her watch. "That's all, just six minutes."

Of course, I thought, why not? Time is just an illusion, like life is an illusion. I looked at Yusef, it was all there in his face. His smile told me that he was glad to see me back safely, but his eyes—his eyes expressed something else. They expressed a knowing, something beyond words, something that told me that he knew somehow, not only what I had been through, but what I had learned along the way.

"Come, everyone, and I'll tell you what happened," I said, trying to break the lethargy. "Oh, Yusef, I didn't come back with Satan's Veil, but then again I did. Satan said that you would understand."

"I know, my son, I know," said Yusef, coming over and embracing me. All of a sudden, the shock that held the rest of the spellbound group in check wore off, and everyone sprang to life, gathering around me, hugging me, and welcoming me back.

24

The Accident

FROM THEIR VANTAGE POINT NEAR THE TOP OF THE RIDGE FACING the mountain, the three Mossad agents were able to see everything that was taking place below.

"Boss," said Avram, "did you see that? The American walked through solid rock, didn't he? Then, six minutes later he walked back out of solid rock. Boss, I'm telling you these aren't normal people. I've never seen anything—"

"Quiet," snapped Jehuda, looking at his map and drawing lines on it with a black marker.

"What's up?" asked Yitzak, looking over Jehuda's shoulder at the map.

"I'm not sure, but I'm going to find out. What are they doing now?"

"They're sitting and talking by the cars," said Avram, refocusing his binoculars and wiping the sweat from his forehead.

"I wish we had our sound equipment," said Yitzak, looking at Avram and then at the map Jehuda was working on. "I'd focus that parabolic dish on the old man and the American, and then we'd know their whole life stories."

"Yeah," said Avram. "Remember the time that we were—"

"Quiet, you two," said Jehuda. "There's something else here that's strange."

"What?" asked Yitzak.

"All right," said Jehuda, pointing to the map. "We've trailed these guys to five places, right?"

"Right," said Yitzak, trying to get a better look at the map.

"All right! I mapped out the five places and . . . ."

"And?" said Avram.

"And, when I connected the five places on the map, they formed a perfect pentacle."

"A pentacle, boss?" asked Avram, not taking his eyes from the little group below.

"You know, a five pointed star with Jerusalem right in the middle of it. Damn! If this isn't a freakin' pentacle, then I'm the pope's stepmother."

"What do you make of it?" asked Yitzak, looking at the pentacle drawn out on the map. "Something occult?"

"I don't know. It's all so crazy. I mean, we've seen a lot of strange things from these guys. I don't know why I should be surprised that . . . ."

"Hey, boss," said Avram, readjusting his position, "the American and the old man are walking off."

"Follow them," said Jehuda, "but don't let them see you. Yitzak, take over and watch the others."

"What? You want me to follow them?"

"Avram, get off your ass . . . ."

"Er . . . right, boss," answered Avram, jumping up and getting ready to move.

Yitzak replaced Avram on the ledge and took over the surveillance of Muhammad, Mara, and Ali.

"Avram, I know that you're one of the best there is at this," said Jehuda, looking him directly in the eye, "but, don't get us busted, all right?"

Avram nodded to Jehuda, turned, and then started to make his way along the ledge.

The ledge was uneven and varied in width, narrowing in spots that barely allowed him passage. He made his way carefully, trying to keep from kicking any of the small stones that were scattered on the ledge to the large rounded rocks below. He managed to keep up with Yusef and Benjamin as they walked and talked. Then it happened: he made a false step, slipping on some loose stones and he came down hard on the ledge. There was a loud cracking sound as he struggled to get to his feet, but it was too late, the ledge gave way beneath him and Avram fell twenty feet to the rocks below. There was no scream, not a sound from Avram as he tumbled with the falling pieces of ledge. The cracking of the shattering ledge, and the sounds of the falling rocks crashing on the large boulders below, caught everyone's attention.

"Avram!" cried Yitzak, training his binoculars on the body of Avram stretched motionless across a large gray boulder. "Oh, Avram . . . ."

Jehuda stood up, put his binoculars to his eyes, and saw Muhammad, Mara, and Ali running over to the fallen Avram. From the left he saw Benjamin and Yusef also converging on his fallen comrade. "Let's go down . . . we're busted. Screw it!" he said to Yitzak.

Yitzak turned, dropped his binoculars, and nodded his agreement. The two of them took off down a small path that led from the ridge to the floor and then ran to where Avram lay.

25

The Miracle

Mara, scrambling up a few small boulders, got to Avram first. She felt for a pulse but found none. She placed her ear to his chest and listened for a heartbeat. "He's dead!" she said, her voice stirring with emotion as everyone else converged on the fallen man.

Immediately, everyone turned their attention to Jehuda and Yitzak.

"Who are you? Why are you here?" snapped Muhammad angrily, looking at Jehuda and Yitzak.

"That's none of your business!" said Yitzak, moving toward Avram's body and being pushed back hard by Muhammad. "Your friend is dead! Who are you?"

Yitzak tried again to get to Avram but was shoved back again by Muhammad even harder.

Yitzak's concern for Avram suddenly turned to rage. He went back at Muhammad and threw a punch, narrowly missing Muhammad's nose.

"Yitzak!" yelled Jehuda, grabbing him around the shoulders. "That's enough! He's dead."

Muhammad was just about to punch Yitzak when he was stopped by Yusef. "Muhammad, don't!" said Yusef sternly. Muhammad dropped his fist, muttering to himself in Arabic.

"Who are you?" asked Yusef.

"The question is who are you," snapped Yitzak. "What the hell are you doing out here and what . . . ."

"That's enough, Yitzak," said Jehuda, still restraining him. "We're not going to get anywhere this way. Now settle down." Jehuda released Yitzak, who was in an intense staring contest with Muhammad. Both men stood with their eyes narrowed, focused on each other.

"These guys are terrorists," said Yitzak, continuing to glare at Muhammad.

Muhammad raised his hand in a fist ready to go at Yitzak. "No, Muhammad," said Yusef. Muhammad begrudgingly relaxed his fist and muttered to himself in Arabic again.

Jehuda took out his gun and trained it on us. "Search them, Yitzak."

"Right!" he said, staring at Muhammad. "I'll start with this guy." He searched all of us, being especially rough on Muhammad.

"They're clean," said Yitzak.

"What about the guns?" asked Jehuda.

"Right. Where are the guns, you two?" asked Yitzak, looking at Mara and Ali.

"They're in the van," said Ali, nervously.

"All right, look," said Jehuda, reaching into his pocket to produce his identification card, which he tossed to Yusef. "We're agents of the Mossad. We've been tracking you guys since you checked the American out of the King David."

Yusef looked at the card and then handed it back to Jehuda.

"Why were you following us?" asked Yusef.

"I did it on a hunch. All of you people were acting strangely."

"Then you were following us all the time?" asked Yusef.

"Yes, all the time, and I want to know what those canisters are that you've been collecting," said Jehuda sternly.

"Don't forget that stick," yelled Yitzak, training his weapon on the group.

"Right," said Jehuda. "Don't you think that everything we've seen you people do since you left Jerusalem would make us suspicious?"

"I could see where it would," said Yusef. Mara walked over to Yusef and hooked her arm through his.

"You either tell us what the hell's going on or we'll discuss this thing back in Jerusalem at headquarters. Either way, we're going to get to the truth. Make it easy on yourselves."

"Yusef, he's right," whispered Mara.

"Very well," said Yusef. "Very well."

"Is it all right with your big Arab friend if we take our man down?" asked Yitzak, challenging Muhammad with a smirk.

Yusef nodded to Muhammad. Muhammad and Yitzak carried Avram's body from the boulder and gingerly placed him on the desert floor.

"Now let's sit and talk, shall we?" said Jehuda.

"Back at the vehicles?" asked Mara.

"No, here. I want all of you people to sit down right here and tell me what the hell is going on," said Jehuda, motioning with his gun toward the ground.

Mara slid over to me and held my hand; I could feel her nervousness as we all sat.

"Well," said Jehuda, "I'm waiting for an explanation."

"It's kind of complicated," began Yusef, looking up at Jehuda.

"Make it uncomplicated," said Jehuda. "Make it simple for us simple folk."

"Well then, simply put, we've been collecting religious relics—"

"There it is, Jehuda, they're looking to get these thing out of the country," interrupted Yitzak, having another staring contest with Muhammad.

"No!" said Mara. "We're not thieves."

"That's okay, child," said Yusef. "Not to worry."

"Well?" said Jehuda.

"Suppose I told you that we were on a special mission for God?" said Yusef.

"I'd say that you were deranged," said Jehuda.

"Well, suppose I can prove it to you?"

"How?"

Yusef turned to me. "Bring him back, Benjamin."

"What?" I said.

"Bring him back to life, Benjamin," said Yusef.

I looked at Avram's body and then back at Yusef.

"Go on, Benjamin. Trust God. It will be all right."

"Are you saying that he can . . ." began Jehuda.

"I'm saying that what I've told you is true," said Yusef.

Jehuda looked at Yitzak. "Why not," said Yitzak, "what do we have to lose? What does Avram have to lose. Besides, remember the lightning and the—"

"All right. Go ahead, but no funny business," said Jehuda.

"Do it, Benjamin," said Yusef. "Trust God."

"But . . ." I began.

"Do it. Remember what you were told, Benjamin," Yusef said, with a small smile. "God will not fail you! You must trust God! Remember, the prophets Elijah and Eli did it. They trusted!"

"Trust God," I said aloud to myself, turning my attention to Avram. Now I would know whether my experiences with Satan in the various Heavens and Hells had been hallucinations or reality.

Everyone inched closer to the body.

"Give him room!" said Muhammad, glancing at Yusef with a questioning look.

I took a deep breath and knelt down beside Avram. I looked at Yusef one last time before I put it to the test. Yusef didn't say a word, he just raised an eyebrow and nodded to me. I nodded back to him and saw tears begin to well up in his eyes.

"What the hell is—" began Yitzak.

"Sssh!" said Yusef, holding his index finger to his lips. "Trust God!"

I stared at Avram and placed the palm of my left hand on his forehead. I closed my eyes and a thousand images flashed across my mind: images of Satan and all of the angels I encountered during my incredible odyssey, things that were said, promises that were made, and most importantly the experiences that I had in the tenth Heaven. That was God! I began to pray, asking God to redeem the life of the man lying dead in front of me. I didn't know what to expect. Suddenly, it came to me in a great flash of knowing. I felt myself simultaneously floating in the great Void of the tenth Heaven and kneeling beside the fallen Avram. A moment later I felt something stir inside of me. It came from deep within the Void of God, and passed upwards through the Sha'ar haAr, through my arm, and out of my left palm. It was the power of God! An almost imperceptible indigo glow encircled my hand and slowly spread to encompass all of Avram's body. A few seconds later I withdrew my hand, knowing instinctively that it was done.

I gazed up at everyone briefly and then down at Avram as he slowly stirred back to life. Everyone's jaws dropped in disbelief. Everyone, that is, except Yusef. He had a gentle smile on his face as he wiped the tears from his cheeks.

"Hi, boss," said Avram, opening his eyes and groggily looking up at Jehuda.

Everyone gasped.

"What the hell?" said Yitzak.

"Not hell," said Yusef, "God!"

"Er . . . how are you doing, Avram," said Jehuda, bending down over him and then turning to look at me with an expression of disbelief.

Mara, with a look of both awe and pride, came over to me, hugged me, and kissed me.

"Hi, Avram. How do you feel?" said Jehuda, smiling, kneeling, and briefly pressing Avram's head against his chest. "You gave us quite a scare. Are you all right?"

Avram moved his head in a small circle and then checked the rest of his body with his hands. "I'm fine, boss. Hey, I had the strangest dream. I . . . ."

"Can you stand up?"

"I think so? Yeah, I'm all right!"

"Good, then get up you son of a bitch!" yelled Yitzak, with a big smile on his face. "Welcome back to the world of the living."

"World of the living?" asked Avram, confused.

"You've had an accident and . . ." began Jehuda.

"Right. I remember falling when the ledge broke and—"

"And you were killed," interrupted Jehuda.

"Killed? Really?" said Avram, shaking his head.

"I'll explain it to you later," said Jehuda.

"Okay, boss, but don't leave anything out."

"Come," said Yusef, clapping his hands, "help the man up, and bring him over to the cars."

Yitzak and Jehuda put their guns away and both of them helped Avram.

"Come," said Yusef, looking at me, "I think that we all need to talk, no?"

Jehuda nodded his agreement, everyone walked to the cars. Ali got there first and arranged the chairs in a circle. Yusef and I sat in two, and the three Mossad agents sat in the others. Muhammad and Ali stood behind Yusef, Mara stood behind me, resting her hands on my shoulders. Jehuda looked at Avram and Yitzak, and then at Yusef and me. "I don't know what to say."

"Why don't you start by telling us what you've seen," said Yusef.

Everyone listened intently to Jehuda tell of the events that he witnessed at the King David Hotel in Jerusalem, and all the subsequent events that took place during their surveillance of us, including his decision to take the Arab bandits out. He even told us about the miraculous things that they had witnessed. Yusef looked on as if he was hearing something that he already knew. Everyone sat quietly as Jehuda finished his story.

"Benjamin, it seems that the government is everywhere, no?" said Yusef, a small grin coming to his face.

I nodded.

"What do we do with them," asked Muhammad, arrogantly. "I think that God should—"

"That is a problem," interrupted Yusef.

"We didn't know," said Yitzak, defensively. "We were just doing our job."

"Could I ask your name?" said Jehuda.

"I am Rabbi Ani. You can call me Yusef. This is Benjamin, and behind us is my good friend Muhammad, his daughter Mara, and his son Ali."

"You value your friend's life very highly," said Yusef.

"Yes, I do," said Jehuda, uncomfortably. "I already knew before Avram fell that you weren't terrorists. Really! But when he fell I had to make a decision. I could either help my friend and blow our cover, or forget about him, and play the game out. My choice was an easy one. In other circumstances, I wouldn't have had a choice . . . I can't . . . ."

"I understand," said Yusef, tugging lightly on his beard.

"What now?" asked Muhammad, still speaking in a threatening tone. "What do we do with them?"

"Do with them?" said Yusef, turning to Muhammad, and then back at me. "We do nothing with them. We let them go away in peace, and I hope that they let us do the same."

"Let us go with you," said Jehuda, looking at his comrades, and then back at Yusef and me.

"No!" snapped Muhammad. "I don't trust them, Yusef."

"We won't interfere with your work," said Jehuda. "I mean, we'll see to it that no one bothers you."

"I owe you my life," said Avram. "Do you think that I would forget that?"

"Please, Yusef," said Yitzak, "let us join you."

Yusef looked at me with a "what do you think" expression on his face. I returned a "why not? It can't hurt" look.

"Okay!" said Yusef, with a small smile. "But we have only one other item to pick up and then we're finished. It's in Jerusalem. No interference, right?"

"I still don't . . ." began Muhammad.

"Please, Muhammad," interrupted Yusef. "God wouldn't let them interfere. You three can join us, but you must follow my instructions. Agreed?"

"Agreed!" said Jehuda with a smile, and turning to his two companions.

"Agreed!" said Yitzak.

"Agreed! And thank you, Benjamin," said Avram.

"Fine, then it's settled!" said Yusef, glancing at his watch. "Go and get your things, Jehuda, and come back as soon as you can. We leave for Jerusalem in a few hours—just after sundown."

26

The Ark of the
New Covenant

SUNDOWN FOUND OUR FOUR-CAR CARAVAN HEADED FOR JERUSALEM. Muhammad, Yusef and I were in the lead, Mara and Ali in the van just behind us, Jehuda in his jeep, and Avram and Yitzak's jeep brought up the rear. Muhammad remained silent the entire uneventful trip, while Yusef pored over the scrolls in the dim glow of the map light. I silently mused over the events of the past week—demons, angels, miracles, beasts, Moloch, the Heavens, the Hells, God. But Mara kept creeping into my thoughts. I loved her.

Staring out the window into the Israeli night, nothing seemed the same to me anymore, not even the darkness. Everywhere I looked I felt the presence of God, I had begun to understand that nothing is separate from God—not even the blackness of night.

Just before we reached the city Yusef had us all pull to the side of the road. He examined the scrolls for a few minutes while Muhammad and I waited to learn something more of the object of that night's quest. I found myself wishing that we had more holy relics to find—I was going to miss the adventure of it all.

Finally, Yusef broke the silence and turned to me. "If what Solomon says is true, and I have no reason to believe that it isn't, then tonight we are going to stand in the presence of the

358

Ark of the Covenant. Imagine, Benjamin, the actual Ark of the Covenant."

The golden Ark had been constructed under the supervision of the prophet Moses as a resting place for the Holy Torah. I could hardly believe that I would get to see it, although the events of the past week made it seem somewhat less far-fetched as the idea might have been only a few days ago.

"Benjamin," said Yusef, glancing at the scrolls and then back at me, "listen to what King Solomon has to say about the location of the Ark:

> Get thee to the Temple Mount
> for at its base somewhere a door,
> That locks the relic none may touch
> lest they the crown of glory wore.
>
> Upon a wall of weathered stone
> a seal exists, but can't be spied,
> It faces Avram's resting place
> and hides a door man's body wide.
>
> To find the entrance stand before
> the withered stones and face aright
> A shadow cast to mimic man,
> beneath the orb of lesser light
>
> Thee who seeks the Holy prize
> must stand before that wall of stone,
> And if thy faith be strong and true
> then, shall the pentacle be shown.
>
> But, be thee warned before thee stir
> that if thy faith be but a lie,
> That thee may grieve by such mistake
> for on that spot then thee shall die.

If thee live, then raise thy arms;
entreat the Lord, then thee shall see,
The seal dissolve to open the door
for only God dost have the key.

"Another one of the great king's riddles," I said, "again filled with enigmas, mystical innuendoes, and danger. I suppose I can't blame him for being so mysterious, I mean after all, the holy relics that we've discovered are more than just priceless arti-facts."

"That's true," Yusef replied. "They are more than priceless in every sense of the word."

"Well," I said with a little smile, "it's just something else we have to figure out. We've done it before, right?"

"Yes," said Yusef, "but we should try to figure it out, or at least part of it, before we enter Jerusalem."

I nodded.

"Muhammad," said Yusef, placing his hand on Muhammad's shoulder, "go out and tell everyone that we'll have to—"

"I know, my friend, I know," said Muhammad, "everyone will have to sit patiently for a while. I'll be back."

"Muhammad, no trouble with our new guests. Right?" said Yusef, peering at him over his glasses.

"Right," mumbled Muhammad.

Muhammad left the Land Rover and went to inform the oth-ers, leaving Yusef and me to discuss King Solomon's enigmatic verses.

"Benjamin," said Yusef, taking off his glasses and wiping them with his handkerchief, "I am truly proud of you. I know what you have gone through these past few days has been difficult."

Yusef's voice cracked with emotion, which started to make me emotional also. "Yusef, I can't begin to . . . ."

"I know, my boy, I know. Now, let's turn our attention to the work at hand."

I nodded.

"All right, we know this," said Yusef, pointing to a particular place in the scrolls, "the entrance lies somewhere at the base of Mount Moriah, that's the Temple Mount, you know. That's clear from the first stanza. Now, the "crown of glory," that's a problem. Okay, we know that the entrance is in a wall that is made of weathered stone facing Avram's resting place. Avram must be Abraham! Well, that's easy enough. Abraham was buried down in Hebron, which means that the wall that Solomon is talking about faces south. Any thoughts, Benjamin?"

"Well, it seems that Solomon made the location relatively easy to find, or at least the approximate location. What do you think?"

"I think that the rest of it we'll have to figure out when we're there," said Yusef, looking at the scrolls and then at a map of Jerusalem. "Yes, that's it! We'll just figure the rest out when we're down there. OK, we should go. Where's Muhammad?"

I turned and saw Muhammad standing by Jehuda's jeep talking to the agent. I was sure that they were plying each other with a million questions. I leaned forward and honked the horn and Muhammad returned. "Maybe I was wrong about them," said Muhammad. "That Jehuda is a grateful man. He and his two friends have seen a great deal and could have interfered with us long before this. Besides, it's better to have them where we can keep an eye on them than to have them lurking in the shadows."

"I think that you're right," said Yusef, raising his brow. "It's better, I agree. As far as them being grateful, I agree with that too. I think that they are true believers. People are more prone to believe what they see with their own eyes than to believe stories told to them by other people. It's all God's doing, no? They did save us from those nasty thieves and murderers. Now, let's go to Jerusalem." Yusef paused for a moment, and then continued. "Oh, yes, Muhammad, you have to take us to the wall on the south side of the Temple Mount. From what I can figure out, it has to be somewhere to the right of the Al-Aqsa Mosque. The best place to park is in the Mount Ophel area, no?"

"I agree," said Muhammad, starting the engine and sticking his arm out of the window, signaling to the others that we were about to leave. "It will place us close. We can go the rest of the way on foot."

"Okay, then, it's settled. Shall we?"

We pulled back onto the road and finished our journey in silence. We finally arrived around ten o'clock and parked in the shadows of an old building on the southern side of Ha-Ophel Road, approximately three hundred feet from the base of the Temple Mount. The night was darker than most, and the shadows cast by the old building hid us well. Out on Ha-Ophel Road I could see an occasional car pass and quickly disappear around the corner.

Yusef rolled down his window and looked up into the night sky. "We'll have to wait," he said, with an air of disappointment in his voice, "the moon hasn't risen yet."

"The moon?" I asked, not quite sure what the moon had to do with Solomon's riddle. "Are you sure, Yusef? Are you sure about the moon?"

"Yes, my boy, quite sure," said Yusef, holding up the scrolls. "In the third stanza Solomon says 'there will be a shadow cast to mimic man, beneath the orb of lesser light.' The lesser light is mentioned in Genesis, chapter 1, verse 16. I know the verse by heart. 'And God made the two great lights: the greater light to rule the day, and the lesser light to rule the night.' The greater light, of course, refers to the sun, and the lesser light refers to the moon."

Yusef directed Muhammad to join the others and tell them that it might take a while, that they should make themselves comfortable. Muhammad nodded and left the Land Rover.

Yusef and I passed the time talking over the events of the last few days and I thought that this would be the perfect opportunity to ask him the one question that I really needed to have answered. "Yusef, will I be able to help you train the Messiah when—"

"My boy, you've been invaluable throughout all of this. Maybe I'll just keep you around. You never know!" he said with a smile.

"Then, you mean yes?"

"We will see, my son, we will see. So, I see that you and Mara are becoming closer, Benjamin? Do you love her?"

"Yes."

"A perfect match, I think. Yes, a perfect match, indeed."

"Yusef, about the Messiah. Will he—"

"So, tell me what you think of Israel, Benjamin."

Just like that he changed the subject as he had so many times before. We wound up talking about everything—travel, theater, marriage, food, sports, and even the degeneration of Western art in twentieth-century America. Finally, at midnight, the moon rose, hanging low over the houses behind us.

"We have to wait just a little longer," Yusef said, looking at his watch. "Maybe another hour. Are you okay?"

"Sure, I'm fine. I'll wait as long as it takes."

Yusef smiled.

We spent the next hour talking about the Ark of the Covenant and how important it was, both historically and religiously, to the Jewish people. Seeing Yusef's face light up every time the Ark was mentioned, I began to truly understand its significance to him.

Yusef looked out of his window at the moon, which was now almost directly overhead. I looked at my watch it was just past one o'clock.

"Come, my boy," Yusef said, opening his door and stepping out into the cool night air. "Let's go find the Ark."

I nodded and exited the car. When the others saw us get out, they came over and gathered around us in quiet but excited anticipation.

"We can't walk along the southern base of the Mount together," said Yusef, looking at everyone. "We'll look like a mob of terrorists sneaking around in the shadows. It will draw too much attention. Everyone wait here, I'll go by myself."

We stayed by the cars, obscured by shadow, and watched Yusef cross Ha-Ophel Road to the base of the Temple Mount.

We waited patiently, watching Yusef walk to the east and out of sight. Ali climbed up on the hood of the Land Rover, while the rest of us stood behind Jehuda's jeep talking. Mara stood next to me as Avram told us about killing Fu'ard and his band at the crevice, and where they wound up putting the bodies. As we were talking, Yusef reappeared and walked west, then back to the east again. Back and forth he walked, disappearing and reappearing, disappearing and reappearing.

Yusef rejoined us after nearly an hour. "I found it!" he exclaimed, waving his hands in the air. "That is, well, I think I found it."

We all gathered around him.

"All right, this is the plan," said Yusef, stroking his beard. "Jehuda, you, Avram and Yitzak must wait here."

"But we can back you up," said Jehuda. "We can . . . ."

"You can do whatever you think is necessary to protect us," interrupted Yusef, "but you must not bring attention to us. Benjamin and I will try to open the entrance. Muhammad, you, Mara, and Ali can come part of the way with us, but you cannot come over to the entrance until I signal, so stay close, okay?"

Everyone went to their places. Muhammad, Mara, and Ali stood in the shadows about thirty yards from the spot that Yusef said contained the entrance. Jehuda and his comrades separated in the shadows and watched for signs of trouble.

Yusef led me to a stone wall at the base of Mount Moriah, about a hundred feet to the right of the Al-Aqsa Mosque. If this wall was weathered at the time of Solomon, then it had held up very well. The stones, in good condition considering their age, stood nearly eight feet high and shone a powdery gray in the moonlight. We stared at the stone wall for a moment, then Yusef broke the silence. "This is it, my boy! The entrance is here. You'll have to be the one to open it."

I looked at the wall and saw nothing resembling a door. "Yusef, how am I supposed to . . . ."

"A shadow cast to mimic man beneath the orb of lesser light," said Yusef, with a smile. "It's a man's shadow cast on the wall by the moon! Clever, no? Now come over here and stand so that your shadow falls on the wall."

I stood so that my shadow fell on the wall. I waited, but nothing happened.

"Now," said Yusef, stepping back from me, "within you, my son, was placed the Spirit of God. You must contact that Spirit! You must make it active, Benjamin. Bring it to life."

I understood what Yusef meant. I closed my eyes and brought up the Breath of the Sha'ar Ha'ar. When I did, I felt the Spirit of God fill me as it had in the tenth Heaven, and as it had when I brought Avram back to life. I felt the power come from deep within the Void of God, up through the Sha'ar Ha'ar, filling my body from the tip of my toes to the top of my head. I was filled with the spiritual power of God. When I opened my eyes I saw a bright silver pentacle materialize on the wall in front of me. "God is within me and I am within Him," I kept repeating. "Nothing exists outside of God. Nothing exists outside of—"

Suddenly, miraculously, the silver pentacle, the seal that King Solomon had placed on this wall so very long ago, broke apart, and the five silver triangles composing it floated outward from its center. When they were each three feet or so from the center, they began to spin and orbit around the center, slowly at first, but increasing in speed until they took on the appearance of the bright flaming trail left by a whirling fire brand. A moment later the whirling triangles stopped, spun in place for a few seconds, and then reunited to again form the pentacle.

A few seconds later, the pentacle began to change color, turning from a bright metallic silver to a deep mystical indigo. I watched silently as it began to pulsate, fade, and then completely disappear. Just as it vanished, a door appeared. I heard a small popping sound, and the door slowly opened six or seven inches. I turned to Yusef and nodded. He smiled at me and left to signal Muhammad, Mara, and Ali to join us. A moment later, the five of us were gathered in front of the entrance.

"No one has been here for three thousand years," said Yusef as he wiped the sweat from his forehead with his handkerchief. "Benjamin, my boy, you must be the one to retrieve the Ark, so you must be the one to go in first. Remember, the Ark contains the New Covenant that the Messiah will give to the people of the world. We can recover the Ark, but only God can give the Covenant to the Messiah, not even an angel can do that. You must be very careful!"

"For God and the Messiah," I said, then pushed the narrow stone door open the rest of the way. It creaked, sending chills down my spine. I started to go inside but stopped halfway in. "Will you let me help you train the Messiah?" I asked, turning to Yusef.

"Go in, Benjamin. Go!" said Yusef, waving me forward. "It's not the time to dally! Go!"

I turned, walked in, and found myself in a very narrow corridor no wider than the door. Solomon had described it well, it was as narrow as a man's body. I expected the hallway to be dark, but it was bathed in a warm indigo light that allowed reasonably good visibility. The walls were black and smooth, and seemed hewn from solid rock. As narrow and alien as it was, I felt no fear. I continued along the path.

At about thirty yards in we came to a dead end, a wall of solid stone.

"This can't be right," I said, turning to Yusef.

"It has to be," said Yusef.

"What now?" I asked. "Did Solomon mention anything about this?"

"No."

"Did he say anything about . . . ."

"All he said was to have faith and . . . ."

"And what?"

"And faith will get you through."

"That's it, Yusef! Faith will get us through. Remember when I passed through the side of the mountain when I went after Satan's Veil? This has to be the same thing. Tell the others."

"Try it, my boy."

I turned back to the wall and closed my eyes, prayed, and confirmed my love and faith in God. I stepped forward and through the wall where the corridor continued. I waited for the others. One by one, they joined me, except for Ali.

"Where's Ali?" asked Mara.

"He didn't come through," said Muhammad.

"What do we do?" asked Mara, concerned for her brother.

"Ali," called Muhammad, pounding on the wall, "trust God! Have faith!"

We waited. Still no Ali.

"Is he in trouble?" said Mara, staring at the wall.

"No," said Yusef. "Ali, remember all that you've witnessed—Aaron's Rod, Samuel's Oil, Avram coming back to life."

A moment later Ali stepped through the wall.

"Good boy," said Muhammad, giving him a hug.

"That was amazing," said Ali. "Wow!"

"Is everyone all right?" I asked, turning to them. I locked eyes with Mara and could see the love and admiration she had for me in her eyes. She smiled.

"Move forward, Benjamin," said Yusef. "Move forward, my son."

We continued walking. About fifty yards in, the corridor turned sharply to the left and widened into a small chamber. Two great angels that I recognized immediately to be Cherubim stood before us. Both had identical faces—fearsome countenances wrought out of the very wrath of God. Yusef stepped next to me as Muhammad, Mara, and Ali shuffled backwards in fear of the two great angels. I felt my heart pounding in my chest as I wondered what would happen next.

The two angels took two steps forward and in great thundering voices said, "Behold! We are the angels, Jael and Zarall, keepers and protectors of the Holy Ark. Drop on your knees in homage to our position and to our might, or we shall destroy you!"

I heard some movement behind me and I turned just in time to catch the others about to drop to their knees.

"Stop!" I shouted. "Don't drop to your knees or we're all doomed."

They stopped, fixing me with quizzical stares.

"No!" I said, boldly pointing to the two great angels. "None of us standing here will bend a single knee to either of you. It is God and God alone that we will bend our knees for, not His servants!"

Mara gasped and Muhammad cleared his throat. I knew that they were thinking I had made a mistake. I waited for the angels to make their play. They didn't move.

"If you mean to kill us for not paying homage to you, then do it, and face God's judgment for your actions!" I said, speaking words that seemed to come from some other source.

The two great angels took a step backward, and for a moment I feared I'd said the wrong thing. Then they bowed respectfully to us. As they did, the great stone wall behind them dissolved, and the small area we were in became a very large chamber. Resting on a gleaming white marble base stood the Ark of the Covenant. It was just as the Torah had described, except that the two Cherubim were missing from its top.

"Everyone! Take your shoes from your feet!" said the angels in unison. "The ground upon which you stand is holy ground!"

As we quickly slipped off our shoes, the angels continued. "Only you may approach the Ark," the angels said, pointing to me with one hand and holding up their other hand up to stop the others from nearing the Ark. "Go to the Ark, for God, the One True God awaits you."

I turned and looked at Yusef. Tears were running down his face as I walked forward to stand before the Ark, uncertain of what would happen next.

Suddenly, the room began to brighten. It grew brighter and brighter until everyone in the room was bathed in the warmest whitest light imaginable. It was just like the white light that I had experienced in the tenth Heaven. I looked around. All I could see were the two angels, Yusef, Muhammad, Mara, Ali, and the Ark of the Covenant. Nothing else seemed to exist—no walls, no floor, no ceiling. Suddenly, the ethereal sounds of the Kadishim surrounded us, their music permeating our very souls. Then, appearing before me was the glowing image of a woman, so magnificent, so beautiful, so radiant, so transcendentally powerful, that I dropped to the floor and lay prostrate before Her. She wasn't just an angel, but was something much more powerful, much more holy.

"Stand, Benjamin," She said, raising Her slender arms.

"I am the Shekinah, the Feminine Aspect of God within the Manifest World," She said in a powerful transcendental voice. "Only you can see Me. Your companions can only hear My voice."

I didn't turn around to look at Yusef, Mara, Muhammad, and Ali, but I knew that they were standing awestruck by what they were witnessing.

"Know that within this Ark, my Ark, do I have a wonderful gift for the world of humankind, that they may hear and obey My Will." As She spoke She slowly raised Her hands and the cover to the Ark lifted and hovered high in the air. I knew that everyone could see the Ark. "Do you know what is contained herein, Benjamin?" Shekinah asked, looking at me, a warm smile spreading across Her face.

I took a deep breath. "It contains the Books of the Law that You have given to the prophet Moses," I said, in a voice that I somehow managed to keep reasonably steady.

"Do you know what else, Benjamin?"

"It contains the scroll of the New Covenant that the Messiah will bring to the world."

"Yusef Ani, step toward Me four paces," She said, Her voice resonating through my soul.

Yusef came up just behind me and a step to my right.

"Yusef Ani," said the Shekinah, gently smiling, "you have done well in the training, very well indeed. I am pleased, Yusef, and very much pleased with your student."

Training? Student? What did God mean?

"The collection of the Holy Objects," continued the Shekinah, "did what they were intended to do and I am pleased with you, Benjamin, so very, very pleased! They have taught you a great many things that you must know. But you have much more to learn, and there is much more to do. This has been only the beginning of your education, Benjamin, there is much for you yet to learn."

God's glorious transcendental radiance bathed me in Her magnificent warmth as Her words continued to resonate throughout my entire being.

"Since the beginning I have sought the Masculine, for I am in need of that completeness. Know, Benjamin, that which I seek shall redeem Me. Though nothing is hidden from Me, I ask you, Benjamin, do you love? Do you have one who will make you complete in all things?"

"Yes," I said, "I do!"

"Then have her stand beside you."

I turned to Mara and smiled. Mara walked up and stood beside me.

"I know that you love each other," said the Shekinah. "As I seek that which will make me complete, you have sought and found. The masculine cannot be complete without the feminine, and the feminine cannot be complete without the masculine, for my needs, my wanting, are woven within the fabric of all of creation. There is nothing better for humankind than that the masculine and feminine be joined as one, merging with perfection in the union of spirit. So shall it be with you and your beloved. In truth, Benjamin, the masculine and the feminine joining is the symbol of My Redemption. My seeking balance is the Tikkun. To think otherwise is a grievous error, for those that do not understand this cannot understand the nature of My Redemption. I had explained My Redemption to my beloved servant Solomon so that he could write it down for all of humankind to see and understand. What he wrote is called *The Song of Solomon*. Know that writing, and know the Tikkun. Understand it and you will understand the love that the masculine and feminine share and the need that they have for union.

"As I once told Solomon, 'I am a rose of Sharon, a lily of the valley.' It means, Benjamin, that I am both the promise of new life and the bringer of finality. I am the very beginning and the ultimate end of all existence. Remember this always. Now join hands Benjamin and Mara."

Hearing the voice of God, Mara slipped her hand into mine. When she did, a bright indigo glow surrounded our hands and slowly traveled up our arms, soon encasing our entire bodies. I felt Mara's spirit merge with mine.

"Benjamin," said God, "Mara shall be a balance for you, for you cannot function in your tasks properly without her. I have given women strength, love, and wisdom. They are, in truth, equal to and the compliment of the man. But both men and women are only half as strong, loving, and wise without the other. Now take a step forward, Benjamin, and reach down within the Ark and take up the Scroll of the New Covenant that you shall soon deliver in My Name to the peoples of the world. You shall be the Messiah that I will send among the nations to deliver My Word and My Promise, that they should turn away from evil, and work for My Redemption, My Reunion with My beloved."

I took a deep breath and I began to realize what was happening. I stepped forward and reached into the Ark and slowly lifted the scroll out of it. I looked at God and couldn't hold back my tears. I was the Messiah that Yusef, for his love of God, was training.

"Now, Benjamin, soon you must bring My New Covenant to the world. You shall teach them, Benjamin, and those teachings shall become a great cleansing river that will heal all whom those waters touch. This is My promise, this is My word: They who are touched by that holy river shall be redeemed and will fear no more forever. They will experience My love and know My Truth for I shall, through that healing river, forgive them of their sins and make Myself truly known to them and they will doubt no more. This promise you will deliver to the people in My name.

"Know this also, as I had once said to the prophet Nathan concerning My beloved servant Solomon: 'He shall be a son unto Me, and I shall be as a mother and a father unto him.' And so I say unto you, Benjamin, 'You shall be a son unto Me, and I shall be as a mother and a father unto you.' Yusef Ani, attend well unto him so that he may do his Holy Work. Now, go from this place in peace, Benjamin, for you have other trials ahead of you and much to learn before you are ready. For the day is coming when you will deliver My Word to the peoples of the world and in that day, they will heed your wisdom. You will bring to the world My love and My promise of eternal life within Paradise. Fear not, my son, for I shall be with you always!"

Epilogue

"TRUTH IS FICTION, FICTION IS TRUTH!" YUSEF ONCE TOLD ME. "Who can know for sure where one leaves off and the other begins? So write the book, Benjamin, and let the world decide. Soon, very soon, they'll know the truth of the matter. Begin the 'Great Healing River' that God had spoken of."

Well, as Yusef first suggested during the course of our acquisition of the holy objects, and at his subsequent urgings, I have written this novel to record the actual events as they happened. He was right, it needed to be written. It is the beginning of the "Great Healing River."

Now, as I write this epilogue, Mara is at my side and Yusef is sitting across from me, peering at me over his glasses, and smiling. I know that I still have much to discover and learn, but that is coming. According to Yusef, the adventures and wonders yet to come will be astounding to behold. I believe him.

Let this then be my final word in this first work: Bless you all and always trust in God! I am here and will be among you soon!

Benjamin Stein
Spring 1997

Appendix

You are about to embark on a great adventure, one that will not only expand your knowledge concerning some of the many arcane powers existing in the world, but, more importantly, actually give you hands-on experience in the use of those powers. The techniques that I've included here have never appeared in print before. You will not find them anywhere else. In fact, I have only taught them to a select few over the past thirty years. I now offer you these techniques in the sincere hope that you will not abuse or misuse any of the powers that you may develop as a result. With the acquisition of such powers must come a mature control of their use. Do no harm in the world and you will be living a truly spiritual life.

You will come to learn, as your abilities in the use of these techniques mature, that the possibilities in their application are as endless as your innate thirst for spiritual knowledge. A whole new world is about to be opened and explored by you. Learn, grow, and be well.

—Richard Behrens

A Word About Practice

As in all new endeavors of this kind, it is extremely important that every step in the execution of each technique be followed to the letter. Familiarize yourself with each of the steps of the particular technique that you want to learn before you begin to practice that technique. Commit the requirements of the technique to memory so that you don't have to refer to the book when you attempt it, or your concentration will be broken and the results may be disappointing. Some techniques will come very easily to you, others will take more time to master. This is the way of things. Don't rush. Take your time, follow all the steps, and success will be yours.

Nefesh Hafsa'kah: Mind Stoppage Technique

The Nefesh Hafsa'kah, or Mind Stoppage Technique, is a safe and effective way of taking immediate control of the Lower Mind. As a prelude to meditation, it offers the meditator a marvelous way of quickly reducing the activity of the Lower Mind, which is so necessary for a good and productive period of meditation. Also, during times of stress and anxiety, it affords the sufferer an effective way of breaking the chain of thoughts that cause and sustain that condition. The Nefesh Hafsa'kah may be used at any time during the course of one's day when the preparation for proper concentration is required.

Step 1   Close your eyes and, exhaling through your nose, expel as much air from your lungs as you can. Hold your breath for a count of ten, or until all thoughts stop. Observe what takes place during that time. Notice how your thoughts decrease both in intensity and volume, eventually disappearing entirely.

Step 2   Once your thoughts have stopped, begin a very slow inhalation. Do not rush that first inhalation, control it. Fill your lungs to their normal capacity and hold your breath for a count of ten.

Step 3   Exhale through your nose very slowly and empty your lungs of air, holding the extreme position for a count of ten, before making another slow controlled inhalation. At this point, your thoughts should have stopped and your Lower Mind becomes quiet. If necessary, you may repeat all three steps.

Sha'ar Lev: Heart Sephira Technique

The Sha'ar Lev, or Heart Sephira Technique, is so called because it is a quick, effective way of empowering the Heart Sephira (Heart Center) with M'retz Na'she, Feminine Energy. The Heart Sephira is located in the center of the chest. The effects of this technique take place promptly. You will immediately feel a sense of peace and focus. You will enter what professional athletes call the "zone." In fact, I have taught this technique to a number of professional athletes in order to allow them to enter the "zone" at will. The Sha'ar Lev coupled with the Nefesh Hafsa'kah or Mind Stoppage Technique will quiet the Lower Mind and allow you to access the magnificent spiritual faculties of the Higher Mind.

Step 1   Do a complete exhalation [through your nose] and hold for a count of five.

Step 2   Do a complete inhalation, filling your lungs to capacity, and hold your breath for a count of five.

Step 3   Place the palm of your left hand over your heart and imagine your arm as being hollow. Now, exhaling through your nose, imagine your breath traveling down through your "hollow" arm, out of your palm, and into your

Heart Sephira. All three steps need only be done once, but may be repeated, if necessary.

Experiencing the Magen or Shield (the aura)

Many of you have had the experience of seeing the magen or shield (also called the aura) of people and objects, but did you know that it is actually palpable and can be felt? It's true. The technique to experience the magen is very simple.

Exercise 1: Experiencing Your Own Magen

Step 1   Place the palms of your open hands approximately 4" apart.

Step 2   Slowly "pump" your hands back and forth. Avoid making physical contact with your palms. If done correctly, you will experience a pressure between your palms. The pressure that you experience should feel very much like the pressure that two magnets exert when their like-poles are brought close to each other. If you feel that pressure, you are now experiencing your magen—your aura.

Exercise 2: Experiencing the Magen of Others

Step 1   Have your partner place both of his hands approximately 4" from your own.

Step 2   Pump your hands back and forth making sure that you do not make physical contact. The pressure that you feel is generated by the contact of both of your magens.

Projecting the M'retz Na'she

Basic Exercise

All magen (shields) radiate M'retz Na'she (Feminine Energy) naturally. However, you can project the M'retz Na'she from yourself in order to bring about a number of interesting phenomena. Here, I have provided you with a basic exercise that will allow you to generate a palpable "beam" of M'retz Na'she. You will need a partner for this exercise.

Step 1   Have your partner stand in front of you with his palm raised and facing you. Note: the distance between you and your partner is not a factor. If you like, you can experiment by varying the distance (i.e., 5 feet, 10 feet, etc.).

Step 2   Do a complete exhalation (through your nose) and hold for a count of five.

Step 3   Do a complete inhalation, filling your lungs to capacity, and hold your breath for a count of five.

Step 4   When you are ready, have your partner exhale and hold his breath (this will increase sensitivity). Now, direct the palm of your left hand toward your partner's palm and imagine your arm as being hollow. Next, exhaling through your nose, imagine your breath traveling down through your "hollow" arm, out of your palm, and into your partner's palm. If done correctly, your partner should experience a great amount of heat in the palm of his hand. That heat was created by your M'retz Na'she striking his palm.

Sha'ar Daath: The Daath Gate

The Sha'ar Daath, or Daath Gate, is located in the center of the forehead between the eyebrows. It is the doorway to many mystical possibilities. Some claim that it is located in the throat, but as you will learn through your own experience, the forehead is correct. Using this technique, you will be able to access the past, present, and future.

A Word About Time Travel

Whether you travel into the past, present, or future, you should know that your status will be that of an observer. You will not be able to interact with what you experience. You cannot, for example, travel back in time and change history. However, you can go back in time and visit a particular historic event and gather a great amount of information concerning that event that has eluded modern history writers. You can even go back to the very creation of the Universe and see for yourself the very beginning of it all.

The future is all there, however, it is important to understand that an infinite number of futures exist at any one moment and that the future is changeable due to mankind's "free will." That is, when you travel into the future, you are traveling into a future based on current conditions. This makes the future a very flexible medium for exploration.

Now, time does not exist merely in a linear way, but exists laterally also. That is, it is not only infinite in terms of past and future, but is infinite in all directions. This means that, besides traveling into the future or the past, you can time travel in the present. So, if you want to see what is occurring some place in the world "now," all you have to do is have those directives brought to the attention of your Higher Mind prior to entering the Sha'ar Z'man, the Gate of Time.

Of course, time being infinite in all directions allows for "angular" journeys through time. That is, time travel involving various degrees of progress either into the past or the future. For now, however, it is best that you confine yourself to journeys in the three major directions: past, present, and future.

Finally, a word about "seeing." A beginner at time exploration almost always has trouble seeing images clearly. Generally, a beginner sees images in blacks and grays. If this occurs, it is because you haven't learned to see "clearly," and that you're attempting to see with your Malkuthian (earthly) eyes, rather than your Yesodian (Higher Plane) eyes. With practice, the transition will take place automatically, so don't become discouraged. When it does happen, you will feel as if you are there! Every action that takes place, every event that you are witnessing will have all the color, all the sound, and all the action that you will be looking for.

Seeing the Past, Present, and Future Via the Daath Gate

Step 1   Perform the Nefesh Hafsa'kah, the Mind Stoppage Technique (page 376).

Step 2   Begin to control your breathing. That is, your inhalation should be slow and protracted. Your exhalation should be even slower. You will do this breathing for a minimum of three minutes. As you breathe in, imagine that your entire body is hollow and that the breath fills your body from the very tip of your toes to the top of your head.

Step 3   When you are ready, take a slow, full inhalation and place the palm of your hand over the Daath Gate between your eyebrows. Pressing your palm lightly against your forehead, exhale and imagine your breath traveling through your hollow arm, out of your palm, and into the Daath Gate. You are stimulating the Daath Gate by infusing it with M'retz Na'she. If all three steps are executed properly, you should find yourself swept deep into the Void of God. You will have the sensation of traveling deep into starless space. Continue traveling until you come to the Sha'ar Z'man, Gate of Time, an irregular round patch of blackness suspended within the Void of God. You should have no trouble seeing it as you travel through the Void. It will be there.

Step 4   Before you enter the Sha'ar Z'man, you must first know exactly what it is that you are seeking. For example, if you are seeking the past, formulate in your mind the specific time and place that you wish to visit. Once you have, then you may enter the Sha'ar Z'man. Follow the same procedure if you want to travel in the present or future. That is, know before you enter the Sha'ar Z'man where and when you want your journey to take you. Of course, you can, if you like, enter the Sha'ar Z'man and leave the time and place of your experience to chance. Of course, if you do that, you can wind up anywhere and in any time period. Even so, you will always be returned to the present.

The Nefesh Kafdan: Uniting the Worlds

Everything exists within the Void of God, nothing can exist outside of it. For the average person, inexperienced in this concept, the Void of God and the physical world manifests as two separate states. This is, of course, unfortunate for the average person. For the mystic, it is an absolute tragedy. With the proper application of the Nefesh Kafdan that can be changed and union, in this regard, can be achieved and experienced.

To experience the Void is one thing, but to truly understand the oneness of all of existence you must unite both worlds. The Nefesh Kafdan will give you that experience. This is accomplished by utilizing the Sha'ar Ha'ar, the mystical gate located in the lower abdomen approximately two inches below the navel. This technique can be used throughout the course of one's day in order to maintain the feeling of uniting both worlds. It will also give you a sense of balance and peace that will not only enhance your sense of harmony, but will lay the groundwork for greater and greater advancements in your mystical endeavors.

Step 1   Perform the Sha'ar Lev (page 377) to quiet your Lower Mind.

Step 2   Inhale through your nose and follow that breath as it passes downward through your "hollow" body. When your breath (inhalation) reaches the Sha'ar Ha'ar, in the area of your body approximately two inches below your navel, visualize a gate that pushes outward as your breath passes through it and out into the Void of God beyond it.

Step 3   Exhaling, follow your breath as it travels from deep within the Void of God, past the gate, up from the Sha'ar Ha'ar, and out from your body. With very little effort, you will experience your breath traveling back and forth between the two worlds with you at the center. Of course, the more you practice this technique the more benefit you will derive from it. You will have the great joy of uniting both worlds.

Tebul Tov: The Good Immersion

The Tebul Tov, the Good Immersion, if done correctly, will bring you into a deep transcendental state that not only unites both the Void of God and the Light Malkuth (the physical Universe), but unites them in such a way as to transcend them both. It is a unique mystical method of quieting the Lower Mind to the point where the Higher Mind comes forward and dominates. When this occurs, you will not only experience the Oneness of all of existence, but it will place you in a state where a great many mystical possibilities exist.

Understand that clairvoyance, telepathy, precognition, and so on are faculties resident in the pristine Higher Mind and do not exist as part of the finite nature of the base Lower Mind. Simply put, when the Higher Mind dominates, the "extrasensory" tools of the mystic are in position and accessible. The proper employment of the Tebul Tov will help you do just that.

Step 1   The first necessary element of the Tebul Tov is that one should have both an abiding love for God and an uncompromising trust in His Word.

Step 2   If possible, place yourself in quiet surroundings, one free from noise and distractions. Eventually, however, with experience, the Tebul Tov can be executed very quickly and even in the most upsetting and chaotic of conditions.

Step 3   Employ the mystical Sha'ar Lev (page 377) to quiet your Lower Mind.

Step 4   Employ the Nefesh Kafdan to unite the Void of God and the Light Malkuth, the world of matter.

Step 5   Enter into the silence and peace created by the Nefesh Kafdan and then "let go," turning your spirit over to God completely and without reservation. By doing so, you will have the unmistakable sense that you have merged with all of existence—that you have merged with God. Since nothing is hidden from God, this "merging" will lay bare, with God's sanction, all the knowledge in existence. With God's blessing, nothing will be hidden from you. This is the power of the Tebul Tov, the Great Immersion.

Tebul Tov Kadishim: The Good Immersion to Experience the Kadishim

Employing the Tebul Tov, one would be able to experience the sweet angelic voices of the Kadishim, the great transcendental Angelic Choir eternally singing their praises to God and declaring to all of existence God's love and glory. Each step must be followed to the letter. Should any element be missing, then you will not be successful.

Step 1   The first necessary element of the Tebul Tov is that one should have both an abiding love for God and an uncompromising trust in His Word.

Step 2   You must place yourself in quiet surroundings, one free from noise and distractions.

Step 3   Employ the Sha'ar Lev (page 377) to quiet your Lower Mind.

Step 4   Employ the Nefesh Kafdan (page 382) to unite the Void of God and the Light Malkuth, the world of matter.

Step 5   Enter into the silence and peace created by the Nefesh Kafdan and turn your spirit over to God completely. If your initial intention was to hear the Kadishim, then your Higher Mind will automatically seek the Kadishim. If it is done with true faith and reverence, then, God willing, you will hear their magnificent transcendental voices pervading all of existence. You have but to listen and you will hear them. Once you experience the angelic voices of the Kadishim, their singing will be with you always. It is an unforgettable experience.

He'stakail Gadol: The Great Scanning

To understand the technique of the He'stakail Gadol, "The Great Scanning," you must realize that everything, whether animate or inanimate, has a magen (aura) or energy field surrounding it. More, the magen radiates M'retz Na'she (Feminine Energy) in all directions. The principles and techniques of the He'stakail Gadol, when properly applied, can readily detect the M'retz Na'she generated by another person's magen. A good rule of thumb concerning radiated M'retz Na'she is this: the more animate the subject is, the stronger and more palpable its magen is and the more M'retz Na'she is radiated by it. In other words, humans have stronger magen than animals and radiate more

M'retz Na'she. Animals, in turn, have stronger magen than plants, and plants have stronger magen than those magen found in the mineral world. This should be not only well understood by you, but patiently accepted as being axiomatic. In using the He'stakail Gadol, The Great Scanning, the quieter your Lower Mind is, the greater the sensation of heat you will feel in your palm when you scan. With practice, the execution of the He'stakail Gadol can take place very quickly, almost instantly. There are many uses for the He'stakail Gadol; the following basic exercises demonstrate just a few of the possibilities.

In the following exercises, your Lower Mind must be quieted. In order to do that, you have three wonderful techniques at your disposal, namely, the Sha'ar Lev (page 377), the Nefesh Kafdan (page 382), and the Tebul Tov (page 383). I recommend utilizing the Sha'ar Lev first. It is the easiest and quickest of the three and, in most cases, should be sufficient in order to bring about the desired results. Remember, the quieter your Lower Mind is, the better the results will be.

Exercise 1: Basic Scanning

Step 1   Have your partner stand 8–10 feet in front of you.

Step 2   You must quiet your Lower Mind. You may perform the Sha'ar Lev, Nefesh Kafdan, or, if necessary, the Tebul Tov. For most people, the Sha'ar Lev should be sufficient.

Step 3   Take a deep inhalation and hold your breath.

Step 4   With your left palm facing outward begin a slow sweeping movement in front of you in a moderate semicircle, from your right side to your left and then back again.

Step 5   As your palm crosses in front of your partner you should experience the sensation of heat on the palm of your hand. What you are feeling is the M'retz Na'she or feminine energy generated by his magen or shield.

Exercise 2: Scanning in Darkness

This exercise is a variation of Exercise 1. Here, the difference is that you will not have the benefit of being able to see your partner. This exercise may be practiced with your eyes closed, blindfolded, or in a totally dark room. It may be done using one partner or many partners. If executed properly, you should have no trouble at all locating your partner(s) in total darkness.

Step 1   With your eyes closed (you may choose to be blindfolded) have your partner(s) stand quietly somewhere in the room. Distance from you is not a factor.

Step 2   Quiet your Lower Mind by performing the Sha'ar Lev, Nefesh Kafdan, or if necessary, the Tebul Tov.

Step 3   Inhale and hold your breath.

Step 4   With your left palm facing outward begin a slow sweeping movement in front of you in a moderate semicircle, from your right side to your left and then back again.

Step 5   Again, as your palm crosses in front of your partner you will experience the sensation of heat on the palm of your hand. As your palm begins to pass him, your palm will cool. When your palm cools you know that you went too far, so slowly bring it back and "zero in" on the source of heat. The source of heat bordered by the areas of "coolness" will indicate your partner's location. When you are sure that you've located your partner, point with your scanning hand and open your eyes. You should be pointing directly at your partner. You may now breathe normally.

Exercise 3: Scanning Through Walls

Radiated M'retz Na'she (Feminine Energy) is not blocked or impeded by physical matter. That is, if executed properly, you should have no trouble at all locating a person or persons hiding behind objects, not even if they are in another room. You should be able, with practice, to tell not only how many people are in that room but precisely where those people are located.

Step 1 Have your partner place himself somewhere in an adjoining room.

Step 2 Perform the Sha'ar Lev, Nefesh Kafdan, or the Tebul Tov to quiet your Lower Mind.

Step 3 Inhale and hold your breath.

Step 4 Face the wall of the room with your partner in it. With your left palm facing outward begin a slow sweeping movement in front of you in a moderate semicircle, from your right side to your left and then back again.

Step 5 Again, as your palm crosses in front of your partner you will experience the sensation of heat on the palm of your hand. As your palm begins to pass him, your palm will cool. When your palm cools you know that you went too far, so slowly bring it back and "zero in" on the source of heat. The source of heat bordered by the areas of "coolness" will indicate your partner's location. When you are sure that you've located your partner point with your scanning hand. You should be pointing directly at your partner. Exhale. Go to the room and see if you were right.

Exercise 4: Scanning a Building

This exercise is very similar to Exercise 3, "Scanning Through Walls," except that you will be standing in front of your house, office building, or some other edifice, scanning for the number and location of persons inside. Coming home at night, for example, you may want to scan your house for any intruders, or if you are a police officer, you may want to employ this technique to scan for suspects in a building that you have to enter. You can also use

it to scan your car at night to make sure that no one is hiding in
the back long before you approach your car. It has many uses.

Step 1   Stand in front of your home or a building of your
          choosing.

Step 2   Perform the Sha'ar Lev, Nefesh Kafdan, or the Tebul
          Tov to quiet your Lower Mind.

Step 3   Inhale and hold your breath.

Step 4   Scan a floor at a time. With your left palm facing out-
          ward begin a slow sweeping movement in front of you
          in a moderate semicircle, from one edge of the building
          to the other and back again.

Step 5   As your palm crosses the front of the building, if there is
          anyone in there, you will experience the sensation of
          heat on the palm of your hand. As your palm begins to
          pass that person, your palm will cool. When your palm
          cools you know that you went too far, so slowly bring it
          back and "zero in" on the source of heat. The source of
          heat bordered by the areas of "coolness" will indicate
          not only if someone is in there, but how many people
          and their exact locations.

HaGe'lah: The Uncovering

The HaGe'lah, the Uncovering, is a technique that is used to find
lost or missing objects. It is a variation of the He'stakail Gadol,
the Great Scanning, and can be used to find lost objects such as
rings, watches, or necklaces. If you've ever misplaced something
in your home, then you could imagine just how useful this technique could be. Of course, the object doesn't necessarily have to
belong to you and it doesn't have to be your home. You could
employ it to help someone else locate a lost or missing object. It
can even be used to find lost or missing persons or sites of oil
and mineral deposits.

Exercise 1: Finding Lost or Missing Objects

Step 1   You must quiet your Lower Mind. You may perform the Sha'ar Lev (page 377) , Nefesh Kafdan (page 382), or, if necessary, the Tebul Tov (page 383). For most people, the Sha'ar Lev should be sufficient.

Step 2   Now, you must have a clear image of what you are looking for. To do this you have to place that thought in your Higher Mind. This is the sequence:
- perform the Nefesh Hafsa'kah, mind stoppage technique
- issue the mental command "clear" to yourself
- mentally name the object that you are searching for. Example: "gold ring," or "my necklace," etc.

Step 3   Employing the He'stakail Gadol, The Great Scanning, scan in all directions systematically (i.e., first in front of you, then turning to your left, the right, etc.). Your are using your palm as a sort of metal detector, sweeping for the lost article.

Step 4   When you feel the sensation of heat on the palm of your hand, zero in on it and pinpoint the location of the lost article.

Exercise 2: Locating Lost or Missing Persons

Step 1   Spread a map of the area you want to search out on a table in front of you. For example, if you want to search a country for a missing person, you would need a map of that country. If you believe that the person is in a particular state, then you would use a map of that state.

Step 2   You must quiet your Lower Mind. You may perform the Sha'ar Lev, Nefesh Kafdan, or, if necessary, the Tebul Tov. For most people, the Sha'ar Lev should be sufficient.

Step 3   As with finding lost or missing objects, you must have a clear image of who it is that you are looking for. To do this you have to place that thought in your Higher Mind. This is the sequence:

- perform the Nefesh Hafsa'kah, mind stoppage technique
- issue the mental command "clear" to yourself
- mentally name the person that you are searching for. Example: "Sam," or "Jennifer," etc.

Step 4   Employing the He'stakail Gadol, the Great Scanning, (page 385) begin scanning, slowly passing the palm of your hand systematically over the map. You will be using your palm as a sort of metal detector, sweeping the map for the lost or missing person.

Step 5   When you feel the sensation of heat on the palm of your hand, zero in on it and pinpoint the location of the person you are seeking.

Note   Suppose that you are looking for someone in the United States and want to pinpoint his or her exact location. This requires that you have three maps: one of the United States, one of the state that you narrowed it down to, and one of the city that the person is in. If you want to find someone and you know that he or she is in a particular state, then you only need two maps, one of the state and one of the city. If you know that a person is in a particular area, but are not sure where in that area they are, then you only need one map—one of that area.

Exercise 3: Locating New Oil Sources, Mineral Deposits, or New Archeological Finds

Step 1   Spread a map of the area you want to search out on a table in front of you. For example, if you want to search a country for new oil sources, mineral deposits, or new archeological finds, you would need a map of that particular country. If you have no particular country in mind, then you can use a map of the world or even a globe.

Step 2   You must quiet your Lower Mind. You may perform the Sha'ar Lev, Nefesh Kafdan, or, if necessary, the Tebul Tov. For most people, the Sha'ar Lev should be sufficient.

Step 3   Again, as with finding lost or missing objects, you must have a clear image of what it is that you are looking for. To do this you have to place that thought in your Higher Mind. This is the sequence:

- perform the Nefesh Hafsa'kah, mind stoppage technique (page 376)
- issue the mental command "clear" to yourself
- mentally name the source that you are searching for. Example: "new oil source," or "new gold deposit," or "Amenhotep IV's tomb," etc.

Step 4   Employing the He'stakail Gadol, the Great Scanning, (page 385) begin scanning, slowly passing the palm of your hand systematically over the map. Again, as in Exercise 2, you will be using your palm as a sort of metal detector, sweeping the map for the object of your quest.

Step 5   When you feel the sensation of heat on the palm of your hand, zero in on it and pinpoint the location.

Note   The larger the map, the better—it will be easier to scan. Naturally, you understand that if you are looking to locate an ancient Egyptian tomb, it would be wise to start with a large map detailing Egypt in the area of the Valley of the Kings. It would not make much sense to begin your scanning in the Arctic Circle.

Glossary

Ain Sof: the unmanifest nature of God.

Ain Sof Aur: the manifest Universe.

B'ehr Ar'ehr: the "temporary well." Repository of feminine energy that must be replenished daily.

B'ehr Shel Chai: the "well of life." The finite source of feminine energy within man's body.

Bene haAur: "Children of Light," the True Workers of Light.

B'ged Ar'ee Shel Nefesh: the "temporary garment of the soul." The human body.

Chutzpah: nerve, moxie, strong will.

C'lee Rayk: "empty vessels" or soulless bodies (*dybiks*).

Diaden Omry: In the demon language, "mother's gift." A reference to the feminine energy that they receive from Lilith eight times a year.

Gehenna Aysh: the Hell of Fiery Damnation, the sixth division of Hell.

Gehenna Ba'arut: the Hell of the Ignorant, the first division of Hell.

Gehenna Chara'tah Gadol: the Hell of Great Remorse, the third division of Hell.

Gehenna G'mul: the Hell of Retribution, the fifth division of Hell.

Gehenna Mavet Gadol: the Hell of the Great Death, the seventh division of Hell. It is only called this by the True Workers of Light.

Gehenna Shadim: the Hells of Demons, the fourth division of Hell.

Gehenna Tachton: the Dark Hell, the second division of Hell.